THE DISAPPEARING ACT

THE DISAPPEARING ACT

A Novel

Catherine Steadman

BALLANTINE BOOKS | NEW YORK

Published in the United States by Random House, an imprint and division of Penguin Random House LLC, New York.

BALLANTINE and the HOUSE colophon are registered trademarks of Penguin Random House LLC.

LIBRARY OF CONGRESS CATALOGING-IN-PUBLICATION DATA
Names: Steadman, Catherine, author.
Title: The disappearing act: a novel / Catherine Steadman.
Description: First edition. | New York: Ballantine Books, [2021] |
Identifiers: LCCN 2020044412 (print) | LCCN 2020044413 (ebook) |
ISBN 9780593158036 (hardcover) | ISBN 9780593158043 (ebook)
Subjects: LCSH: Disappeared persons—Fiction. | Actresses—Fiction. |
British—United States—Fiction. | Hollywood (Los Angeles, Calif.)—Fiction.
Classification: LCC PR6119.T436 D57 2021 (print) |
LCC PR6119.T436 (ebook) | DDC 823/.92—dc23
LC record available at https://lccn.loc.gov/2020044412
LC ebook record available at https://lccn.loc.gov/2020044413

Canadian ISBN: 978-0-593-35869-6

Printed in the United States of America on acid-free paper

randomhousebooks.com

1 2 3 4 5 6 7 8 9

First Edition

Book design by Susan Turner

For Clementine—and the hours we spent together in the British Library's First Floor Reading Room.

The place is unreal. The people are unreal . . . Even the streets and buildings are unreal. I always expected to hear a carpenter shout "Strike" and the whole place come down like a stage set. That's what Hollywood is—a set, a glaring, gaudy, nightmarish set erected in the desert.

—ETHEL BARRYMORE,
America's "First Lady of the Theater," on Hollywood

When we are struck at without a reason, we should strike back again very hard; I am sure we should—so hard as to teach the person who struck us never to do it again.

—CHARLOTTE BRONTË, *Jane Eyre*

THE DISAPPEARING ACT

Have you ever asked yourself what kind of story the story of your life is?

I always thought mine would be a coming-of-age story. A small-town girl making it in the big city, like Melanie Griffith in *Working Girl* or Dolly Parton in *9 to 5*. Sure, I'd struggle for everything I achieved, but in the end my plucky can-do attitude would ensure I'd triumph over whatever obstacles stood in my way.

Like *Legally Blonde* or *Pretty Woman* or *Pride and Prejudice,* the story of my life would be an uplifting comedy, in turns fun and moving and aspirational. I'd be strong and spirited and a riot to be around. I'd be beautiful and smart and kids would love me.

That's what I thought. But now—looking down at the gun in my hands, feeling the heft of it, its cold reality in my palm—I'm not so sure I got the genre right.

In fact I'm not even sure I'm the main character anymore.

1

The Good with the Bad

SOMETIMES, NO MATTER HOW HARD YOU TRY, YOU JUST CAN'T DISAPPEAR. There's nothing you can do to melt back into the crowd around you no matter how hard you wish you could.

The tube carriage rattles and jolts around us as we clatter along the tracks deep beneath the streets of London. And I feel it again, the familiar tug of the stranger's eyes on me, staring.

I've been in their house. Or at least they think I have, but I don't know them. We're friends already, or we're enemies, but I don't know which. I'm part of some story they love or hate. I'm part of the story of who they are. They've rooted for me, cried with me, we've shared so much, and now I am right here in front of them. Of course they're going to stare. I'm the unreal made real.

On the fringes of my awareness I feel the figure finally break the connection and whisper to the person beside them. I try to focus on my novel, to let my breath deepen and the story wash over me once more.

All those gazes, like robins alighting on me and fluttering away, wary but interested. I know people always stare at one another on the tube. But these days it's different.

The carriage rattles on shuddering around us.

Since the show started airing, four weeks ago, I'm lucky to get through any journey without some kind of interaction from strangers. A shy smile. A tap on the shoulder. A selfie. A handshake. A late-night drunken gush. Or a hastily scrawled note. And sometimes even, quite confusingly, a scowl.

I don't mean to sound ungrateful; I love my job. I genuinely can't believe how lucky I am. But sometimes it feels like I'm at the wedding of a couple I don't really know. My face aching from meeting so many well-meaning and complicated strangers, while the whole time all I want to do is bob to the bathroom so I can get away and finally relax.

I don't feel threatened by attention, exactly, I know I'm safe.

Although, of course, it's not always safe. I learned that the hard way, a month ago, when the police showed up in my living room after countless calls and emails, finally taking notice when my agent stepped in.

He'd been waiting outside the theater, every night. Not particularly strange or concerning. Just an ordinary man.

I'd leave the stage door tired from work. I'd gone straight from filming on *Eyre* into *A Doll's House* in the West End. At first he just wanted a signed program, and then a chat, and then longer chats that got harder to leave until finally he was following me to the tube station still talking. I had to start leaving with friends. I had to be chaperoned. One day he couldn't stop crying, this stranger in his fifties. He just walked behind me and my friend, silent tears dripping down his slack face. His name was Shaun. I'd tried to sort it out with the police myself but it wasn't until my agent received a package that they took it seriously. He was just a stalker. Not even a stalker really, just a lonely man trying to make friends. I told the police that, of course, but they insisted on following it up, issuing an official warning. I think his wife had died recently.

They wouldn't tell me what was in the package he sent. I jokingly asked if it was a head, and they all laughed, so I guess it can't have been a head. I felt guilty about what happened; the friendlier I had been, the worse it had gotten and the more I strengthened his perceived connection to me. I hope he's doing better now. I wish they'd just told me what was in the package straightaway, though; instead I spent a week imagining the absolute worst. Weird photos. Skin. Teeth. Something his wife had owned. It was just a stuffed toy in the end and a slightly unsettling poem. But it's hard not to think the worst when you're trying not to think the worst.

I know not everyone is strange. But some people are.

At the next stop as I gather my things and disembark, a few eyes follow but when I surface at Green Park and the cold February air hits me, cooling my flaming cheeks, I chalk today's trip up as a success. No incidents this time, no drunken football chants demanding I "Say it! Say it!"

Who knew *Jane Eyre* had a catchphrase?

Who knew Arsenal supporters read Brontë?

And yes, in case you're wondering—much to my shame—reader, I said it.

"YOU'RE LATE," MY AGENT, CYNTHIA, smirks as I plonk down into the restaurant seat opposite her.

"Sorry. Tube," I counter.

She's already ordered us two glasses of champagne. I eye the chilled bubbles in front of me greedily. "Are we celebrating, again?" I half joke as I shrug off my coat, but her silence makes me raise my gaze.

"You could say that. Yes," she says, grinning before pointedly sipping from her champagne flute. "I got a call this morning," she purrs, placing her glass down calmly. "From Louise Northfield at BAFTA. A heads-up if you will . . . Louise and I went to St. Andrews together; we tend to keep each other posted—she loves you by the way.

So the word on the street is . . . though they're not announcing the nominees until a month before the ceremony, which is in May, but . . ." She pauses for effect. "You're on the BAFTA list. Nominees. For *Eyre*. Best actress."

For a moment her words don't make sense to me. Then they slowly shuffle into meaning. I feel the blood drain from my face, then my hands, and in its place a rush of serotonin floods in, the like of which I have never felt before, crashing through me.

"Holy shit." I hear the sounds come from me, distant, as I fumble with a shaky hand for my champagne and gulp down a cool, crisp mouthful. The light-headedness only intensifies. Seven years I've worked for this. This is it. This is what I wanted. "Jesus Christ," I mutter.

"That's what I said." Cynthia chuckles, grinning from ear to ear. "Now here's the really good bit. All the other nominees are over fifty, and they've all won before."

I sober quickly, brought up short. "Wait. *Is* that good?"

"Yeah, it is," she says with a laugh. "People love *discovering* actors, even if they've been knocking around for years. Plus, you've got great credits, pedigree, even though this is your first major leading role. You're academy catnip. A safe bet that seems like a wild card. And everyone will be rooting for you, nobody needs to see one of the 'Ladies in Lavender' win another bloody award."

I let out a nervous laugh and take another swig of my drink. Seven years of auditioning has taught me never to get my hopes up but right now I can't help it; my happiness bubbles up, irrepressible.

Cynthia catches the waiter's eye.

"Could we get a selection of everything? Just, whatever the chef thinks," she says airily, as if that's a thing that people actually say in restaurants. "Nothing too big, just a light lunch." She looks to me questioningly. "Is that okay, hon?" The waiter's gaze follows suit. Both deferring to BAFTA-nominated me.

"Okay, sure, yes, that sounds great," I reply, and the waiter heads off with total confidence in what I'd personally consider to be a very confusing order.

Cynthia leans forward on the table businesslike.

"This is all going to be new for you, and to a certain extent it's new ground for me too. I mean, Charlie Redman won best actor in, what, 2015? But it's different with men, they just show up in a suit. Best actress is trickier. I'll be fielding calls about you as soon as the press release lands in April. So here's my thinking. We've got two months to kill in the meantime. I don't want you tied up filming, I need you free for bigger meetings with this on the horizon. We're going to ride the crest of this. So how do you feel about a little work trip to LA so we can drum up some studio interest? Nom's still unofficial but we can certainly drop some hints."

She clocks my expression and changes tack.

"Sorry, I'm firing a lot at you, aren't I? It's a lot to take in. Here." She raises her champagne flute and clinks mine. "One thing at a time. Congratulations, Mia, you clever, clever thing."

Cynthia has been my agent, advocate, and therapist since I graduated. We've weathered some soaring highs and soul-destroying lows together over the years. In some ways we're unbelievably close and in others we're almost strangers. It's an odd relationship, but then it's an odd industry.

Her energy suddenly changes. "Oh, and I heard about George by the way," she says, her eyes searching mine, alive with curiosity. "That's so exciting for him! He must be over the moon."

I feel the smile slip from my face. I literally have no idea what she's talking about. George? My George?

To my knowledge not much is happening for him. In fact, if anything it's slightly insensitive of Cynthia to bring it up. George hasn't had an acting job for eight months at least and he's an absolute wreck, if I'm honest.

I met George on my first big job—a movie adaptation of *Tess of the d'Urbervilles*—six years ago and we've lived together pretty much from the get-go. We both had tiny parts in *Tess* but our scenes were with the Hollywood star they shipped in to play her and we couldn't believe our luck, and we couldn't believe we found each other. We bought our flat last spring but after that things sort of dried up for George, right around the time they picked up for me. But that never seemed to bother us. Because George isn't competitive like that.

"What do you mean?" I ask.

She looks confused for a second, then frowns. *"Catcher in the Rye."*

My heart skips a beat—*my God*—I remember the day we taped two scenes in the spare room. That was well over a month ago. George's Holden tape. But nothing came of that. I remember the weird art house direction we took pains to create for the Dutch director we were both desperate to work with, the way the script had changed the ages of the central characters, modernized the story, and transposed it into a university parable set in twenty-first-century New York.

I struggle to get up to speed.

George sent the tape. He got the part. And he didn't tell me.

My mind flashes back through the last month. I think of George sitting quietly in the kitchen reading, leaving the house early to meet friends, rejoining the gym, smiling again after months of depression and . . . *shit*. He didn't tell me he got it. He knew all along and he kept it to himself.

He must have had so many meetings, and chemistry reads, and screen tests since then. He sent the tape before Christmas. Why the hell wouldn't he tell me? How the hell didn't I notice?

I realize I haven't responded to Cynthia yet. "Yes! Sorry. Yes, I know, right! He's a . . . he's a bloody genius."

"I couldn't believe it when I heard. My client Zula's in it too. She's only got a small part but she started rehearsals last week, said she met him yesterday at the cast read-through. Said he looked great. God, he must be so relieved. It was all looking a bit desolate there for a bit, wasn't it?"

"Yeah, no, I know. So great!" The words are coming out of my mouth but all I can think is: *Why? Why didn't he tell me he got the part?*

And then a thought solidifies, and the answer is suddenly very clear, the solution as ludicrously obvious now as it was impossible to imagine seconds ago. "I forget, Cynth, who else is in it again?" I ask as casually as I can. "George told me but I completely . . ."

"Yes, the love interest is—God!—I'm so terrible with names. Naomi Fairn, yes. Chris Fairn's daughter. She's twenty-one, I think, first job since modeling. Seems good, but even if she's not, she'll look amazing in it. Tell George not to worry at all, she'll hold up on camera."

And there we go. I take a slug of champagne and try not to look like my entire life is crumbling.

"Filming starts in, what, a week?" she asks, oblivious to what is happening to me. "I bet they're putting him up somewhere gorgeous in New York, aren't they?" And with that I gently push back from the table, make my excuses, and head to the ladies' room. Somehow managing to keep a smile on my face while I do it.

LOCKED IN A MARBLE-LINED BATHROOM stall, I google: *Catcher in the Rye casting news.* Nothing announced yet. *Yet.* My stomach rolls.

I think of George quietly watching the TV next to me last night, the same as ever. Texting. Now I wonder who.

I google her face.

Holy shit.

Things start to fall into place.

I tap on the least glamorous shot Google Images offers me in an attempt to work out what Naomi Fairn actually looks like. It's a makeup-free shot from an impossibly cool magazine. I study the beautiful wrinkle-free planes of her face, and I want to die.

None of those things ever seemed to matter until now.

I read on. Even her parents are cool. Both gorgeous, both actors. Her dad basically was the 1990s. I think of my dad, Trevor, bicycling around the Bedfordshire countryside in an anorak.

With trembling hands, I tap out a message to George, hit send, and unlock the cubicle door. Standing in front of the vast washroom mirror I look at myself, checking my eyes to see if it's possible to tell that my heart is cracking open just by looking.

You can't.

I guess I am a good actress after all. I straighten up my hair, reapply some lipstick, and take in my twenty-eight-year-old reflection. And the face of Jane Eyre stares back at me.

I know what she's thinking, because it's what I'm thinking.

We're so fucked.

2

Stranger at the Door

FRIDAY, FEBRUARY 5

I'M HOME ALONE, HOURS LATER, STARING AT MY TEXT TO GEORGE.

> Why didn't you tell me about the job? x

I could have said a million things but I didn't, I said that. And he hasn't replied. So when I hear a knock on the front door—even though he obviously has his own key—I'm convinced it will be him: rain-soaked, sad, and contrite, prepared to explain everything away.

It might sound naive, given the circumstantial evidence, to expect this whole thing to be a purely innocent misunderstanding, crossed wires, but hope has gotten me this far in life. Every *no* I've ever received, in my mind, was almost a yes. And all I've ever really needed was an *almost a yes*.

I turn the latch letting a gust of wind and rain into the warmth of the house. But of course it's not George standing on our doorstep, it's a smiling stranger in a red bomber jacket.

"Hey. Mia, is it?" He's about my age with an easygoing manner and a warm Irish lilt.

"Yeah?"

He looks down at a damp and crumpled piece of paper in his hand. "So, I'm supposed to be collecting George's things."

"George's things?"

We both stand there in silence for a moment as I try to make sense of the Irishman's words. When it clicks, fear chases my confusion and then just as suddenly I feel the calming certainty that I must be misunderstanding what's going on here. And yet my grip on the doorframe tightens.

"I'm really sorry, but who are you?" I ask. My voice has a faraway distant sound. Perhaps it has decided it doesn't want to live with me anymore either.

"Sorry, right. I'm Andy." He extends a hand warmly. "I work for, um, Fantastic Movers." He cringes at the company name as I numbly shake his hand.

"Right, okay," I manage, then clear my throat. "I see. And is George coming to—?"

Andy's handsome face creases into an apologetic frown. "I wouldn't have thought so, no."

Two hours later the living room is pockmarked with missing chairs, books, and pictures. Shapes left in the dust that I hadn't even realized was there. The front door is gently pulled to by Andy and once I hear his engine start, I finally release the hot angry tears that have been silently choking me from inside since he entered the house.

George has gone. He's left me and this is how he's done it. After six years of love, or what I thought was love.

No reply to the text I sent him as Andy packed away his things. No answer to: *What the hell is going on?* But then I suppose—actions speak louder than words—it's pretty obvious what's going on.

A thought occurs to me and my thumb hovers over the Instagram search icon on my phone. I know this way madness lies. If I start down this road things will get very painful, very quickly, and yet in a way I want the pain. Pain will fill the room with something at least now that Andy has gone, taking all of George's things with him.

I tap out her name . . .

Her verified account springs up. Her curated, muted-tone online existence exactly as I would have imagined it. Naomi Fairn and her achingly cool life. There's a post from two days ago, a Polaroid photo of a script with her pale hand obscuring the title card, a plain gold band on her middle finger, clear nail polish, and the sleeve of a gray hoodie.

@Naomifairn: New job. Can't say yet but this one's special.

The crop emoji. I always thought that one just represented a generic crop but now on closer inspection I see it is actually supposed to symbolize rye. A fun clue for her intrepid followers. I'm suddenly reminded that she's only twenty-one.

I scroll through her earlier posts looking for him, looking for anything that can explain my now empty house. Something catches my eye. Posted last week.

@Naomifairn: Shadows.
January 29th. Hampstead Heath.

A photo of two people's shadows elongated in the winter sun along a path in Hampstead Heath; the tips of her white Converses are in shot and, partially obscured, to their right, the edge of the other person's shoe. My stomach flips; I know that shoe. I pinch and zoom, hunched over and squinting at the phone screen like an octogenarian in my lonely kitchen.

A scuffed navy Adidas. His shoe. I was there the day he bought them. I've gathered them up, abandoned about the house, and put them away for him a thousand times. My heart yawns wide deep inside my chest followed sharply by the acid burn of anger.

He left me for her. How could he think it was okay to do this to me, like this? After everything we've said and been to each other. Six years. No word. No explanation. Just gone. The anger inside me twists around itself, a beast ready to scream.

I exit Naomi's account and put my phone up on the kitchen counter. Best to leave it there for now.

I concentrate on my breathing. I try to fight the fresh prickle of tears stinging my eyes. I need to stay calm.

I can't blame Naomi for this. God knows if George even told her about me; she might not even know I exist. I tell myself I can't blame her because I remember being twenty-one, I remember being in love. I need to remember it's him not her. He left; he wasn't taken.

She is twenty-one and George is thirty in November. In the interests of self-preservation, I leave that thought there because that's someone else's problem now.

I let my eyes play across the kitchen, across our things. The ones left behind. Shouldn't we have more to show by now: more than a flat, and a kettle, and a toaster, and a smoothie maker? I know it's not a decision for right now but I wonder if I should sell the flat. I guess it is mine. I put the deposit down and my name is on the mortgage. We're not married after all. I've been covering the full mortgage payment for the last five months anyway. I've been covering most things for quite a while now. In a way, I guess, he hasn't really been here for quite some time. I wonder how on earth I will tell anyone what's happened without dying inside. Without being forced into the role of victim. I am not a victim.

My anger stretches taut again. How could I have been so stupid to love him? To trust him?

I sit up straight, take a breath, and try to refocus. I need to work out what I'm actually going to do.

There was a reframing trick I used to use when I hit a dead end working on *Eyre*. When things threatened to overwhelm me. When I suddenly felt the weight and responsibility of carrying Charlotte Brontë's story. Whenever a scene wasn't working or I was too cold or tired or scared I'd ask myself—what would Jane do? Not what would I do. But what would Jane do if she were here, now.

So I ask myself: *What would Jane do?*

And without a second thought, I know. I've lived with her now for so long.

In the book Jane asks herself: *Who in the world cares for you?* The answer is: *I care for myself.*

I need to care for myself.

She would cut her losses. She would protect herself. Jane would move on. Cauterize the wound to protect from infection. That's what I need to do: control the fallout, change the story he's written me into.

If I were Jane, I'd send a letter, an email. I'd secure another position, far from here. I'd move on and I'd adapt.

I think of my one lifeline, my bright bolt of good news in the darkness. The next few months are going to hurt, but I'm going to be okay. I will not play the role he's cast me in. I will write my own story.

On the counter my phone sits silently. No word from him. Not even an apology. Nothing. I am not even worth a sorry.

Jane would not crack, or cry, or drunk-text. Jane would focus her mind.

I breathe deep and think only of two letters . . .

LA.

And with that thought I pick up my phone and dial Cynthia's number.

3

Another Country

SUNSHINE AND A FRESH CALIFORNIA BREEZE HIT ME AS I DESCEND FROM the plane. London's February chill long forgotten, five thousand miles behind me, as I pull in a lungful of spring air and squint up into the cloudless azure sky above.

I wriggle out of my cashmere jumper and fish my sunglasses from my bag as I follow the other passengers across the hot tarmac of LAX toward the terminal.

Cynthia called yesterday, to finalize the details of the trip, just as I was deep-cleaning the flat, desperate to erase the final traces of George's abrupt departure. Still no call, only a text, four pointless words: *Sorry. I had to.*

Had to lie, had to cheat, had to run away. But if he can, so can I.

"Right. First things first," Cynthia had explained. "I spoke to a couple of the studios over in LA. Now, they're all eager to have general meetings with you—but Universal in particular wants to talk to you about a new project."

"Universal Pictures or TV? Are there sides?" I'd asked. Sides are the pages of script that casting directors send actors to learn for their auditions.

"Ha. Sides! They won't even tell me what the project is let alone the role. It's a film, that's all I know at this stage. And they just want 'a chat'—no audition. Which could mean a number of things. *But* they love you, they seemed very concerned about who else you'd be meeting over in LA and for what. It's Kathryn Mayer you'll be meeting, she's a new division president at Universal, she's building a production slate for next year. I don't want you to feel any pressure obviously, but this is a big deal, Mayer hardly ever meets actors. Apparently she adored *Eyre,* she got hold of a screener. Have a Google of her."

Although I've never braved LA before, I know that right now actors from all over the globe are migrating here for the three-month period of pilot season. Every television network in America will be hustling to grab the best, or cheapest, or most in-demand actors they can to fill their roster of new shows for that year. And all those actors end up auditioning for the same roles. It's a fire sale. Contracts are offered, careers are launched, dreams get made . . . and some get broken. Not everyone who flies over can get what they came for, not everyone can get what they deserve. Luckily I just need to get away from my life, a distraction, and I'm guessing I'm going to get that in spades.

She talked me through some of the selected shows and roles she's scheduled for me during the three-week trip. And the American agent she's arranged to represent me.

"Michael Spector at United. He's good. I've got a couple of US clients with him and he's really on it. Very savvy. Let me know how he is and we can shop around if it's not a fit."

Handheld name signs pepper the LAX arrivals barrier, and I'm surprised to spot the familiar swirl of my own name held by a woman in a sharp trouser suit. She catches my eye, gives me a bright smile of recognition, and makes her way over, smoothly, her hand extended.

"Mia? I recognized you from the press pack they sent me. It's Leandra from Audi. It's so great to meet you. How was your flight?"

Her hand is cool and strong in mine. Her freshly blown-out hair and crisp business suit putting my comfy travel wear and puffy eyes to shame.

"Sorry, Leandra. Did you say you're from *Audi*? The car company, Audi?"

"Yeah." She lets out a breezy laugh. "I guess someone must have dropped the ball on this one. We reached out to your agent. Let me show you to your vehicle."

A quick call to Cynthia confirms the matter. Audi is loaning me a sports car for the duration of my stay. All I have to do is Instagram it. My stomach flips at the thought of it. I explain to Cynthia that while I theoretically have an Instagram account, I have never actually posted anything and have absolutely no followers. At which stage Cynthia informs me that I now have a new verified Instagram account set up in my name to get posting on.

Leandra keeps the conversation easy and light as she leads me out of LAX into the daylight. A shiver of excitement jolts the sadness out of me as the sun hits my bare arms again, warming my air-con-chilled skin. Gone is the airport smell of chlorine; in its place recently cut grass carries on the Los Angeles breeze. Fresh beginnings.

I devour the scenery hungrily. A flurry of new information, palm trees, yellow cabs, signs for companies I've never heard of, even the people here look different, less tired than back home.

"First time in LA?" she asks.

"Yeah, it is. But I've heard great things!" I turn on a smile.

"My only advice," she confides cheerily. "Make sure you're wherever you need to be in LA before five-thirty P.M. and then stay there until after seven. You do not want to be caught in an LA traffic jam. Trust me. There's nothing else in the world like one."

"So, always leave early in LA? . . . Like Cinderella!" I offer jokingly.

She considers for a second before laughing. "Yeah, actually. *Exactly* like Cinderella. Got to keep those wits about you. But I can guarantee you that this car will never turn into a pumpkin. Even if everything else turns to rags." She gives an odd little chuckle. I'm certain she's joking but in spite of myself I shiver at the cold pessimism of the comment. There's a bright beep tone as she depresses the key fob in her hand and my attention flies to the sleek black car in front of us as its whole roof slowly peels back, folding in on itself with balletic precision. I'm definitely not a car person but even I have to admit it's bloody sexy. I think of my own basic four-year-old Ford Ka, covered in snow, back home, with its fabric seats as standard and its sliding sunroof, and I have to stifle a giggle.

Twenty minutes later, suitcase stored away in the trunk, I slide my leather seat forward, take a deep breath, and pull the $200,000 car out onto the correct side of the road. Making sure to keep my wits, very much, about me.

4

It's a Sign

THE VIEW FROM THE THIRTY-FIRST FLOOR OF MY BUILDING IS DIZZYING. It's the first thing that hits you as you enter the apartment: it's on the corner of the building so more than half the room is sheer glass, floor-to-ceiling, suspended more than three hundred feet above bustling Downtown LA. Up here we're slightly higher than the Statue of Liberty. Or so Miguel, the Ellis Building's porter, tells me as he lays my bags down with a smile. George never liked heights, he would have been nervous up here but he would have tried to hide it. Luckily, I'm not scared of heights; I'm not sure how much sleep I'd be getting up here if I were. But the view is nothing short of mesmerizing.

Beyond pristine glass Los Angeles stretches out, from up here a world in miniature, its sprawling smog and heat haze spellbinding if somehow not quite real. From the crisp cool of my luxury accommodation, I can make out LA proper for the first time in all its monstrous glory.

An arid industrial hub strung together by highways, thick clogged arteries pumping out to the vast studio lots along the horizon and their sticky-tarred multistory parking garages. Closer inland the low makeshift wooden skyline intermittently gives way to the odd gleaming glass tower like mine, while out toward the hills glittering crystalline pools sparkle in the sunshine in random configurations like scattered jewels. It's beautiful in its way. But then it would be nothing without the story that comes with it. It would be just another California city without the borrowed magic of those that pass through. Then as if on cue, I see it, hazy on the far horizon, emblazoned on the lush green rise of the Hollywood Hills, instantly recognizable. Nine white letters writ forty-five feet high. The whitewashed sign that launched a thousand ships and the rocks they ran aground on. The siren song.

"It used to light up, you know?" Miguel chirps following my gaze. Weirdly, I had read a bit about the Hollywood sign in the in-flight magazine on the journey over. I know that originally it was just an advertising banner for a housing development called Hollywood-land, but I didn't know about the lights.

"Really?" I ask and try to imagine the two-story-high letters glowing out across the city.

Miguel nods energetically as he struggles to retract the extendable handle on my suitcase.

"Yeah, it was completely covered in lights, over four thousand twenty-watt bulbs, it used to light up the hills in the 1920s. Used to flash, pulse, you know, like a heartbeat. HOLLY—WOOD—LAND." He puffs, finally releasing the bag's temperamental handle, narrowly avoiding trapping a finger.

"You're an actor, right?" he asks cheerfully as he offers me my new apartment keycard.

"I am."

Miguel nods sagely. "Yeah, me too, you know. I've been acting for, maybe, about ten years now." The porter's eyes sparkle as they stare out through the glass to the white letters in the distance, then he turns back to me with a quick grin. "You know the story about the actress and the sign, right?" he asks breezily.

"No, I don't think so." I try to recall any industry gossip I might have heard recently but my mounting jet lag stops me from fully investing. "What was it? Which actress?"

"Oh no, it's just an old story. From the '20s. This theater actress. She jumped off the sign. It's such a tragic story. Every now and then I think of her when I see it, you know."

"Oh God," I say looking out at the sign once more. The height from the letters to the sloping hills beneath seems monstrous even from this distance. "That's awful."

"Yeah, she came to LA to do a small part in a movie and after that movie they called her in for this huge lead role. You know, a really big part. So she screen-tested and everyone was sure she'd get it but then there was a disagreement between the producers and they went with this other *unknown* actress instead and that *unknown actress* turned out to be Katharine Hepburn! That role was Katharine Hepburn's big break instead of this girl's. Then the studio canceled her contract a few days later. So she jumped."

I shake my head, unable to think of a more appropriate response to Miguel's tale. "Wow, okay."

"Yeah, I know. But the real kicker? The thing that gets me every time? Three days after they found her body in the ravine a telegram arrives at her place from the studio. Turns out the contract canceling had been an administrative error! And they want her to come back in for another huge part. They wanted her to test for another lead role." Miguel shakes his head and then a thought suddenly occurs to him. "Actually, ha, she was British too. Like you!" He grins innocently.

Thanks, Miguel.

AFTER MIGUEL LEAVES I TRY to shake off his creepy story as I wander the state-of-the-art apartment. I take it all in hungrily, the muted

Scandinavian design, the low wool-upholstered furniture, a security video entry monitor in the hallway, discreet wall-mounted plasma screens in all the rooms, oversized coffee-table books. This apartment must be costing someone an absolute fortune. Why on earth they are putting me up here, I do not know. I wheel my case into the larger of the two bedrooms and dig my mobile out from my handbag.

I feel my insides squirm as I remember I'm supposed to start posting things on Instagram during this trip. Hashtag-gifted. Oh bloody hell. After years of holding out, I really thought I'd gotten away with not getting dragged into the Insta-bubble. But I guess there really is no such thing as a free lunch. I'll have to double-check with Cynthia if an iPhone apartment photo shoot is somehow part of my accommodation deal. It's starting to look like my new social media account might be doing all the heavy lifting this trip. I try not to think of Naomi's account; I will not check her grid again, not today. I feel the loneliness beginning to seep back in and I briskly head back into the kitchen.

On the countertop I find a package of essentials: filter coffee, snacks, and a fruit basket with a note from my new American agent Michael.

Welcome to Los Angeles, Mia! Looking forward to meeting you in person tomorrow. M Spector.

Next to his gift is a bottle of Perrier-Jouët champagne, another note attached to its dewy glass, from the producers of *Eyre:*

Congratulations on the "top-secret" award news!! You absolute star! You're a winner to us already. Thanks for all your continued hard work x

A warm feeling spreads through me at the reminder of my good news as it wakes up and stretches inside me.

I send a quick message to my friend Souki who I know is in LA right now too. I do not mention George. After all, I can tell her if I see her. But I'm not ready to let my thoughts go back to him right now. The point of coming here was to move on. I need to keep things light, easy.

I haven't spoken to Souki in months—another quirk of the job—but she's exactly the kind of person I should be hanging out with right now. Fun, exciting, and not at all hard work. We basically lived together for three months while we filmed an indie horror movie on location in Bulgaria two years ago. The people you work with tend to become an instant family on acting jobs. You're thrown into close quarters in strange new countries, which means high-stress bond-forming relationships happen fast. There's only so many hotel dinners you can share in a row without the polite veneer of professionalism slipping into comfortable familial frankness. Souki and I had a blast—on a job that wasn't. Though we may drop in and out of each other's lives, our bond is eternal.

An email from Cynthia updates me on the details for the Universal meeting with Kathryn Mayer, which will be at the end of the week—they still won't let anyone see a script, which of course only adds to the mystery and allure of the meeting.

In the meantime I have a magazine photo shoot for *Eyre* scheduled for tomorrow morning and my first LA audition in the afternoon. Two big scenes. Eight pages of mostly my lines in dialogue as an overworked female Boston cop who discovers her new husband is involved in historical rape allegations. Sounds intense, but I do get to dust off my Boston accent, which is always fun. I give the empty apartment my best "Car park. Car park," with New England vowels.

I decide to take my audition sides up to the building's outdoor pool on the thirty-second floor and combine line learning with a post-flight/pre-bed swim. I wriggle into my swimsuit, shrug a beach cover-up over myself in case I run into any other apartment residents, and slip into sandals.

I catch a glimpse of myself in the bedroom mirror, my pale British skin, my tired puffy eyes. I think of Naomi Fairn and try not to compare. But I do. Then like a chain reaction I'm thinking of them together, talking, eating, laughing. As if I never existed. And all I got was four words. I warranted no warning or explanation from a man who, I imagine, couldn't really care less what happened to me now. I've been thrown out like old clothes.

I force myself to stop. I must not obsess. What's done is done, there is nothing more to be learned from circling back and back and back. The habit that has served me well in my career—that need to unearth the fundamental meaning in any human interaction, to rehearse and rehearse until everything finally makes sense—will not serve me here. He left. He didn't love me. He found someone else. There is no more. That way madness lies.

I grab a towel, a bottle of sunscreen, and my script and head up to the roof terrace. I need to keep my mind away from the dark places it longs to go.

5

Diving In

MY JET LAG MEANS I'M UP BEFORE DAWN THE NEXT MORNING.

Lying awake staring at the light seeping slowly in through the corners of the blinds sends my thoughts in dangerous directions. I rehash the first night after George left. I'd started to worry. George hadn't sent me his four-word text yet; that wouldn't come till the next day and Andy from Fantastic Movers had long gone. In the quiet of my flat I'd suddenly been convinced that something was wrong. The idea blossomed that perhaps something bad had happened to George; perhaps Andy hadn't worked for Fantastic Movers. I'd been so convinced at the time that something else had happened, after all, that I'd even made a call to George's friend Harry to check George was safe. I cringe in my crisp LA sheets as I recall the conversation. George was fine, Harry told me. And while Harry couldn't tell me if George was seeing anyone new—it wasn't his place—he gave me his sympathy on our breakup. And of course registered his personal disapproval of George's methods though he had been the one to help George unload Andy's truck at the other end. They'd gone to the pub after.

They'd gone to the pub.

I fling back the covers in a flash of rage and get dressed to head up to the pool for a predawn swim. I need to burn off this anger, this shame.

As I push open the heavy pool terrace doors and head out into the fresh California air, I feel a welcome ripple of excitement as I remember my BAFTA news. I snuggle it tightly inside me. I remind myself that my LA adventure is only just beginning, and just like that a Christmas-morning feeling dawns.

The rooftop is empty except for me, and I take a moment to look out over the glass barriers at the edge of the building. Below, the city is just beginning to wake. Apart from Miguel and the receptionist I haven't seen another soul in this apartment block so far. But then that's not a huge surprise given I only arrived yesterday evening.

I shed my layers down to my swimsuit and let my still-bed-warm skin sink into the cool pool water. The splash and ripple around me is the only noise as I glide smoothly through the blue-green water.

I pause after a few laps, half in half out of the water as I watch the sun rise across LA, my chlorine-stung eyes hazy as I take in its streaks of lilac and peach. In the new silence I can just make out the distant rumble of the highways beneath the sound of my own breathing, as the poolside cabana's curtains dance gently in the morning breeze.

I push myself in the water again, sinking into a rhythm that pushes away all other thoughts. Blocking out everything until there is only the present and the water and my labored breath.

Mind cleared and body warm with post-exercise ache, I head back down to my apartment and shower off.

MIGUEL SEEMS HAPPY TO SEE me when I head down to the building's valet station to collect my car.

"Auditions?" he asks with a knowing look.

"One this afternoon. CBS."

He grimaces as he hands over my car keys. "That's in Studio City.

You'll be fine on the way out but watch that rush-hour traffic on the way back. It's a killer. I hope you like listening to podcasts," he jokes.

"Thanks for the heads-up," I say with a chuckle. "I'll download some!"

The audition's not until the afternoon, so first I'm on my way to an abandoned 1930s diner in Echo Park for the midmorning magazine photo shoot. The magazine's called *Atelier* and after an hour in makeup, I look like the sort of person you might see in a magazine called *Atelier*. A company security guard fastens $1.3 million worth of air-con-chilled Boodles diamonds around my neck while a team of wardrobe girls lifts the delicate train of the gown I'm wearing into the corner booth of the dusty atmospheric diner. I'm arranged artfully in situ against the mint green of the art deco background. Incongruous hip-hop music is pumped up, and a fan is sourced to keep us cool under the hot lights. Finally the helpers and crew drop away until it's just me and the photographer and a wall of bass-y music. As the camera flash pulses, I try to forget that I'm no Naomi Fairn. I try to forget my anger and my shame and the fact I'm all alone and instead I focus on the shoot and I do my fucking job.

There's a costume change. The atmosphere is buzzing on set, smiling faces, easy conversation. Somehow I'm pulling it off. They can't tell that all I really want to do is put on an oversized sweater, hide at home, and eat cupcakes for a month. The next outfit is subtle, my haute couture gown replaced by a caramel oversized Victoria Beckham suit with vertiginous barely there heels, my hair tumbled chicly to one side. The next setup is at the bar counter, my sharp stilettos digging into the vinyl padding of one of the stools. And suddenly for the first time since George left me, I start to have real fun, slipping into creative mode with the kind of gratitude I usually reserve for post-filming baths. Jane was right. I can do this. I'm already starting to feel better.

During the next coffee break I shrug off the caramel jacket to reveal the matching bustier beneath. I kidnap one of the makeup artists, a skinny blue-haired nineteen-year-old called Marchesi, and we sneak off to do an impromptu Instagram shoot of me and the Audi in the diner car park. Cheeky I know, but (a) I might never look this good again, and (b) I'm under strict orders to post about the free car. What's a few more pictures while I'm already at it?

I know George will see these photos but for the few minutes we shoot them it's not about him. It's about me. How I feel. How I want to be. Marchesi is grinning like a kid, which he pretty much still is, when he hands me back my phone. The pictures look fucking great.

I post one of me looking slightly off camera, hair partially obscuring my profile. I'm leaning, longer and thinner than I actually am, against the side of the car. The only indicator of where in the world I am is the In-N-Out beverage cup hanging loosely by my side, although the morning light has given everything that unmistakable California glow. I click share. Fuck you, George.

TWO HOURS LATER, ON THE other side of LA, I'm standing in an almost empty office space, the room devoid of furniture save for: eight metal-and-fabric office chairs holding eight seated CBS executives, a large camera tripod, and a harassed-looking casting director quickly shuffling through different character scripts.

"Well, thank you for asking me to come in to read." I direct my attention to the only executive who has acknowledged me since I entered the room. "It's a great script."

He gives me a magnanimous half-smile, seeming to agree with my good fortune on being here at all, before he dives back into his iPhone.

The other seven execs, two of whom I'm thrilled to see are women, are still completely ignoring me. I stand and wait as they talk among themselves, leafing through photos or tapping away at laptops and phones. Luckily any dignity I may have had wore away about five years ago while I auditioned for adverts. I stand, invisible, awaiting direction.

The harassed casting director, in a final flurry, roots out the correct script scenes, tuts, adjusts his camera, and finally looks up at me, almost surprised to see I'm still here. He flaps his script pages, triumphant.

"Okay. Shall we just go ahead then, Mandy?"

"Mia," I correct, cheerfully.

"Sorry, what?" He looks genuinely confused at my meaning. A couple of executive heads rise from their separate endeavors too and stare at me—it's almost as if the wall had started talking.

I try incredibly hard not to giggle. "No, nothing. That's great. Yes, let's go for a take. Ready when you are." Equilibrium is restored.

I give my shoulders a quick roll, crick my neck, and try to put myself in the body of an overworked and exhausted female cop in the middle of a grueling investigation. Officer Bethan O'Neill. I let my limbs loosen, my face slacken, and I stop trying to cover my jet lag and the frantic emptiness I've been, almost successfully, ignoring since Andy arrived on my doorstep three days ago. I simply let my weariness become visible.

The casting director, oblivious, takes his reading position next to the camera tripod and presses record. A red light flashes on. He gives me a nod. In the brief silence that follows a couple of executives look up and finally I feel eyes on me. I start talking.

The first scene is easy, station banter with my loudmouth Boston-Irish cop partner, McCarthy. A chance to see my character's fun side but also the toll the job takes on her as one of the only women in a male-heavy environment. The irony of my present executive-ratio-ed situation is clearly visible to no one but myself.

The casting director, standing in as McCarthy, delivers one of his lines and I wait a beat longer than I should to reply. Executive eyes rise again, I give my McCarthy stand-in a well-timed *look,* and a couple of the executives involuntarily laugh.

I chase their laughs with a couple more and the remaining dipped heads start to grudgingly lift. And suddenly everyone is listening. I win. The next scene is trickier. I take a position kneeling on the scratchy office floor while the casting director adjusts the camera angle for the next setup. This one is a scene from the final episode of the whole series. Everything has come to a head and we find Officer O'Neill's husband pointing a gun at her having just shot McCarthy in the chest in a desperate standoff. O'Neill's husband has reached the end of the line; backup is on its way but right now she is all that stands in the way of his escape. As the scene starts, O'Neill dives to administer first aid to a wounded McCarthy as her husband levels his gun at her.

The camera's red light flicks on.

With shaky hands, I administer first aid to the prone body of an invisible McCarthy as he slips in and out of consciousness, blood pumping from his wound. I look up at my husband stand-in and start to talk.

The scene is going fine until I hear something raw in my voice. There's an almost imperceptible crack in the way I tell my husband that I still love him. And the full force of the words I'm saying hits me, the sadness of them, because after everything the man I love has done, *I do* still love him. It's pathetic but it's true. I do still love George. Even though he's deliberately hurt me, even though he left me for dead, I still want him so much. I miss him so much. And suddenly I'm talking to my George. The barriers between O'Neill and me disappear and this is my chance to talk to George, even if George looks like a forty-year-old gay casting director. And suddenly all the script's lines, as hackneyed as final-episode lines can be, are eloquent and fluid and exactly the questions I long to know the answers to — but I know can never really be answered.

Why did you do it?

Why did you lie to me, for so long?

When did things change between us?

He tells me he's not the man I thought he was. But I never thought he was anything but himself. He tells me he tried for too long to be something he wasn't.

I ask him what kind of a man he *wants* to be.

George looks away, his eyes won't meet mine. And then I tell him that if he goes, I won't follow him. I tell him to go. To run away. I don't care where.

He looks at me sadly, he doesn't believe me, he thinks I'll make things harder for him. I suppose, in a way, that was always our problem. He isn't going to go without hurting me. He'd erase me rather than run the risk of having me get in his way.

So I make my decision, kneeling over my wounded friend, to do what I have to do to survive. My husband looks away for a second, and in that moment I pull my hidden weapon from the back of my waistband and turn it on him. He freezes. I hold him in my sight, finger on the trigger. And suddenly I—Mia—I realize I would do it too. If this really were George, if he had done this, I would do this. I feel a hot tear roll down my face and I let my weapon recoil back in my hands.

When I look up, the execs are staring back at me, rapt, and George is gone.

I had forgotten about them.

The casting director turns off the camera with a nod.

I hastily wipe my eyes and scramble up from the carpet. I take a breath and dust gross office floor crumbs from my knees. God, what a weird job this is.

Realizing the show is over, executive eyes flutter hesitantly back to iPhones and laptops. I get a couple of *fair play* nods and a broad smile and a thumbs-up from one of the women as I gather my things and say my goodbyes.

Once we're out in the corridor, the casting director pulls me to one side, close and conspiratorial. It's a bit closer than I'd ideally like as I'm pretty sure my mascara has run and I'm strongly aware that I need to wipe my nose. But I'm interested to see where this is going.

"That was *fan-tastic!*" He clutches my upper arm firmly for emphasis. "Seriously. You in town for a few more days? God, tell me you are?"

"Yeah. Three weeks, actually." I smile.

"Fantastic. You . . . *missy*"—he jiggles my upper arm again for emphasis—"are my new favorite actor." He says this with a level of intensity that, I'm not sure he is aware, could have been specifically designed to terrify British people. Also, I note, he still has absolutely no clue as to what my name is. I am apparently now called *Missy,* not that it really matters. "I'll call . . ." He flounders for a second. "Who are you with over here again?"

"Michael Spector at United."

"Oh, interesting, okay." He nods knowingly. "I know Michael . . ." He winks.

God knows what that implies. I'm pretty sure Michael is married with kids.

"Great," he continues. "I'll talk it through with these guys, and I'll call Michael. I wanna get you in for everything on my list. Well, not *everything* obviously. I mean, no one wants that." He gives me a wry smile. I like this guy. He's a lot to take, and my upper arm is a bit chafed, but I like him.

"That would be brilliant, Anthoni. I'd love that." He squeezes my arm again.

WHEN I GET BACK TO the studio's car park and start the car the dashboard clock says it's six-fifteen. Shit. Rush hour. I remember Leandra's advice. Miguel's advice. Bugger. I should definitely download a podcast for the trip. I turn off the engine and grab my phone from my handbag. After selecting a couple of things, I find myself opening up my Instagram account.

My breath catches in my throat. I have 1,287 likes since I shared my first post at the photo shoot four hours ago. Holy crap. I look at the follower count: 8,932. I don't recall how many followers I had before I posted but it definitely wasn't that high.

I scroll through the small profile photo-circles of my new followers. Who are these people?

Every now and then I see a face I recognize, another actor, a few friends, even weirdly some cousins I haven't seen in years, but the photos are mainly of strangers. I skim their smiling faces and feel bizarrely elated. It's an odd feeling, a weird sense of kinship, of acceptance by a new tribe. I suppose this is why people get so into all of this. It feels pretty good knowing all these people are interested in my life. Even if my life is just me advertising a gifted car.

Almost nine thousand followers in a few hours. That seems good, although now that I think about it, I recall Naomi Fairn's numbers being up in the high 100k's. I'm thinking about George again. And just like that my thumb flies up to the search bar at the top of the likes list and taps in George's name before I can stop myself. No matches.

George hasn't liked the photo. Obviously. I sincerely doubt he's even seen it. But I wonder if she has. I tap on her profile and scroll-search for clues once more.

After a good bout of Insta-stalking I tap on George's profile. There's a new photo. My breath catches and I move the phone closer. A candid cast shot from the *Catcher in the Rye* rehearsal room last week. He's surrounded by the rest of the cast, his arm casually slung over her thin shoulders as they both beam at the camera. I feel a hot burn of my rejection twist inside me and read the official *Deadline* casting announcement beneath it. They must be in New York already. There together. Filming starts in four days. Everyone we know must know he broke up with me by now.

There's a tap on my driver's-side door and I yelp in surprise. Jesus Christ.

It's a studio security guard. I lower the window.

"Everything okay, miss?"

I glance at the dash clock: 7:03. Oh God. *I've been obsessing for over forty-five minutes.*

"Sorry, lost track of time. I'm . . . I'm just leaving now." I fumble with my seatbelt and throw him as sane a smile as I can muster.

He looks at me slightly concerned. "Okay, ma'am. You have a good rest of the evening."

6

The Favor

"They *LOVED* you!" The call comes at seven a.m. a day and a half after my first audition. My agent Michael is calling from his car on the way into the United offices in Beverly Hills. His voice is bright, full of excitement. "*Anthoni* loved you, and he's—well, he can be— tough sometimes."

I can imagine.

I towel off my morning swim hair with my free hand as Michael continues. "So they're probably going to want to screen-test on that next week. You and two other actresses. That's the early word. This is a great start, Mia. One hundred percent hit rate so far." He cheers.

No pressure then.

Today's first audition is for a Mars terra-forming expedition that goes wrong. The meeting is in a small casting office in North Holly- wood. I set off early, local talk radio on low in the car as I mumble out lines like "Check the O_2 regulators, we're losing isotopes through the main coolant vents. The whole system's degrading." Rose At- wood is a British biochemical engineer with a love of horse riding and ballet—I know, what a well-rounded character I hear you cry. But hobbies like that make for fun pre-production prep.

The satnav blasts me up the 101 highway, through the hills, the sun high in the spring sky, the traffic blessedly thin. Once I'm off the highway, I wind through the palmed and leafy boulevards—the skyscrapers of Downtown far behind me. It's easy to forget that, outside the vast industrial studio complexes and soaring glass towers, people are just living their lives out here.

North Hollywood has a different feel, more lived in, realer, somehow. Out of the car windows I see people out walking, coffees in hand, dogs in tow, women in high-end athleisure wear with neat ponytails, $500 sneakers, and rolled-up Pilates mats.

Cynthia texted me a link to a *Daily Mail* article this morning. The subject line: A HEADS-UP. The article was a sidebar puff piece with candid shots of George and Naomi grabbing coffee together in New York. His arm pulling her close, a peck on her cheek. Wool hats, gloves, and rosy-cheeked smiles. The news is out. George and Naomi Fairn are a couple. The texts start rolling in from back home. And I thank my lucky stars that Cynthia has a Google alert on my name.

On Instagram my post has over three thousand likes and my followers are creeping up at just over 16k.

There's no way of knowing if George has seen it, to know if he's checked to see how I am. Actually, there's no way of knowing who's been checking to see how I am at all. I think of Shaun, my theater stalker from back in London; he could be following me under any name and I'd never know. I wouldn't even know if my stalker was stalking me on here.

When I get to the casting address there's on-street parking and I gratefully pull into the only free space as another car leaves. Before I head in I promise myself that I will stop thinking about the article and the happy couple.

The casting suite is a block of units encircling a fountain courtyard. I follow the CASTING ROOM signs up some wooden stairs, hoping

the place won't be as depressing a venue as yesterday's scratchy car-
peted office space. But as I open the door I realize the inside definitely doesn't live up to the promise of the beautiful courtyard below.
It's just another rented office space hired out for pilot season.

Straight-backed office chairs line the waiting room. There are
five actors here already, spaced out around the seating, three of them
women, all brunette, all my age, all potential Rose Atwoods. We all
look weirdly similar. Of course that's the point of castings, but for a
second it throws me how similarly we're dressed too. Tight jeans, silk
blouses, hair up. I guess the character of Rose Atwood isn't exactly
hard to dress for. The two men waiting are both tall, thin, wiry, both
awkwardly perched on too-small seats as they pore over their lines.
I'm guessing they're reading for Marcus, the coms specialist who's on
the autism spectrum.

A notably attractive receptionist works on, unfazed by my arrival
as she sorts through stacks of sides and résumés. Judging by her model
looks I'm guessing she's an actor too, although currently in her second job. I make toward her but she heads me off. "Sign in over
there." Without looking up she points a thin tanned arm back in the
direction of the door where a folder lies open on a chair near the
entrance containing two sad crumpled pages.

"Right, okay," I say as her thin arm falls back to its task. "Thank
you." One of the Roses looks up at the sound of my accent, clocks
my expression, and lets out a snort of conspiratorial laughter.

Suppressing my own giggle, I head over to the tatty sign-in folder
to do as I have been told. Squatting awkwardly in front of it in order
to write, I add my own halfhearted scrawl to the other completely
illegible names already present. What possible use this record could
be to anyone I do not know.

Behind me one of the two audition room doors opens and another gangly Marcus exits the audition room, his expression deeply
troubled. I dodge as he strides purposefully past me, eyes firmly fixed
on the door, shutting it loudly behind him. A few startled eyes follow
his progress past the window as I take a seat next to the friendly Rose.

"Well. I wonder how that went then?" I whisper to my new friend.

She blurts out a laugh again, the ebullient sound so incongruous in the space that even the surly receptionist looks in our direction.

As if on cue the other audition room door opens and a Rose Atwood exits. Her audition clearly has gone better than the last Marcus's. She throws us a supportive smile as she gathers her things, and after a moment a casting director's head pokes out of the audition room she just left, scanning the remaining Roses.

The casting director frowns. "Is there a Samantha?"

The Rose nearest the receptionist desk rises hastily, smoothing her tailored trousers and grabbing her script. "Uh-huh. That's me," she says brightly before they both disappear into the audition room.

The waiting room noticeably relaxes as the door closes behind them. I check my watch; my time is meant to be twelve fifteen but it's already twelve twenty. I have another audition across town after this one. I do the math. There are still two more girls waiting ahead of me. Let's say they each take twenty minutes. I should be done in about an hour. I resign myself to the wait and dig out my mobile phone, keying in my passcode. But I promise myself no social media. Just email and texts. The girl beside me shifts and when I look up, she too is on her phone hastily tapping out a message.

Another Marcus is called into the other room and I find my mind wandering back to George. I need a distraction and for some reason the story that Miguel, the apartment building's porter, told me yesterday comes to mind. That story about the sign keeps coming back to me in bursts and I can't help but wonder how much of what he said was fact or if it's all just generic Hollywood mythmaking.

I tap the words *British actress* and *Hollywood sign* into Google and read.

Turns out it's true—the actress jumped after Katharine Hepburn got her part. This actress could have been Katharine Hepburn, could have had her career, if things had gone differently. The British actress had given up everything to travel to Hollywood, alone; no friends, no partner, she'd bet it all, and she'd almost won. I shiver at the grue-some details of her death, unsure why I am so fascinated. Thinking she'd been laid off, she left her belongings neatly stacked beneath the sign, climbed the service ladder on the letter H, and leapt out into the night sky.

Her carefully folded suicide note read:

I am afraid, I am a coward. I am sorry for everything. If I had
done this a long time ago, it would have saved a lot of pain. P.E.

I shake off the memory of George's four-word message and read on defiantly.

Apparently, a few days after she jumped, a female hiker chanced upon her things beneath the sign and then found her unidentifiable body in the ravine below and called the police. There's no record of that hiker's name. She was gone before the police arrived. I find my-self wondering why anyone would just leave a crime scene after such a traumatic discovery. And more to the point, how on earth could the police have been sure that the British actress had jumped in the first place? A few words in a note? What if she was pushed? The note wasn't even signed; it was initialed.

The sound of a throat being cleared on the other side of the wait-ing room interrupts my thoughts. "Sorry, am I next or . . . ?" a Rose inquires, her voice reedy. "'Cause my time was like eleven forty-five and that was forty-five minutes ago."

The receptionist huffs out a sigh, unreasonably irritated by the question. "They'll call you in the order you arrived. So yeah," she smirks derisively. "I guess you'll be next."

Bloody hell. I'm not sure I can take sixty minutes of passive aggres-sion. I make a decision and rise from my seat as inconspicuously as possible.

"I think I'm last so I'll just wait outside for a bit, if that's okay?"

"Sure, go for it." The receptionist shrugs.

Outside I take a seat on a bench in the sun and let its warmth wash over me. I open my iPhone inbox and scroll down to this afternoon's audition at Warner Bros. It's a film about the first female students at Harvard Medical School in 1945. I skim the scenes again. They are fantastic.

I'm halfway through running my lines when a voice snaps me back to reality.

"Good call, it's better out here. Mind if I join you?"

When I look up, the friendly Rose is standing in front of me gesturing to the bench beside me.

"Yeah, yeah, of course." I shuffle up as she sits down beside me.

"Well, that was tense." She smiles, nodding back toward the casting office, her New York accent thick with vocal fry. She pulls out a packet of cigarettes and extends it in my direction.

"I don't smoke," I say in a tone that bizarrely suggests I'm not cool enough to do so, but then, I suppose, my new friend is disconcertingly cool. I take in her incongruous Rose Atwood outfit. She is not a natural Rose, though I have no doubt she could play her, but there's a curl to her smile that suggests she couldn't be further from the character in reality. And there's something incredibly familiar about her. I must have seen her in something though I can't quite put my finger on what it might have been.

She flicks her lighter open in one smooth roll of the wrist and lights her cigarette. Then flicks it closed and takes a drag, a thin gold bracelet jiggling against her watch. "You're British, right?"

I smile. "I am. New Yorker?"

She chuckles. "Yep."

"How are you finding it out here?" I ask.

"LA?" Her eyebrows crease momentarily before she answers wryly. "Good days and bad days, you know."

"Yeah, I think I'm getting that. But it's only my second day so . . ."

"Newbie." She grins and grabs my wrist, in mock-solidarity, with her cigarette hand. I can feel the warmth of her cigarette tip close to the skin of my forearm as she continues, suddenly intrigued by me. "First time in LA? Oh my God. Jesus, how's it all going?"

Her grip releases as she takes another drag and I look down at my unscathed arm. I realize I haven't been touched by another human being since that casting director yesterday. I miss human contact. I had forgotten how, even toward the end of our relationship, George and I had been pretty tactile with each other. Close on the sofa, legs entwined and arm about my shoulders. I force the thoughts away.

"Yeah, it's my first time. So far so good. How many times for you?"

She flashes me a mega-watt smile then rolls her eyes in answer to my question. "God knows, I've been out pretty much every year since I was a kid. Think I've got it cracked now, though." She barks a laugh. I like my new friend. And I could definitely use a new friend out here. She's a lot tougher than her compact frame would suggest. And that confidence. I bet she doesn't take shit from her boyfriends. I bet people don't just leave her without a word.

"Sorry, I'm Mia, by the way," I say extending my hand.

She shakes it with another tinkle of bracelet. "I'm Emily." She grins. "You were at the CBS thing yesterday too, right?"

"Yeah," I say, surprised. I hadn't seen anyone else in the waiting room.

"Yeah." She chuckles. "I saw you in the lobby. Thought we'd might end up going for the same stuff. I get the feeling we'll end up seeing a lot of each other this trip." I study her features now with fresh eyes. She's right, we are similar. I suppose all the Roses here are. But now that she's pointed it out, I realize that must be the reason I thought she looked so familiar—because she is. She looks like a slightly more streetwise version of me. It's inevitable we'll see each other around at auditions; it's a small industry. "Where you staying?" she continues.

"Downtown, you?"

"Oh, it's a . . ." She pauses a moment, taking another drag on her cigarette. "I just picked an Airbnb as close to the 101 as I could find.

Not my first rodeo," she says, raising her well-groomed eyebrows for effect. I've only been here forty-eight hours but already I know the 101 gets you everywhere.

"Any LA tips?" I ask.

"Yeah, avoid rush hour!" She puffs, a smirk creasing her features. "But I'm guessing you've heard that one. Oh, and don't get too involved with anything. Things tend to turn on a dime out here. It's pretty much a mud fight."

Along the gangway the casting office door swings open and the most recent Rose strides away briskly. One down, another two to go. When I look back at Emily she is glancing at her watch, troubled. She's worried about the time too.

"You got another audition after this one?" I ask.

She looks up at me, momentarily surprised by my question.

"What? Oh no. Just a video call." She frowns, seemingly unsettled by the thought. She catches my concerned look and recovers quickly. "No, it's just, my parking is almost up." She smirks and takes the final drag on her cigarette before stubbing it out on a planter pot. "You got something after?"

"Yeah, I've got one over in Burbank."

"At Warner Bros.?"

"Yeah."

"Right, I heard about that one," she answers but I can tell she's not listening anymore. Something really is bothering her. The casting office door bangs open again and another Rose exits.

Well, that *was* quick.

Emily and I share a glance as the latest Rose disappears down the stairs.

"Uh-oh," Emily mutters and checks her watch again. "That can't have gone well."

A casting director pops her head out around the door.

"Who's next? Ready?" she trills before disappearing back inside.

"Oh shit," Emily groans, still eyeing her watch. "Do you wanna go in first? I am actually going to have to top up my parking or I'm going get a ticket. I'll run and do it now and you can take my place, okay?"

The suggestion knocks me off center for a second. I'd almost forgotten I was even here for a casting. I can't go in next; I can't even remember what we're supposed to be auditioning for. I'm not ready. My mind whirs as I try to work out how the hell I can politely decline and come up with—"No, no, it's fine. You go first. I can keep an eye out for parking attendants." As soon as I say it, I know we both know I have no intention of doing so. I change tack. "I'm sure the car will be fine. Even if the meter's run out they won't give you a ticket straightaway. Go on in, it'll be fine." I wonder if it's completely obvious that I couldn't care less about her car, I just don't want to go in next.

But she doesn't seem to notice as she flops her bag down onto the bench next to me and starts digging around inside for her keys.

"Urgh," she groans. "I don't know if I should chance it. It's a rental car and I literally have no idea what I'm supposed to do if it gets clamped or towed. My agent sorts car stuff out for me. I don't drive in New York." She turns to me, clearly preoccupied. "Seriously, it's fine if you want to go in first, I don't mind. I just need to feed the meter."

She's quite worried, her earlier confidence strangely absent. I feel my guilt rising. Might she get towed? I hadn't considered that. I don't know what I'd do if that happened to my car either. "Do they do that in LA, tow you, if your parking runs out?" I ask.

She's still not really listening as she fumbles for her wallet. "Dunno, but I don't want to find out."

The casting director reappears. "Whenever you're ready, ladies," she chirps passive-aggressively before disappearing again.

I feel my stress levels rising now. I'm not going in next with the casting director in that mood. No way. And it's out of my mouth before I can stop it. "I'll feed the meter for you. Just go."

Emily pauses mid-bag-scramble. "Seriously?" She seems suddenly caught off guard as she takes a second to think it through. "Uh.

Okay." She flicks a glance down to the wallet and keys in her hands, realizing she'll have to hand them over to a stranger.

And suddenly I find that I'm now the one trying to convince her. "It's fine," I assure her. "It'll only take me a second. It's just downstairs, right?"

"Yeah." Her forehead creases as she looks back toward the audition room, her wallet held tight in her hand. Then her eyes land back on me decisively. "Yes. Okay. Okay, great! Here." She hastily hands me her wallet. "It's the meter for the white Chevrolet. Oh, and take these just in case you have to move it to the next bay if it's reached a limit or something." She quickly pushes the car keys into my hand too. Then she straightens her outfit and grabs her script. "Great. Thanks. I owe you one. It's Mia, right?" She beams over her shoulder. I nod and she slips into the darkness of the casting studio.

I find her car two spaces from mine. A clean white Chevrolet as basic as a rental car comes.

The parking meter has no minutes left on it. I squint at the faded digital readout. It ran out twenty minutes ago. Why the hell didn't she come down and top it up earlier? I suppose she got her timings wrong. There's no fine yet, thankfully. I scan the street for traffic wardens but I have no idea what a California traffic warden looks like so quickly give up. There's no one on the street anyway.

I carefully read the blurb on the parking meter. I put two hours on my car when I got here. But it doesn't say anything about exceeding a maximum stay on her bay so I guess I don't need to move her car for her, thank God. It suddenly occurs to me how annoying and time consuming that would actually have been as the bays here are full and I wonder why on earth she would suggest I do that in the first place. And why on earth she gave a complete stranger her bank card. I guess neither of us is particularly good under pressure—which, I note, might not bode well for our choice of career.

As I fumble through her wallet I wonder why I felt the need to do this. I guess I felt obligated. I don't know. I couldn't help notice the break in her cool. The change in her demeanor—the genuine fear. I think getting this audition could possibly mean more to her than it does to me. Although I have to remind myself that I didn't offer to help solely for her benefit. I just didn't want to go in early without being prepared.

I slide her card into the slot, select another hour on the meter, and Emily's parking meter dial shoots up to one forty-five.

And all things considered, I head back to the casting office feeling pretty good about myself.

7

A Rose by Any Other Name

FOUR BRAND-NEW ROSES TURN TO LOOK AS I REENTER THE WAITING ROOM.

There's no sign of Emily. I check my watch. That only took about five minutes so she'll still be in there.

Thankfully I have time to check over my scenes again before I go in. It's then that I realize I don't have my bag with me anymore. I feel a rush of blood to my face—everything is in that bag, my wallet, keys, phone—and try not to think about what the hell I'm going to do if I've lost them as I leap from my chair and hurry back out into the sun. I feel inquisitive eyes follow me as I dash out, but thankfully as soon as I clear the doorway I see its soft crumpled leather nestling safely next to the bench's armrest. Disaster averted. I grab it and head back inside to a bank of staring Roses. I take a seat, ignoring my audience, dig out my script pages, take a breath, and start to skim the scenes one last time before I go in.

After a few minutes the audition room door opens a crack and I hear the mumble of voices beyond growing in volume. Emily must be done. I can hand back her keys and wallet before I go in, maybe we can exchange numbers and grab a coffee. It would be great to have a friend out here—if nothing else I'm sure she could teach me a thing or two about navigating LA. I take a last-chance look at myself in the mottled mirror across the room, smooth down my hair, and straighten my silk blouse as they exit the audition room.

It's not Emily, though. The actress the casting director leads out is one I haven't seen before. They exchange goodbyes as I gawk at them completely baffled. I lean forward to look around them hoping to see Emily emerge behind. Though why she'd be in with another actress is beyond me. The room behind them is empty. Emily must have gone into the other audition room. Perhaps she wasn't here to read for Rose Atwood after all.

A strange dread starts to stir inside me. This is weird. I try to think who she might be auditioning for, maybe Melaya Tulli, the ship's medical officer. I look around the waiting room but nobody else here could possibly be auditioning for that role. Melaya is clearly a Hispanic character, and Emily was most definitely not Hispanic.

The actress who isn't Emily turns and gathers her things from one of the waiting room chairs. Emily's car keys are still clenched in my hand.

"Is there a Mia?" The casting director turns and looks up from her list.

Bugger. I rise from my seat and plaster on a smile as I plunge the offending car keys into my pocket. "Yes, that's me." I smile, telling myself that it's fine. She'll be in the other audition room. They were running over time-wise and started using both rooms. That must be it.

I let my shoulders relax and head into the casting suite, leaving my jacket and bag behind, trying to clear my head of everything not pertaining to Mars as I go.

Twenty minutes later, I reemerge into the waiting room, my eyes readjusting to the daylight, my heart rate still elevated from screaming into the soul-less abyss of space.

The casting suites must be soundproofed as I didn't hear any of the earlier Roses screaming at the end of their scenes. My eyes scan the waiting room for Emily.

She's not there.

I head outside to the bench, but it stands empty in the warm sunlight. Maybe she went to the restroom. I go back inside and scan the waiting room again. One of the Roses stares at me curiously as another is called in.

I leave my things and follow the RESTROOM sign behind the reception desk down a very long corridor. The women's restroom is the third door along the empty cream hallway. I push its heavy-hinged door and enter. A fresh scent of bleach and synthetic lemon hits me. It's a large industrial bathroom, eight cubicles, the stall doors floating above freshly mopped polished-concrete floor. All of the work units in the building must connect and share these facilities. The end cubicle's door is closed.

The clack of my heels echoes around the space as I enter. And suddenly I feel shy.

"Hello?" I hazard, my voice a reedy British apology. I grimace at the sound of it. "Emily?" I ask hopefully.

No reply.

I crouch low, squatting, in the middle of the restroom floor, my heeled boots and the taut knees of my skinny jeans making things unnecessarily difficult. I duck my head low until I can just about see under the closed door, my ponytail skimming the bleached floor.

Behind me the main restroom entrance bangs open and the Rose who was just staring at me in the waiting room is suddenly confronted with the vision of me squatting, legs akimbo, in the middle of an abandoned restroom. Excellent.

I rise with slightly more difficulty than a woman of my age should be experiencing. The Rose looks at me with a frown etched deep into her brow.

"Hey," I offer, hoping that saying something normal like *hey* will convince her I'm not completely insane. She looks unconvinced.

"Um, *hey.* Are you all right? Should I get someone?" she asks carefully.

"No, just looking for someone. She's probably outside," I reply as breezily as I can.

"Oh, okay. Then can I just get past?" She gestures to the cubicles beyond me and I realize I'm entirely blocking her way. I give her a wide berth and she heads for the closed cubicle on the end, pushes it open easily, and slides the lock firmly behind her.

There was no one in here. I've been talking to myself.

I check my watch and head back outside hopefully. The sunlight makes me squint after the darkness inside. This is really weird. Could she still be in her audition?

I get a sudden burst of annoyance, partly due to the time this is taking and partly due to the look I just got in the restroom. This is all starting to get a bit silly now. I definitely do not need this today. I turn on my heels, head straight back into the casting office, and march up to the willowy receptionist with purpose.

"Hi," I blurt. "Is there a girl called Emily in there?" I point unambiguously toward the Marcus audition room.

"Excuse me?" she bites back at me, incredulous.

"Are the casting directors seeing actresses in both rooms?" I clarify. The receptionist frowns, my meaning escaping her, so I continue. "Listen, I'm looking for a girl who was here before. Emily. I was sitting with her. You saw us. I have her car keys and her wallet. I need to give them back to her. Is she in there?" I gesture to the Marcus room again.

"No," the receptionist answers, her eyebrows high. "They're only seeing guys in there."

Fuck.

"Oh right. Okay." Faltering, I scan the waiting room faces again. Gazes scatter away like pigeons. I'm clearly making a scene.

It suddenly occurs to me that Emily might be waiting for me by her car, and I kick myself for being such an idiot. I give no one in particular a nod and stride back out into the sunshine.

Outside I let out an exasperated sigh. This situation is really starting to stress me out. I check my watch. It's 1:32. My next meeting is at three in Burbank and I need to eat before I go or my lines might not come out.

Down on the sidewalk there's no sign of Emily.

Fuck.

Out of options, I stand at a complete loss on the empty pavement, casting my eyes impotently in both directions. She could have popped into a convenience store or a café along the block to grab something quickly but there aren't any shops or cafés in sight, just office buildings. But I have her wallet, so she wouldn't be able to buy anything anyway. I look back at the car, just as it was before, and root out its keys from my pocket. Just generic rental keys and an Avis fob with the number plate details. Where the hell would she go without her wallet and keys?

There must be a rational explanation. She mentioned a Skype call; perhaps it came early. She definitely seemed concerned about it. Perhaps it was much more important than her audition and she had to find a quiet spot to take it?

It makes sense but I feel my annoyance bubbling to the surface again. Because now I have to wait out here on the sidewalk until she finishes her call like an absolute mug. I feel the frustration building and try to disperse it with a tense wander along the line of parked cars. And ask myself what undeterrable, fiercely self-sufficient Jane would do? She would have said no in the first place. Why didn't I just do that? Jane counter: no point in retreading that when you can just say no now.

I stop in my tracks. That's the solution. I head back to the audition room, grab my stuff, and wander back out to Emily's car. Plonking my bag on the hood, I ferret out a pen and tear a section of paper from my script to scrawl her out a note.

Hi Emily,

Sorry, couldn't find you anywhere and had to dash. Hope your casting went well. Left keys & wallet with the receptionist.

Best, Mia x

I tuck it beneath her windscreen wipers and briskly take the stairs back up to the casting office to leave her things.

There's only one Rose left in the waiting room and I'm unsurprised to see it is not Emily. I wander up to the reception once more with as much lightness of touch as I can.

"Hi, me again," I trill, as if we've both had just about enough of me for today, and I plow on. "Right, so, I can't find that girl. Emily. She gave me her car keys and wallet. I'm guessing she'll be back for them soon but I have to go—so I'm just going to leave them here with you, if that's okay?" I plonk them down on the counter between us. She looks at them for a moment before gazing back up at me.

"Who gave you their *keys* and *wallet*?" she asks, incredulous, disapproval written clearly all over her face.

I sigh internally. "I don't know her full name. Emily something. She was auditioning before me. You saw her. She asked me to feed her meter."

The receptionist's expression turns to one of mild disbelief. "And you *did*."

This time my sigh isn't internal. "Yeah, yeah, I did."

She shakes her head, I presume at my naïveté. "Okay, well, you can't leave her valuables here."

For a second I think I've misheard her. "Sorry, what?"

"I mean, we can't offer to take legal responsibility for someone's car and wallet, can we? Obviously."

I hear the unspoken addendum to her statement: that I probably shouldn't have either. I breathe through my irritation. I hate this day.

"Right, so what you're saying is, I can't leave them here for her with a note?"

"No. You can't," she says simply. And then, perhaps feeling the harshness of this, adds, "Well, you could leave a note here, I suppose."

"I guess that would be something. Right, I'll leave her my phone number and I guess she can call me and get the keys whenever."

She slides me a pen and a Post-it pad and I scrawl out my phone number and name.

"You'll give her this when she comes back?"

The receptionist eyes my writing. "Yeah, sure. What was her name again?"

"Emily."

"Surname?"

"I don't know."

The receptionist frowns again. "Did you look in her wallet?"

It hadn't occurred to me. I rifle through the card holder and find only the bank card I used earlier.

E. A. Bryant.

"It's Emily *Bryant*? Sound familiar?" I say looking up. The receptionist shrugs. "I suppose she could have a different stage name?"

Behind me the entrance door bangs open and we both turn to look. Another brunette actress arriving to audition for Rose. She bends to sign in.

"Oh!" the receptionist blurts and my attention whips back to her, her face lit up with excitement for the first time. "Look at the signing-in file. She'll be the name just before yours, right?"

I'm guessing she's never actually looked at that signing-in file. I don't hold out much hope but I head over quickly and grab it. I find my own name buried halfway up the page already. Above it only illegible scribbles. Pretty much any of the signatures could say Emily, or Em, or E. The receptionist joins me, craning in to see.

Her excitement melts. "Oh. Okay."

"You must have a master list of auditionees, though, right?" I ask. "Everyone who's auditioning today. Can't you just look at that? There can't be that many Emilys on the list, can there?"

The receptionist balks slightly. "So I don't actually have anything to do with the casting. I just work for the studio space. I just . . . Well my duties are more focused on the suite facilities themselves than anything else. I'm sure the casting directors have some kind of list. Maybe ask through your agent, though. I mean they're pretty busy right now. Sorry I can't help more." She gives me a rallying shrug. "But you can definitely leave your note and if an *Emily* does turn up I'll pass it on."

Outside I dither for a moment by Emily's car. It's 1:54 and still no sign of her. Her parking time is up again. And so is mine.

I make a decision, top up her meter, and amend the note under her windscreen wiper.

Hi Emily,

Sorry, couldn't find you anywhere and had to dash. Hope your casting went well. ~~*Left keys & wallet with the receptionist.*~~

Couldn't leave your stuff with receptionist and I've got a meeting across town now—so I've still got them. Left my number at reception. Call me as soon as you get this and I'll get them to you asap.

Best, Mia x

It's just as I wedge the tightly folded note back under her windscreen wiper that I feel a hand grab my shoulder.

8

Passerby

MY HEART LEAPS INTO MY THROAT AND I SPIN, COMING FACE-TO-FACE with the hand's owner.

It's not Emily, with her gleaming chestnut hair loosely tied back in its low bun. It's not even the receptionist with more unhelpful suggestions. It's a man. A tall and conspicuously handsome man wearing a suit. His brown hair is rumpled, his intelligent eyes crinkled with mild amusement at my shock. He's looking at me like I know him. His smile denotes a level of intimacy between us that I am absolutely certain we do not share. I don't know why but I suddenly find his confrontational attractiveness just as infuriating as Emily's absence. Because I really don't have time for all this right now.

"You okay?" he asks, his voice warm. There's genuine concern in his tone and I realize I've been lurking around the parked cars long enough to draw attention.

I give him a look I hope conveys that this is really none of his business. "Yes, yes. All good. Thank you." I notice I'm leaning hard into my accent like a particularly indignant Maggie Smith, but this only seems to amuse him more.

"Car trouble?" he asks, and I realize a conversation is happening whether I want one or not. He's not going anywhere. I take a breath and dive in.

"No. No car trouble. I was at an audition and the girl before me needed someone to feed the meter for her car so she gave me her wallet and keys and now she's gone."

"Ah! I see . . . so, then—gone girl?" he says with a mock seriousness that, if I wasn't so annoyed and late, might have elicited a laugh.

But I am, so it doesn't.

I raise my eyebrows in acknowledgment of the joke and brace myself for more hilarity. "No, ha, very good. But yes, actually, she is gone. Which isn't ideal. And now I have these." I hold up her wallet and Chevrolet keys.

He nods, sagely, and points behind me. "I work across the street." I turn to look at the glass and plant-wall-covered work unit opposite. "I've been watching your progress so far." His smile turns sheepish, or, as sheepish as, I'm guessing, a former college athlete's smile can ever really turn. I frown slightly at his confession but he counters with a light shrug. "Slow workday."

He appears to be waiting for me to say something or maybe continue with my story but I have no desire, or time, to do that. I turn back to my note and re-wedge it firmly. "Well, thank you for your concern but I have to go." I give him a tight smile as I grab my bag and root out my own car keys. "Running late."

Undaunted by the brush-off or just oblivious to the nuances of British social interaction, he continues brightly.

"So what's the plan? I'll keep an eye out. Who are we looking for?"

We?

I suddenly wonder if I'm going mad. Is this guy really not reading my signals or am I losing my touch? I open my car door and turn back to him.

"Right, well . . . Um . . . ?" I realize I don't know his name, but he's ahead of me.

"Nick."

Of course. Of course, it would be something like Nick.

"Okay. Well, Nick, I appreciate your concern but I've left a note and everything is under control so we're fine. Thank you." I think there's a firmness to my tone but, again, judging by Nick's amused expression, somehow my desire for him to bugger off is still miraculously not getting through.

"Wait, so, you're just leaving with this woman's wallet and keys?"

I freeze momentarily, one leg in the footwell, one on the sidewalk. I suppose he's right. I am leaving with her property, and actually I haven't really waited that long. Put like that it doesn't sound great. I retract my leg from the car and turn back to Nick.

"Yes, okay, I see your point. But I can't stay any longer. I really do need to go. I've got another meeting. I've left a note with someone about the keys and wallet, they're passing on my phone number, so it's all sorted out. Okay?"

He raises his hands in casual defense. "Yeah, sure. Just trying to help. I'm sure you've got it covered." He smiles gently. "I hope it all works out." He studies me for another second before nodding and turning back up the street. I feel guilt rise inside me. The only person who's genuinely tried to help me today and I've essentially told him to fuck off.

"Nick. Wait, sorry." I call after him. He turns back to me, eyebrows raised. "You didn't see her, did you? Earlier?"

He looks down for a second seeming to weigh the pros and cons of getting involved with the crazy British woman again. When he looks up his face is different somehow, serious for the first time.

"What did she look like?"

I'm not sure how to answer that. Not because I don't know, I do, I would recognize her anywhere, but because the truth is she sort of looked like me, or every other woman that entered the building opposite his today. Shit.

"She was about my height, brown hair tied back, blouse, jeans, heels."

He's grinning again. "So exactly like you!"

I look down at my outfit and back up at him wryly. "Yeah."

"Okay. It was a casting, right? Well, if it helps, I'm pretty sure I only saw you loitering around the cars. You've got a certain way about you." His eyes crinkle around the edges again. "You're quite . . . British-y."

What the hell does that mean? Am I stumbling around LA like some cake-addled Bridget Jones character or something? I hold his gaze. "You know *British-y* is not a real word, right?"

He laughs. "Noted. But the point stands. Plus no one else has been hanging around here, except you. You'll have to take my word for it. But I can keep my eyes out, I'm here at the office until"—he looks at his watch—"about six this evening. If she comes back, I can pop out and give her your cell number or something? If that helps?"

I think of the receptionist upstairs, and decide an extra pair of eyes would help. But it'll mean I have to give him my number. And I'm not entirely sure I should be giving it out to any more strangers today. I give him an apprehensive look.

"Okay, listen," he adds, registering my concern. "Why don't I just give you *my* cell number? That way if you don't hear from her by this evening you can check in with me to see if she came back. Sound good? Sound safe?"

Bizarrely just the acknowledgment of my safety somehow puts me more at ease. And perhaps he's right. What harm could me taking *his* number do? It's easy to hide your caller ID on an iPhone, the police showed me how to do it after my problems with Shaun the stalker.

"That would actually be really helpful, Nick. Thank you. Yes. If you see her then let her know they have my details at reception and she can call me. That'd be great." I feel a twang of regret at having been so obstructive up until now. He's just a nice guy trying to be nice. I unearth my phone from my bag and jab his digits in as he reels them off.

"And what's her name?" he asks as I save his contact.

"Emily. She said she had a video call or something to do, so I'm hoping it's just that."

"You got a surname for Emily? We could google her, get an agent contact?"

"The last name on her card is Bryant. So if she doesn't call this afternoon, I'll get my agent on it, I guess. But hopefully she'll show up." I feel my stomach rumble. It's 2:08. I might just have time to grab lunch en route if I leave now. "Nick, thank you. Really appreciate your help but I absolutely have to go or I'm going to be late."

"Casting?"

"Yeah. Burbank."

"Jesus. Okay, good luck with that. Rather you than me." He grins.

I slide into the leather seat of the Audi and start the engine. I can't help but watch his sharp suited figure recede in the rearview mirror as I join the flow of traffic back toward the freeway.

I just have time to hit an In-N-Out drive-through and ravenously inhale a cheeseburger and fries on the way to Burbank. I might have to acquaint myself with the apartment gym if this keeps happening.

When I get to the Warner Bros. parking lot I have only ten minutes to spare. I check the surrounding vehicles for inhabitants and once I'm sure the coast is clear I wrestle off my blouse and pop on a short-sleeved cashmere jumper. I need to go from the near-future, fictional Mars terra-former Rose Atwood to the real-life Raquel Eidelman, in 1945, one of the first female students ever accepted at Harvard Medical School. I swap my jeans for slacks and slip into some low pumps, stuffing my clothes into the back footwell. Then I flip down the sun visor mirror, loosen my hair, and fluff it out, letting its natural wave do its thing. Finally I apply a deep-plum lipstick to my lips, comb through my thick brows, and spritz a healthy spurt of perfume to cover my burger shame.

Done. I give myself a look in the mirror. I throw a few of Raquel's lines at myself with a warm American hum. Then I pop the door, grab my bag, and wiggle with intent straight into my next appointment, ready to slam the patriarchy 1940s-style.

9

New Friends

I'M STILL RIDING HIGH ON THE BUZZ OF THE SECOND AUDITION WHEN I get back to the apartment building that evening.

Three network executives, who'd all seen *Eyre,* and three scenes that flowed in all the right places. It couldn't have gone better. Them asking about my availability at the end had been the icing on the cake.

I drive into the Ellis Building's underground car park and catch sight of Miguel at the valet station. He gives a cheery wave as I pull up and jogs over to meet me.

"Mia, Mia, lovely Mia, it's so very good to . . . see ya," he sing-songs through my open window. I cut the engine as he appraises my broad smile. "Oh? It's a good day, huh? Nice casting?"

"Yeah, I think so, Miguel," I say tentatively, not wanting to jinx myself. As I get out of the car, he assesses my audition outfit and nods his approval.

"Nice. A 1940s part, right?" he guesses.

I nod. Correct.

"Okay . . . Secretary?" he hazards. "Politician's wife?"

"Harvard Med."

"Oooo! Nice!" He does a finger slap, delighted with himself.

"Yep." I grin, his energy infectious. "Feeling pretty good."

"Damn straight." He slides into the car with my keys to valet-park. "Well, you let me know how it goes. I want to know what they say. But if your getup is anything to go by"—he nods to my 1940s hair and makeup—"you got *options,* girl. You know what I mean?"

It's only when I get into the lift that I realize, in all of today's excitement, I've misplaced my own apartment keycard. I head back down to reception to get another card coded.

UPSTAIRS, I DUMP MY STUFF and head straight for the fridge. I'm in the mood for something fancy. I definitely deserve it after the day I've had. But as I pull my chilled bottle of gifted Perrier-Jouët from the fridge door compartment, it suddenly occurs to me that my bag was left unattended today. Did I lose my key or could someone have taken it? I pause with the fridge door still ajar as I scan the apartment, the chill from the dewy bottle in my hand making me shiver. The empty apartment stares back at me, silently, exactly as I left it this morning. Nothing out of place. Besides, no one could have gotten past the reception downstairs without being noticed. I shake off the eerie feeling that someone else has been in the apartment. No one stole my apartment card; it probably just fell out of my bag when I was rushing around today. Why steal a blank white card and leave a wallet and phone? I grab some grapes from the fridge compartment to go with my drink.

I pop the champagne cork and let a puff of effervescent sparkle loose before carefully filling a single flute. A memory of New Year with George flashes through my mind but then I suddenly realize I haven't thought about him since that first audition today. Not once since then. All thoughts of the article Cynthia sent me this morning watered down to nothing. Well, almost nothing.

If anything is worth celebrating then it's that. Outside the light is fading and I toast the twinkling city lights beyond the glass of the apartment, taking a cool sip of fizz as I wander to the bathroom to run a hot bath. I bequeath myself: self-care.

Salts in, steam rising, I hear the familiar ping of a text message from my bag in the living room and suddenly Emily and everything that happened earlier today comes back to me.

Oh shit, her stuff.

I look at my already nearly drained champagne glass. If it is her, I can't drive anywhere to meet her tonight. I feel a strange thrill of excitement. I cannot wait to hear her excuse for disappearing—the reason an adult woman would leave all her money and her only method of transportation with a complete stranger for a whole day. I mean where the hell did she go? That thought, and the fact that I'm suddenly dying to talk to someone about this beyond-weird day, propels me back into the living room. I think, after this, Emily and I could become pretty good friends. I mean, in script terms, it's a pretty great best-friend meet-cute.

I skip into the living room, towel tight around me, pour myself another quick glass, and tip the contents of my audition bag out onto the sofa.

High-heeled boots, makeup pouch, white blouse, my wallet, Emily's wallet, Emily's Avis car keys, my water bottle, folded-up audition pages, and my phone. The lit-up screen showing a text from a number I don't recognize.

"Oooo!" I plop down next to the pile of stuff and read.

Weds Feb 10, 6:36pm

Hi Mia, this is Delilah from reception at Casting Ground Zero. Thought I should let you know: nobody collected your note today. We're closing up now but I'm in tomorrow so will pass on your cell number if she shows up then. Del x

I stare at the text, unblinkingly.

What? Emily didn't show up. My eyes find her wallet beside me. Her car keys with their Avis key fob containing its hastily penned number plate info. What the hell happened to her? With no money and no car.

I shiver and reflexively take a sip of my drink, the sound of the bath thundering on in the other room. What should I do? Should I call Michael and tell him what happened today? But I don't want him to make trouble for her with her agent. I'm pretty sure if something bad happened to her someone else at the studio would have noticed.

I have a habit of assuming something terrible has happened to someone when in actual fact they're just ghosting me. George was absolutely fine, just moving house and having a drink in the pub without any intention of ever speaking to me again.

So perhaps Emily is fine, too. Maybe she has another bank card in a coin purse, or Apple Pay, who knows. Perhaps she'll get in touch tomorrow. I should probably wait until the morning and reassess.

I head back to the bathroom to turn off the water, warm steam hanging in the air. Maybe something just came up, an emergency, perhaps she got a call and didn't make it into her audition. I know if anything happened to my family, I'd be off instantly, leaving everything behind me. But the thought niggles slightly because how would she have gotten anywhere in an emergency without her car and her money? I suppose someone could have picked her up, or she could have ordered an Uber on her phone . . . Whatever it is, it won't be a mystery for too long. If she doesn't contact me by tomorrow then I'll pass her things on to her agent through my agent. None of it is really my business. If she'd thought about me today half as much as I've thought about her, I'm pretty confident we wouldn't be in this situation.

And with that thought I tap on some music, slip out of my audition clothes, and sink into the hot bubbles of the bath.

Half an hour later my self-care session has moved to the bedroom. Thick toweling robe on, dark chocolate selection box on my chest, and old *Sex and the City* reruns playing on the TV. The idea of ordering in some kind of udon is playing at the back of my mind when one of Carrie's ill-advised shoe shopping excursions is unceremoniously interrupted by the loud electrical buzz of my apartment door bell. I bolt up reflexively, scattering chocolates across the bedding.

Someone's at the door.

The clock under the TV reads 7:12. It's not so much the hour that bothers me—it's the fact that I literally know no one in LA except Souki and she doesn't know where I'm staying.

I grab my phone, slip it into my robe pocket, and pull the robe tight around me. The buzzer fizzes loudly again as I pad out to the apartment hall. The security monitor next to the front door is illuminated and there is a woman standing in the hallway outside my door, holding something in her hands. Closer to the screen I take in her features. Dark-brown hair pulled back from her face, a white blouse—and for a second I'm certain it's Emily.

But then there's no way she could know where I live. She doesn't even know my full name, let alone my address in LA. I squint at the monitor, the figure's features slowly making sense. It's the building's front-desk concierge. I let out a breath I hadn't realized I was holding and swing open the door.

She greets me with a warm smile. Her name badge is partly obscured by the large package she is cradling, and despite having seen her every evening since I arrived, I realize I can't for the life of me remember her name.

"Hi, Mia," she says. "Sorry to bother. This just came for you. Someone dropped it at reception—it wasn't Michelle but it seemed pretty urgent so I thought I'd bring it straight up."

"Okay," I reply, baffled. I assume someone called Michelle must have delivered my welcome gifts to the apartment before I arrived on Sunday.

The tightly bound packet in her arms crinkles, the brown packing paper soft in her hands, something angular hidden within. There are no postage marks on it. No need if it was hand-delivered. I see my name written in neat precise black Sharpie across its front in handwriting I don't recognize. I try to think who on earth would be dropping off a parcel for me at seven o'clock at night. My agent perhaps, it could be scripts. But he'd just email them.

I realize she's waiting for me to take it or at least acknowledge her effort in bringing it up for me. I'm sure it's not part of her job description to cart people's stuff directly to their doors.

"Shall I?" I ask, taking the heft of it from her. "Thank you so much for bringing it up here—" I spy her name badge now. "—*Lucy.* I really appreciate it."

She beams. "No problem at all. It's a bit slow downstairs at this time of the evening, gave me something to do! I'm guessing you've noticed the building's pretty quiet at the moment."

She's clearly bored and in the mood for a chat. I shift in my doorway, the package awkward in my arms, but I have to admit my curiosity is piqued.

"It's funny you say that, I was thinking exactly that this morning. It does seem oddly quiet here." She gives me a conspiratorial smile. "Did they build this place on an Indian burial ground or something?" I joke.

"You know what, they may as well have." She laughs. "No, it's, actually—" She stops herself abruptly, like a Transylvanian villager suddenly thinking twice about telling me about the local landlord. If a peal of thunder sounded now, it wouldn't be entirely out of place. I let out a compulsive giggle at the sudden campness of the situation.

"Wow. That bad, huh?" I ask.

She flushes slightly. "Pretty sure I shouldn't be telling you this. Are you, like, a nervous person? Do you get anxiety or . . . ?"

I shift my heavy mystery package in my arms and briefly consider. "Nah, I think I'm pretty sturdy. I suppose it depends what it is."

She considers before continuing. "Basically, during construction on the building some state geologists discovered that there's a minor fault line running between Wilshire and Ninth. Right where we are. There was an article in the *Los Angeles Times.*"

It's not what I was expecting. "What, like an earthquake fault line?" I ask. "Under us? Here?"

She snorts out a little laugh as my voice leaps an octave.

"Yeah. But the fault line's inactive, so the city decided it was fine to carry on construction. Apparently they can stay dormant for up to three thousand years, so . . . I think we're probably fine. But a lot of buyers read the article and pulled out of buying apartments. We opened last year and not many people actually moved in. Most of the apartments are foreign-owned, Asian investments, just sitting empty. We've got a couple of short-term lets over pilot season like you and a few out-of-town studio executives are renting up on the top floor but aside from that, I'd say there's only about twenty full-time residents."

"Out of how many apartments?"

"Two hundred."

"Wow. No wonder I don't see anyone. How can the building stay open?"

"Investors?" She shrugs her ignorance. "As long as I've still got a job, I don't ask." She answers before she addresses my expression. "It's totally fine, I promise. Seriously, I would not be working here if I thought for a second that the whole place might fall in on me. LA hasn't had a proper quake since the 1990s anyway. And if there was one then it wouldn't really matter where you were in the Downtown area. There's a lot of high-rises to topple."

Well, that *is* a comforting thought. I think of the view behind me through the living room window, LA sparkling in miniature out in the darkness, three hundred feet up in the night sky with nothing but cool evening air between me and the concrete beneath.

"Fantastic!" I round up, raising my package in thanks. "Well, good night then, Lucy! Sleep well!"

She gives a friendly chuckle as she heads off down the hall. "My conscience is clear. You said you weren't a nervous person!"

She rounds the corner, disappearing back toward the lifts, and I stand for a moment alone with my package, its handwritten label ominously staring back at me. I shiver in my bathrobe as I head back into my three-hundred-foot-high death trap.

10

The Whole Package

I LAY THE PACKAGE ON THE RUG IN THE LIVING ROOM AND SIT CROSS-legged before it. A present perhaps, from Michael, or from Cynthia back in London. An apology from George.

I don't know why but I'm reminded of Shaun, my stalker, and the package he sent. The police officer in charge of the case told me, "If anything turns up at the house that you're not expecting then give us a call." I try to remember if he said to open it first or to *definitely* not open it. But that's irrelevant really as there is absolutely no way Shaun my theater stalker (a) knows I'm staying here, or (b) is weird enough to follow up on that knowledge. At least, I assume.

I fish my phone out of my pocket and check my emails. Nothing new from Cynthia. But there is a new email from Michael just forty-five minutes ago.

Mia,

Just got a call from *First Class* (the Harvard med series) after you left the room today. They LOVED you. It's looking good for this one. An offer has gone out for the professor, they're trying for name, but all the female roles are still in the mix. Should hear tomorrow. They're showing tapes to the network in the morning and pushing for you hard. That Boston series is coming back with a screen-test offer tomorrow too.

Also, as I mentioned in my previous email, Universal is emailing over some prep materials for your meeting with Kathryn Mayer. So keep an eye out. No idea what they are, they won't tell me, and they want you to sign an NDA—I've attached below. E-sign it and shoot it back to them direct, details below.

M. x

I scroll up through my emails for his last one—I must have missed it—but all I find is one he sent yesterday. Perhaps he forgot to send it or it bounced back. I look back at the package. Very odd. Prep materials. I click on the NDA, drag my E-signature into the pdf, and send to the email address attached. Then I tear into the package, liberating a thick stack of bound paper heavily watermarked with my name. A script. A thick fresh script. I read the title page. *Galatea.* Can't say the name rings a bell.

I shake the packaging for more information, and two recordable DVDs plop out onto the rug. *Pygmalion* is scrawled in Sharpie across one label and *My Fair Lady* across the other. I root around in the packaging for more and find a compliment slip with the Universal logo; my eyes flick down to the signature. Assistant to Kathryn Mayer.

Dear Mia,

Please find enclosed confidential preparatory materials relating to your forthcoming meeting with Kathryn Mayer.

Kathryn has asked me to make these resources available to you with a view to discussing the title role in the proposed production, the adaptation of which will be based on the original idea by George Bernard Shaw.

Kathryn is keen to stress the reimagining of Shaw's masterpiece will be modernized reflecting a 21st-century sensibility. Hence her desire for collaboration and your thoughts. She is also keen to stress the project will be adhering to Shaw's amended ending so will strongly diverge from the material provided, and previous productions, in tone.

Also, enclosed is an early draft of the screenplay, please note dialogue and scenes will change.

We hope you enjoy the material and we very much look forward to meeting you in person on Friday.

Kind regards,

Jimmy Torres
Assistant to Kathryn Mayer

As I read, the plot of *My Fair Lady* comes back to me. Rex Harrison barking orders at a doe-eyed Audrey Hepburn in the 1960s blockbuster, where an arrogant British phonetics professor wagers he can turn a Cockney flower girl into a princess. It was a musical. My blood runs cold. Oh my God please let this not be a musical! I think back to my one day of a cappella singing on *Eyre,* how my cheeks flushed so much that the hair and makeup department had to stop filming to deal with my redness. Jane was supposed to be embarrassed, sure, but not visibly on the verge of an aneurysm. I feel my heart thumping at the mere idea that I might be asked to sing at the Universal meeting. I flick through the script desperately scouring for songs but thankfully find none.

I tap *Galatea* into my phone and Wikipedia tops the searches. The myth of Pygmalion and Galatea. A sculptor, Pygmalion, creates a statue of the ideal woman out of ivory. He names it Galatea and falls in love with it. And then Galatea comes to life. Every man's dream.

My mind instantly flashes to Naomi Fairn and I immediately feel guilty. She can't help being who she is. *Don't hate the player, Mia, hate the game.*

I heft the script in my hands. I suppose I had better get reading.

I'M TEN PAGES FROM THE end, propped up in bed, when my phone pings. I check the screen and I'm surprised to see the name of an actress I haven't seen in years, Bee Miller. I sent a generic, I'm-in-town WhatsApp to almost every actor in my contacts, but I wouldn't have necessarily expected her to get back to me. The text says she's in LA too and she suggests grabbing brunch tomorrow morning in Venice. It's a bit of a drive and we've never been close friends but I could definitely use the distraction. If there's one thing I don't need any more of it's time alone. All I have to do tomorrow is background research on this new script anyway. I fire back a response and we make a plan.

As soon as I've read the screenplay's final line I flip the manuscript to inspect the title page once more.

Bloody hell. I stare at it, floored, as I smooth my hand over its silky paper. Wow. This is good. This is a very, very good part. This could be it. The big one.

I try to think why Kathryn Mayer could have thought of me for this role. But then it's obvious, it's because of Jane. Kathryn Mayer wants Jane Eyre to play the lead role in this film. That's who she wants to meet on Friday, not me, not Mia from rural Bedfordshire. Not Mia whose boyfriend left her with four words less than a week ago. Not Mia who hasn't touched another human being in days except for the odd arm squeeze. Kathryn doesn't want me. Yes, that makes more sense. Kathryn Mayer wants Jane Eyre—with her self-worth, her fierce independence, and her unwavering dignity—to be the lead in her studio's new film. Well, luckily, I can do that. I can play Jane in my sleep and if Jane can get me this job, this film, then I'll be her for as long as I have to.

I look down at the bright new script. It's not a musical, it's a

tragicomic feature film with complex and incredibly human characters. An award-bait part for an older actor and the role of a lifetime
for a younger actress. The role of a lifetime. And instead of fear coming with that thought, I feel only hope, pure and clean and bright. I
can do this part. I already know how to do every scene in this script.
The words are mine.

I just need to reassure Kathryn at the meeting. I just need to be
who she wants me to be.

My phone pings loudly in the silence of the apartment. I look at
the screen. The text is from another unknown number.

The situation with Emily floods back to me. Her things, my
promise to return them.

But she doesn't have my number. She never went back to collect
my note.

Tentatively I tap the text.

Weds Feb 10, 10:57pm

Hey. Nick here. Sorry, to contact you like this . . . I got your number from the
casting studio this afternoon. Just wanted to let you know I paid her meter till
tomorrow. A parking attendant showed up and I sort of went with my gut.
She should be okay for parking until midday tomorrow. Excuse the number
theft. Just wondering if everything worked out? Nick

I'm not really sure how to respond. I imagine him lurking outside
the casting studio until Delilah left and then accosting her with some
story of chivalric good-deed-ery in order to get my number. But
then I remember that he works directly opposite her building and
he is stop-in-your-tracks-and-take-a-good-look attractive. Delilah
probably just offered him my number straight off the bat. And if I'm
being completely honest with myself, he isn't exactly stalker material.
Stalkers aren't usually above-averagely handsome men with good
jobs. At least not in real life.

It is also kind of sweet of him to pay Emily's meter.

I find myself suddenly wondering if Nick is interested in me. If after George anyone ever could be. Is this Nick's stab at making a connection? Will we one day, bleary-eyed, be telling our grandchildren this story of how we met? I hope not, because I'm not in a good place to start any kind of relationship right now. Even a holiday fling. And after George I'm sure as hell not going to go out with a man more attractive than me.

I let my thumb hover over the message keyboard, regardless. He's probably just being nice. Talking to him can't hurt and I have an overwhelming urge to discuss today's events with someone.

I type.

> You're a terrifying man, Nick. But thank you for letting me know. And thanks for paying the meter. No word on Emily though. Hopefully she'll surface tomorrow. If not I'll get my agent to contact hers. Weird that she hasn't missed her wallet. All very strange. Hopefully she's fine and just flaky. M

I type an x after my name, then delete it, then hit send. His gray dots pulse. I wonder what his job is, if he's involved in production in some way. But maybe he has nothing to do with the film industry— all sorts of people live and work in LA. He could be an architect. I try to imagine him at an elevated desk, his head bowed, squinting at floor plans. No, he doesn't seem the sit-down-all-day kind of guy.

His reply bursts onto the screen.

> I didn't even ask the receptionist for your number btw. She just gave it to me?! No problem about the meter. I kind of have history with parking attendants around here anyway. I'm slightly concerned about this Emily situation, all a bit strange, but I guess you're right to give her the benefit of the doubt. Let me know if I can help in any way. Nick

His pulsing dots disappear. I guess that's that for tonight. It's eleven P.M. People with real jobs need to get their beauty sleep, I guess. And I should probably call it a night too.

I lift the heavy *Galatea* script from my legs and place it carefully on the desk in the corner of the living room. Outside, the lights of Hollywood twinkle magically all the way to the hills. I think of the distance from the apartment window to the ground below. I think of that actress's dive from the blinding Hollywood sign into the darkness beyond and shiver.

I pull the heavy curtains closed and remind myself that fault lines can be inactive for years—I'm not going to fall. I'm safe up here in my sparkling tower. And I'm almost certainly nothing like her.

11

The Abandoned Car

THURSDAY, FEBRUARY 11

ALL 110 POUNDS OF BEE MILLER SITS ACROSS FROM ME IN THE SERENITY Cloud Buddhist tearoom in Venice Beach. Our brunch consists of chili-flaked avocado on rice cake and a pot of Himalayan salt tea. I am clearly being punished by the universe for yesterday's In-N-Out burger.

Bee nibbles her smeared green rice disk. "I just don't get it," she protests, mid-flow. "They offered it to *her*. I know you're not supposed to say it but she has two chins, Mia. She literally has two chins."

She's telling me about the screen-test part she lost to another actress on Monday. A new superhero-origin-story TV series.

She shrugs comically before continuing. "What am I supposed to do, get two chins? And I mean I know she's not up to my standard physically, she can't do action. How is she going to do the fight scenes? After two seasons of *Final Conflict,* it's pretty clear my stunt work is going to be better than hers, right? She's done, what, like a day of harness work in that crappy time-loop show. Was she even a series lead on that?"

It's hard to know what to say so I just nod and sip my disgusting tea and try to think Serenity Cloud thoughts as the café around us buzzes with similarly fraught conversations.

"I mean, bless her," she continues with terrifying earnestness, "I know she really struggles with her weight but how are they even going to film her? Like from what angle? They'll have to shoot all her scenes from above."

Something inside me flutters. I think I should probably say something now.

"I don't know, Bee. She seems pretty in shape to me. And I'm not exactly a model myself, if you know what I mean."

Bee's eyes flare wide and innocent as if I've accused her of a hate crime. "Oh my God, Mia," she blurts apologetically. "Please . . . I am not talking about you. You look fantastic. You're naturally thin. And I would never even—God, you must think I'm such a bitch. But, I mean, this is an action series I'm talking about, you know. It's based on a comic book. The costumes are basically latex. It's not an issue for you, obviously, you do more *Austen*-y stuff anyway. I'm just saying, for her this series is going to be an *uphill* struggle. She's really going to have to keep on top of it. I'm guessing production will have to hire a nutritionist for her. She is going to have to work really hard. Really hard. That's all I'm saying." She bites into her rice cake diplomatically.

I nod, pause for a moment, then try to wrangle back the conversation.

"So aside from that, how have you been finding it?"

She looks up from pouring more salty tea. "LA?"

"Yeah. It's got a weird vibe, right?"

Her perfect little features pucker. "Weird how?"

"I don't know. Empty," I say. "Perhaps I'm just not going to the right kind of places?"

"Oh God, I don't know, I've been too busy to notice. Literally it's lines, tapes, meetings, and parties. It's exhausting. I'm actually getting a bit puffy on it. You know, you try to drink enough water but it's never enough, is it? Are you using ice in the morning?"

"Ice?"

"Yeah, on your face." She looks at me expectantly.

I'm not sure how to reply as I don't know what exactly I'd be doing with the ice on my face. "It's good for my puffiness," she adds, with her completely un-puffy face. "You dunk your face in a bowl of water with ice in. You do it first thing, like as soon as you wake up. It feels *so* good."

I push my now browning avo rice cake around the plate. "Nice. Okay. I will give that a go." God, I would kill for some bacon. "So talk to me about these parties. Work or . . ."

"Work, kind of everything out here is work, right? Yeah, my agent has basically been sending me to them. Well, it's like 'oh, so and so is going from the agency do you want to tag along'—that kind of thing." She leans forward across the table. "They are really handsy over here, right?"

I feel my eyebrows shoot up. "Handsy, like—?"

"Uh-huh." She nods meaningfully.

"In public?"

"Kind of, yeah. Sometimes you get a warning but I mean what are you going to do? Best thing is just not to get caught alone with anyone, or if someone gets a bit grabby just make an excuse to get away or make a joke of it. It's a minefield, but then isn't everything?"

There are a million things I want to say, but of course I say none of them.

"They're super useful, though. The parties. You get to meet a lot of faces. If you want I can get you invited to the next one I go to?"

I cannot think of anything worse. "You know, I'm not sure my jet lag is up to it yet, Bee. But thank you so much."

She suddenly seems to realize that she hasn't asked me anything about myself. "But what about you? How are you?" I can tell by her tone that she knows about George and Naomi. There's no way she hasn't seen the photos. I'm amazed she's kept quiet this long. That's the one good thing about being single now, the whole fucking world won't know everything that happens in my private life from now on.

"Yeah." I answer brightly, knowing full well the danger of pack animals showing weakness. "I'm really good actually. Keeping busy, trying to get on with it to be honest."

"I can't believe he did that, Mi." There it is. But I'm not going to take the bait and ask her how she knows. She continues regardless. "But I suppose if he was going to leave you for anyone then Naomi Fairn is a pretty good choice. She basically looks like an angel, right?" I pray that's a rhetorical question and I'm not supposed to answer. "I mean, imagine if he'd left you for someone less attractive. She's ridiculously sexy too, bloody hell. You are dealing with it *so* well, Mi. I'd be going absolutely mad, have you seen her underwear shoot for La Perla on Instagram?"

I sip my tea, shake my head, and try to work out how to end this sojourn in hell.

"Anyway, you're going to be fine," she assures me. "You'll get something great out here and before you know it you'll be on to the next."

Outside the café we promise to catch up next week but as I trudge back to the car park a broken woman, I vow to never ever brunch again.

In the car I pull a banana from my bag and gorge, ravenous after my dry and salty breakfast. Maybe I'm just not cut out for LA. Maybe I'm not cut out for relationships.

My phone pings in my bag. I lazily tip it out onto the passenger seat and continue to concentrate on my banana. It's Souki. She wants to meet up tomorrow. Thank God, an actual friend, but I'm way too drained to reply. Instead I scroll absentmindedly through my new messages and pause to reread Nick's. I feel a little stir as I think of his eyes, his smile, the collar of his shirt against his neck. The way he found my irritation amusing. The way he spoke to me. He was flirting, wasn't he? *Bloody hell.*

My eyes catch a glint of metal on the seat beside me. Emily's keys.

And my stomach tightens as I remember the reason Nick and I met in the first place. I still haven't heard from her. Her wallet and keys stare back at me accusingly. She's been without them for almost twenty-four hours now. How did she get home? And suddenly, for the first time since she disappeared, I get the sensation that something bad really has happened to Emily.

And with that thought I start the engine and update the satnav. I'm going back to sort this out.

I DON'T SEE THE CAR at first, and for a second the relief is overwhelming. I imagine that earlier this morning, roadside assistance helped her pop the locks so she could drive home. Her bank cards canceled and new ones issued. But as I pull along the street past a brown delivery van her car comes into view. She didn't come back for it.

I park farther along the street, shut off the engine, and think. I should call Michael at this stage and drop Emily's things off at his office. He can contact her agent and pass them on to her. I look into my rearview mirror at her car sitting there, in the California sunlight, as if nothing were out of the ordinary.

The clock on the dash reads 11:28. Nick topped up the meter until noon. Half an hour until it runs out. Without thinking I grab my wallet, her car keys, and mine and get out. I'm across the road in a couple of strides. My plan is to top up the meter but as I approach a thought occurs and before I know it I'm depressing the door fob, the electric clunk of the lock responds, and I'm opening her car door.

My thinking is this. Perhaps there's something in the car with her information, some way of contacting her or at least verifying her name is actually Emily Bryant so I don't sound completely mad when I talk to Michael on the phone.

I dive into the passenger seat as if I own the car and scan the backseat. A sweater. Gray marl with an NYU logo. Some old scripts. In the front cupholder: a pack of gum, sunglasses, pocket tissues. I lean forward and pop the glove compartment. And there it is. The car rental document. I feel a smile burst across my face. Just call me Miss Marple.

I slide it out and unfold the carbon-copy paper. Name, address, phone number. Jackpot.

Something in my peripheral vision catches my attention. I see a figure approaching fast in the rearview mirror. I spin in my seat just in time to catch a young man's eyes as he power-walks past my open door with a white poodle in tow. My heart is racing. I have no idea if what I'm doing is illegal but it feels like it might be.

I don't know how the American legal system works and I don't want to find out—best to quit while I'm ahead. I hastily fold the rental agreement, slip it in my pocket, and exit the vehicle. Once it's safely locked, I feed the meter up to the limit of midday tomorrow and head back to my own car.

Inside I crank up the Audi's air-conditioning, the sweat rolling down my back from my brief stint of sleuthing. I let my pulse settle as I pull the rumpled paper from my pocket and smooth out its wrinkles on my thigh.

Customer name: Emily Bryant
Address for duration of rental: 1929 Argyll Avenue, Los Angeles, CA 90068

Her name, the same as the bank card. And an address. It occurs to me that I could pop over to her apartment right now and drop off her keys and that would be the end of it. I reach for my seatbelt but then something stops me. I should probably try to call her first. I check the rental document for a number and find one at the bottom of the page in tight neat scroll. Her cell number.

I type the digits in carefully and press dial. The ringtone burrs, once, twice, three times then connects to answerphone. I bite my lip and then speak.

"Hi Emily, it's Mia from the Mars casting yesterday. Listen, I don't know what happened but somehow I totally lost you." I hear myself let out a nervous laugh. "I'm guessing . . . something came up, but don't worry I still have your wallet and keys and the meter is all paid up until midday tomorrow. So hopefully the car will be fine there." I pause, not really sure how to continue. "So listen, when you get this, can you call me back? Anytime, and we can arrange a hand-over. I'm hoping this is the right number for you, but if I don't hear back from you, I'll let my agent know what happened and pass all your info on to him. I'm going to get your stuff back to you if it kills me." I let out another joyless chuckle in the silent car. "Anyway, this is my number. Call me. Oh, it's Mia, by the way." I hang up and frown as I add her name into my phone contact list.

I'm doing the right thing.

12

An Unexpected Visitor

THURSDAY, FEBRUARY 11

I'M MAKING FAJITAS WHEN THE TEXT COMES THROUGH.

Necessity means I've managed to keep myself busy with research for the Kathryn Mayer meeting at Universal tomorrow. My mind only strays from the DVDs Kathryn's office sent me occasionally to respond to texts from Nick asking if I would like to grab coffee this week. With no lines to learn for tomorrow I've had time to make copious script notes and familiarize myself with the scenes in general, and I'm feeling as ready as I'll ever be for whatever tomorrow may hold.

It's after six P.M. when my phone finally pings and I hop over to it, spatula in hand, half expecting it is, half knowing it isn't, Emily. I swear, if it wasn't for the physical fact of that empty white car parked in North Hollywood, I'd start to wonder if I'd made Emily up completely.

I'm half right. The text isn't from Emily, it's from my friend Souki. Asking: Do I, or do I not, want to go on a Hollywood Homes of the Stars four-by-four tour around LA tomorrow afternoon?

I burst out laughing at the incongruity of the question, choking on the spicy fug of fajita seasoning filling the kitchen. Souki knows me too well. The idea sounds like tacky, tourist heaven. I cannot think of anything I would rather do tomorrow, after the most stressful meeting of my life, than sit in a four-by-four and listen to a tour guide talk complete nonsense while we gawp at A-listers' houses.

I shoot back an affirmative and pop my tortilla wraps in the oven to warm. It's early for supper but I want to get an early night tonight. After eating, I'll lay out my outfit for tomorrow, take a bath, then head to bed to reread the script and hopefully be asleep by ten. That way I'll be bright-eyed when the alarm goes in the morning.

Belly full and bath running, I select a silk camisole for tomorrow to go under an oversized Ganni suit paired with some sharp heels; I want to look smart. It's a business meeting, after all. And while I'm sure Kathryn can imagine me playing Cockney Eliza in *Galatea,* I want to convince her I can play post-makeover Eliza too.

My phone buzzes on the nightstand, and I wander over expecting to see Souki's name.

But as I get closer, my breath catches in my throat. Instead of Souki's name I see Emily's. It's her.

I grab the phone and sink down onto the edge of the bed to read.

Thurs Feb 11, 6:43pm

So, so sorry about yesterday. Long story . . . Goes without saying, I am a complete disaster. Thank you so much for looking after the car. You are an actual lifesaver. Can I collect my wallet and keys tonight? Xxxx

I stare at her words for a long time. My first thought, though ghoulish, is simply *Thank God she's alive.* Which is a strange thought considering that it hadn't explicitly crossed my mind that she wouldn't be—not consciously anyway. Not enough for me to raise any kind of alarm or tell anyone what had happened. And yet, there the thought is.

The mind immediately goes to strange places when strange things happen, I suppose. A cascade effect. Our ideas of what's possible in the world shift up to meet the new reality. But she's not dead. She's not even missing. She's right here talking to me; I've let my imagination run wild, untended, over the last two days, when the truth is, I just need to return this woman's things.

I tap out a response.

> So glad to hear from you! Yes, no problem at all. We've all been there. Could you pop over to mine and collect tonight x

The dots pulse.

Of course. What's your address?

My thumb hesitates over the keypad for a second, as I consider whether it might be better to meet her in a more neutral setting, somewhere a bit more public. After all I don't know her. I don't know her situation. But then meeting in a public place means getting in the car now and driving somewhere and staying out way too late the night before the most important meeting of my life. The last thing I want to do is head out to some random bar or diner. I don't think I can reasonably ask her to wait until tomorrow. God knows how she's managed this long without money or a car. It's not as if I'm here on my own, Miguel and Lucy are just downstairs. Every inch of this building seems to be covered by CCTV anyway. Seeing her here should be perfectly safe.

I type out my address and hit send.

Her gray dots pulse for a long time. Then finally a response.

Great. I'll be there in 30 mins. X

I suppose the silver lining to her coming here tonight is that there's no way I'm going to have time to get nervous about tomorrow's meeting.

I flick on CNN, watching the minutes count down to her arrival and wondering if I should have changed out of my sweats and into something more suitable for company. But then I don't really want her coming into the apartment; it's getting late and while I had thought we could have been friends before now it's probably best if I don't get too involved with whatever weirdness is currently going on in her life. To be honest I should have probably handed her things in at the police station or something. Most people would have by now.

I grab her wallet and keys and place them ready on the entrance table, next to the security monitor.

I mute the TV when the intercom sounds, and head out to the hallway to answer the security phone.

"Hi Mia, it's Lucy at reception. We've got an Emily down here to see you?"

It's strange hearing Emily's name coming out of someone else's mouth, and immediately my worry about the whole situation is halved. Emily is just a person, an ordinary person, standing downstairs at reception, talking to Lucy. I'm suddenly certain that whatever happened to Emily yesterday will be something underwhelming and disappointingly banal.

"Okay, great. Thanks, Lucy. Could you send her up?"

"Sure, no problem."

Only after I hang up the phone do I remember that the rental document I stole from Emily's car is still downstairs locked away in my car.

Shit.

I dither for a second before dashing into the living room to grab my Audi keys, but just as I pick them up the door buzzer sounds. I don't have time to go and get them. She's here.

I see her on the video monitor in grainy black and white. She's dressed differently from yesterday, which isn't particularly unusual, but for a microsecond it throws me. Though her hair is tied back in the same loose bun and her same minimalist Nike rucksack is slung over her angular shoulder, just as it was.

I open the door with a smile. "Emily! Hi."

The words come before I really see the woman in front of me. She was looking the other way on the monitor and now that our eyes meet for the first time I know instantly: This isn't her. This isn't Emily.

"Hey! Good to see you again," the woman says, giving me a broad beautiful smile. I feel my features ease into a smile in reply while my mind races to make sense of what the hell is going on. Her voice sounds exactly the same as Emily's. Her creaky New York vocal fry. Her hair, her rucksack, her tinkling bracelets all the same and yet . . . Her face is extremely similar to Emily's but it's not *Emily's*. What the hell is going on? I study her features—full lips, chestnut hair, thick brows, a smudge of eye shadow, and pale skin—all like Emily's, but not.

I must be just misremembering what Emily looked like, right? After all, I only spoke to her for a few minutes almost two days ago. I could definitely have misremembered her. She just responded to the name Emily as well. It would be beyond weird if she wasn't her.

The woman hitches her rucksack pointedly and I realize I'm staring at her.

"God, sorry," I apologize, having to tear my eyes away from her. "It's been a really long day. Jet lag!"

"No, no, it's me who should be apologizing. Seriously. Thank you so much for taking care of my car, Mia. I really appreciate it."

For a second I wonder if this might just be a friend of Emily's, but why would she have her bag, her jewelry, her voice. Why would a friend of Emily's be pretending to be Emily? That's ridiculous, it's definitely her.

I shake off the thoughts. Flustered, I grab for her wallet and keys on the table next to the door, giving her a reassuring smile. "Got everything right here." But I catch myself just before handing anything over. As desperate as I am for this weird situation to be over, I wonder how Jane would handle this and I pause. The woman in front of me hasn't even told me what happened to her yet. Why she disappeared on me. Where's she's been all this time. It's still all a complete mystery.

"Can I ask what exactly happened yesterday?" I ask. "I mean, sorry to be rude, but where the hell did you go?"

There's a subtle flicker of annoyance behind Emily's eyes. "Ah, yeah. I guess I owe you an explanation, right?" She smiles apologetically. "I've kind of been having a bit of man trouble, so to speak. It's complicated. I'm so sorry about the whole thing; getting you involved, putting you out." She shakes her head at what I assume is the ludicrousness of her situation. "Basically, after you went down to feed the meter, I got a call, from my ex"—she rolls her eyes—"so I took it in the restroom. It was kind of an emergency and you were in your audition by then so I had to get an Uber across town to go sort it out straightaway rather than wait for you to finish and get my keys. I should have waited, or left a note like you did, but it was pretty time-sensitive. Anyway, the whole thing went on for ages and my phone ran out. So I only got your message when I finally got home and charged my phone this afternoon. It's been intense"—she raises both hands, ringed forefingers crossed—"but hopefully I'm rid of this guy now."

Jesus. I guess I was wrong about her not being the sort to take shit from boyfriends. But then I suppose even Jane took shit from her boyfriend.

It's a vague story and I find it difficult to believe something could have been such an emergency that she'd have to leave her bank card with a complete stranger. But then conveniently she hasn't actually told me what the emergency was. Again I feel Jane nudging me on. The plastic contours of Emily's car keys sweaty in my hands, I decide that I deserve to know more. I've spent a day and a half of my life worrying about her.

"What did you have to sort out exactly?" I ask, my tone blunt.

She's caught off guard by the directness of the question. I watch her realize that I still have her keys and wallet and she doesn't have any choice but to answer. This woman who doesn't quite look like Emily.

"Oh, okay. I broke up with my boyfriend a few months ago," she answers dutifully. "But he's turned up in LA the other day. And I got a call from someone in the building where I'm renting an apartment." She shakes her head. "It was a neighbor, the woman next door. She was calling because a *man* was climbing in one of my windows." She gives me a quick tight smile, and I can see where this story is going. "So I asked the neighbor what he looked like and she described my ex so I told her to tell him she was calling the cops. So she tells him that and he freaks out and he falls off the window ledge. He hits the ground at a funny angle, and he's flailing around, yelling, and I can hear her shouting at him down the line and then he goes quiet. Completely blacked out. Turns out he broke his ankle. She tells me she's calling an ambulance but I tell her not to because I know he doesn't have health insurance because he's still on my joint insurance. So I tell her to wait and then I look around for you in the waiting room but you've gone into your audition already so I called an Uber. I get back to my place, grab him, and take him to the ER, and then we're there for like twelve hours. I had to call his family and tell them what happened. Which was the worst. Then I rang my insurer and had him taken off my policy afterward. And then my phone died." She sighs heavily, her story complete. "So that's what I had to sort out."

I feel embarrassed for making her tell me.

"God. That sounds awful. Is he okay now, your ex?" I ask.

"Yeah I guess." She shrugs wryly. "Although, kind of not my problem anymore."

"Here," I say, passing her the wallet and keys with a sympathetic smile.

She pockets the wallet with one hand, then she looks down at the keys in her other hand and nods a thank-you. "Great. Thanks again.

Oh, and thanks for paying the meter. That was nice of you. Not many people would have done that. I should reimburse you."

"Well actually, I can't take full credit for paying all—" My eyes catch the glint of something in her open palm, the hallway lights reflecting off an Audi badge, and suddenly I realize I've handed her my car keys instead of hers. She waits for me to continue, and when I don't her eyes drop to the keys in her hand too. But she's looking right at them oblivious to the mix-up. How does she not know that they aren't hers?

My blood suddenly runs cold. I didn't misremember her. This isn't Emily.

The woman's forehead puckers. "Is everything okay?" she asks.

"I think I gave you my own car keys there, by accident."

She looks down at them again and seems taken aback. "Oh, right?"

"Yeah, see, those are for an Audi. What type was your car again?" I ask innocently, though of course I know perfectly well.

Her eyebrows shoot up at the implication of the question. "God, I literally have no idea. It's just a rental. It's white?"

She hands back my keys unconcerned. I can't tell if she's the worst liar in the world or if I'm going completely mad.

"Could I grab mine then?" she asks, and I realize I'm just staring at her again.

"Sure." I grab her set from the table beside the door and hand them over. "Here. Sorry about that." Somehow my voice sounds normal but my thoughts are going at lightning speed trying to work out what the hell I'm supposed to do.

"Great." She smiles and slip the keys into her rucksack. "Thanks again, for everything, Mia. I owe you one."

I don't have much time left. If I'm going to say something. If I'm going to confront her it needs to be now. "We still on for that coffee this weekend?" I blurt.

She looks at me startled, but quickly recovers. "Oh yeah, God, I almost forgot we said we'd do that. Yeah, sure." She shakes her head at her own flakiness. "Yes. Text me, let me know when and where. I'll be around."

I watch her back as she disappears down the corridor, my breath high in my chest.

Emily and I never made a plan to have coffee. But then Emily would have known that. And Emily would almost certainly have recognized her own car keys.

I don't know who that woman was but it wasn't Emily.

13

The Offer You Can't Refuse

FRIDAY, FEBRUARY 12

WHEN THE ALARM GOES OFF THE NEXT MORNING I FEEL WORSE THAN before I went to bed. Worry, nightmares, fear.

This is not the state I wanted to be in to meet Kathryn Mayer. Regardless, I drag myself from my warm sheets and try to expel last night's weirdness from my mind, at least for now. I'll have to get to the bottom of it after this meeting, because right now I need to focus. I stumble into the bathroom bleary-eyed and wriggle into my swimsuit for my head-clearing morning swim.

In the cool morning air, I slip into water and try to push Emily from my mind. But the same questions keep circling around my thoughts: If that wasn't Emily then where is she? And who was the woman who came to my apartment last night? But these are question I don't have time to answer. I can't let my mind go there. I need to focus on Eliza. I need to focus on my meeting. It might be the biggest opportunity I ever get. As I scoop my way through the water, I let George take Emily's place in my thoughts instead. I force myself to focus on him and Naomi. He'll be starting filming today on the

East Coast. With her. His big opportunity. I let my anger fuel me. I'm going to get this job. I'm not going to let anyone take away my shot. I hold that thought in my mind as I slip through the crisp water. And finally George too dissolves away as, out of breath, I feel my mind clear. I pull myself from the water and head back down to the apartment to get ready.

Back in the apartment there's a text message from Nick.

Emily's car is gone. Did she contact you? Nick x

The woman who came here last night must have taken it. I wonder if I should call him and tell him what happened last night. I check the clock and realize I just don't have time. I tap out a quick reply instead and jump in the shower.

Yes. She came over to collect keys last night. Bit strange.
Can't talk right now tho. Got a meeting at 10. Mia

Once I'm ready I grab my car keys and bag and head to the table to pick up my script. Except it's not there. The table is completely bare. I look underneath and then turn a quick circle on the spot scanning the living room floor. Gone. It was definitely there yesterday evening. Unless . . . I head back to the bedroom. It's not there either. I pause in the hallway flummoxed. What the hell did I do with it? I don't really need it for the meeting today, but the fact that it's gone is extremely strange. I didn't take it out with me yesterday so I can't have left it somewhere. Did I put it somewhere weird? I head back into the kitchen and check the counters, the cupboards, and then the bin. Only fajita leftovers greet me. God knows why I'd have thrown it out but I'm at a loss as to where else it could have ended up.

Could someone have been in here? I know the apartment is serviced so perhaps a cleaner cleared it away thinking it was a used script. Maybe I left the packaging on top of it and it looked like rubbish, but I can't remember. My eyes instinctively examine the rest of the room but everything else looks the same. I guess the cleaner could have been here; it's hard to tell as it was pretty immaculate anyway. I freeze for a second suddenly remembering my lost keycard. Could someone else have been in here? A shiver runs down my spine. I try to remember the last time I actually saw the script. Was it yesterday afternoon or yesterday morning? If I saw it last yesterday morning then a cleaner could easily have been in while I was out. I catch sight of the kitchen clock and start. I'm running late. I need to go. I can check to see if a cleaner came in yesterday with Lucy once I get back later. That's probably all it is. I'm just on edge because of the strangeness of last night, I tell myself as I head out the door.

The drive to the studio is busy but relatively painless. I make it in time, retrieving a photo pass from the studio gate and heading into the pristine marble-lobbied building where an assistant collects me and guides me briskly up to Kathryn Mayer's floor.

My heels clack out a reassuring heartbeat as we head across another lobby and enter a bustling open-plan office spanning half of the building's footprint. We wind our way around busy desks until we reach the open door of a corner office. The assistant disappears inside and swiftly reemerges.

"Kathryn's ready to see you now." He smiles and gestures into the warm sunshine inside Kathryn Mayer's office. I take a breath and head in.

She stands as I enter, an athletic woman in her early fifties in a well-cut gray trouser suit and a brilliant white shirt, her perfectly styled hair graying gracefully at the temples. She walks around her desk and greets me with a warm handshake.

"Mia. It's great to finally meet you. Take a seat." She indicates the chair behind me and turns to pour me a glass of water from the pitcher on her desk.

"So tell me, how are you finding LA?" she asks, handing me the glass.

I take a welcome sip before answering brightly, "Well, the weather is amazing."

She lets out a throaty laugh. "That's very diplomatic of you. Ha, yeah, LA's something else all right but the *weather's* fantastic." She raises her eyebrows in solidarity and takes a seat at her desk. "If I'm honest, I try not to come into town unless I have to at this point. I only do two days a week here at the studio then work from home the rest of the week. I always advise young actors, when it comes to LA, get in late, leave early." She smiles, adding lightly, "If you stay too long that's where the trouble starts."

I can't help but think of what happened last night. Have I stayed too long already? I've only been here six days. I take another cool sip of water and try to refocus. "Yeah, it's definitely different from London, that's for sure. But it's been an interesting few days." I give a wry smile.

Her intelligent eyes study me, searching for something, and then I remember who she was expecting to meet today. She's only ever seen me as Jane Eyre, so I let Jane's steady gaze meet hers. She smiles, satisfied.

"This is exciting," she says, almost to herself, then leans forward, elbows on the desk. "So, *Galatea*. What do you think?"

"It's a great script. *Perfect*. And I think it's perfect for now."

She nods as I speak. "You've watched the movies we sent?" Her brow crinkles as she waits for my thoughts.

"I did. And I remembered watching the Rex Harrison version as a kid. It's a fun film, but obviously *of-a-different-time*," I add pointedly. "And from what I can gather the film is pretty much the opposite of what Bernard Shaw wrote. I guess something like Spike Jonze's *Her* is actually closer to what Shaw wrote, in terms of the object becoming the subject. The ideal becoming a living breathing autonomous reality who can suddenly choose for herself."

A bright smile flashes across Kathryn's face as she slams a palm down enthusiastically on the desk. "Yes. This is why I wanted you. This. Yes. This is good. And you're right that's the kind of ending we want. The teacher educates the student, she learns everything he teaches her then works out she's too good for him. That's the story.

A new kind of makeover movie. Sandy puts on her Lycra catsuit and realizes she can definitely do better than Danny Zuko, the man who wanted her to change in the first place, and instead she heads off to find a real equal."

I fleetingly think of how George left me for someone cooler, someone prettier, someone younger, and I feel my confidence wobble beneath me.

Get your shit together, Mia, I tell myself. *Because, if you remember correctly, George sat around the house in his underwear for most of November.*

Kathryn is still talking, oblivious to my momentary internal flutter. "So let me tell you the production plan so far." She pulls a portfolio across the desk and opens it between us.

"I want a female director and a top-notch female crew. We're tying down a director today, oh, and there's an offer out on Professor Higgins." She looks up excitedly. Her energy is infectious: any remaining nerves I may have had fall away. "You wanna know who we've asked?"

I scooch forward in my seat to better see the portfolio before her. "Of course!"

She grins and spins the book to face me, her index finger pressed below a name.

"Top secret of course." She grins "And it's only an offer, so we'll see."

A shot of pure adrenaline shoots through me as I read the name printed above her finger. *Oh my God.* I look straight back at her.

"Will he do it?" I blurt.

She grins. "Maybe. He's very picky these days—he hasn't worked in two years —but he likes the idea. A lot. That's all I'm going to say."

I feel my cheeks flush and my head lighten. If he says yes, and if I somehow pull off this meeting, then—

I need to calm down. I take a gulp of ice water and Kathryn chuckles.

"I had the exact same reaction," she says. "Anyway, what I want to do, Mia, is get you to test for this."

I immediately sober. Oh God, no, not testing. The never-ending marathon of *testing*. First screen testing, then a chemistry reading, then waiting to hear, then retesting, then studio executives opining, and then the possibility that after all that, it falls through as it so often does. But Kathryn's already ahead of me.

"Wait, before you go down that road, hear me out. I just want *you* and *him* testing. Just a chemistry read, both of you in a room, on film. This isn't an open call. Listen, I've seen your stuff; I know what you can do. And I've sent *him* your stuff. It'll just be you and him, in some scenes together, and we see how it goes."

She's sent him screeners of my work. One of the best actors of the last generation has seen my work. I feel a warmth rise up inside me at the thought, my feeling of dread abating.

"He wants casting approval on Eliza if he signs. So we'll work on making this happen together, right? You and me. You give me one chemistry read and hopefully we can go straight to offer. Either way it'll be one hell of a ride. You up for it?" She places her palms down lightly on the portfolio in front of her, like a blackjack dealer, and grins.

14

Stars

SOUKI'S READY AND WAITING WHEN I PULL UP OUTSIDE THE SAD-LOOKING Hollywood Star Tours building, a bundle of energy, her doll-like features framed by a bush of wild blond hair, her petite frame snuggled into a cashmere tracksuit, headphones slung casually around her neck.

After a flurry of hugging and effusive greetings, Souki roots out our tickets and we join the queue forming beside the safari truck. Inside the truck is bench seating that can comfortably carry the seven of us currently queuing. It's an eclectic group with Souki and me, three chatty southern soccer moms, two cheerful Indian gentlemen, and one Korean student.

Our tour guide arrives full of energy, sporting a Hollywood Star Tours shirt and a microphone headset, shaking each of our hands individually as we board the truck and take our seats. Souki flashes me a grin.

"This is *everything*," she whispers. "I love that we are doing this!" I stifle a giggle as she pulls me in to another tight rugby-tackle hug.

"So, Mi . . . I have questions," she says after releasing me. "(A) Why has it been so long, (b) are *you* going completely mad out here too? and (c), in the interests of full disclosure, I've heard about what happened with George."

Everybody knows what happened with George.

"Okay, well to answer (a): Sorry it's been so long. Work, I guess. And (b) yes, I definitely think I am going a little bit mad out here." I run through her questions as lightly as I can. "And do you mind if we do (c) a little later? Bit of a downer." I make a joke of it but I really don't want to lose my good mood yet and rehashing the breakup is guaranteed to do that.

She nods understandingly. "Sure, later. But yeah, I know what you mean about going loopy. I've been in LA for three weeks now, and I swear to God I'm starting to forget how to be a normal human being. It's a bio-dome of bullshit out here."

"You've done three weeks already? Are you going home soon?" I ask, suddenly terrified to lose the one person I've actually felt comfortable being around for days.

"Yes, thank God! My flight home is on Sunday morning." Souki stuffs her headphones away in her rucksack and slips on some sunglasses. "I cannot wait to get back to London. I just want people to be a bit rude to me again, you know? I don't know how many more times I can believably say 'Have a great day' to complete strangers without cracking up."

I let out a laugh just as the tour guide flicks on his sound system and a high-pitched wail of feedback fills the air. Hands fly to ears and faces pucker. *Here we go* . . . I mouth over the noise and Souki snorts with laughter.

"Sorry, folks, technical difficulties!" the tour guide booms as the driver starts the engine. "Okay, gang. Welcome to the Hollywood Star Tours, rated *the* number one Hollywood stars' home tour for the third year running by Tripadvisor." Souki nudges me grinning and gives a silent double thumbs-up. And I can't help but feel a little thrill of genuine excitement as he continues. "My name is Phil and I'm your guide today, so if you enjoy the tour then feel free to post a re-view, good or *bad*—I'm joking of course!" A spatter of chuckles from the group as we cast off from our moorings and join the flow of traf-fic, sailing westward, toward the hills, the warm sun on our faces.

I hear the low hum of Phil's voice, the soft cluck of camera shut-ters, and the honeyed drawl of American passengers' voices. When I look up, the palm trees of Sunset Boulevard are gliding by above us, backlit by blue, and with the sun on my skin and the breeze on my face, Hollywood rolls past.

We stop at Grauman's Chinese Theatre, littered with buskers in worn-out costumes, cut-rate Spider-Men and plastic Darth Vaders, out-of-work actors in sweaty Halloween suits. But somehow the glamour of Hollywood holds, as, undeterred, Phil tells us sparkling tales of golden-age magic. Stories of Oscar-night starlets stepping from gleaming limousines. Unbelievably, the refracting shimmer he weaves with words begins to settle over the tourist-packed piazza before us. We disembark to try to fit our feet and palms into the hand- and footprints of long-extinguished stars.

The tour continues, we head north, stopping periodically on the manicured edges of lush palm-obscured mansions. We peer through custom-designed gates at questionably appointed design projects and pipe dreams: castles in the sky, Swiss mountain lodges transported to the California sunshine, whitewashed Mexican villas, glass infinity houses teetering on craggy cliffsides. We catch glimpses of lives only, but Phil fills the gaps as we rumble up higher into the hills.

Between the houses of the stars, I tell Souki about George. The whole Fantastic Movers extended version. Though I edit out the tears, and self-recrimination, and Instagram sadness. She shakes her head at it all but has the good grace not to try to cheer me up with platitudes. Instead conversation moves on to auditions, we discuss Bee Miller, we talk about how strange it is to be so far from home. An ocean between you and your real life.

At the Hollywood sign we pull up to a dusty layby and disem-bark. Whether you buy in to the magic of Hollywood or not, this close up, the sign is something. Each letter the height of a five-story building. As I look up at the giant letters soaring above us I find myself thinking of the story Miguel told me on my first day, the story of the actress who jumped.

The tour guide apologizes for the mess around the sign, some kind of city workers' strike, and my concentration falters. I catch myself gazing down into the sunless ravine beneath us as he talks, thinking about how long that actress's cold body lay there, broken and undiscovered.

Souki hauls me from my reverie, demanding photos with the sign, and after a whirlwind of Instagram content creation we lounge spent on the sunbaked rocks and post. Finally she leans back, tilting her face fully into the sun.

"You're okay, though, right?" she asks, out of nowhere, and I know she means George.

But it's not George that's my problem. My thoughts have circled back around and snagged once more on Emily. Emily and the strange things that have happened since I met her. I think of the woman who came to my apartment last night. And make a decision.

"Something weird happened the other day," I say, meeting Souki's gaze.

I tell about the parking meter, about Emily disappearing, about the woman, and after I fall silent Souki inhales deeply before speaking.

"That *is* weird," she says with finality. I can't see her eyes past her sunglasses. She looks away for a moment, out toward the hills, before continuing. "Please don't be offended by this, Mi." She looks back at me. "But it kind of sounds like you're lonely—which is totally understandable—what happened the other week was beyond awful. George is such a shit. He's a terrible, terrible person. No wonder you're feeling like this. And he still hasn't even called you, has he? Or explained himself!"

This is exactly where I did not want this conversation to go. What I just told her has nothing to do with George but I realize anything I say to the contrary will make me sound overly defensive and somehow prove the point. I take a calming breath before speaking. "Agreed. But George didn't make the girl I met at the audition disappear and he definitely didn't send a complete stranger to my apartment last night, Souk. So I'm not sure how he's relevant."

She removes her sunglasses and wipes them with her top. "I'm not saying he's relevant to that situation. I mean you used to spend all your free time with George. I'm just saying maybe you're focusing too much on stuff that you normally wouldn't? You're a very driven person, Mi, and when you decide to do something you tend to get— not obsessed exactly, but preoccupied, and now you suddenly have all this time on your hands."

"So you're saying none of what I've told you would have bothered you?" I ask her carefully.

"Honestly?" she asks. I nod her on. "I wouldn't have helped her in the first place. It kind of sounds like a weird situation."

"I just didn't want to go in next!" I protest. "I wasn't ready and if I'd gone in then I would have been flustered and not gotten it."

"And did you get it?" she parries.

The question pulls me up short.

"No," I confess. "No, I didn't get it."

"Yeah, look, I love you, Mi, but do you think maybe you've just let yourself get distracted by this random person? Is there a chance that this actress was a just a bit of a flake and that she sent a friend to pick up her stuff last night because her life is messy?"

I consider Souki's question before responding. "But the woman last night was actually pretending to be her! She told me this whole involved story about a boyfriend in the hospital—"

"Yeah, people are fucking weird out here, Mi," she interrupts. "Don't get involved. Please, tell me you'll drop this. Please." She looks at me plaintively and suddenly I know she's right. I'm obsessing over the elusiveness of a complete stranger rather than the elusiveness of the man who was supposed to love me more than anyone else. And she's right about another thing. If George and I were still together I wouldn't have even noticed Emily at that audition the other day. I would have been focused; I wouldn't have been so desperate to find some kind of distraction.

"Okay," I decide. "You're right. I will drop it." I exhale noisily and smile as Souki leans in to give me a warm, sun-cream-scented hug.

As we wind our way back down into the city, I mention Nick, careful not to go back over how we met two days ago.

"Is he American?" she asks.

I purse my lips to keep from grinning like an idiot and nod.

Souki raises her sunglasses theatrically, eyes aflame with interest. "Do I know him? Is he an actor?"

I know he hasn't really expressed any interest, he's just been friendly, but I let myself run with the idea of getting slightly more friendly if the possibility's there. A little holiday romance might keep me out of trouble.

"No. He's definitely *not* an actor." I laugh. "I don't know what he does but he's got an office in North Hollywood," I say lightly. "So, normal job, I guess."

Souki fully removes her sunglasses now and high-fives me. "Yes babes! Yes! Is he ridiculously hot?"

I nod, somewhat pained. "Uh-huh," I confirm. "Which is not ideal."

"*Why* is that not ideal?" Her forehead creases in disbelief.

"Because—oh God, this is embarrassing—because I promised myself I wouldn't go for another guy hotter than me." I know what's coming before the words are out of my mouth.

"Not true. And babes, that's the dream anyway! The absolute dream. But listen, and trust me on this, George was nice-looking, sure, but *you* can do so much better, Mi. And I don't mean, like, a 'nicer' guy; I mean a 'hotter' guy. Like, okay, do you remember Jamie Vintner when we were on *The First Crusade*?"

"Yes, why?" Of course, I remember Jamie Vintner, the insanely good-looking but mortifyingly boring series lead. He was supposed to have been in an on–off relationship with a well-known British model. I noticed in the airport duty-free that he's now the face of Burberry.

"Yeah, well, he kept asking about you on set. I didn't say anything at the time because he was a weirdo and you were serious with George. But Jamie kept going around asking us all how long you and George had been together and stuff. He cornered Alice in her trailer for like forty-five minutes. If I'd known what a shit George was back then, I'd have arranged a bloody candlelit dinner for you and Jamie at unit base."

I beam back at Souki. She's a good friend. God, it's pathetic how cheered I am by the idea of Jamie Vintner fancying me; his boring-ness aside, it's pure catnip for the soul. Souki is right, my self-esteem needs some serious rebooting. A little work/holiday romance might do me wonders. I could ask him out for a coffee or something.

BACK AT THE TOUR DROP OFF point Souki hugs me tight and tells me to take care of myself and I promise her that I will as we part ways.

In the car I check my phone. It's the first time I've allowed myself to check it since leaving Universal. I feel a buzz of excitement as I see I have three missed calls, one from Michael, one from Cynthia, and one from Nick. Michael and Cynthia must have heard from Kathryn's office already. A bright joy crests inside me as I listen to his ebullient voice message and then hers.

"Well, you clever clever thing!" Cynthia trills joyfully. "It looks like we're in business. She *loves* you. The studio loves you. I had to sign the NDA to even get them to tell me the part but I'm looking through the script now. And boy-oh-boy, this is a big one, very very exciting for us. Now listen—let me get on the testing contract and I'll get straight back to you with details."

I've said yes to the screen test, of course. Like a seasoned gambling addict, I've laid all my hopes for the future on a single square, not for the first time. The least I can do is enjoy the soaring high I'm feeling right now before I inevitably lose everything on a roll of the dice. Though maybe not this time.

Bursting with happiness I tap on the missed call from Nick. I guess he's wondering what exactly happened with Emily last night. I did mention it was odd but now after talking to Souki and in the warm midday sun the whole Emily incident seems, well, a bit silly. I open the new text from Nick.

Hey. Tried to call earlier. Just wanted an update. On our missing girl but mainly on our coffee plan. I'm going to be even more honest and say, this might be the most exciting thing that's happened on the street opposite my office this entire week. Hell, this entire month even. Hope your meeting went well! Give me a call if you're free. Nick

I grin at the screen, quickly tapping out a reply.

Sorry I missed your call. The Emily update is kind of a long story. The coffee update shorter. Free to talk now?

His gray dots pulse for a second then stop and suddenly my phone bursts to life, pumping out the FaceTime ringtone at full volume.

He wants to do a video call, Jesus.

My heart rate shoots up as I fumble open the visor mirror and check my reflection. It's all still there, just as I left it, albeit slightly messier than this morning. I gingerly tap accept call and a bright patch of blue sky and the edge of Nick's face fill my screen.

"Hi!" I call and he finally looks at the screen.

"Sorry, hey! Thought I should probably take this outside, one second," he says, adjusting the phone angle so that I can see his full face. He smiles as our eyes meet. "Hey stranger! What's the scoop?" I can't tell if it's the intrigue of our Emily sleuthing he's enjoying so much or if he's just genuinely pleased to see me. I remember Souki's advice to stop obsessing over Emily and I consider avoiding the whole subject with Nick from now on, come what may. If he loses interest then that would certainly answer that question. But then I have to tell Nick something and round off the whole story—I mean, he knows Emily's car is gone.

"Emily sent me a text last night and then she just came over to collect her stuff," I say, keeping it light and as underwhelming as possible.

"Wait, how did she get your phone number?" he asks, brows knitting. "Did she finally go back to the casting studio and pick up your note?"

I sigh internally. Nick doesn't know I stole Emily's rental document and called her. And now that I think about it, I still have her rental document. I flip open the armrest beside me and it stares back at me. *God, I'm a crazy person.*

"What is it?" Nick asks, reading my expression from the screen.

"Right, don't judge me but I went back to her car yesterday and found her contact information in the glove box. I rang her."

"Great idea. And she collected her stuff?"

"Well, kind of." I pause, unsure whether to fully lie in order to drop the whole subject or tell the truth and risk prolonging its airtime. I know I promised Souki I would drop it but surely Nick, an LA resident, would be a great litmus test in terms of whether I've blown this whole thing out of proportion. I tread carefully. "Right, this might sound mad, but it wasn't Emily who collected the stuff."

His forehead creases. "Oh, she sent someone else to collect the stuff for her?"

"No, no." I'm not explaining this well at all. "A woman turned up saying she was Emily but it wasn't her." Nick looks even more confused. I try again. "Someone who looked very similar to Emily showed up pretending to be Emily. She said she *was* Emily but she wasn't."

Nick raises both eyebrows. "Whoa. What! Okay. I wasn't expecting that. Someone was pretending to be the girl you think disappeared!" he says, incredulous. "So what did you do? You didn't give this woman Emily's stuff, did you?" I go quiet. "Oh shit. You did."

He gives me an appraising look. "You didn't even say anything to her, did you?" He bursts out laughing. "You just pretended it wasn't happening, didn't you? God you're so British! Okay, so you just gave this complete stranger Emily's things rather than cause any embarrassment?" He's joking but that is pretty much exactly what happened.

I go to speak but stall. It's funny how everyone is always an expert on what you should have done after the fact. I fumble for an answer. "Yeah, I did. Well, actually, I was flustered so I accidentally gave her the wrong car keys first and that's when I knew it definitely wasn't her because she had no idea the keys I gave her weren't hers. It was such a weird situation that up until then I wasn't sure, I thought I might've just misremembered her face. But if you're using your car for everything, every day, rental or not, you recognize your car keys. But yeah, as I say, I got flustered and gave her Emily's stuff."

He shakes his head in amused disbelief. "You gave her someone else's wallet! Even though you knew it wasn't her—?"

"Hey!" I protest. "Give me a break. I only met Emily for ten minutes, days ago. I'm not bloody Rain Man, I don't remember every single face I've ever seen. I wasn't certain it wasn't her until I *was* certain. And even then, she was probably just a weird friend of Emily's or, I don't know. She had the same accent as Emily, she looked pretty much the same. It's not as if I handed over Emily's stuff to three kids stacked in a trench coat! She looked really similar. And then I guess I just thought she must know her."

"Fair enough." He grins. "But why would she pretend to be Emily? Wouldn't Emily have just mentioned that her friend was coming around to get her stuff?"

The conversation is not going the way I had hoped. Any chance of us dropping the Emily mystery seems to be fast disappearing. "I don't know. Maybe she's just flaky?"

Nick snorts a laugh. "That's certainly one way of putting it!" he quips then takes in my stony expression. "Aren't you even a little concerned?"

I feel my resolve wobbling because of course I am. Or at least I had been, because why would Emily's friend pretend to remember me and then tell me that bizarre ex-boyfriend story? I try to stack up a reasonable explanation in my mind. But as far as I can see there is no reasonable explanation for any of this. Unless, of course, Souki is right and Emily's friend was just a run-of-the-mill LA weirdo. Then a thought begins to form. "There was something else," I add. "I kind of caught her out." The corners of Nick's mouth edge toward a smile as I continue. "She was pretending to be Emily so I tested her. I pretended we'd made a plan to meet up for coffee. We hadn't actually made a plan but she said she remembered and she still wanted to meet up. She had no idea I was bluffing, she remembered us making that plan."

He studies my face a moment before speaking. "You're really worried about this, aren't you?"

I guess I haven't dropped it. And now he thinks I'm fully mad. I feel my face flush. "No, I just . . ." I stutter to a halt because I am worried all the valid points Souki made have now somehow melted away and I feel like I'm right back where I started. I'm definitely messed up because of George, and perhaps I am obsessing about this to distract myself, but if the woman who took Emily's keys last night wasn't Emily then who was she, and why was she pretending to be Emily? She could have been anyone and I gave her Emily's things.

"Maybe you should speak to the police?" Nick says, jogging me back to the here and now.

The idea of involving the police makes my stomach flip, instantly throwing the harsh light of reality onto everything; either Emily is fine and I'm making a fuss about nothing or she is missing and a stranger came to my apartment to collect her things. If I have even a vague suspicion that something is wrong here, shouldn't I mention something to someone? Nick's right but I promised Souki, didn't I?

"Urgh, I don't know if I should get dragged into all this. I'm just supposed to be here to get a job!"

"That's the spirit, champ." Nick laughs, sympathetically. "Listen, it's up to you, only you know what you saw. As far as I'm concerned . . .

I think it's pretty weird that a woman goes missing for two days without a wallet or car and only surfaces after you manage to track *her* down. But like I say, it's up to you."

I hadn't thought of that but he's right. She only got in touch after I called her, after I mentioned passing Emily's things on to my agent. It could be that threatening to attract attention was the only reason someone replied to me at all. Suddenly the whole situation seems a little more concerning than it did before.

It can't hurt to speak to someone, can it? All I'd need to do is register a concern.

"I'll think about it," I say.

Nick looks at me seriously for a moment before nodding. "Okay. Do. And let me know what happens."

15

Missing Person

FRIDAY, FEBRUARY 12

THE LAPD WEBSITE OFFERS HOTLINE NUMBERS FOR ALMOST EVERY conceivable criminal activity. Back at the apartment I scan through the list to find a number that fits but I'm not exactly sure what it is that I'm supposed to be reporting.

I can't report an abandoned vehicle anymore because there isn't one. And the stranger last night collecting Emily's things definitely wasn't a robbery. I click on the non-emergency hotline and take a slug of hot coffee.

I've seen enough BBC dramas to feel like I might know how this goes. If I'm reporting a missing person I know they'll need: her surname, her last known location, her vehicle registration number, and her home address. So I keep her car rental document close at hand in case I need it. I take a deep breath and carefully dial. As the phone rings I reassure myself that, if it comes to it, the police can check who exactly came to my apartment last night from the building's CCTV footage.

. . .

AFTER HANGING UP, I PACE the living room. I wasn't expecting the call to go that way at all. I try to slow my heart rate but it's a losing battle, there's too much caffeine and adrenaline coursing through my system. Trying to relax is not going to cut it.

I head to the kitchen, chug back a tall glass of tap water in an attempt to rid myself of a suddenly intensely dry mouth, then stand there frozen thinking over what was just said, the police officer's words fresh in my head.

I need to talk to someone about what just happened. I check the time on my phone. It's after seven, Nick should be finished at work. He might even be home by now. I realize I still know nothing about Nick, what he does, where he lives, even if he's single. Though if he's not then I'd have serious concerns. And he doesn't wear a wedding ring. I bring up his number and pause. Who else am I going to tell? I'm absolutely certain Souki would not like this.

The call tone pulses for a few beats before Nick's face fills the screen. The image is dark for a second before he reaches overhead and clicks on his car's interior light, his face thrown into relief by the shadows. I make out the multistory car park in the background behind him. He looks distracted, like I've caught him in the middle of something.

"Hey! Sorry to keep calling," I say quickly, my tone businesslike. "I just wanted to let you know that I spoke to the police. The LAPD." His focus sharpens at my words so I continue. "It was a bit daunting, but I think . . . I think I did the right thing?" It's a question, not necessarily for either of us to answer, but a question nonetheless.

"Oh right! Okay. And what happened, what did they say?"

"I told them about paying her meter, and her disappearing, and I told them I'd had her things and I was worried something might have happened to her because she didn't show up. They basically weren't interested, they said it's not a crime to be missing and unless I had evidence that an actual crime has taken place, blah, blah, blah. So I told them about the woman who pretended to be Emily. And then they suddenly got *really* interested."

"I'll bet they did. And?"

I hesitate for a second, part ashamed, part fearful of the series of events I've set in motion. "They said I should go to a local station and physically file a missing persons report. And they said they're going over to Emily's house. Now."

"Seriously? Now? They told you that?"

"Yeah, they said they were sending a car over to check the address. They said if someone stole her wallet and keys, then it's a valid cause for concern." I shudder at the thought of Emily answering her apartment door completely oblivious to any of this, wondering who the hell called the police on her.

"Anyway," I continue, "they said they'd go over and if anyone's there then they'll ID them and ask about the wallet. They said they'd let me know one way or another if there's an issue."

Nick is silent for a moment, the seriousness of the situation sinking in. "Wow. Well, fingers crossed you're wrong, I guess."

"Yeah. I really hope she's home and fine, you know. Even if they tell her some crazy British woman called the police on her. I just want to know she's safe. I'd want someone to do the same for me, if it was the other way around."

Nick gives me a rallying smile. "Me too. She's lucky she met you. Not many people would have bothered to do this. I doubt she would have expected you to either. Don't worry, you definitely did the right thing."

I feel a flush rising up my neck and realize that's all I really wanted to hear. I've done my bit and now I really can drop it. I wander, phone in hand, away from the harsh kitchen lights toward the twinkle of LA beyond the glass. The glittering city lights fill the screen behind me.

"Thanks for the advice," I say, genuinely grateful for his help. A horn honk sounds from his audio, and my attention turns to his situation. "Are you on your way home?" I ask.

He looks out at the car park beyond his window and sighs. "No, not yet, there's been a bit of a problem at work. I'm down at the studio." He says it in a way that assumes I know what it is he does but this is the first time he's given me any indication of what his job is. It's funny but I still get the feeling, just like that first time we met, that he thinks we know each other much better than we actually do.

"Studio?"

"Yeah, there's a problem with one of the films we're doing." My heart sinks slightly at the mention of a film. I don't know why but I really did think Nick was separate from that world. "Actor trouble," he continues. "He's stopped filming, it's a long story, but here I am."

"Nick, I literally have no idea what you do."

He blurts out a laugh. "Oh, okay. Really?" He chuckles incredulously. "Well, this is embarrassing." He holds my look for a second trying to judge if I'm being serious. "You really *don't* know who I am, do you? No idea. This whole time?" He shakes his head briefly. "Well, I suppose it's not that unexpected, can't say it's the first time it's happened. We met, I think, about two years ago at the *Scott of the Antarctic* premiere in London. It was only a brief hello—"

I feel the blood drain from my face. Nick knows George. *Scott of the Antarctic* was George's last big role before things dried up. George played one of the explorers on Scott's last expedition. It was a decent supporting role, it should have gone somewhere, but it didn't even though the film did well. And I met Nick at the premiere? I desperately try to place him.

"Oh my God, I'm so sorry, Nick, I had no idea. Did you work on *Scott*?"

He looks genuinely surprised. "Did I work on *Scott*? Erm, yeah, you could say that. I sort of produced it, Mia. Nick Eldridge. You don't remember meeting me at all, do you?"

My stomach flips like I've just missed a step, like I've just realized the whole floor is completely transparent. Nick is Nick *Eldridge*? I plonk down gently onto the sofa nearest the vast windows. Outside, Hollywood glows like dying embers.

Oh God, how could I have been so stupid? Nick isn't just the lovely, easygoing, sexy all-American Nick I've been talking to over the last few days. He's also the fucking film juggernaut, cutthroat, super producer Nick Eldridge. A man who buys up film rights from under people just to stop them from making anything even vaguely similar to what his production company is working on. Everything he touches turns to gold but he's notoriously single-minded. My mind whirs as I desperately try to pair up the two images I have in my head: this Nick and *the* Nick Eldridge.

Holy fucking shit. I've been flirting with him, and acting like a complete fucking moron, and I had no idea who he was. I want the fault line beneath the building to open up and swallow me whole.

I catch sight of my pale face in the tiny box at the top of my iPhone screen. A rabbit in the headlights. There's no getting around it. "Oops?" I offer. Because what the actual hell am I supposed to say. Thankfully, he laughs.

"Don't worry, it was two years ago and you had a lot going on. It happens surprisingly often—producers don't tend to lodge in people's minds the same way actors do."

The terse way he says the word *actors* brings me back to what he was saying before my world-class social blunder. "So what's the problem at the studio then?" I ask.

"The lead actor won't go back on set for the night shoot until the sound guy is fired."

"What? Why? What did the sound guy do?"

"God knows. Hopefully, he told the actor to get his lines right and stop wasting everyone's goddamn time." He shakes his head, drained. "Sorry, not helpful, I know. But I mean, why can't people just do their jobs?" He smiles wanly. "Don't worry, I'm not going to lead with that when I get to the set."

I laugh. God, he's cute. There's something ridiculously sexy about his world-weariness. And I realize that I don't think I can marry the two different versions of Nick together, and I don't think I want to. I like the Nick I met two days ago too much to let him change into someone else.

I know it's totally inappropriate to ask but I can't help myself. "So what exactly are you going to say to him when you get there, Nick Eldridge?" My tone is confrontationally flirty. *Start as you mean to go on,* I figure, and if I do intend in any way to "go on" with Nick I want to make it clear that our dynamic isn't going to change just because I now know who he is.

His eyes twinkle and crease around the edges in the car light. "Oh, I see. I see how this is going to be." He smirks. "What would you suggest I do? Any actor-handling tips from the front line?"

I feel a warm rush of blood through my chest and if I was in any doubt before, I'm not now. Nick likes me. I suppose he must have liked me to recognize me after a brief meeting two years ago. I clearly stuck in his head. I try to remember the night we must have met. *Scott of the Antarctic* was George's first premiere, and it was a lot to take in; he took me as his plus-one. I was so proud of him. After years of dreaming, it was thrilling for one of us to suddenly have achieved something real, something tangible. I remember it feeling like magic was being dusted over our lives. I remember what I wore. It was the first time I'd been given a gown to wear, a figure-skimming dusty-pink Giambattista Valli gown, its deep V making my pale skin look almost translucent. I don't often feel it but I felt I looked good that night. I could tell by the way George clung to me as he guided me through crowds of people I didn't know. It's no wonder I don't recall meeting anyone that night when I remember how in love with George I was back then.

"Do I have any actor-handling tips?" I smile. "Afraid not, Mr. Eldridge. If I knew how to deal with actors I'd bottle it and sell it. I certainly wouldn't be giving it away for free."

He laughs, his eyes alive. "Well, it was worth a try." He looks away a second, thinking. And when he looks back he seems decided. "Listen, Mia. Is George still—"

I know what he's going to ask so I save him the effort. "No, he's not."

He nods his understanding. "Okay. That's good." He studies my face for a moment, perhaps looking for reassurance before the fact.

But that's not the way we're going to do this and he knows it. "Let's skip the coffee. Can I take you out for dinner, Mia?"

"I would love that."

"Tomorrow?"

"Yeah, text me. Go save your sound guy. And I'll see you then."

AFTER THE CALL IT TAKES me a full minute to remember why I called Nick in the first place. And suddenly all I can think about is what is happening right now at a small Airbnb out by the 101 freeway.

16

All Is Well

THE NEXT MORNING I FORCE ON MY SWIMSUIT AND DRAG MY HEAVY body up the service stairs to the pool, hoping a short burst of exercise will kick away the fug of sleep after another bad night.

I shiver in the dawn breeze as I drop my robe and slip into the warm pool water. I thought about texting Emily in the early hours but I couldn't think what I could possibly write and to whom I might be writing. I try to imagine what might have happened last night somewhere out across the glowing brilliance of Los Angeles. I try to imagine Emily's rented apartment by the 101, functional, easy, magnolia-painted walls, veneered floors, plug-in air scents to cover cooking smells. I might be wrong but I'm almost certain I'm right.

As I glide through the water, I imagine the police knocking on her front door and no answer. Their knocks echoing through dark empty rooms, past open suitcases, rumpled sheets, and used script pages. Emily gone.

But in the same breath, I can also imagine the opposite. The soft hum of a Netflix show, Emily pausing to answer those knocks, tying her hair back as she cautiously opens the door. She retrieves her license from her bag after a few questions from the police, handing it over with a mixture of bemusement and annoyance. The officers apologize for the inconvenience and Emily returns to the warm glow of her apartment to live her life in peace.

God, I hope that is what happened. I don't care about the fuss I've caused if that is how it went last night.

I dive down under the surface and let the water play across my face, my eyes held tight shut against the chlorine. It is silent down here, silent save for my own movements, my heartbeat thumping in my ears.

I break the surface to the sound of my phone ringing from my discarded robe. I heave myself out of the water and hop across the chilled flagstones to grab it.

I towel-dry an ear and answer. "Hello?"

"Hello, this is Officer Maria Cortez from the Los Angeles Police Department. Can I confirm who I'm speaking to?"

I straighten and hastily pull on my robe with my free hand. "Yes, of course. Mia Eliot."

"That's great. Okay, Ms. Eliot, so I'm just following up on the report you made last night. Would now be a good time to talk?"

I look about the deserted pool terrace, its cabana curtains fluttering gently in the breeze, and pull my robe tighter around me. "Yes, now would be fine, thank you." I sink down onto one of the deep cushioned loungers and try to stay calm.

The officer continues, friendly but professional. "Okay, so, the good news is we can confirm that Ms. Emily Bryant is now in possession of her wallet, her car keys, and her car so no further actions will be taken in regard to the report made by yourself."

She is silent for a moment. I wait for more details but none come. Is that it?

"So she was there then? Emily?"

There's a pause before the officer responds. "I'm sorry, ma'am?"

"Sorry, I just . . . I was wondering if the officers who went to her apartment spoke to Emily herself. If she was there. If it was definitely her." I realize I sound fully mad but I'm not sure Officer Cortez knows the fundamental aspects of the whole Emily situation.

"Ma'am. I can only tell you what's written here in the report. Emily Bryant was present at the location; she was in possession of her wallet and her vehicle. The officers at the scene were satisfied and there were no grounds for further investigation."

"Right." I know I shouldn't push it but I can't help myself. "So the officers checked her ID?"

"Ma'am, is there a problem here? Is there something I should know?"

"No, I just wanted to make sure it was definitely Emily they spoke to. I know it sounds strange but I'm slightly concerned it might not have been."

"Well, yes, they would have checked and confirmed her ID on the scene. So if the woman they ID'd is not Emily, then we'd be talking about a much bigger crime here than auto theft. Do you have any reason to believe the woman we spoke to is not who she says she is, Ms. Eliot?"

I shiver in the breeze, my wet hair icy cold now, my forearms goosebumped as I try to figure out what crime impersonating someone is, exactly. Is it fraud? Whatever it is I'm not sure being the only witness in a criminal investigation would be a great career move for me this week. But if I push this that's what I'll be.

"No, no. I'm sure if they checked, it's all fine. Thank you for letting me know. Oh, and what happens to the report now?"

"It's been closed. It's in the system but as far as anyone's concerned it's gone."

"Okay. Great, thank you, Officer Cortez."

"You're welcome. Have a great day." The line goes dead.

BACK IN THE APARTMENT I hop in the shower, letting my cold skin warm under the water. I can let this go now. I have enough on my plate without adding in a police investigation. Emily is fine. They assured me Emily is fine. Order is restored.

I towel off and head into the pristine marble kitchen to make breakfast. Halfway into the room I stop dead in my tracks. My laptop sits open on the kitchen counter. I stare at its blank screen. I didn't leave it there last night, did I? I left it charging next to the sofa as I usually do. The charging cable lies abandoned on the thick carpet. Did I forget to plug it in last night? A little shiver runs through me as I remember my missing script yesterday morning. Another thing seemingly moved in the night. I had meant to ask Lucy yesterday if the cleaners might have been up to the apartment. If they came up while I was out, they easily could have mistaken the script for rubbish underneath all that crumpled packaging. They could have thrown it out. I'd meant to ask Lucy but after the meeting at Universal and seeing Souki the whole incident had gone from my mind.

I stare at the laptop's lifeless screen, and the more I think about it the more certain I am that I did plug it in before bed. And one thing's for sure, cleaners don't come in the night and move laptops. Did someone come in here last night while I was sleeping? Could this have something to do with Emily? Or am I being completely crazy?

I head over to the computer and tap the cursor; the screen lights up showing the desktop. I look along my app dashboard. Nothing is open, nothing appears recently used. But if someone did use it then they would have access to everything. Everything is here: email, messages, FaceTime, contacts. The hairs on my arm rise at the thought of what could be possible with all that information.

Instinctively I head straight into the hallway and grab the intercom phone. It rings twice before a male receptionist's voice answers. "Hello, front desk, how can I help?"

"Hi there, could you tell me if anyone was let up to my apartment last night?"

"Were you expecting someone?"

"No, I just wasn't sure if, perhaps, someone had come past reception last night and come up?"

"Not if you weren't expecting them, ma'am. We only let residents come and go freely within the building. We would have called up to you if you had an unexpected visitor and checked you were expecting a guest. We take building security very seriously."

"So no one could have sneaked past and—"

"No ma'am."

"Okay. Oh, and what days does the cleaner service the apartments?"

"Tuesdays and Thursdays."

"I see. Thank you."

I place the receiver back in its cradle. Cleaners did come the evening the script must have gone missing. So that potentially solves that. But it certainly doesn't explain how my computer got up onto the counter.

But if no one unaccounted for went past security last night, and my computer was moved, then that means whoever moved it either lives or works in this building. For some reason my mind immediately flies to Miguel, Miguel who knows when I'm coming and going, Miguel the actor with so much interest in my career. I feel a twinge of guilt. Miguel might be a bit overfriendly at times but I really don't see him as criminal. Then there's Lucy, the concierge, but again she's hardly the stereotypical criminal—though she could definitely get into my apartment if she wanted to. But why would she? Why would anyone?

I try to recall the details of last night after my phone call with Nick but they blend with the previous night's evening routine. It must have been me who moved it. There's no way someone could have come past reception last night without being seen. And Souki's right that I've just replaced one preoccupation with another. I won't let myself fixate on George so I'm fixating on everything else instead. I have jet lag, I'm busy and stressed and sad; I'm probably responsible for moving my computer. No one came in last night, and the police have told me categorically that Emily is fine. I need to stop leaping to ridiculous conclusions and focus on why I am here.

There's a very urgent email from Cynthia on my laptop asking me to respond as soon as possible. Kathryn Mayer has set the chemistry screen test for Monday morning and Cynthia needs me to okay the time immediately in order to confirm with the studio. I send her a quick confirmation and ask if she can get another script sent to me though it's clear from her email she still has no idea who I'll be testing with. I guess it's just between Kathryn and me—and him, of course—for now. A fizz of excitement shoots through me at the idea of working with my co-star. He has screeners of my work; he's actually sat down and watched me in *Eyre,* and he still wants to screen-test. He must have liked it, which means a lot, especially from someone like him.

Cynthia's email tells me not to worry about parts that I've already auditioned for over here; everything must come second to this. But there's no mention of which *Galatea* scenes I need to prepare for the screen test yet, so it looks like I'm free for the day. A full day off.

At a loss for how to fill it, I scan the rest of my inbox and find an old email from Michael: an invitation to attend a gifting suite this afternoon at the Sunset Tower Hotel. I'd been hoping I might be free but hadn't expected I would. Because it's the week running up to the Oscars, gifting suites are cropping up all over town—and as *Eyre* starts to air on streaming services in the US within the next two weeks, I've obviously been added to someone's PR list. I've been to a gifting suite before with George and understand the concept, but this could be my first official time.

Essentially PR companies invite actors in popular shows and films to a series of hotel suites in order to receive free gifts. And not just goodie bags either but larger things: holidays, luxury brand endorsement, villa stays, island-hopping, private jet usage. A good gifting suite does not pull its punches. Depending on what type of actor or celebrity you are, you're offered a certain color and tier of pass that you have to wear around your neck on a lanyard. I'm sure whatever list I'm already on specifies my preordained gifting level.

Much to my shame I feel a thrill of excitement. I may like to think I'm a relatively egalitarian, un-shallow person, but when push comes to shove, I have to admit I love sparkles and presents just as much as the next person.

The suite opens at noon, which gives me something to do before the screen-test scenes arrive, but I really don't want to go to this alone. I dash off a quick text to Souki and slip into a jewel-toned outfit: emerald cashmere sweater, deep-amethyst pants and slip-ons, finishing off with a clean makeup look and my thick hair tied back into a loose bun. It's a PR event so I know there'll be photographers there for the brands, and while I'm sure there'll be more interesting people for the photographers to snap than me, it's worth being camera-ready just in case.

A text lets me know Souki can't make it, she's meeting her agent for lunch. I look in the mirror and my heart sinks: all dressed up, no place to go.

I definitely don't want to go alone but, other than Souki, I really don't know anyone in LA. I can't ask Nick to be my plus-one—that would be the most embarrassing first date ever, not to mention we said we'd go to dinner. I scour my phone for a last-minute savior but at the back of my mind I already know there's only one person guaranteed not to turn this event down, even at such short notice. She may not be the perfect brunch companion but I can't think of a better gifting-suite ally than Bee Miller.

WE MEET IN THE LOBBY of Sunset Tower Hotel at noon. Bee, camera-ready, dressed in a minuscule doll-like playsuit, with sheer black tights and ankle boots, looking every inch a millennial Edie Sedgwick with the wide eyes and thigh gap to match.

She clutches me in a tight sinewy hug and gives me a lipsticked peck on the cheek. "This is so exciting, babes. I did one of these last year at the W, West Hollywood, for *Final Conflict,* but this one is better—I asked around. This is a really good one." Her hot flushed cheeks are my only clue to the excitement bubbling beneath her implacable poise. "So I asked at reception," she continues, her tone businesslike. "It's on the fourth floor, we get our passes up there. Apparently, I get a plus-one guest pass but I'm going to have a word with PR up there. See if I can get a proper pass. I got that new show, by the way, the one I was telling you about the other day."

"Oh," I say as delicately as I can. "I thought they'd offered it to Poppy Fenchurch?"

Bee pulls a tight little face. "Yeah, they did. I'm actually quite annoyed about the way they went about the whole thing to be honest. Apparently I was always the showrunner and the studio's favorite but the director went with Poppy Fenchurch, for some unknown reason, and then Poppy pulled out anyway. I got the call last night. Poppy's doing a film instead, God knows what, anyway, I think it's all worked out for the best. I'm going to have to keep an eye on this director, though, God knows how she got the job."

I struggle for a response before settling on, "That's great! Congratulations." Though I'm pretty certain neither sentiment fits the news Bee has just told me entirely.

On the fourth floor Bee disappears into a back room with two PR assistants and emerges victorious with a Gold-tier pass, the joy of her acquisition barely dimmed by seeing my Platinum version.

"Oh babes. You got Platinum. Nice. So listen, we need a game plan. If there's something you're not into then grab one for me anyway, okay?"

I let out a laugh. I don't know why but I really was expecting an actual game plan. Still, there's something refreshingly straightforward about Bee's attitude to life that sits well with me after the last few days I've had. I don't have to worry about her intentions at least, and for the next few hours I don't have to think about Emily, or the apartment, or George, or my screen test. And with that we're ushered past security and into the glittering belly of the beast.

17

Gifted

An entire floor of the five-star Sunset Tower Hotel has been taken over by super brands. Every room is filled with concession tables, each with discreet tier pass color-coding to signify who is allowed what and save our blushes.

My eyes drift through open doorways, as we glide along the corridors, taking in the glittering tables of high-end jewelers, brightly colored fashion lookbooks, designer bags, and concessions offering monthlong villa residencies, private yacht chartering, skiing vacations, and Learjet rental. There's something almost scary about it: being surrounded by luxuries that in real life are so far beyond my pay grade.

The atmosphere from room to room is calm with quiet, discreet conversations between brand liaisons and lanyard wearers. There are faces I recognize, faces that anyone would recognize. Stars, big and small, beautiful and handsome, wander past, just living their everyday lives, as if they weren't the people they clearly are.

"Holy shit!" Bee's viselike grip latches onto my forearm. "Do you know who that is?" she rasps at me under her breath. Her eyes direct mine up the corridor to an incredibly tall blond actress who is laughing at a joke one of the PR liaisons has just told her. It's clearly a rhetorical question as I'm certain half the population of the world would know who it is, and when I look back, Bee's gaze has already moved on, scanning the milling clientele for more. "This is definitely a good one, Mia," she adds quietly, lost in her own haze.

I lose Bee at the Cartier stand and wander on through the rooms, stopping briefly to hear a talk at a personal trainer concession. But as I listen to nutritional advice from the towering muscle-bound athlete in front of me, something catches my eye. It's just in my peripheral vision at first, but the uncanny sense of import turns my head before my rational brain understands what I'm seeing. I turn just in time to catch sight of a sweep of chestnut hair leaving the room. Emily.

And without a word I'm following her into the next room, the bemused personal trainer left in my wake. I scan the faces in the connecting room but she is not one of them. I spin in the crowd wondering if I saw her at all.

And then, as the security guard by the door shifts, I see her. She's bent over a jewelry concession inspecting one of their pieces closely, her focus down.

My stomach flips. It's her, not the woman who came to my apartment two nights ago. She's here, she's okay. Curiosity, relief, and a twist of anger propel me forward. I approach briskly, my mind desperately trying to work out what the hell I'm going to say to her. Before I can reach her she rises, oblivious, and makes to move on. A jolt of panic shoots through me and before I can stop myself, I grab her arm.

"Emily?"

She turns and, as in a nightmare, I realize I'm firmly grasping the upper arm of an incredibly well-known A-list celebrity who is clearly not Emily Bryant. The actress looks back at me startled before the security guard next to her shifts between us and I immediately release my grip.

"Oh my God. I'm so sorry. God," I babble in apology. "I thought you were someone else. A friend. Sorry-sorry-sorry."

"Okaaay," the starlet drawls, staring up at her security in response.

"I'm going to have to ask you to move right back, miss," her security guard rumbles down at me tactfully, at least doing me the service of not drawing too much attention to us.

I feel my cheeks burn neon. "Of course, of course," I mutter, backing up as the pair make their way past me, back into the room I just left.

I let out a held breath and scan the people around me. Eyes flutter away. My shame is palpable but thankfully no one is looking anymore, though they're all very aware of what just happened. Classic LA: everyone knows something weird is going on but we're all pretending we didn't see it happen.

I make a quick exit, finding myself drawn toward the reassuring darkness of the room opposite. Inside I let myself relax, feeling the flush of embarrassment in my cheeks slowly ebb away. I need to get a handle on myself. I need to forget about Emily or I'm going to do something really stupid. I know I need to drop it, so why can't I?

Because something about it still doesn't sit right. I swear I just saw her. I can't just drop it. If Emily isn't okay, if something terrible happened and I'm the only who saw, how can I drop it? And however crazy it sounds, I can't help feeling that it could have just as easily been me who vanished that day—and if I had who would have noticed? Not George. Not my family or friends thousands of miles away on another continent. Maybe Cynthia would have noticed after a day or two of missed emails. Perhaps Souki, but then we hadn't spoken in months. And if they had noticed would they assume it all had to do with George? That I'd flipped out because of him and disappeared? I quickly shake off the thought because *I* didn't disappear. And *Emily* didn't disappear either. The police told me she's fine. I did my bit. I need to move on.

In the darkness of this room, a cinema screen plays an exotic beach resort trailer. Caribbean waters lapping a pink-sanded beach, tall palms swaying, slow motion, in the tropical breeze. I take a deep breath in and slowly let it out. Maybe once all this is done, I'll take a break. Get my head straight. What could ever go wrong in a place like that?

The redheaded concession assistant looks up as I approach, her gaze dipping to my lanyard where she finds her answer. Her smile widens, perfect and white, as our eyes meet.

"Hi there! How's your day going so far?"

"Fantastic, thank you. Is this a resort?" I ask, taking in the other spotlit portfolios spread across the stand: palms against bruised sunsets, idyllic waterfalls in leafy groves, twinkling beach lodges, and cool clear waters.

"Not as such, we work in conjunction with the real estate branch of Christie's auction house." She hands me her card. "We're gifting private island stays today. Is that something you'd be interested in?" She grins, possibly at the ludicrousness of her own question.

"Yes. Yeah, that would definitely be something I'd be interested in," I answer hesitantly, certain I must be missing the catch here.

"Fantastic," she nods, businesslike. "So let's see what I can offer you." Her eyes go to my lanyard again, this time noting my name as well as my tier. She cross references her clipboard.

"Right, so," she says, laying some brochures out before me. "This is an exciting one, we can offer you a two-week stay on Leda, a private island in Greece. This one's got real pedigree: you'd be staying in the fully serviced main house, which was built in 1960 and has since played host to everyone from the Beatles to Sir Winston Churchill."

Not to look a gift horse in the mouth but I suddenly realize what section of her list I must be on. I'm on the "classy" British cultural heritage list. As far as these guys are concerned, I'm basically the swinging '60s, tea bags, and beans-on-toast. Greece is great but I was hoping for something a bit closer to this hemisphere and preferably not haunted by the ghosts of old British men.

She catches my hesitancy and flips open another brochure, spinning it toward me. "Or, if you're more of a beach person?"

I soak up the two-page spread of warm sand and jade waters. "Yeah. I think I am," I say, hopefully.

Ten minutes later I leave the stand with an information pack and a penciled booking for the private Bahamian island of Bone Fish Cay, private jet flights and island chef included, still a little unsure how it happened or why. And all of this for the price of an Instagram post or two—I feel a stab of guilt at the excess of it all but quickly remind myself that the point of booking a holiday in the first place was to take my mind off things and try to relax.

I find Bee deep in conversation at the Burberry concession, a small red Cartier gift bag and a large Gucci one swinging from her tiny wrist. After another hour of perusing and nabbing, we call it a day, wandering back out into the California sunlight bag-laden with our hauls.

Back in the car after our goodbyes I start the engine and think about getting back to work on the script. It's only when I look at the GPS that I realize how close I am to the 101.

Emily's house. Curiosity, like creeping ivy, wraps itself around the idea as it forms. I zoom in on the GPS map. Perhaps I could just drive past, check if her car is there. Perhaps I did see her here earlier, that flash of chestnut hair disappearing into another room; maybe she saw me and left and went home? Who knows. But I'm so close to her apartment, it can't hurt to swing by, I might even see her from the street. A quick look at her place can't hurt. I tap the address into the satnav and it tells me the building is only twenty minutes away. I tap start journey and roll out onto the open road.

MY HEART STARTS TO FLUTTER as the satnav destination dot draws closer. I'm suddenly not sure what it is I'm trying to achieve here. The police said everything was fine. But I suppose that's the problem, I don't trust that they knew what they were looking for. If I can just see Emily's face for myself, I'll know. If I can be sure it's not the woman who came to my apartment the other night, then I can put the whole thing to rest.

When I take a left onto her street, I slow. There's on-street parking both sides of the mainly residential avenue, cars tightly parked
bumper-to-bumper. According to the satnav, Emily's building is at
the end of the street. I keep my eyes peeled for the bright white of
her Chevrolet rental as I approach but there's nothing, no white cars
sticking out among the silver and black Priuses and Hondas. Her
building comes into view on my right, a two-story 1960s prefab with
a concrete staircase leading up to the entrance. The building is
dwarfed by high-rise apartment blocks looming on either side so that
it appears to stand alone, an innocent relic of simpler times in a sea of
architectural brutalism. The building's entrance is obscured by an
overhanging tree and remains a mystery as I sail past. If I can't even
see the entrance, how am I going to see her face? I realize I need an
actual plan, or I'm just a lonely tourist driving around pointlessly.

I pull off the avenue and start to loop back around for another
pass when I see the PARK HERE sign, painted massive and garish onto
the side of a strangely geometric 1960s building.

LAST
CAPPUCCINO
BEFORE THE 101

>>> PARK HERE <<<

Without a second thought I swing the car into the car park and
find a space. This is ridiculous. I'm not achieving anything by slinking around her neighborhood like a creep. I turn off the engine and
consider my options. I flip up the armrest and stare down at the
neatly folded rental document. I've certainly got an excuse to pay her
a visit. I take it out and straighten it, some of the carbon-copy dust
coming off on my fingers.

Or I could just go back to my apartment and forget about the
whole thing. But what are the chances I'm going to forget about

what happened the other night? I'm the only person who knows that Emily disappeared, and I'm the only person who knows she never came to collect her things. I need some kind of closure on this. I need to focus over the next few days, I can't be wondering what happened to Emily. Either she's fine or she's not, and if she's not then I report a bigger crime than auto theft to Officer Cortez. I report it and leave it to someone else.

And I don't need to sneak around, I just need to give her back one last thing.

I slip my phone out of my bag and type.

> Hi Emily, it's Mia again. Sorry to keep bothering you. I still have your rental agreement. Accidentally kept hold of it the other day. I'm just around the corner from you—I can drop it in now if you're about? X

I tap send and my words fly off into the ether. I stare at my reflection in the windscreen. Jane looks back at me. My phone pings.

> Hi! Thanks for doing that. I'm actually out at the moment but you can just drop it in my mailbox. X

I frown at the screen. Then type.

> I was actually hoping to say hi, if you're about? Xx

Her gray dots pulse . . .

> Oh, okay. Right. Well, I'll be back at the apartment in, say, 45mins. Can you wait that long?

My resolve solidifies as I type.

> No problem, I'll see you then.

18

Emily's House

As I make my way up the concrete steps toward the tree-shaded entrance to Emily's building I realize I have no idea which apartment is hers, the rental document having given me no further information than her building number.

Once in the entranceway I head over to the mailboxes, examining the names on each. The building comprises only four apartments and number four's label, recently replaced, reads BRYANT. The door is directly next to the mailbox wall.

I take a step back from its peephole, not expecting to be at this stage of my plan quite so quickly. I dig out Emily's rental document from my bag as a kind of talisman and draw my hand back to knock. But one step ahead of me, I hear the latch unlock abruptly and the door swings away from me before I can make contact.

"Sorry, I could hear you rooting around out there." I hear Emily's voice before I see her and my heart leaps in my chest. "The walls are pretty thin." She smiles as she steps forward into the light.

After everything that's happened over the last few days, in spite of all my dark imaginings, and in spite of fearing the police were wrong, I really did expect to see the original Emily smiling back at me. But she isn't.

This must be who the police ID'd last night, the woman who turned up at my door two nights ago. Emily's bracelet dangles from her wrist as she leans against the door. I recall Officer Cortez's words—*if the woman they ID'd is not Emily then we'd be talking about a much bigger crime.*

I realize I haven't spoken yet and the woman's smile wavers in the awkward silence I've created.

"Oh, here's your—" I blurt, thrusting the crumpled rental document between us. She looks down at it unconcerned before carefully taking it from my hand.

"That's great, thanks. I actually returned the car yesterday. But thanks for dropping it around," she says.

I feel my eyebrows shoot up. "Why?"

She holds my gaze for a second and for the first time since meeting her, I get the feeling she knows I know she's not Emily.

She gives a slow blink before speaking. "Listen, do you want to come in for a second? I could make you a coffee or something. We never did have that *coffee date,* did we?"

The absolute last thing in the world I want to do right now is go into the dimly lit flat with her. But I'm suddenly at a complete loss as to how to express that in a socially acceptable way. After all, she doesn't exactly look threatening in her Lululemon yoga outfit and grippy socks. And besides, I came here for answers, didn't I?

I pull myself up short, because no, I didn't come here for answers. I came here to see if Emily was okay. I came here for closure so I could forget about the whole thing and concentrate on work. But now it's pretty clear that Emily is not fine. I can either try to find out what the hell is going on or get back in my car and call Cortez. But what if they send the same officers back and she fools them again? I suppose the only way I'm going to find out what's really going on is to do it myself.

"Yes, that'd be great," I say. "Thanks." She ushers me in past her and I hear the *clunk* of the latch dropping as she pulls the door closed behind us.

The apartment isn't what I was expecting. As my eyes adjust from the sunlight outside, I see it actually has a light and clean IKEA aesthetic. The brilliant white of the walls is softened by the rich emerald of houseplants, ferns, and hanging succulents dotted along bookshelves and low coffee tables. Littered used scripts, half-drained coffee cups, and the odd item of discarded clothing are the only signs of inhabitance in the ordered minimalism. "I returned the car because Ubers are just easier, you know. Parking in LA is too much stress," she says with a sigh as I follow her through to the eat-in kitchen.

She returned Emily's car, and no one batted an eye. I don't know what the hell is going on here but I resolve that I will not leave this apartment until I find out.

We enter a kitchen with its original 1960s design, mint green, with a round-edged sink, arched chrome taps, and a freestanding gas hob cooker. A '60s housewife's dream and clearly where the apartment's millennial modernization stopped.

The woman clicks on the kettle and pulls out a chair at the Formica table, gesturing for me to do the same.

But I don't.

She looks at me curiously. "Is something wrong," she asks, "you seem a little . . . ?"

I could just come out and say it. I could, or I could play along a little longer and see where this goes. There's still the possibility I've gotten all this wrong. In which case I have hounded this poor woman, stalked her, reported her to the police, and now I've forced my way into her house to confront her with my own complete delusion.

"No, I'm fine." I smile. "Just jet lag." I pull out my seat and sit down opposite her. "So how's the ex-boyfriend with the dislocated ankle?" I ask brightly, knowing full well that he's completely made up.

She hesitates and then shrugs. "I'm sure he's fine. He's not in LA anymore."

"Gone back to New York?"

"Yeah." She nods. "You're from London, right?" she asks, pleased with her knowledge.

"Yeah. Whereabouts are you from in New York?" I ask lightly, watching carefully for a hint of something in her eyes. She doesn't disappoint: her eyes shift away from mine.

"Pretty central," she answers quickly. "You know New York well?"

I shake my head. "Not really. Only been once." I notice something out of the corner of my eye as the kettle rattles to a boil and clicks off behind her. It's an ashtray. Clean and neatly tucked on a shelf. The woman rises and lifts a cafetière from a cupboard and sets about adding coffee. My eyes scan the kitchen table, counters, and shelves but find no lighter, no cigarettes, no butts.

"Could I bum a cigarette?" I ask, my voice slightly louder than anticipated.

"Sorry, I don't smoke," she replies, engrossed in her task and oblivious to the relevance of her answer.

And the words fly from me before I can stop myself. "Sorry, I don't mean to be rude, but who are you?"

She turns to look at me, confused. "Sorry?"

"Who are you?" I ask simply.

She stares at me wide-eyed before answering. "I'm Emily," she says, her confused gaze holding mine. She wants to know where I'm going with this, how far I'm going with this. But it's telling that she doesn't ask me why I would ask something like that. And if I was Emily I'm pretty sure that would have been my first question. But she remains silent.

"No, you're not Emily, are you?" I ask. "I think we both know that."

The woman blinks, dumbfounded, and I suddenly wonder if I'm acting completely mad. From her expression it's impossible to tell if she's been caught red-handed or if she's terrified of the madwoman in her kitchen.

But I've come this far, so I continue. "Why are you pretending to be Emily?" I demand.

The woman's gaze falters, her eyes darting past me to the door. She's scared. I notice a tremble in her hand and my resolve wobbles.

When she looks back at me there is a nervousness to her, but no fear. She's calculating what to do next. There's a subtle tell, a look behind her eyes that I recognize from years of improvising scenes with other actors. A look that tells you that your scene partner is trying to preempt where you're going in the scene so they can figure out their own path through it.

And it's that tiny glimmer that, finally, tells me I'm right about all of it. This woman isn't who she says she is.

I play my ace card. "You know I was the one who called the police, right?" Her confidence suddenly falters. She isn't Emily. She isn't. I push on. "If you don't tell me what the hell is going on, I'm going to call the cops again, now, ok—"

Her fear crescendos into exasperation. "All right!" she blurts, suddenly slamming the packet of coffee she'd been holding down on the counter, her change of energy jarring me not nearly as much as her sudden change of accent from New York to a thick Texas twang. Jesus. I step back, spooked.

"Okay. Good for you," she says, hands raised in angry surrender, her body language completely different, all hint of the person she was a moment before gone. "I'm not. Well done, you want a fricking medal? Unbelievable. You are one strange person; do you know that? I give up. I quit, okay? Happy?"

I try to make sense of what's happening right now but without any clues, I don't get very far. "I'm sorry, what?" I hear myself ask pathetically.

"I'm sorry, what?" she echoes back at me in a painfully accurate British accent that makes me cringe inside. She shakes her head dismissively at my confusion and continues in her Texas drawl. "I can't help not doing it exactly right if you only give me a day's prep, can I? I'm doing the best I can and for the money you're paying, I know for

a fact you won't find anyone better than me. Seriously, I don't get what you want. You ask me to turn up and do a bunch of weird shit with you and then you start calling the cops. I thought the cops were part of it when they turned up! But they were real! Do you know how much trouble that could have landed me in? I mean, why would you do that?"

All I can do is stare, and then I choose my words with care. "Look, I'm afraid I have absolutely *no idea* what you're talking about. I don't know who you are. I thought you were Emily, but you're obviously not. I'm just looking for Emily. Actual Emily."

"What? What the hell are you talking about?" she shouts, her features scrunched in disbelief. She squeezes her eyes shut and blows out a long, loud breath before opening her eyes again. She gives me the time-out sign. "Okay, that's it. Time out. I'm done. I'm quitting, okay? I quit. Just keep the money, I'll call my agent and tell her to pay you back, you strange, strange person." She starts to remove Emily's earrings from her ears and thumps them down on the table.

She's *quitting*? My mind scrambles to catch up. But as I watch her I realize there's something about the way she's removing her earrings. It reminds me of being in a dressing room after a curtain call. And suddenly the whole situation sharpens into focus. This woman is an actress, an actress being paid to play Emily. And she thinks I'm the one who hired her. For a terrifying second, I wonder if I did hire her, if somehow without realizing I have gone completely mad and all of this is down to me. Have I created an elaborate distraction to keep myself from cracking up after George left me? But that can't be true if only for the simple fact that I wouldn't know how to begin hiring someone in LA, even if I had gone mad.

"Wait, stop!" I burst as she hastily continues to remove Emily's valuables. "I am not part of whatever this is," I say, gesturing to the situation. "I definitely didn't hire you, okay? I am a real person. I'm not role-playing."

She stops unhooking Emily's bracelet and raises her eyes to mine. "What? You're not the person who hired me?"

"No."

"And you didn't call the cops on me?"

I pause, unsure of how to answer. "No. I did call the cops but I didn't hire you. I was looking for the real Emily Bryant and you showed up instead. I only met her once so I wasn't a hundred percent certain you weren't her until just now. That's why I called the police the other day, I wasn't a hundred percent sure about any of it, but I had a feeling there was something weird going on."

Her expression sobers. "There's a real Emily?" she asks, her tone concerned. "What do you mean you were looking for her? Why were you looking for her?"

I hesitate to explain everything that's gone before. "Basically, I've been looking for her for four days. She left her wallet and car keys with me at an audition and then she just disappeared. So I looked in her car, found a phone number and address, and called. Then you showed up at my apartment. I wasn't sure if I was imagining it—you look quite like her, you sounded like her. I suppose my only theory is that whoever hired you is trying to cover up the fact that Emily disappeared at that audition. I think I was one of the last people to see her."

"Shit," she says almost to herself and sinks back down into her chair.

"Do you know who actually hired you?" I ask, delicately.

She looks up at me, embarrassed. "No." She shrugs hopelessly. "I thought it was you. The job came through my agent and I taped the scenes they requested and sent it back through them. Just like a normal taped audition."

"What scenes did you do?"

"It was, like, similar to when I came to your place."

"Someone scripted our interaction? Before we had it? How is that possible?"

"Well, no, obviously, it was like a sort of scene outline. They gave me a character breakdown for your character as well as mine."

I feel my blood freeze. "They did what?" I exclaim. I suddenly realize that I am a part of this whether I like it or not. Whoever hired her knows about me; they've been watching me, following me maybe. I think of my apartment and how things have been moved around the last two days. Whatever happened to Emily involves me now too, and whoever hired this woman hired her to deal with me. "Do you have my character breakdown?"

She bites her bottom lip as she weighs the requests. "Yeah." She's reticent but gives a dutiful nod. "I'll get it," she says, rising.

In the living room she drops down onto one knee in front of the sofa and roots around underneath, finally coming up with a tatty cracked leather handbag. Her own things, hidden "offstage." She rises businesslike and hands me a dog-eared padded envelope.

"So this is everything I have. Breakdowns, scene guides, everything. My agent sent them all through."

She hands me the packet of papers and I take them.

"Your agent must know who hired you, right?"

"I guess," she answers, then catching my expression adds, "Oh, should I . . . I can check."

I nod her on, astounded that even at this point, she still isn't leaping into action to find out what the hell is going on.

She pulls out her iPhone, hesitantly. "Do you mind if I take this in the other room?" she asks, indicating the bedroom beyond.

"Yeah, sure." I understand. If I were her, the last thing I'd want to do is discuss this situation with my agent in front of me. She heads off into the other room, closing the door behind her. I wait until I hear the soft mumble of her voice then make my way back to the kitchen.

A few minutes later she returns, her brows knitted. "Okay, so, I spoke to her and . . . she's not exactly sure who hired me. She's never heard of the company before. The payments are coming through but she doesn't have a name or anything like that. She's going to call them now on the number they gave her and see if anyone picks up. She said she'd call me back straight after."

She sits back down opposite me at the table.

"That's great. Listen, thanks so much for doing this."

"No problem," she says.

One question keeps snagging in my mind, and as a silence descends I decide to broach it.

"Can I just ask? What kind of acting job did you think this was?" I try to keep the bewilderment from my voice but it's hard given the situation we've both found ourselves in.

She gives me a defensive glance. "Well, they told me it was supposed to be immersive theater. Site-specific, you know, like you're playing a character in a real setting and you interact with other actors in character but also with members of the public. I've done a bunch of it before. I did this interactive reconstruction of Marilyn Monroe's final day up near her old house in Brentwood a couple of years ago. I just had to act out her last day, errands around LA, her meals, everything. The 'audience' bought tickets and followed me around to all the different locations. It was pretty dark. But people are really into true crime at the moment so, you know, you go where the work is."

I nod. I do know. That's why I'm here in LA, after all.

"That was a weird job. This, though . . ." She chuckles. "Until today, this has, comparatively, been easy. They gave me the keys to this place in the information pack. Basically, I've been sleeping here, and then when they need me, they text me a location and a scene synopsis. A couple of scenes were in the breakdown they sent me originally." She points to the envelope between us on the table. "So I've just been showing up and playing whatever scene they tell me. To be honest everything was going fine. You seemed to be the only other character and audience member following the story, though." She pauses and shakes her head. "I genuinely thought those cops were other actors. Goddamn it, that's embarrassing."

"And you didn't question who was paying you until now?"

She looks back at me surprised. "Well, up until about twenty minutes ago I just assumed you were! You're the only familiar face I've seen." She hesitates. "I was starting to get a bit creeped out by you, to be honest. I assumed maybe it was some sort of role-play. Maybe you used to know an Emily, an old friend, relative, I don't know, I was trying not to overthink it. I would have pulled out but the money's been good."

"How good?"

"Good. Well over SAG rates. And it's a hell of a lot less soul destroying than waitressing through pilot season."

"What did you do with Emily's car?" I ask.

"They told me to return it to the rental place. They pre-paid for it so I just drove it over and handed the keys back."

Another piece of evidence connected to Emily's disappearance conveniently tied up.

The mobile phone in her hand bursts to life, piercing the fresh silence between us and setting us both on edge. Our eyes connect, both instantly wary of who might be calling.

She checks the screen. "My agent." She sighs and lets out the tension of our equally held breaths before answering. She rises and heads out of the room to take the call in private.

I wonder if I should call Officer Cortez, tell her everything that's happened. Surely we should involve the police at this stage. I decide I should wait until the actress comes back. I realize I don't even know the woman-playing-Emily's name.

I slide the padded envelope closer and there it is on the address label. Joanne Prince. I pull out my phone and google her name. Her face appears in Google Images, it's definitely her. I scan down through her credits: guest appearances on popular shows, a couple of *CSI* something-or-others, and a ton of theater. I see her Marilyn credit. She is who she says she is. At least that part of the mystery is solved.

I slide my phone back into my pocket as she returns.

"The company paying me is paying through a personal account apparently, it's not even a company, and my agent can't get through on their number. It just keeps going to voicemail. Which is not a great sign—but I gotta say, at least they paid. She's going to keep trying and she's emailed them to say I'm pulling out of the job. They're going to realize whatever they're doing has gone wrong." She looks worried. "Why would someone want to do this?"

"I don't know. I'm hoping there's still some kind of rational explanation," I say. She looks unconvinced and I suppose I have to agree with her. "But it's getting harder to think that."

"Yeah," she says quietly. The kitchen descends into silence for a moment, and when she speaks again the sound makes me jump. "Right, so my agent said to just leave it with her, she'll get me out of the contract. If it's okay with you I'm probably going to go now." She heads back into the living room.

It takes me a second to make sense of what she's saying. She's going to leave without getting to the bottom of any of this. "Er, okay," I manage as I follow her through. "How should I get in touch with you? About all of this?"

She's down on one knee again rooting for her things under the sofa. She pauses to look up. "Yeah, I'd actually prefer if you didn't contact me. I mean if that's okay? I'll just follow up through my agent, I think."

She pulls out a faded denim jacket and a pair of worn trainers from underneath the sofa and shakes them out. Her own clothes.

She's genuinely just going to go.

"But how will I find out who was paying you? Or . . . anything?"

"My agent said it was just an account number. No name on the transfer." Joanne sits on the edge of the couch and tugs on her trainers. "I mean, if you're really worried about this girl you could report it or something? Listen, I'm just going to leave the apartment keys here on the table and get going." She hesitates, taking in my expression. "I mean, it's up to you if you want to stay and get involved but I'm going to quit while I'm ahead."

Her words throw me. Do I want to stay and get involved? Do I have a choice or am I already tangled up in this?

I realize Joanne is waiting for me to say something.

"Yeah, that's fine, I'll stay a minute and lock the door when I leave."

She rises, now shrugging on her denim jacket. "Great. Okay then. Good luck with . . . everything."

"Can I at least get your phone number, in case? Your agent's?" I ask, even though I'm certain a quick Google search will supply me with the latter.

"No offense, but no way am I giving you my number," she says over a shoulder as she breezes out the door, disappearing into the fading evening light.

The door clunks shut behind her and silence falls over me and Emily's empty apartment.

19

All That Is Left Behind

SATURDAY, FEBRUARY 13

I COULD JUST LEAVE LIKE JOANNE.

I could call Souki; she's not leaving LA until tomorrow. I could ask her what the hell I'm supposed to do but I can't because I promised her I'd drop the whole thing. I already know exactly what her answer would be anyway. Leave.

I could call Cortez. But what would I say: I didn't trust her colleagues so I went to Emily's house and there was an actress pretending to be her living in it?

Worst-case scenario, she'd think I was mad, best-case scenario I'd have to hand over Emily's apartment keys, give them Joanne's name, and forget about it. My involvement in the investigation would be over. And I might never know where Emily went.

I let my eyes linger on her apartment, on her belongings, on the potential trail of evidence Emily might have left behind. I'm no detective; I'm quite sure messing with evidence isn't a great idea.

I dig out my phone and scroll back through my call list to Cortez's number. What's the worst that can happen if I report this? I take a deep breath and press dial.

When the call connects I can hear the clamor of station life through the receiver before a voice answers and then after a few transfers I'm finally speaking to Cortez.

"Hi there. It's Mia Eliot, we spoke this morning?"

The muffled hubbub on her end of the line fills the quiet apartment around me as she tries to place my name.

"Right," she answers. "Yeah, missing persons report. How can I help?" She sounds busy, clearly irritated that my call has come through on her direct line.

I buckle up for a bumpy phone call and start to explain this afternoon's events from the beginning.

"OKAY. I CAN DEFINITELY UNDERSTAND why that might have raised alarm bells," she concludes after I finish. "Sounds like you've really been going above and beyond for this Emily person," she adds, and I'm pretty sure from her tone that it's not a compliment. "And from what you've told me, it's definitely something we'd look into," she continues. "Why don't you pop into the station tomorrow morning and we'll fill out a missing persons report and look at the whole thing."

"Of course," I reply. "But what should I do in the meantime?"

"In the meantime?" she asks, baffled by the question.

"Well, yeah, I'm still in her house."

"Then I'd suggest you leave her house. And if you still have a set of her keys, then bring them along tomorrow. That'd be helpful. Although, having said that, we'd need to get Emily's, or Emily's landlord's, permission to enter the property anyway so . . . but yeah, probably best if you head home now and come in to report the incident tomorrow."

I feel completely immobilized by her words. They can't seriously expect me to just go home after this. Someone was hired to *act out* scenes with me. Someone gave Joanne a character description of *me*. And Emily is gone. "But what if something's happened to her? Am I safe?"

"I would have thought so. You know, technically, going missing isn't a crime, and the only reason we'd investigate this is if there's solid evidence of a crime. What you're telling me now about someone impersonating Emily might be evidence of something or it could just be that Emily doesn't want to be found; again, not illegal. So unless you know of an actual crime? Because this could just be a prank she's pulling, we don't know, believe me I've seen worse. Anyway, come in tomorrow, we'll go through the procedures and see what we see. Okay?"

Not really. "Yeah, okay." I sigh.

"Oh, and bring a photograph of her. Whatever you've got."

I have nothing. My eyes scan the room for one.

"Will do. Thanks, Officer Cortez."

"It's Maria. We'll see you tomorrow."

I CAN'T SAY I FEEL any better after I hang up. I suppose in my head they'd send a squad car straight here and dust the apartment for prints and open an in-depth investigation immediately but then things don't work like that in the real world, do they.

Joanne is going to be more than a little annoyed at me if I give the police her name tomorrow but I don't think she'll go as far as to deny she was involved. If she does, I'm not sure where that leaves me. Because if Joanne is removed from the chain of events that led me here, then it might be assumed that I stole Emily's apartment keys from her car or broke in.

My mind fizzles along that track. If I had access to her apartment I might have been the woman the cops ID'd here the other night. Might I have been the woman impersonating her? I know for a fact I fit Emily's description; everyone at that audition four days ago did.

But I'm sure Joanne won't deny it. It's one thing to want to avoid hassle and quite another to lie to the police. I shift on the sunken-seated sofa. Besides there'll be an email chain on Joanne's computer and her agent's linking her here. And she was caught on CCTV in my building collecting Emily's things. I wander back into the kitchen to retrieve Joanne's padded envelope full of evidence.

I weigh the packet in my hands. I should take this and give it to them tomorrow too. And I should leave. Cortez is right. I've already wasted too much of my own time on this. It's not like I don't have anything to do out here. I think of Joanne slinking out into the evening light, free. I could just go. It's clear nobody else is as concerned about this as I am.

But then that's not true. Somebody else is very concerned about this, about what I know. They are so concerned that they've gone to great lengths to make me think Emily is still around. I can't help but wonder what they'll do now that I know she's gone.

I finger the papers inside the envelope, pulling one out absent-mindedly.

It's Emily's character description.

CHARACTER: (Emily) Brunette, late twenties, attractive, native New Yorker. Emily Bryant is an actress pounding the pavements in search of that elusive golden ticket, her big break. While she's got all the sass and grit you'd expect from a girl who grew up in the big city there is also a soulful and quiet confidence to Emily. And although she's quick to make friends she never really lets anyone get too close. As this immersive role develops we will come to realize that Emily is living with a secret that may force her to abandon everything she values . . . or face the consequences.

Jesus, this is meta. A shiver runs through me.

Without stopping to think I grab the package and root through until I find what I'm looking for. I take a breath and read.

CHARACTER: (Mia) Brunette, late twenties, pretty,
British. Mia Eliot is the classic innocent abroad. Having
found success in her native England she travels to LA,
on her own, to land the role of a lifetime.

I spin and look around the empty apartment suddenly possessed by the eerie idea that I am being filmed. Right now. I scan bookshelves, the corners of the room.

I've heard stories. I know there are whole sections of the Internet given over to secretly filming women, that iPhones get duct-taped under sinks in Starbucks, that laptop cameras get hacked and set to broadcast. My eyes skip to Emily's computer on her desk. The tiny black camera aperture above the lifeless screen stares blankly back at me. I march over and slam the lid.

The idea that I might have been deliberately led to where I am now comes into my head. Someone could be back at my apartment, right now, doing God knows what. Waiting for me, maybe.

I pull out the rest of the papers and inspect them. They're scene breakdowns. My eyes scroll through them.

> • Proposed car collection scene. Emily retrieves
> her rental car from outside a casting studio after
> disappearing for two days. She may meet a concerned
> receptionist, whom she'll need to reassure. The
> receptionist may express concerns over Emily's sudden
> disappearance. Emily should appear rushed and under
> pressure to return her rental car before her parking
> lapses.

That was the morning Joanne collected the car from North Hollywood. My eyes leap to the next.

> • Avis rental return. Emily returns the pre-paid vehicle
> and explains she no longer needs it for the full period.

She asks for her card to be refunded if possible. If this is
not possible, she is willing to lose her deposit.

God, Joanne must have thought this was the weirdest and most
boring job in the entire world. I turn back to the previous page.

> • <u>Proposed café scene.</u> Emily meets Mia (an actress she
> met at an audition) to collect her wallet and her car
> keys. Emily thanks Mia for her help but is reticent to
> talk about her personal problems. She may allude
> passingly to family or relationship issues.

I stop reading. It didn't happen in a café. This is exactly what happened at my apartment two nights ago. Joanne played out this scene
with me without my realizing. Aside from a different location our
interaction was almost exactly this. Someone planned our meeting
ahead of time. A chill runs through me and I spin around suddenly,
feeling phantom eyes on me. But of course I am alone. At least I am
right now. This is fucking weird. My fear for Emily is now wholly
superseded by fear for myself. How far does this story go? How does
it end for me? I desperately flip through the scenes looking for more
containing my name. And for a horrifying moment I get the feeling I
might find one describing exactly what I'm doing at this moment. My
heart pounds and everything else slips away except for the words in
front of me as I skim. Breath held, I turn to the final page and read.

But the scenes don't make it to where I am now. The last page in
Joanne's stack relates to a potential police scene she "acted out" the other
night. Whoever organized this pack thought of everything. Well, everything up until the police verifying her ID. I imagine they assumed that
after that verification, I would be satisfied. I would stop. But I didn't.

I wonder if they know I am here. But the only way they could
know that is if I'm being watched. I head back to the laptop and flip
open the lid. The screen remains lifeless, not even turned on. Then I
bend and search under the desk for a camera, but there is nothing

except laptop wires. I move on to the bookshelves searching for re-cording equipment, following my instinct through the living room and into the bedroom.

I check the wardrobes, behind the curtains, under the bed. Stuck to a lamp on the bedside cabinet, I find a photograph. Two women hiking. Emily on the right, and beside her another woman about the same age. A friend perhaps, or a relative. Though why this other woman hasn't noticed Emily's disappearance, I do not know. Or per-haps she has noticed? I give the photo a tug and the adhesive putty holding it in place loosens, coming away. I flip the picture over; on the back are the words ME + MARLA. I pocket the photo and keep searching the bedroom. But there's no filming equipment, no tiny filament cam-era holes in the paintwork or light fittings. No one is watching.

Whoever hired Joanne probably won't realize something is amiss until they get the email from Joanne's agent. I pause. Unless . . .

I turn on my heels and head for the front door, pulling it open and staring up into the stairwell. No CCTV cameras. I scan the other apartment doors, listening for inhabitants within, but I hear only the low hum of the 101.

I look out toward the street, but the view is shielded by the over-hanging trees. There are no windows looking back in this direction. No one is watching. I remind myself that whoever sent Joanne to my apart-ment two nights ago knows my name, and they know where I live.

Back in the kitchen, I notice rotten fruit in the fruit bowl, ob-scured by Joanne's chair earlier, bruised and furred. Perfect spheres of green and white fluff, once apples, or oranges, now just the ghosts of them. Emily hasn't been here for days.

A shiver runs down my spine as it occurs to me that whatever happened to Emily could now very easily happen to me.

I cast my eyes around her place one last time, taking in her things, her books, her clothes, her slowly perishing groceries.

And then I see it, next to her laptop, half hidden under an audi-tion script. An iPhone.

Emily's iPhone.

20

Proof

I HEAD BACK TO MY APARTMENT TAKING A DELIBERATELY COMPLEX route, bending back on myself several times, slowing and changing roads whenever I feel a car too close behind or if I notice one following for more than a block. I'm half expecting someone to swoop in and snatch Emily's phone and laptop from the seat beside me. I try not to think about the fact that wherever Emily is, she has no phone, no wallet, and no car. I try to shake the thought of the actress who jumped from the sign and her carefully stacked possessions. Her broken lifeless body lying undiscovered in the Hollywood Hills.

At the back of my mind I know my elaborate route home is ultimately useless as whoever hired Joanne already knows where to find me; they sent her to my apartment two nights ago, after all. I texted my address to Emily's phone. I curse myself for not asking Joanne if she had been the one using Emily's phone to contact me or if I'd been speaking to someone else via those texts.

Even though they most likely know my address, I'll still be safer back at the apartment with its CCTV protection and Miguel and

Lucy keeping a watch than out here. It would be so easy for someone to carjack me right now, driving down dimly lit roads; they'd leave no trace except my abandoned car. And at this stage I'm under no illusions that my car wouldn't disappear, too, just like Emily's. There are no doubts in my mind that given half a chance, LA could swallow me whole in one night.

As I pull into the Ellis Building's brightly lit porte cochere, I feel the tension in my shoulders release slightly. I catch sight of Miguel wandering over to greet me, and his small talk buoys me as he helps wrangle my long-forgotten gifting-suite bags toward reception. Still, I'm careful to keep one bag in particular close, feeling the reassuring weight of Emily's things digging the cloth straps of a gifting tote sharply into my shoulder.

UP IN THE APARTMENT I turn on all the lights and pull the curtains, blocking out the bone-white sign looming in the distance over LA.

I unfurl the cables and plug in Emily's laptop, laying out her phone, her photo, and Joanne's padded envelope on the glass coffee table. Then I grab a notebook and pen.

I look down at my stolen goods, a sliver of doubt creeping into my resolve. I remind myself that all I want to do is speed things along. Because once I hand over Emily's keys to the police tomorrow, it could take them days, weeks, to get the correct permissions to enter her apartment and start to look for her officially. If I can just find something useful to tell or show them tomorrow, then we could be one step closer to finding out what happened to Emily four days ago and where she is now.

But where to start. It's not like I've done this before. I've researched a role but never a person. I realize my heart is still racing from the drive back; I need to calm down first. I head to the fridge to grab a quick snack, and crack open a beer to steady my nerves. The vague remembrance that I have the most important screen test of my life on Monday wafts through my mind, but then I still don't have any scenes to prepare so I'm not technically able to work on it yet. I promise myself that as soon as the scene numbers arrive, I will focus entirely.

I sit down on the floor in front of the coffee table, pull the notebook closer, and ask myself the question: why do people disappear? I jot down the word: *accident.* Then add: *(rushed to hospital)?* But quickly cross it out. If Emily had an accident in the brief slot of time between my leaving the studio and my returning to it, I'm sure somebody at the casting studio would have noticed, somebody would have helped her, and an ambulance would have been called. But no one batted an eye when I got back to the casting office—Emily had simply dissolved into the ether.

No, something else must have happened. Perhaps something odd happened in the casting itself. I jot down: *audition room.* After all, strange things happen in auditions all the time. I struggle to imagine what could have tipped hers over the edge to the extent she'd just up and vanish. There's no way of knowing what was said in that darkened room, though, as each casting suite was soundproofed. Which isn't unusual, the last thing a casting director wants to do is to hand, say, Steven Spielberg a bunch of audition tapes with another actor's muffled screaming in the background. Filming is ninety percent waiting for background noise to stop, so soundproofing at studios is essential. Nothing to be suspicious of in the slightest, but then most actresses don't disappear after going into casting rooms to tape.

I recall the final scene of that Mars audition: everyone who auditioned ripped out a desperate animal roar into space and nobody in the waiting room heard a peep. Anything could happen in that room and we wouldn't have known. That's the point of soundproofing. I shudder at the thought.

And now that I think about it, the casting studio receptionist didn't seem to have any idea who was coming and going from the rooms. I feel the blood drain at the idea that someone who wasn't supposed to be there could have gotten into that room with her. And I remember her pleas for me to go first. Did Emily have a feeling something was wrong, is that why she was so keen to switch places? Yes, her parking meter had run out when I got there, but it had been on empty for a full twenty minutes before and yet she made it seem urgent. But I said I'd go feed her meter and she went in. If I had agreed to go first, would I have disappeared in her place?

I try to remember the casting director. She was in her mid-twenties, short, with a kind, round face. Hardly intimidating. I think she said her name was Claire, but I could definitely be wrong about that.

I scrawl the name *Claire* out on the notepad. While I'm guessing she had nothing to do with Emily's disappearance, she might have been the last person to see her after me. She can confirm whether Emily made it in to that audition room. She might even know what happened after.

Because there's the strong possibility that something stopped her from going in. I think of the excuse Joanne-as-Emily gave for disappearing—of her getting a phone call about an injured boyfriend—and while I know it's just a story she came up with on the spot, it's entirely plausible that a phone call did drag the real Emily away. An urgent call that would require immediate attention. My eyes flick to her phone on the table.

I know exactly when she disappeared, so all I'd need to do is check the last call before then. Emily even told me she was expecting a call after her audition. Perhaps that call came early.

I pick up her phone and gingerly tap the screen. A passcode keypad appears.

I stare at the screen hopelessly, my own blank expression reflected back at me. I have no idea what her code might be and I'm guessing there's no way to bypass it. I scrabble over to my own bag on the couch opposite and pull out my phone. I google *bypass iPhone locked screen*.

A couple of hokey videos about unlocking come up. I watch one until it becomes obvious it's nonsense then head directly to the Apple website instead.

The website tells me it is possible to bypass the locked screen but if I do that it will wipe the whole phone. Which obviously is the exact opposite of what I want to do. There's also an option of trying to retrieve her call log through iCloud on her laptop, and for a moment my heart skips a beat, but as I read on it becomes clear I would need her iCloud password to do that—which I also do not have.

That only leaves trying to guess the six-digit number and I'm reminded of a horror movie I once watched where the hero, needing to open a stranger's phone, simply holds it up to the light; as he tilts it we see the fingerprint traces of a code on the phone screen. Then he traces the fingermarks and the screen opens. Easy-peasy.

Apprehensive, I raise Emily's iPhone screen toward the light and tilt it.

The screen is a mess of indecipherable finger smears impossible to read. I console myself with the fact that though I can't open it, I can hand it over to the police tomorrow. Perhaps they'll have a way of accessing her call log that I don't. But the idea that I might never know if they do spurs me on in a different direction.

I put the phone to one side and spin around her laptop. I might not be able to see her call log but I know I can read her iMessages from her computer.

I take a breath and depress the power button, praying that, now charged, it still works.

The screen flares to life. I inhale sharply as the Apple symbol appears and then opens onto her home screen. No password protection. I let out a little cheer in the silence of the apartment and allow myself another slug of cold beer as I watch the desktop icons load.

Emily's desktop settles. It's a mess, crammed with script files, self-tape thumbnails, and casting breakdowns. Compared with my relatively ordered laptop, Emily's is enough to break me out in hives.

I click on the iMessage icon on the dock and for the first time something actually works. All of Emily's text messages appear on the screen.

21

Not the First Time

THE APPLICATION OPENS SHOWING EMILY'S TEXT CHAINS TO THE LEFT. Names I do not recognize, the people in her life unknown to me. At the top are the people she was in contact with recently, the people who should have noticed that she's not around anymore.

I see my own number, second from the top, replying that I'll be over in an hour.

Above it another message, received this evening, and its conversation chain opens up filling most of the screen—the contact name is *Dad*.

My stomach flips. I hesitate, unsure if I should read on. Up until now it hadn't occurred to me that her family might already be looking for her. Officer Cortez didn't mention anything like that on the phone. If Emily's disappearance had already been reported she would have mentioned it unless, I suppose, it was reported in a different state. I scroll up to the last reply Emily made on Wednesday before she disappeared.

Weds Feb 10, 12:04pm

Sorry I missed your call. Just heading to a casting, I'll call when I can.

No worries. Lemme know how it goes. And . . . break a leg?

Yesterday, 8:17am

Hope the audition went well?? Any news on the big one?

Yesterday, 7:43pm

Tried to call. Know you're busy. I'm watching the game tonight so I'll try you tomorrow. I want to hear about that big job.

Today, 6:49pm

Everything going good? You're probably driving. Call me back xx

What job is he talking about? She must have been waiting to hear back about something. Curious, I scroll further up the conversation to find out more, roll back as far as January before I notice something odd. I stop scrolling abruptly.

To my surprise there's another large gap in the conversation between her and her father. A gap where she didn't reply to any of his messages for almost a week between the sixth and the twelfth of January. So Emily's gone missing before.

The days preceding the gap read:

Fri Jan 1, 12:04am

Happy New Year honey! Hope it's a good one

Sat Jan 2, 11:27am

Sorry for not calling New Year's Eve honey. It got a bit out of hand at the bar. D'ya have a good one? Love ya kiddo xx

Love you too dad. Yeah, sorry, things are a bit crazy here right now too. Talk soon

No worries. Don't work too hard. Call me when you can

Mon Jan 4, 3:15pm

Things calmed down yet? Lol! You still hanging out with Marla? You guys have fun over New Year? It's good to know you got company out there.

Yeah, she's fun. Listen dad, I don't want to jinx it but there's this big job, and it's kind of out of the blue. It's a big part, it could change everything. Anyway, I'm gonna find out by the end of this week. If it comes through I'll head back home to celebrate before It all starts x

That's such great news honey. I'd love to see you either way. Let me know when you might be coming back home & I'll book some days off work. We'll do some stuff

Weds Jan 6, 08:02am

They're letting me know this evening . . . I'll keep you posted. Dad, this could be so good!! Can't wait to tell you x

That's the last text she sends before the six-day gap. Again the job is mentioned, and I can't help feeling that's relevant. To disappear on the exact same day you're expecting to hear life-changing news has to be more than a coincidence.

Receiving bad news could definitely explain her sudden absence.

My eyes instinctively flick toward the living room window to the sign I know hides behind the heavy drawn curtains, and I think again of the actress who jumped from it. People kill themselves over bad news.

And yet Emily couldn't have heard she'd lost the job because she was still talking about hearing a month later. Something else must have happened that day. I scan back up the messages and note down the name *Marla,* the friend her father mentions, on my pad. It's the name on the back of the photograph I took from Emily's apartment too. They were obviously close. It might be worth trying to contact her, I'm sure she will have noticed Emily's disappearance by now. She might even have an idea where Emily is.

I read on. After the six-day gap Emily starts responding to her father's texts again:

Tues Jan 12, 2:54pm

Sorry for the radio silence! Things got a little complicated, but the good news is I'm fine and that job I was telling you about is still looking good. So, fingers crossed. Apparently, I have to wait until they cast the male lead to get my contract offer X

Em-Em. It's great to hear from you! Got a bit worried when I couldn't get hold of you. That does all sound complicated but I've got everything crossed for you. And let me know about dates to book off work. Looking forward to seeing you.

Weds Jan 13, 12:56am

Probably not going to get the chance to fly back and see you before the job starts, dad. If it even happens. Sorry x

Weds Jan 13, 7:04am

That's okay honey. No worries at all. Work comes first. Maybe I'll fly out for Easter? If you're not off jet-setting by then!! Keep up the good work. I'm real proud of you. Dad XX

I stare at her words on the screen. She doesn't even try to explain the absence. And he doesn't push her on it. But whatever happened in that six-day gap made her change her mind about going home to see him.

The fact that Emily disappeared for six days a month ago and eventually reappeared should give me some kind of reassurance but doesn't.

I look away from the screen, suddenly aware of the similarities between Emily's situation and mine. We're both far from home, separated from friends and family, trying to further our careers, and while Emily was imminently expecting big news I have my own screen test, my own big opportunity, on Monday morning.

Two women on the cusp, waiting to hear about the role of a lifetime—the thought of it sends a shiver through me. I can't help but wonder what role she was waiting to hear about. I open her mail app and scan through her inbox going back to the sixth of January, the original day she was supposed to receive the news. I click on an email from her agent sent that day.

From: Rogers, Asst
Sent: Monday, January 6, 2021 10:47 AM
To: "Emily Bryant" <EmEmbryant@gmail.com>
Subject: RE: Self Tape: EMILY BRYANT / SUNDAY CLUB

Self-tape received. Great work!

Danny Engels
Office of Bernice Rogers

That's it? It certainly doesn't sound like the kind of email an agent would send to someone expecting huge news that day. And it's not even from her agent, it's from her agent's assistant. Which is odd considering, in my experience, agents tend to get pretty hands-on when clients start doing well. I jot down *Danny Engels* on my list.

I pull up Google and search *Sunday Club,* the project mentioned in the email subject, just in case that's the role. A *Deadline* casting announcement from mid-January pops up and a row of headshots smile back at me, cast and ready to film. This clearly isn't the job Emily was excited about, it's just a standard network pilot, a couple of weeks' filming at most, nothing groundbreaking.

A wave of sadness floods through me as it suddenly occurs to me that she may have made up this potential job entirely—or that the job she's talking about might not be an acting role at all. She might have been waiting to hear about an entirely different life-changing job. But whatever it is, it features heavily before both disappearances.

I head back to her message app hoping to find messages between Emily and her friend Marla, certain that they must have discussed Emily's new job.

I don't find her name anywhere on messages. But as I scroll through I find a relatively recent conversation with an unnamed number. I open the chat.

Fri Jan 1, 12:02am

Happy New Year bish!!! Sad I had to bail. Got to tape tomorrow. Bleurgh! Drink all the drinks for me.

Done

*Hiccup

Lol.

House guy's not still bothering you, is he?

Nope. Guess he found someone drunker?! Or more ambitious. lol

Okay. Well if he comes back, hide. Text me when you get home x

Fri Jan 1, 11:48am

What time you finish last night? How are you feeling 🤮 ?

Fri Jan 1, 3:48pm

That bad huh?

Sat Jan 2, 9:12am

Listen, sorry I bailed on New Year's. Forgive me? Brunch?

Sat Jan 2, 5:26pm

Sorry Marla. Just seen these.

Not feeling great.

Hahaha! Still?! How much did you drink girl?

Sat Jan 2, 9:57pm

Em, is everything okay?

Sun Jan 3, 8:04am

Can you meet me at the coffee shop?

The piercing ring of the security monitor phone rips my attention from the screen, causing my heart to pound high in my

chest as the sound tears through the apartment again, high and insistent.

It's nearly eleven P.M. I stumble up and head out to the hallway monitor, mildly annoyed at the interruption, but when I see the screen is blank my blood runs cold. Somebody has disabled the security camera and I can't see who's standing outside my door.

My mind races as the tone angrily blares again. Lucy must have let someone up without checking—why would she do that, they said they never did that? I edge toward the door's tiny peephole, possibilities flooding through my head, half expecting to see Cortez, or Joanne, or even Emily on the other side of the door. I pray it's any one of those people over the possibility that this visitor may be someone else entirely.

I take a breath and lean in to look.

22

When No One Is Looking

MY EYE FOCUSES THROUGH THE PEEPHOLE AND I PULL UP SHARPLY. THE hallway is completely empty.

There's no one there.

The security phone screeches loudly beside me again and I realize what I've done. It's just a call from reception; no one is outside the door. But why isn't the hall camera working? It usually lights up even for an intercom call.

I lift the receiver and it's Lucy's voice I hear.

"Hi, Mia, sorry to bother you this late. We've got another package for you down here, it just arrived from Universal, a new script and revised script pages for Monday? They said it's urgent, but it's after eleven P.M. on a Saturday so I didn't know if you'd appreciate a courier or me bringing it up in person this late."

"Oh right! Thank you so much. Should I maybe come down?" I answer, trying not to betray the huge relief I feel at the fact that Lucy refused to let a stranger up to my apartment.

"No, it's fine, I can bring it up. I just wanted to check you were okay to be disturbed this late."

"Yeah, that would be fantastic, thanks, Lucy. Oh, and there's something up with my security monitor. It's not working."

"Oh. Okay, I'll take a look at it when I come up."

Revised pages for Monday? I hang up and dash back into the living room to check my emails but there's nothing about new scenes from either Universal or from my agents, which is odd. Nobody thought to tell me I'd have entirely new scenes to learn for Monday.

The package Lucy delivers is exactly what she described, another large packet similar to the first stamped with the studio logo. Once she hands it over I direct her to the broken monitor and its lifeless screen. She carefully removes the casing around the unit, revealing the circuitry beneath.

"Hmm, I thought it could be something simple like a dead battery," she says, her forehead creased in concentration, "but it looks like these are hooked up to the mains." She shrugs and carefully replaces the casing. "That's annoying, but nothing to worry about. I can get someone from maintenance to take a look on Monday, if that works? I usually call up to check if someone arrives for you, anyway."

"That would be fantastic," I reply, my tone breezy, even though the thought of having no security monitor until Monday is deeply unsettling given what I now have sitting open on my coffee table. At least I can be assured Lucy is downstairs preventing anyone from randomly wandering up here in the night. And then there's the security cameras along the hall. I can only pray that they'd be enough to put whoever hired Joanne off paying me a visit. I try not to think about the extreme coincidence of my camera going out after the very peculiar day I've had.

As soon as Lucy leaves, I double-lock the door behind her and carry my new script into the kitchen. Inside I find a note from Kathryn's assistant, mentioning having already emailed me the scene numbers for Monday and the new pages, but now sending everything in hardcopy, too, just in case it's easier for me that way.

I never received that email.

Kathryn's assistant also includes a schedule in the package for the day of the screen test, which I have also never seen. For the first time, I find out that the call time for Monday is ten A.M. for hair and makeup, to start filming at noon. If I hadn't just received this package I would have had no idea what scenes to prepare or when to arrive on Monday morning.

I've been deluding myself up until now; it's not a coincidence that my most important emails are somehow not getting to me. I think of Cynthia's unusually urgent confirmation email and wonder if perhaps it wasn't her first attempt at getting through to me.

Without a thought I get up, walk straight out to my apartment hallway, and depress the door handle. It's locked, as it should be. I shake my head at the thought but for a second there it seemed entirely possible that the apartment door lock as well as the security monitor might have been deliberately tampered with.

But nobody would be able to get into the apartment while I was out; they wouldn't even let a courier upstairs just now. I must be having a problem with my server? Or could someone be accessing my email remotely?—but all my emails come direct to my mail app. I'm obviously no computer expert but other than a run-of-the-mill server problem, I can't think of another rational reason I haven't been getting emails.

Then it hits me. My computer isn't necessarily the issue here; you can access emails via your phone too. I head back into the kitchen where it sits innocently on the countertop and try to remember if I left it unattended at any point today around Joanne. But my phone is password-protected, there's no way she'd be able to open it even if she wanted to. Could it be that in the general chaos I somehow accidentally deleted my own emails? Not such a crazy thought given that I am apparently the only person other than cleaning staff who can get into this apartment. Am I getting so distracted I'm making these stupid mistakes or am I missing something? Either way I might have almost lost the most important job of my life.

I shake off all thoughts of Joanne, Emily, and emails and pull out the new script pages to take a look. It takes a moment to refocus before my work-brain kicks in. Thankfully the scenes they want me to do are the ones I half expected, and the dialogue has changed only slightly from the previous draft of the script.

There are three scenes to learn, and I have only one full day to prepare. It should be enough if I focus but I'll need to get my head straight and back in the game.

I look at the oven clock. It's too late to start learning lines tonight. Besides, I need to work out what the hell I'm going to say to the police tomorrow about the whole Joanne/Emily situation. I wonder for a second if I can delay going into the station—after all, this audition on Monday could change my life. But then I don't think I could live with the idea of Emily not getting the help she might need. Besides, if I report it early tomorrow, I can put it to bed once and for all and have the rest of the day to focus on the script. Which gives me tonight to find out as much as I can about Emily's disappearance.

My eyes stray back to the open laptop on the coffee table as I feel myself being dragged back into Emily's life.

I head over to the open laptop and skim through the messages.

Marla left Emily at a New Year's Eve party and didn't hear from her properly for the next two days.

I pick up where I left off.

Sun Jan 3, 8:04am

Can you meet me at the coffee shop?

I can be there in 30 minutes?

Thank you x

Then nothing until that night.

Sun Jan 3, 7:21pm

For the record I say do what your heart tells you.
This is your life, your choices.

But please be careful & call me straight after. I'm here if you need to vent.
Anytime!

Thanks. You're a good friend, so, thank you. God, I wish we'd
met in high school! I know this is the right way to do it . . . at least for me.
It's their mess, they can fucking fix it.

Mon Jan 4, 2:15pm

I'm here. Nervous.

Shit, okay. Don't be nervous! You've got this. You know what to say, you've
covered everything.

Em, you know you don't have to do this right?

I do.

I want to do this.

Mon Jan 4, 2:45pm

Done. It's an offer. And I have everything they just said on my phone.

My eyes snap to Emily's mobile phone on the table beside me but
there's no way I can open it.
I read on.

Okay. Is that admissible?

Let me know when you are safe home.

> Home. Wow. Holy shit. I don't know if it's admissible but it's enough, if you know what I mean. I actually feel better! I was scared I wouldn't but I do. I think this is going to work.

Fucking hell you've got balls!

How were they?

> They were weirdly businesslike. They listened, then they had a discussion, and then they made an offer.

What did they offer?

> They gave me three options. I'll tell you this evening. But they're good. If it works then in a way it'll all have been worth it.

Worth it?

> Well . . . not for nothing.

Tues Jan 5, 10:08am

> Just got a call. They're pulling out.

Do they know you have the last meeting on your phone?

> No.

Tell them

Tues Jan 5, 10:22am

It worked. They're consulting legal.

Tues Jan 5, 12:09pm

It's back on. They want me to go in again tomorrow and sign an NDA, then they'll sign the contract.

What time tomorrow? Should I come with you?

I'll be fine. It's at the studio. 9am.

You're keeping the recordings until the deal's done, right?

Of course.

Weds Jan 6, 8:42am

I hope you don't think the worse of me for any of this. I know I should be doing this differently. I know it's not the right way but, as messed up as it is, this might be my only chance. I know I'm good enough and if something can come of all this then why not take it with both hands? Life's hard enough you've got to catch breaks wherever you find them, right? xxx

I'm behind you whatever. Don't worry about what anyone else thinks. Just look after yourself, Em. At the end of the day, if no one else is paying your rent no one else gets a say!

And be careful today—they're clearly capable of anything. Call me after.

Weds Jan 6, 10:05am

How did it go?

Weds Jan 6, 11:01am

Em? How did it go?

Weds Jan 6, 11:46am

Let me know you're okay.

Weds Jan 6, 12:07pm

Right, I'm coming over

Weds Jan 6, 12:42pm

Where are you?

Weds Jan 6, 1:39pm

Em, where are you? I need you to call me asap.
Just let me know you're okay? xx

Thurs Jan 7, 5:04pm

Got your Airbnb woman to let me in. I know where you are now. Just stay
there. I'm coming. Wait for me. Please don't do anything xx

I try to scroll down but that's where the messages end. There have
been no more messages to or from Marla since the seventh of January.

I stare at Marla's final message to Emily. God knows how she
worked out where Emily went. But it occurs to me there's a chance
that Emily may have gone back to wherever it was now.

I suddenly have the overwhelming desire to dial Marla's number
and ask her if she found Emily. I take her number from Emily's screen
and add it into my phone.

And at the risk of her thinking I'm completely insane, I tap out a message and press send before I change my mind.

Today, 11:15pm

Hi Marla, my name is Mia, you don't know me but I got your number from Emily. I know this is a weird question but do you know where she is? She went missing on Wednesday. I'm pretty concerned.

I reread the words I've just sent out into the ether and wonder if I've made a terrible mistake. Because they haven't messaged each other since January, I'm guessing that Marla will have no idea Emily is missing again. I find myself asking why they have stopped talking to each other but then I realize there's no way to know if Marla didn't disappear that day as well. The fact that I can't open up Emily's phone and check if the two called each other is beyond infuriating.

If I could open the phone I could listen to that recording of the meeting, too. Emily clearly had evidence of some kind, worth keeping.

And if I could just get to that call list, I could see who it was she spoke to last and when. I pick it up again, turning it in my hands as if there might be a secret way to unlock it, like a Chinese puzzle, but it's just a regular iPhone.

Wherever Emily went for those six days, she reappeared on the twelfth of January and continued her life as before: she attended auditions, sent and replied to emails, and sent her agent self-tapes, new headshots. I click open the photo attachments, and relief floods through me as I see her face. Real Emily's face. After questioning myself for so long I was half expecting to see Joanne staring back at me but it's most definitely Emily, the girl I met four days ago, looking happy and healthy and real. And for the first time since she disappeared I feel a rising panic because she's gone and no one knows but me.

From skimming her emails after the twelfth, I can see she came back from wherever she went with a renewed vigor. Either her plan worked or it didn't and she had to come up with a better one.

I think back to the day I met her at the audition. She seemed confident, friendly, happy to be there but we're actresses, aren't we, it's not hard to put on a professional face.

I sieve through what I can recall of our conversation for anything telling. The only thing that springs to mind is the call she mentioned she was waiting for. If only I could get on that bloody phone and see if she got that video call just before she disappeared for the second time.

Then a memory surfaces. I recall Zooming George every day while I was away filming on a fantasy film in Romania. I'd Zoom him every evening on my phone in my freezing-cold trailer on the grounds of Bran Castle in Transylvania until I realized the calls weren't included on my data plan. Then I started Zooming him back at the hotel on their Wi-Fi at night instead. I downloaded the desktop version and found to my despair the previous call durations. My entire call log was viewable from the laptop.

I open up the finder on Emily's computer and search for Zoom.

The icon appears and I click on it. On the user name and password screen her password details autofill; all I have to do is click. The Zoom screen bounces open, her account filling the screen.

I see her last call. From this Wednesday.

Moon Finch Multimedia   10 Feb 2021   Call ended 2m 52s

I tap on the call and the call time appears: 1:18 P.M.

This is it, the call she was expecting, a call that came while I was still in that audition room.

I pull up Google and search *Moon Finch Multimedia*. It's a production company. I forgo their website and head straight for their Internet Movie Database page to see what they've produced. They're easy to find and as I scroll through their credits I realize that a lot of the big films I've watched over the last few years have been at least partly produced by this company. They've worked with or through most of the studios.

It looks like they're the developmental arm of a larger company.

I take a closer look at their logo: a small plump bird silhouetted in front of a full moon, its beak held high and open, mid-song. It's a familiar logo, I'm sure I've seen it countless times in opening credits without even noticing.

Emily spoke to somebody at Moon Finch for almost three minutes before she disappeared four days ago.

They could have been calling her about the job she was waiting to hear about. They may have given her bad news. Or good news, she could have rushed off to meet them—though she wouldn't just abandon her car and her things, especially if she had to travel to meet them.

I tap on Moon Finch's in-development credits. There are thirteen projects in pre-production. I look at a few but most are still untitled with only a director or a lead attached. If she was waiting to hear back about the lead in one of these films, then she was right, a job like this truly could have changed her life. Which leads me to ask, what the hell happened on New Year's Eve that warranted such a job offer?

Did she overhear something she shouldn't have; did she see something?

Whatever happened I now know that Emily spoke to someone at that production company from 1:18 to 1:21 on Wednesday the tenth of February and then disappeared.

I pull up the staff page for Moon Finch. There are nine executives working for the company and three executive assistants. Of the executives, five are male and one is female. I jot down their names on the notepad. It's only a hunch at the moment, nothing more, but I have a feeling I don't need to write down the woman's name.

One by one I google their photos and study their faces. Faces that under normal circumstances I'm sure would look completely innocuous now take on all the shades of misdeed. Men who could be husbands, fathers, or brothers now become leering and capable of anything. I study the face of the man who appears to be the primary producer at Moon Finch, Ben Cohan, but it's impossible to tell anything from looking.

I don't recognize a single one of them, though I can see I have auditioned for some of their previous films. It's funny who and what sticks in the mind and what refuses to be pinned down. After all, I now know I met Nick two years ago and I didn't recognize him at all when I met him again this week.

If a production company of Moon Finch's caliber was willing to offer Emily an opportunity of that magnitude, then I have to wonder what she had on them.

I turn to her emails for some kind of answer. Finding nothing in her inbox, I run the cursor down Emily's neatly archived mail folders until I reach the computer-generated folders at the bottom of the screen. RECOVERED, DELETED, DRAFTS.

I dive into the DELETED folder, hoping that her trash hasn't been recently erased, but I'm not in luck. The file is empty, as is DRAFTS. I don't exactly know what the RECOVERED folder is but I click on it next.

The file is full. I stare at the emails, every email the same, all duplicates. Every single email is from Emily to Emily. There must have been an error in sending so she sent and re-sent over and over. There's no subject in the subject bar, and every single email has two attachments. There's eighteen of them, identical.

I open one. It's empty except for the two attached files. One labeled: Bel Air.m4a. The other: San Fernando.m4a.

Emily sent two audio files to her laptop from her iPhone. One must be the meeting she recorded. I know a couple of the major studios are out in the San Fernando Valley where the second recording was obviously made. But the first recording, Bel Air, is a mystery.

Emily must have deleted the email that actually made it into her inbox, but her laptop somehow managed to recover copy upon copy upon copy of its duplicates here.

I tap on Bel Air.m4a and it opens in Voice Memos.

Its creation date is 1 January this year. My breath catches. Emily made an actual recording of whatever happened on New Year's Eve. Whatever is on this forty-nine-minute-long recording must be the leverage Emily used to secure the offer of a lifetime.

23

New Year's Eve

SATURDAY, FEBRUARY 13

I GRAB A CUSHION FROM THE SOFA, TURN A FRESH PAGE IN MY NOTEPAD, and hit play on the New Year's Eve audio file Bel Air.m4a.

At first there is only silence. I increase the volume and the room slowly fills with the comforting ruffle of white noise. The muffled sound of bass music through a wall, the reverb and screech of voices having fun in other rooms, with the scrape and rustle of a pocket in the foreground.

A party from the safety of a pocket or bag.

Now the sound of a voice close, the words not quite distinguishable. I pump up the volume further until a male voice comes into focus, the tone cloying, coaxing.

My blood runs cold. Oh God . . . I think I know what this is. I listen for the female voice, the female voice that must be there, and I pray it's not Emily's.

The sound of the door to the room opening causes a flood of party noise that is quickly muffled as the door closes. A second male voice asking a question.

Then a female voice closer to the recorder—a murmur, followed by a groan. I strain for words.

"I don't feel good. Can I get some water?" the voice whispers.

It's Emily.

The second male voice across the room gives a muffled utterance, his tone dismissive.

"Well, if you don't want to be here then leave," the first male voice snaps back at him, his soft coo now acidic. He turns back to the woman, his voice tender again. "You need some water, sweetheart? Let me help you."

The sound of water hitting glass. The man by the door says something out of hearing. The sound of someone glugging back water thirstily, catching their breath, and gulping back more.

"Whoa, whoa. Slow down," the soft male voice says. "Have you taken something?"

"No. Just so thirsty." Emily's voice, it's recognizable although thickened, distorted slightly, by alcohol or drugs I presume. My thought immediately backed up by her words. "I think, someone put something . . . my drink. It all feels . . . too slow."

The sound of a bed or sofa creaking as someone sits down near her. "Slow is fine. We're not going anywhere, are we? It's nice here just . . . us, right?"

I shudder at his words, his tone mocking in its tenderness. My hand darts out to the keyboard to stop the audio—I've heard enough—but I hesitate as I hear:

"Who is he?" Emily asks hazily.

The sound of the closer man turning, a pause. "Don't worry about him. He's a friend. We're all friends, right?"

The sound of Emily flopping back into the cushions. "Yeah, I guess. Where's Marla?"

"I don't know who that is, sweetheart."

The voice by the door says something and the door opens; sounds of the party flood the room then muffle as the door closes again. The second man is gone.

"Look at you," he says, his voice flat and suddenly much closer. "You're very beautiful, but I suppose you know that. You didn't like me earlier, did you? But I think you like me now."

"No—I need to . . ." Emily slurs.

My hand shoots to the space bar and I stop the recording. I don't need to hear any more. I know what this is and I feel sick to the pit of my stomach. It's a recording of Emily being raped. That much is clear.

I bolt up quickly from the floor, putting instant distance between me and the computer as if continued proximity might, in some way, imply tacit collusion. My blood fizzles with completely useless adrenaline, even though I know that I can't help her. I can't stop what happened over a month ago from happening.

The audio is only six minutes in, there's still another forty-three minutes or so to go.

I know I should put the computer away and pass this straight on to Cortez tomorrow. I don't need any of this in my life. It's not appropriate for me to listen to it at all. I can just draw Cortez's attention to the audio file and let her do the rest. But I would have to tell Cortez that I accessed a missing woman's private emails. I can't help think of the News International phone-hacking scandal, when a journalist accessed a missing girl's private voicemail. What I've just done is no different, is it? Should I really be telling the police I've done that? It might be nothing but if it's something then I've broken the law and people will find out.

It occurs to me that I could tell Cortez that Emily told me about the rape herself; I would just have to pretend we were good friends rather than minor acquaintances. It would only be a white lie.

But then if any of her actual friends came forward after that it would be fairly obvious I lied. Although I do appear to be the only person looking for Emily.

I realize I'm holding my breath, my shoulders high and tensed, like a trapped animal, like a cornered boxer. I need to think straight.

I shake myself out and take a couple of deep, slow breaths. Then make my way back over to the computer, thinking through the options.

I could put it away and hand it over to Cortez tomorrow saying only that I think something happened to her on New Year's Eve and leave it at that. Hopefully they would eventually find the recording and act on it.

My mind skips to the image of the actress who jumped from the sign, her body undiscovered in a gorge in the Hollywood Hills. Surely time is an issue if Emily is missing. And someone going missing after recording their own assault is a very different proposition from someone going missing after a bad audition. I need to tell Cortez about the rape; I can't in good conscience keep it to myself.

I let out another held breath at the finality of my decision.

Right, in that case, if I'm going to report it then I need to know the facts. Reluctantly I sit back down at the laptop. There is no way in hell I am going to force myself to listen to the recording in its entirety, that much I know. But I can skip through it for information.

I look at the visual readout of the recording: its peaks and troughs. I can skip to the sustained mid-range levels, they'll be spoken word. If I avoid the sharp spikes of the clip readout I should avoid any shouts, or screams.

I skip to the next extended mid-level section. And press play.

"Yeah, come in," the man says.

The door opens, the sound of music, party poppers, and laughter, then muffled quiet again. Two men out of range by the door, voices low.

"Don't just stand there then," the man continues. "Lock it."

There are three men in the room with Emily now. I make a note on my pad.

Emily is saying something. I strain to hear.

"I need to go now. I'm supposed to—" I can hear the hazy fear in her voice; she's trying to stay calm, trying not to escalate the situation. Protecting herself in the only way she can in that room. "I just need . . ."

The sound of a scuffle. "No, no, no. You're staying. And we are going to have a nice time." The sound of clothing and a sudden flurry of movement from Emily. She's trying to get away in earnest.

"Hey, hey. Be good. Be nice."

"No." Her thick voice sharpening in focus, the soberest it's been so far. Fear clarifying the situation. "Stop. Get the hell—"

"Ben, it's too loud." The voice comes from across the room and is answered by the sound of a slap.

Emily yelps.

Ben. I scrawl the name down quickly. I flick back a page in the pad to the name Ben Cohan, a producer at Moon Finch, and underline it hastily.

The recording is overtaken by deafening rustling as Emily struggles. I skip the audio away from the noisy peak onward to the next conversational-level section and play.

Emily is crying softly. I try to block it out and listen only to the words. Crying, heavy sobs, the whine of an injured animal, gasping breath.

"I need Mike. Get Mike here," the man says, his breathing ragged.

I feel sick.

"I called him when I went out. He's waiting downstairs," the voice by the door replies. "You want me to get him?"

"Yeah, chuck me that blanket," the man answers, his tone business-like. The audio muffles once more as another layer of something covers the device. "Guess this isn't the evening you had planned, right?" the man mumbles closer to the recorder.

Emily lets out another sob and I abruptly stop the audio.

I take a breath, trying to calm myself. I'm not there and yet my body is reacting as if I am. As if I'm trapped there with her, trapped forever in that room unable to get away.

I try to bring my mind back to the job at hand. I now have two names: Ben and Mike. The name of the man who assaulted Emily is Ben and in some way a man called Mike is involved. I still don't know who the man by the door is, though.

I skip to the last burst of conversation.

"Jesus Christ." A new voice enters the room. He sounds disgusted and yet manages to maintain a businesslike tone. This must be Mike. "Okay. Put her in the bath, Joe," he orders, staying back at the edge of the room and orchestrating from a distance.

Joe must be the name of the other man in the room when it happened.

"Leave her in the water then give her this," Mike says.

"What is it?"

"Ben, leave the room," Mike orders.

There's a silence and then the sound of a throat being cleared and I don't catch Ben's answer. After a moment or two the door to the room opens and closes.

"Did he use protection?" Mike asks. There's a pause before he says, "Good."

"What is this?" Joe asks.

"It's fine. It won't hurt her. It's just insurance," he reassures him. I hear a muffled sound from Emily. "Put her in the bath, shower her off, then fill it, give her that, and leave her. Not too deep, I don't want anyone dying in his house. Come get me when you're done," the voice instructs, efficient and clearly on the clock. He doesn't sound like a guest at this party. The sound of rustling. "No, leave her clothes where they are, dipshit."

The sounds of a now unresponsive Emily being lifted and moved away from the recording device. The audio rolls on oblivious to the exit of its main characters as the thunder of running water begins in the adjoining room.

I sit listening to the rush of unseen water, dumbstruck by everything I've just heard.

Jesus Christ. Emily was drugged then raped, then drugged again and left naked, for God knows how long, in a tub of cold water.

She must have known someone had drugged her at some point and she had the foresight to activate her recording app. She probably tried to call Marla. If only I could check her call log. She must have been so scared. I listen to the muffled sound of the New Year's party bubbling along beyond the walls of that room; to be so close to people but not be able to call for help.

Then suddenly I'm ripped away from the audio by a burst of sound from behind me. My heart leaps into my throat as I spin at the sound of my iPhone vibrating against the granite of the kitchen counter. I see from the oven clock it's just before midnight. I stop the recording and make my way over to the counter cautiously. It's a video call from Nick's phone.

I pause. After everything I've heard tonight I'm not sure it's the ideal time to talk to him.

I hesitate, as the shrill ringtone continues, then look back at my pad on the floor. I have names to give Cortez tomorrow, I have a laptop, I have a phone, and I have an audio recording. That should be more than enough.

And I don't want to go to bed tonight thinking about what just happened in that recording. I need to clear my mind.

I hit accept call and Nick's beaming face fills my screen.

24

Intruder

I WAKE WITH A START TO THE SOUND OF MY ALARM CLOCK. IT TAKES ME a second to orient myself after having slept so deeply. Last night floods back to me: Emily's hazy voice, the sound of distant running water, and her fear.

I shut off the blaring alarm and pull the warm covers up over my head, cocooning myself for a moment in calm stillness. I remember what it is I have to do today. I think of the forms I'll have to fill out and the story I'll have to share.

I yank back the covers and let the cool apartment air wash back over me. I have to think positively, it's going to be a long, hard day otherwise.

After speaking to Nick last night, I googled the directions to the LAPD Headquarters on West First Street. It's not far. I could walk but, for some reason, I much prefer the idea of driving.

I'm glad I answered Nick's call. It took my mind off everything else. He told me about the incident with the lead actor who held up filming the night before. Nick's a good storyteller, funny and easy to listen to. But the moral of his tale was: at the end of the day, everyone is replaceable. He's right, I suppose, everyone is replaceable, but then that would have to include him, Emily, and me too.

I spring from the soft hold of bed, hoping to leave all those thoughts behind in the crumpled sheets. After I've handed everything over to Cortez, I will head back here, learn my scenes for the screen test, and get my head back in the game.

I agreed to let Nick take me out for an early dinner this evening. I'll be back in time for an early night, and it should keep me distracted enough not to get too nervous before the screen test.

I forgo my usual early-morning swim and instead hop under the warm flow of the shower. I want to get down to the station and get this done as soon as I can.

Dressed and looking as respectable and sane as I can manage with a wardrobe full of audition clothes and event outfits, I wander into the still dark of the kitchen/living room to make a quick breakfast. The giant curtains are still tightly drawn over LA as I left them the night before. I tug back the massive folds of fabric and let golden light flood the apartment, my stomach lurching as I look down through the glass at the miniature city below, one palm braced, hard, against the glass. When I pull away a full palm print remains. I stare at it for a second, thoughts of Emily rattling around in my mind.

I turn back to the apartment, letting my thoughts rake over what I need to tell Cortez, and I head to the kitchen. It's only when I return to the living room area, with a hot coffee and a pastry in hand, that I notice Emily's laptop is no longer there.

I spin on the spot scanning the surrounding furniture. Panic flashes through me as I slam down my breakfast onto the table and drop onto all fours to scan beneath the sofa. Nothing. I rifle between sofa cushions and under script pages, I shake out the sofa throw. It's not here.

I try to think straight, to calm myself, because it must be here.

Somewhere. I search the living room floor again, and that's when I realize that Emily's phone isn't here either. I freeze. This time I definitely haven't moved things myself.

I let my eyes travel back to the coffee table. Emily's apartment keys, rental agreement, and photograph are no longer here either.

I grab my handbag from beside the sofa and empty its contents out onto the floor, hoping that somehow some of what's missing will tumble out. It doesn't.

My hand flies to my mouth. Oh my God, there's no doubt about it now, someone really did come into the apartment last night while I was asleep. And while I was in the next room, they took Emily's things.

My eyes fly to the hallway. And I'm off, my socks skidding across the slippery wooden floor toward the faulty security system. I pull up sharply in front of the door but nothing is out of place. I try the door handle; it's still locked.

Whoever it was must have come in with a key. I think of my lost keycard a few days ago then dash into the bedroom trying to keep my breathing calm and steady. Next to the bed, my own laptop is plugged into the wall; my phone is on the sheets beside my pillow. My things are here, only Emily's are gone. Whoever came in to the apartment last night was after her stuff alone.

I head back into the kitchen dumbstruck and notice that my hands are trembling. I'm in shock. I head to the sink and blindly pour myself a glass of water from the filter tap. And it's as I tilt my head to drink that I notice the notepad propped up against the fruit bowl. On a fresh blank page, in handwriting I do not recognize, a message:

BE VERY CAREFUL WHAT YOU DO NEXT

I splutter out half a mouthful of water and then cough the rest up into the kitchen sink as I fight to get my breath back, grabbing a kitchen towel to mop myself down.

I carefully pick up the note. It's written in thick black Sharpie pen on the notepad I was using last night. I turn the pages back and, just as I suspected, all of the notes from last night are gone. Whoever did this had enough time to get everything they needed and to write this without anyone even noticing. They could have done anything.

Jesus Christ.

I pull myself up onto a counter stool, my mind racing.

Be very careful what you do next.

I could just fly home, couldn't I? I could forget all about the screen test, and Emily and Cortez, and just go home. Cynthia would be annoyed but she'd get over it, especially if I win the award in May. And if Kathryn Mayer and the studio are interested in making an offer then we could just reschedule a screen test once I'm back in London.

But I know that's not true. No matter how much anyone *likes* you out here, everyone is replaceable. If I don't stay for that screen test, I will lose that part. A role that would change my life. So no, I can't fly home. I need to stay for the screen test; I need to get that role.

But I could report everything I know to Cortez after the screen test. Report it and then run back home. Although I'm not sure the LAPD would let me fly home straight after I've told them all of this. I'd be the only lead they had in the disappearance of Emily Bryant. If I tell Cortez everything, I'd have to stay even longer and I won't be safe. I'd have given whoever wrote me that note a very clear reason to come back.

I finally have to admit to myself what I have been too scared to admit up until now: wherever Emily is, I don't think she is alive anymore. Whatever game she was playing, she was playing with the wrong people and their patience ran out. The favor I did for her on Wednesday, that one decision I made, put my life in danger too. I've never wanted to cut and run so badly in my entire life.

I wish I could go back in time and change things: I wish George hadn't gotten that job and run off with that girl. I wish I was back in freezing February London, oblivious to Emily and everything that happened to her. I wish I was safe. But I'm not.

The silence in the apartment is deafening. I hear my blood pumping in my own ears.

I have no one to blame for this situation but myself. I curse myself for carrying on my search for Emily much longer than anyone else would have. No one I know would have kept going. I know for a fact that Souki wouldn't. Bee wouldn't. George wouldn't.

I'm not putting my life in danger to report a crime that even the victim wouldn't report. I am not fucking dying for this. It was Emily's job to report what happened to her, it is not mine.

And with that thought I stand, straighten my clothes, and head into the bedroom to make a call. I grab my phone from the duvet with the intention of calling Cortez and letting her know that I won't be coming in but when I look at the screen I see I have a message I hadn't noticed when I woke up.

A fresh flutter of dread dances inside me. Of course, it could be anyone texting me, a friend, my parents, work, but something tells me it's not just anyone. I take a breath and open the app.

It's Marla replying to the message I sent last night.

Today, 2:57am

You need to stop whatever you're doing. I know you think you're helping but you're not. Trust me. Don't get involved with these people. Forget Emily. Delete my number.

Shit.

I reread her message several times. She clearly knows Emily is missing and that something very strange is going on. That hadn't occurred to me until now: that other people might be well aware of Emily's disappearance but have clear reasons for not getting involved. I imagine how what I've been doing over the last few days must look to Marla; I've been out here stomping around, drawing attention to myself, like I'm deliberately trying to put myself in danger.

Marla knows exactly what is going on. She's a real friend of Emily's and she's telling me to stop. If anyone should be reporting any-thing to the police it should be her, not me. She knows what happened on New Year's Eve, she knows how at risk Emily was and the danger-ous game she was playing with the men who took advantage of her. I should definitely take Marla's advice. I do not want anyone else coming into this apartment. I do not want to disappear.

I take a moment, screw my courage to the sticking place, and type.

Today, 7:32am

Understood.

Two minutes later I'm explaining my decision to Cortez.

25

Not Safe

CORTEZ IS HAPPY FOR ME TO DROP THE MISSING PERSON REPORT, AND why wouldn't she be. I tell her I've been in contact with a good friend of Emily's who informed me that she was aware of Emily's situation and that I wasn't helping. I made it clear to Cortez that I wouldn't be coming in to report anything, because, it turns out, it's none of my business.

After the call I immediately head down to reception.

The day receptionist is a man with short blond hair and a tightly pursed expression. I've never seen him before but then I'm rarely in the building at this time of day. It never occurred to me that Lucy wouldn't be available to me twenty-four hours a day but I realize now she must only work the night shifts. She will have left already.

The receptionist looks up warily as I approach. "Hi there, can I help you?"

I hesitate for a second, unsure how exactly to go about getting what I need from him. Whoever came to my apartment last night will have been caught on CCTV and I want to see who it is. I might not be able to help Emily with her problem but I can sure as hell help myself and if I can find out who is threatening me or at least what they look like, then I'll be a lot safer. Though the thought of seeing them on film entering my apartment makes what happened last night suddenly all too real. I obviously can't tell the receptionist what happened; he looks pretty alarmist and I can't risk him just calling the police on my behalf, at least not until I know what I'm dealing with. I need to play it extremely safe.

"This is a strange question," I begin, leaning casually on the counter, "but do you know if anyone came in the building really late last night? I think someone was pounding on my door or something in the middle of the night."

The receptionist's puckered expression shoots up into an arch mask of incredulity. Another actor no doubt. "That certainly doesn't sound like the kind of thing that usually goes on in this building but I really wouldn't know what happens here at night. I work days," he replies, gesturing to what I can only assume is *the day*. "Sooo . . ." he continues expansively and then stops speaking entirely.

I wait for him to continue but that appears to be the end of his input on the subject.

"Is there any way to find out who it might have been?" I try.

He shrugs. "Lucy might know."

"Right. Okay . . . and what time will she be back?"

"What day is it . . . ?" he mutters and stoops to check a green binder just beneath the counter. "Sunday, Sunday, Sunday . . . Lucy is in from six." He looks back up at me triumphantly.

I wait for more but again there's nothing.

"Okay, so could you perhaps take a quick look now at the CCTV from my hallway last night and see who it was? It would have been between two A.M. and four A.M."

His expression hardens. "I'm afraid I can't do that, ma'am. I'm not authorized to look through security footage. You would need to contact the management company about that directly."

"Oh, okay. Could you maybe ask Lucy, when she gets in, if she remembers someone coming in at around that time then? It was the thirty-first floor. And it's Mia Eliot, apartment three one zero eight."

He looks at me for moment before sighing loudly and grabbing a pen and a stack of sticky notes. "Mia El-i-ot . . . apartment number?"

"Three one zero eight."

"Three one zero eight. Right . . . unwanted visitor two A.M. to four A.M. Question mark."

I think this is as good as I'm going to get from him. "Right. That's great, thank you for your help. And Lucy's definitely not in until six P.M.?"

"No, she is not."

I guess I'll have to wait until six then.

BACK IN THE APARTMENT I call Cynthia in London, who's surprised to receive a call so late on a Sunday night. Without giving reasons I ask her to find me new accommodations as soon as possible. I'm guessing it'll be for tomorrow night now at this short notice, unless I'm willing to check into a regular hotel—though I'm not sure how much safer that would be than here. At least here there aren't all those people coming and going through the night. And when I speak to Lucy, I'll make sure she changes my door code and that's she's on high alert if I need to stay tonight.

Cynthia agrees to find new accommodations for me without hesitation, asking only if everything is all right. I tell her I'm fine but request that she find me somewhere with very good security, I'm pretty sure she fills in her own blanks. It's unlikely she's missed the news about George and Naomi Fairn's new relationship so I'm sure she's got plenty to speculate on. I reassure her I'm still focused on work and I'll be going to the screen test tomorrow but I tell her that I'll need to leave LA the day after the test. Reassured and relieved that I haven't flown off the rails, she agrees to arrange a flight home for me for Tuesday.

With an escape plan in place I dive into my script knowing that, come six o'clock, I'll know who exactly is threatening me and I should be in a better position to protect myself with the help of Lucy.

I manage to get four hours of line learning done before my phone pings with a text. Nick wants to know if *Sushi is okay?* I stare at the message, confused, then remember the dinner plan we made last night for this evening. I had completely forgotten. He says he's booked us into a new restaurant. It opened on Friday and, he jokes, it's hard to get a booking there, let alone on Valentine's. I check my phone's locked screen, and he's right, today is the fourteenth of February, Valentine's Day. I don't know how on earth he's managed to book us in somewhere like this on one of the busiest nights of the year. In spite of everything that's happening, I feel a little thrill of pleasure at the idea that he's tried so hard to impress me. He says he'll pick me up at five.

I start to compose a text to cancel the plan but stop. Lucy isn't in until six P.M.; if I go out for an early dinner, I can be back here by seven. If the message I left her gets passed on, she might have had time to find the footage from last night by the time I get back. And God knows, it would be good to get out of this apartment.

Also, it crosses my mind that if I told Nick half of what was going on with me, he'd probably insist I stay over at his place tonight. And while I'm not sure I know him well enough for that just yet, the thought is reassuring.

I manage another four hours of script work before he arrives and I feel I'm in a very good place when he pulls up, bang on time, in the apartment's porte cochere.

He gives me a beaming smile through the windscreen and I slip into the passenger seat beside him. His car is understatedly expensive, smelling of new car leather and his cologne. The hairs along my arms rise being suddenly so close to him.

"Hey, you!" He looks me up and down appreciatively. Clingy black silk dress, gold hoop earrings, and hair up. I thought I'd better at least try to fit in with the crowd I'm sure we'll be seeing at this newly opened it-restaurant.

"I forgot, you *do* scrub up well," he jibes.

"Ha-ha, very funny. Shame you came straight from work, though," I volley back eyeing his clothes. It's a cheap shot, he looks ridiculously good, but I see a reassuring flicker of hesitancy in his eyes before he realizes I'm joking.

"That's the spirit," he grins. "Oh, and lest we forget, happy Valentine's Day."

As we drive, conversation comes easily. Just being this close to him in the passenger seat is oddly intimate.

His scent is so different from George's. Nick smells of soap, a clean woody orange fragrance. It reminds me that Nick has lived a whole life unknown to me up until now, the thrill of that unknown sending a fizzle of excitement through me. I'm going on an actual Valentine's Day date. I don't think I've ever actually been on a date before. I'm not sure British people do them.

I mean I've been to a bar, or the pub, with people or gone for drinks after work but I've never met a relative stranger for a dinner date and been picked up for it.

I haven't been outside all day and to my surprise the light is already fading. It's magic hour, and Los Angeles is beginning to make its slow transition into the twinkling dreamscape it becomes at night.

As darkness falls, we roll past the gargantuan billboards and flashing neon signs that make up Sunset Boulevard and West Hollywood, safe in our leather-clad cocoon.

NDA or not I tell Nick more about the screen test tomorrow and who I'll be filming with in the morning. And to my utter delight he nods as if what I'd just told him was the most normal and natural thing I could have said.

"Yeah. You're great casting for that role. Kathryn Mayer producing, right?"

I nod, masking my joy that he didn't bat an eyelid at my name and my male co-star's being in the same sentence.

"Yeah, she makes great decisions," he continues as I watch his handsome features in profile. "That's why the studio snapped her up, she was independent before, apparently her deal was a big back-and-forth, took a few months to persuade her to move. She's got great taste. These are the kinds of casting decisions studios should be making instead of leaving it up to independents to introduce talent into the system. I mean if I had a dollar for every studio head who complained that established stars cost too much and have too much creative control, I'd sell up and buy an island." His eyes flick to me in the tail-lit darkness, my expression dour. He clarifies. "Don't get me wrong—I'm all for creative control for actors. I think it's important. I just don't want to be held hostage on my own movie. There's a line between creative collaboration and fiefdom."

"The *actor* being the fief in this analogy, right?" I say, making it clear in my tone that entertainment industry fiefdoms don't historically tend to be ruled by actors, or actresses.

"Point taken," he agrees. "But maybe the less said about abuses of power between producers and actors on a first date, the better?" he offers, jokingly. "Anyway, *that guy* is in prison somewhere in upstate New York. Most fiefdoms don't tend to last long."

It's a joke, one in questionably poor taste, but he's right: the last thing I want to talk about is sexual abuse. And tonight less than ever, given everything I heard yesterday. So I let the subject drop into a silence that only lasts a moment before Nick's iPhone bursts to life through the car speaker system.

His eyes flick to me apologetically as it rings. "It's my line producer. Do you mind if I take it?" It's a genuine question—he's seriously contemplating not taking a work call in case it's rude. I wonder if years of living with George have inured me to such rudeness. George would have just picked up a work call—George always picked up work calls. Nick mistakes my surprise at being asked for reticence. "There's probably more problems on set but I can call them back later," he says.

"No, no, it's fine, seriously! Take it." I nod him on encouragingly and he lets the caller's voice fill the car.

I turn my attention out onto the nighttime sky past the window, vaguely aware of the background hum of their conversation. Unbidden memories from last night flit through my mind: Emily's breath whispering through my head, the echo of the distant party, sounds of laughter and music.

I can understand why she didn't report it. And while it's impossible to know what I would do in similar circumstances, I can understand her thinking. She didn't want to fuck up her career, she didn't want to rock the boat. All reasons I might have had for not getting involved with this if I hadn't been threatened anyway. There's always that fear that by diving into the murk, you'd somehow become tarred and feathered by it too.

I'd imagine she didn't report it because she didn't want a court case, she didn't want more indignity, she didn't want justice in that sense, she just wanted what she'd always wanted, a proper career. I guess she felt she was owed that, at least. But blackmail is a crime too. I don't know if I agree with what she did but I certainly understand why she might have done it.

26

St. Valentine

WE PULL UP OUTSIDE THE CONCRETE-AND-GLASS STRUCTURE. A VALET takes Nick's keys in hushed tones and we are led into the roughhewn-floored reception of an achingly modern restaurant.

The space beyond is hard and minimalist and beautiful just like the diners inside it. Its polished-concrete floors give way to panoramic glass walls with under-lit terraces beyond. All around us the quiet, cool hum of conversation babbles.

We're up in the hills, though from the view alone I couldn't tell you where exactly, having wound up endless snaking roads to get here. Beyond the glass, LA sprawls out into the distance beneath us, glowing bioluminescent as plankton in a lake.

We are guided out to the candlelit terrace, and to a front-row table overlooking the twinkling city. I'm struck by how beautiful LA is from a distance, like a fading ingénue with just the right lighting once the harsh light of day has passed, its gray arterial freeways, bald-patch car parks, and low sun-bleached buildings all melted from sight, leaving behind only the winsome sparkle in Hollywood's eyes.

. . .

WE'RE PARTWAY THROUGH OUR SECOND course and swapping stories about growing up in small towns when the free drinks arrive.

"Compliments of Mr. Chapman," the waiter says, placing them on the table between us.

Nick scans the crowded restaurant, finally alights on someone, and gives a curt nod. I follow his gaze and meet the eyes of a burly man in his mid-forties at a booth behind the glass of the restaurant. He's with a very attractive, very thin, very young woman. She's on her phone, her soft blond hair falling across one cheek, completely uninterested in her dining partner. He gives us a tight grin and tips his head in acknowledgment, his eyes locked with Nick's—half challenging, half collegial. Nick raises one of the recently delivered champagne flutes and tips it in thanks. The interaction complete, their gazes break.

Nick leans in. "That's Ben. He's a producer. He probably recognizes you."

My blood runs cold. *Ben.* The name on Emily's recording.

That hushed authoritative voice saying, "Ben, leave the room."

I look back at Ben across the bustle of the beautiful restaurant. He doesn't look like his picture on the Moon Finch website, he looks a good twenty years older, tougher. But why would he need an up-to-date photo—he's not an actor, is he?

"I've never met him," I mumble. "How could he recognize me?" I watch the man across the restaurant slice into a hunk of Wagyu steak, plunge the resulting fleshy clump into his distracted mouth.

Nick gives a surprised chuckle and my gaze is drawn back to the table. Nick is smirking at me. "He knows you because he's Ben Chapman and you're a BAFTA-nominated actress . . . remember?"

It takes a moment for Nick's words to really reach me through the haze of my fear. I release the breath I hadn't realized I was holding, because he's not the Ben from Emily's recording. The man gazing in our direction across the restaurant is not Ben *Cohan,* he's Ben *Chap-*

man. And now that I think about it I've seen Ben Chapman's name scroll by on the credits of countless film. I've seen it on emails, press releases, and casting breakdowns for years. He's a heavyweight in the industry, with the power to make and break careers. I look back at him across the crowded room; he looks nothing like the photograph on the Moon Finch website, and now that I look again the girl with him is smiling as she shows him something on her phone. He gives her a jovial avuncular smile before digging back into his meal. He's not the awful predator of my imaginings. And there's no law against dating someone a third your age.

When I look back, Nick is studying my face in amused disbelief. "Of course he recognized you," he continues. "Unless he's been living under a rock I'd say he'd be well aware of your work." He gestures to the restaurant as a whole now. "I'm guessing ninety percent of the people here know who you are, Mia. You're either hirable to them or you're their competition. You're not in London anymore, this is hardball. The industry is always on out here. But then people only come to LA for one reason, and whatever they say, it's not the weather."

My eyes scan the poised faces of diners around us as they talk, sip their drinks, and push their hundred-dollar sushi around their plates. It's got the production values of a high-end perfume ad, the clothing colors all in the same palette, the characters clearly defined, the location spectacular. And the product they're selling, I guess, is what? Success? America's greatest export: a dream. And yet hardly anyone here is smiling. In theory everyone eating here has made it, except there's a furtiveness beneath all this, a fear that somehow it might all slip through the fingers. Or be taken, by someone else. Actors and directors and producers, oh my!

Nick's right, I see it now. Everyone here is on show but they're also here to watch the show. Hollywood as the performance and the audience rolled into one.

I recognize a few well-known faces scattered through the restaurant crowd. A balding character actor I've loved watching for years stands by the up-lit bar, red wine in hand, nodding in agreement as one of his group holds forth.

I see a young indie actress in a booth near the terrace windows, surrounded by female assistants and her manager, as she unwraps a tissue-paper-packed present with delight.

On the smoking terrace a controversial actor-director is guffawing in a group of men.

But it's clear that the actors are not the real VIPs here, they aren't the ones with the real money or power. Other eyes, watchful, appraising eyes, flick over the shoulders of their dinner companions and take everything in. These are the people who keep Hollywood running.

"God, this place is packed with them, isn't it?" I turn back to Nick. "How can you stand it? It must be like having dinner in a work canteen. If everyone at work wanted to eat your dinner. And take your job. And live your life."

Nick laughs. "That's funny." He shrugs boyishly, eyes intent on me. "I thought you might like the food? And, you know, the chance to get the full Hollywood experience. What kind of producer would I be if I didn't bring an actress to a place like this?" I feel a flush rise up my neck. He brought me here to impress me or at least give me what he thought I wanted. Which makes me wonder if Nick has had many real girlfriends or if he's just dated a lot of aspiring actresses who wanted all of this. "A lot of people would kill to be here with this crowd," he continues, his tired eyes playing over the bustle around us. When he looks back at me, he catches my expression, my eyebrows raised sky-high, and he's laughing again. I clearly am not one of the people who would kill to be here, present company excepted. "To be fair, I had a feeling you weren't like a lot of people. Well, I kind of hoped you wouldn't be."

For a second I wonder if Nick is already in love with Jane. If that's what he sees when he looks at me. But then, I reason, I was Jane wasn't I, aren't I? That was me on the screen, nobody else. I shake off the thought and take a sip of my ice-cold free drink.

The conversation moves on to other things and by coffees we've circled back to my screen test tomorrow.

"Are you nervous about meeting him? Your co-star?" Nick asks.

"A bit, if I'm honest. I really want him to like me. Is that lame?" I ask, sipping my sharp coffee. I know I should have ordered a jasmine tea or something to stand any chance of getting an early night and being well rested for the test tomorrow, but it tastes so good. I can already feel the buzz of caffeine kicking through me.

Nick shakes his head. "No, it's not lame." He smiles and stirs some sugar into his espresso. "You want some insider info on him?" he asks cautiously.

I feel a yawn of dread open in the pit of my stomach, unsure if I can handle any more insider revelations. I don't think I could deal with it if Nick told me my potential co-star was a terrible person.

I take another hot sip of coffee and nod. After all, being prepared is half the battle.

Nick leans forward with a mischievous grin, clearly enjoying seeing a moment of, no doubt refreshingly novel, vulnerability. I'm guessing most of the people he deals with have skins so thick that nerves are nothing more than a distant teenage memory.

"He's actually a really sweet guy," Nick says with a smirk, and I feel a wave of relief flush through my body. "He's very down-to-earth, easy to work with, crews tend to love him."

"And the whole *Method* thing?" I probe.

"Oh yeah. Apparently, he just starts doing it the first time you meet him. Not like full character, costume and all that, but he'll set your relationship up in real life the same as it is in the script." He tips back the last of his coffee. "It's kind of a love story, *Galatea,* right?"

Not exactly.

But I'm guessing Nick hasn't had access to the actual script, and the previous versions of the story have tried to turn it into a love story. "Yeah, sort of," I say, moving the conversation on.

"Yeah, so he'll be setting up that relationship with you from the get-go."

"Okay. That sounds . . ." It sounds a little terrifying considering Higgins and Eliza's relationship, but it will certainly make my job playing her much easier. I'll hardly need to act if he's giving me all of that already. Yes, put like that, it's a gift. Plus, I'll get to watch him work from day one. I feel a shiver of excitement. This is what I wanted. This is it. "It sounds great. I'm not amazing at small talk anyway so he'll save us both the effort," I joke.

"Oh, and he loves biscotti, apparently," he adds. "Remember all that stuff about him living in Italy in the '90s? He likes to have biscotti with his morning coffee, always has it on set. Just a heads-up, but if you swing by Guidi Marcello's on the way to the studio tomorrow— I'll text you the address—you can pick some good stuff up." Nick pulls out his phone. "I'll drop Marco there a quick text, let him know you're coming in and who you're buying for. He'll get you the right brand."

I can't keep a grin from spreading across my face. "You're really good at your job, aren't you?" He looks up at me, caught off guard, uncharacteristically bashful, and for the first time since we met I have a very real flash of what we could be like together, as a couple. Without hesitating I lean forward and kiss him. The restaurant and all its people and politics and pretense disappear around us. It is just his willing lips and mine. When I pull back there's an achingly sexy, slightly surprised look in his eyes. I want him so much it hurts. *You're in a restaurant,* I tell myself, *it's just a first date; you barely know this guy.*

Nick's face cracks into a smile and I fail to suppress a giggle. I'm so happy.

"Shall we get the bill?" he asks, quietly.

I nod. "Yeah, if I stand half a chance at getting any sleep before tomorrow, we'd better," I answer, gently. I can't go home with Nick tonight, even if I'd like nothing more than to do that and then stay there with him indefinitely. Even if I need to enlist Lucy as a night guard and to barricade my own apartment door, the most important thing is that I am rested and ready for tomorrow. I can't let myself be derailed by threats and I certainly can't let myself be derailed by horniness.

When he pulls up outside the Ellis Building to drop me off, he takes my cool hand in his warm one and squeezes. It's strange but I haven't felt this close to another living person in a while, not even to George in our final year. I try to remember the last time a man took my hand; ironically George's first premiere comes to mind.

A cloud passes over my thoughts as I remember that I'm leaving LA after the test tomorrow. I can't stay and I might never see this man again. I lean in and kiss Nick once more, desperately.

The sound of a car horn blares in the far distance, breaking the spell. As I emerge from the car I feel the safety of his gaze on me, taking in the delicate fabric of my dress as it clings and shifts with the contours of my body, until I disappear into the apartment building.

27

Video Footage

SUNDAY, FEBRUARY 14

Lucy is ready and waiting for me at reception when I enter, her sober expression bringing me back down to earth with a jolt. She obviously got my note.

"I heard about the issue last night," she confirms as I approach.

"Thank God. And did you see anyone come in at around that time?"

"No one. Just your assistant," she says. "No one else came in."

"My assistant?" I repeat straight back at her.

She seems momentarily baffled by the question. "Yeah, Michelle, your assistant."

The air is sucked completely out of me. "Lucy, I don't have an assistant," I hear myself say. I try to maintain my composure, completely dumbfounded, but my heart is already hammering, my body fizzing with instinctive panic as the implications of what she is saying begin to spiral out of my control. "I don't even know anyone called Michelle," I continue. "Okay. Is there a chance you might be mixing me up with another person, another apartment?" I can hear the desperate hopefulness my voice.

Lucy lets out a nervous laugh. "No, of course not, I'm talking about *Michelle*. Your personal assistant, Michelle."

I involuntarily slam a palm down onto the counter. "Lucy, I *do not* have a personal assistant. I just don't have one, okay? I don't know anyone called Michelle."

I watch the meaning of what I'm saying seep into her, and her face slowly falls. "Oh," she says in a tone that tells me I am not going to like what's coming next.

I take in a slow breath. "Lucy, has somebody called Michelle been going into my apartment?"

Lucy's eyes have a low-key wildness to them as she nods, her lips pursed. "Yeah," she answers.

A silence falls across the counter as the full ramifications of that pass silently between us.

"Okay," I finally manage.

"But she had a key. She said she was your assistant." Lucy shakes her head slowly in disbelief at what seems to have transpired.

She had a key. She had my lost apartment key from four days ago. I think of Joanne. Has Joanne been paying me nighttime visits? Whoever it was has had my key for four nights. How many times have they been in?

"When did you first meet Michelle, Lucy?" I ask. There's a thinness to my voice.

She hastily consults the calendar beside her. "Okay, okay. Michelle first came in on . . . on Wednesday afternoon. Yeah. You were still out and . . . she said she just had to quickly drop something off for you."

Lucy bolts up, suddenly remembering something. "Wait, I checked with you!" she blurts and leans over to her computer, tapping furiously at the keyboard. "Yes. Here. I checked she was with you. I promise you. See? You sent that email, remember?" She looks up at me, her face a mixture of relief and indignation. "You told me she'd be coming. You said to let her up."

"I did what?" I say, incredulous.

"Yeah," she replies, her eyes fluttering quickly across her blue-lit screen. She nods triumphant and turns the screen to face me. "Here. Look. See. You emailed me."

On the screen is an email. It's from my email address to reception. It's an email I did not write. I shiver in my silk slip dress in the air-conditioned lobby and read.

From: Eliot, Mia
Sent: Wednesday, February 10, 2021 1:05 PM
To: "reception" <Reception@Ellisbuilding.com>
Subject: Visitor—Apartment 3108

Hi there,
Just to let you know I'm expecting a visitor to the apartment in the next half hour or so.

Her name is Michelle and she's my personal assistant so I'd really appreciate you letting her straight up to the apartment. She needs to drop off something important. She has her own key to let herself in. Give her a quick call on the cell number below if there's a problem as I'm just about to go into a meeting. But she should be with you shortly, she's on her way over now.
Mia Eliot

A phone number is at the bottom. I look up at Lucy completely horrified. "I didn't write this."

Lucy's features crease in disbelief before she takes in the serious-ness of what I'm saying; it's clear from my tone that I have genuinely never seen this email before.

"But that's your email address, right?" She points to the screen.

I nod. "Yeah, it is," I mumble, "but I didn't write that." Some-one wrote an email from my email address. It was written just after one o'clock on Wednesday. That was the day of the audition where Emily disappeared. I must have been in my audition at that exact time. I left my bag unattended twice that day. Once outside while I fed the meter and once in the waiting room while I auditioned. All my things were there while I was in that casting room, for a full thirty minutes. Anyone could have accessed them.

My hand flies to my mouth. "Oh my God," I hear myself pant. Someone took my phone and used it during those thirty minutes. I snatch at my clutch bag on the reception counter and desperately try to fumble out the phone. It's passcode-protected. How could they have worked out my passcode?

Regardless, I check my SENT MESSAGES folder. It's empty; the whole SENT box has been deleted. God knows how many emails they've sent and to who.

They must have worked out my code and they've had full access to my emails, my messages, everything since. Then they found my address from my emails, stole my apartment keycard, and came here. And I know for certain they've been in my apartment more than once. They took my script, deleted my emails, and left me that note. God knows what else they've been doing.

I turn back to Lucy. "How many times has Michelle been here?"

"I'm not sure. I can check in the logbook, we note down all deliveries and visitors."

"Did she come a lot, Lucy?" I insist.

She hesitates, biting her lip before answering. "Yes."

"Did she have anyone else with her?"

Lucy's expression darkens before she answers definitively, "No."

Thank God. Suddenly the image of Joanne springs to mind again. "Wait. Did Michelle look anything like the other girl who came to visit me? On Thursday?" It's a crazy thought, as it would have been incredibly risky on Joanne's part to try to get past Lucy as both Michelle and Emily.

Lucy thinks for a moment before shaking her head. "No. Well, I suppose they were both brunettes and about the same height, but they were quite different as people. Michelle was a lot more—I don't know—she was really friendly, chatty, we spoke a lot—" She breaks off, aware of the irony of her character appraisal. She hesitates, an idea clearly coming to her.

"Here, follow me," she says, turning and disappearing behind the reception area into an alcove housing a more functional work space. A large desk laden with paperwork is flanked by a video security system with four small screens showing constantly shifting images of the building's lobby, lifts, car park, hallways, pool, and gym. Lucy's going to show me footage of Michelle.

She takes a seat, tapping through the system, until she locates last night's lobby footage and switches one of the screens to playback. We both watch the footage as residents I don't recognize come and go at double speed. It turns out there's actually quite a few people living in this building. It just goes to show how lonely a city can be; I've never seen a single one of them in the flesh before. The time code in the top right-hand corner speeds past midnight. She slows the playback as we hit 3:50 A.M. at reception.

My gaze flickers to Lucy's screen-lit face and I can't help but question why on earth she would let someone, even a personal assistant, up to someone's apartment at four in the morning.

"Lucy, why did you think an assistant would be coming up to my apartment in the middle of the night?" I ask as delicately as I can.

She glances at me. "I don't know. I mean . . . you're an actor. It's LA. I didn't ask. Could have been emergency mineral water for all I know."

My gaze is pulled back to the screen as a dark figure enters the lobby. She strides up to reception and gives Lucy a wave. They're talking. The woman is wearing tight black jeans, a black Celine hoodie, and an unmarked baseball cap that her long dark ponytail swings from. I can't see her face from this camera angle, and to give Lucy credit this woman really does look like an assistant dashing in to run a quick errand. She leans across the reception counter chatting to Lucy, who smiles and nods.

The camera angle of the footage changes and I see the front of her now, the peak of her cap still masking everything but her mouth and chin.

Lucy fast-forwards the footage. The woman is now in the lift, her baseball cap still obscuring her face, and then suddenly the woman is looking up to check the floor number. In fast forward it's only a flash of her features and then it's gone. My arm shoots toward the screen but Lucy is on it, already rewinding until the face is frozen on screen looking up at us.

My breath snags in my throat. I know this woman very well.

"Oh my God."

The woman on the screen is Emily. The girl I met at that audition four days ago. The girl who has been missing ever since. The girl who was drugged and raped just over a month ago and who I had assumed might now be dead because of it. But she's not dead; she's there on the screen very much alive. About to break into my apartment.

Emily was here. And she was here more than once.

"Keep playing the footage, Lucy. Go to my hallway," I tell her and blessedly she doesn't question me. I watch as Emily rounds the corner of my corridor and approaches my door. I imagine myself sleeping soundly within. She pauses briefly outside the door, and then the green door light flashes and she slips quietly into the apartment. Lucy taps the footage into double time again and we stare at my closed apartment door as the timestamp above speeds along. There's movement as the door reopens, the timestamp showing that eleven minutes have passed since she entered. She reemerges and in her hand is one of my old Whole Food bags, laden. Inside are her things: her laptop, her mobile, her rental documents, and the photograph I unstuck from her bedside table. She stole back the things I took from her apartment.

I feel a sudden flush of shame. She came to take back the things I stole from her. I can hardly accuse her of theft.

But then she didn't just enter my apartment once, did she? I think of my broken security monitor. She's been breaking in for four days.

I've been missing emails; she's been sending emails, moving things, taking things, and that message. God knows what else might have gone missing that I haven't even noticed yet.

My mind scrambles for an explanation for all of this. She must have seen me tap in my iPhone passcode while I was sitting next to her in the waiting room and then she rifled through it, found my address, took my key, and emailed Lucy her lie. All while I fed her meter and auditioned. But why? Why use my phone that day, why take my key, why keep coming back? I have nothing to steal.

I take a breath and try to make sense of this tangle of facts. Emily didn't disappear, she was coming here as Michelle. She must have hired Joanne to collect her things from me and play out those scenes. Perhaps she knew she couldn't get past reception as both Michelle and herself. So she wrote those strange character breakdowns and scenes that Joanne showed me and texted Joanne instructions on where to go next in her place.

Emily came straight here after emailing Lucy from my phone. That's why I couldn't find her after my audition. She kept me busy looking for her while she searched my apartment. But what was she looking for on that first day?

Lucy's voice breaks my concentration. "Do you recognize her?" she asks. "Michelle?"

I nod. "Yes. That's—" I catch myself in a lie. I can't tell Lucy this is Emily because she still thinks the woman she let in three nights ago to collect her keys is Emily. I could explain the whole story but I'm not sure that would do me any favors. She misreads my pained expression for concern and shoots out a hand for the desk phone.

"I'll call the cops," she offers, lifting the receiver, fingers poised to dial.

"No," I blurt out. My mind is racing to put everything together without misstepping. Emily isn't missing but she's certainly pretending to be. The recording I listened to was real. Her emails were real. The Zoom call from Moon Finch seems to be the thing that set all of this in motion. Perhaps she really did mean to disappear that day but

I had her wallet and keys. Perhaps that's why she went into my bag. I should have dumped them back in there before I went into my audition, but for some reason I pocketed them. She couldn't find them so, perhaps in the hope of getting them back later, she stole my apartment keycard.

But she wouldn't have been able to take back her car keys and wallet from my apartment that first day because I was still at the casting. So she must have wanted to check out how possible it would be to gain access. And then the next day she wouldn't have been able to take them back either as I took her things out with me all day. Emily knew if she wanted her things back she'd need to collect them from me directly, as I kept leaving the building with them on me. But that would have meant showing up here as Emily Bryant, so she sent Joanne instead. Emily Bryant is hiding.

After Joanne collected Emily's stuff Emily would have realized I still hadn't returned her rental document. I'd accidentally locked it in my car. So she had to come back again.

"Has this got something to do with the woman who lost her wallet?" Lucy asks, placing the chunky cream receiver back into its cradle.

"Yeah, I think it might," I reply carefully. "I hate to put you in this position, Lucy, but could you let me try to speak to *Michelle* before we report this? I don't know exactly what's going on yet but I am pretty sure I'm missing something very important here."

Lucy weighs my request, concern creasing her brow, but I sense she's aware that calling the police means admitting she let someone into my apartment without checking their ID properly, email or no email. Finally she nods, returns the monitor screens to their live feeds, and swivels her chair back to me.

"Well, the footage is there, if we need it. It gets wiped after a month but you're fine until then."

"Thank you, Lucy, I really appreciate this. I need to speak to her before I drag in the police."

She shifts in her chair. "I know it's not my place to say this," she says carefully, "but I really think you should just call the cops. I don't know if she's your friend or something but she's been here a lot and she's obviously very convincing when she needs to be."

I take in her concern. It must seem crazy from Lucy's perspective for me not to report this, but that note left for me this morning wasn't left by whoever took Emily, it was left by Emily herself.

BE VERY CAREFUL WHAT YOU DO NEXT

I had assumed it was a threat, but what if it was just a warning? She must know by now that I've heard the recording. Could she be warning me off reporting her disappearance, her rape, in case whoever she is hiding from right now comes for me next? She knows firsthand how dangerous those men are. Perhaps in her own strange way, Emily is trying to protect me.

Marla had said as much when I contacted her too. She'd told me to let this go, that while I might think I was helping Emily I really wasn't. But I don't know how I can explain that to Lucy.

"I hear what you're saying," I explain, "but it's very delicate. I don't know yet, but I think the woman in the tape is in some kind of trouble. I know it sounds crazy but I think she might be hiding from someone. I don't want to make her situation worse. Or mine." Her face slackens. I definitely haven't eased her concern. "Could you just let me see that email she sent again?" I ask.

She looks momentarily surprised by the request but rises nonetheless and leads me back out to the lobby reception.

I jot down the cell number written in the email and thank Lucy once more.

"Oh, and it goes without saying, please don't let her back up to my apartment," I say firmly. "Don't let anyone upstairs for me anymore, at all . . . no matter what they say. And could you make a note on the system for the daytime reception team too? Oh, and can I get a new door code for tonight?"

"Of course. Not a problem," she replies. "Again, I am so sorry about all of this. Even with the email I should have checked her ID first. I should have confirmed with you in person."

"It's fine, Lucy, seriously. I mean how could you possibly have known?"

I head upstairs with one clear thought in my head: *The sooner I get out of this place the better.*

28

It's a Test

MONDAY, FEBRUARY 15

MY ALARM BLASTS EARLY AND I GROAN AWAKE.

I did not sleep well. I didn't even turn out the lights until well past one A.M. and then only after barricading the front door with an armchair with one of the bedside tables piled high on top. It wouldn't have stopped Emily, or anyone else, from getting in—if they somehow managed to get past the now impeccably vigilant Lucy—but it would have certainly slowed them down and definitely woken me up in the process.

I roll out of the tangle of sheets and head, half dead, to the warm cascade of the shower, letting it slowly bring me back to life.

I'd stayed up late, instinctively going through all of my belongings and double-checking my passport, trying to think of any other reason that could explain why Emily took my key on Wednesday. But nothing was missing. I checked the phone number I took from her email, and it matched Emily's cell number. I texted and I emailed her on the email address I got from her laptop:

From: Eliot, Mia
Sent: Sunday, February 14, 2021 12:57 AM
To: "Emily Bryant" <EmEmbryant@gmail.com>
Subject:

I know you were in my apartment.

And I know what happened on New Year's Eve.

I am so so sorry about what happened to you but I don't understand why you stole from me, or why you made Joanne come here, or why you repeatedly broke into my apartment. What is going on? Are you hiding from someone?

I haven't contacted the police yet but if I don't get some kind of explanation—and I know you can read this—I'm reporting it all.

After my shower I slip into the clothes I picked out for the screen test. I know I'll be in full costume and makeup all day but I want to look good when I arrive at the studio. I leave my skin fresh and makeup-free, though. I pull my hair back into a slick ponytail and I'm ready.

I decide to grab breakfast on the go. I don't want to spend any longer in this apartment than I have to. I need to get out and into the fresh California air. I grab my phone, car keys, laptop, script, and bag, and head off.

IN THE CAR PARK BENEATH the building Miguel dashes off to get my car. While he's gone I find the pin-drop Nick sent me for the Italian deli. Biscotti. I'm going to follow his advice and swing by to grab that first-day gift. It's not something I usually do, but knowing that it is a thing people do in LA has somehow emboldened me. My thoughts stray back to our date last night and I can't help feeling a twinge of sadness that I'll be back in London by tomorrow night. I find myself wondering absentmindedly if Nick would ever consider moving to England.

Somewhere deep within the car parking structure there's a loud, choking, mechanical noise spluttering away. I can't see where it's coming from but a knot starts to form in my stomach. The noise stops for a second and then there's another cataclysm of throttled croaks. After a brief moment of silence, I see Miguel bobbing back over through the car park, his expression confirming my worst suspicions.

"It won't start," he puffs, clearly more surprised about it than I am.

Refusing to let this turn of events affect my pre-game focus, I tell him not to worry, pull out my mobile once more, and order an Uber to Guidi Marcello. Nothing is going to throw me off course today, not car tampering, not anything. I will get there on time and I will do a good job, even if I have to get through the ten plagues of Egypt to do it.

It's only in the back of the Uber that I let myself think about what the car means: either Emily did this or whoever she's hiding from did. Is it a warning? I push the thoughts away. Regardless of who is responsible I need that car fixed. I shoot off a quick email to Leandra at Audi explaining the mechanical problems with the car as Miguel described them before I left. I ask her to arrange for a mechanic to take a look at it while I'm working today; that way I can drive myself to the airport tomorrow.

Email sent, I heave my *Galatea* script out of my bag and dive back in.

Forty-five minutes later we pull up outside the glass shopfront of Guidi Marcello. Inside is packed higgledy-piggledy with produce from all across Italy, walls of ruby-red wines from Tuscany, Sicily, and Venice. Amarones, Chiantis, Cabernet Sauvignons, and Barolos. Giant wheels of fresh Parmigiano Reggiano DOP and salty Pecorino

Romano, misty glass-fronted fridge cabinets stacked with caramel-ized cured meats, fresh egg pastas, and jars filled with olives. My stomach groans at the sight of it all and the scent of freshly brewed coffee in the air.

I follow the soft *plumph* of shelves being stacked through the maze of overflowing aisles until I find a young dark-haired man in his twenties. He looks at me, surprised to see a customer.

"Hi, is it Marco, by any chance?" I hazard.

A smile breaks across his face. "Of course. And you are Mia. I have some good things for you at the register. Come." He rises from the stacking stool and slips past me back to the cash register, where he hefts a small selection of packets from a shopping basket up onto the counter. "Okay. So, biscotti. Cantucci. We have, from Prato, Italy, this one is the best. Handmade at Antonio Mattei." None of that means anything to me but he proudly presents an intense cobalt-colored package with blue string and golden lettering. It looks great. "Or just as good—but for me, not so good." He winces, comically. "The Seggiano Cantuccini Biscotti, from Tuscany also." He presents a clear packet with ten slices of golden-amber biscuit within. "Same price."

"Easy choice then." I smile, pointing to the bright blue of the Antonio Mattei packet. "I'll go with your favorite."

Fɪғᴛʏ ᴅᴏʟʟᴀʀs ʟɪɢʜᴛᴇʀ ʙᴜᴛ ɴᴏᴡ with a coffee, a pastry, and a multiple-Oscar-winning-actor peace offering in hand, I slide back into my Uber.

At the studio gates, I dust the pastry crumbs from my clothes and head into security to sign in. Twenty-five minutes later I'm in the hair and makeup truck, a friendly makeup artist working on my elab-orate updo for the first scene. It's the scene after Eliza successfully fools the royal court into believing she's a Hungarian aristocrat so I need to look like one. When she's finished working on me, she turns me back around toward the mirror proudly and I see her work for the first time. My complexion is bright and flawless, she's brought out my eyes with hidden lashes, my hair is piled high in a glossy Edwardian updo, and all is finished off with an understated pearl tiara. Worthy of a Hungarian princess or, at least, a counterfeit one. I rise and pull the makeup artist into a tight hug, and she lets out a throaty laugh. If I don't get this role it certainly won't be because I don't look the part.

Next, I'm taken to costume in a temporary dressing room in the studio building. It's a blank room with nothing but a space heater, an armchair, and a clothing rail with my three costumes.

I strip down to my underwear and a team of people from the costume department hoist and hoick me into my Edwardian corset and gown. My waist now a good three inches thinner, I slip easily into the antique ivory fabric of my ball gown.

As the costume designer and his team fuss around the hemline and sleeves, I give myself a look in the full-length mirror. I look like a nervous bride, my skin pale and cheeks flushed from the exertion of being laced in so tightly by two wardrobe assistants. But it's a relief to see I no longer look like Mia, I no longer look like Jane—I look like Eliza.

Once I'm ready, I'm led to set. But I'm told my co-star isn't quite ready yet. I hand the runner my little pre-shoot gift and ask him to drop it off at my co-star's dressing room. He winks at my ingenuity and trots off with the bright-blue packet in hand.

A full forty-five minutes after our original start time my co-star arrives on set, in the production runner's wake. He's studying something written in a small moleskin notebook as he approaches, and when he looks up his eyes find mine.

He takes in my costume, hair, and makeup, and gives me a tight smile. "Very good. Very good indeed," he remarks, in an accent not his own. He's already in character, just as everyone said he would be.

They storm past and the runner gestures for me to follow too. I trot behind them dutifully in my Edwardian heels and corset, struggling for breath, as they stride out onto the brightly lit soundstage.

On set things move quickly. We discuss the scene with the director then block through a rehearsal. I check which lights are mine with the camera operator and what is being favored in the first shot, and after final checks—and "Quiet on set," has been called—the soundstage bell is rung. We take our first positions, behind a false front door, ready to enter. The set quiets around us and in the fresh silence my co-star leans in and whispers, his tone sincere, "Thank you very much for the biscuits by the way, much appreciated." His character has dropped for a second and he gives me a warm smile. "Oh, and break a leg."

With that, we hear the director's voice blare loud from the darkness beyond the studio lights.

"And . . . action."

29

New Information

MONDAY, FEBRUARY 15

TWO SCENES DOWN AND I'M WALKING ON AIR BACK TO MY DRESSING room, my heart fluttering light in my chest, my face aching from suppressing my happiness. He is so good. He makes me so good. I'm terrified to think about how well it's all been going so far. I even saw Kathryn Mayer give me a covert thumbs-up between takes from the dimness behind a camera monitor.

We have an hour for lunch, and while they've told me I can take it in my dressing room, I'd prefer to get some fresh air after being in the studio for so long. With the help of a wardrobe assistant, I wriggle free from my corset, slip on some joggers and a hoodie, and take a stroll out onto the lot.

My eyes take a moment to readjust to the glare of the California sun as I breathe in the cool spring air. Then following signs, I wind my way through the studio lots in search of the studio coffee shop.

Coffee shop located, I inhale a pastrami sandwich and a bag of potato chips before heading back across the lot with an ice-cold Frappuccino in hand. And that's when it happens.

I feel the antique hair comb fixed onto the back of my second updo loosen and I'm too slow to catch it as the delicate tortoiseshell-and-rhinestone piece hits the tarmac of the lot. I watch a single rhinestone pop from its setting and skitter along the ground. *Damn it.*

It's as I bend to pick it up that he knocks into me, sending a splash of Frappuccino cascading down my hoodie and jogger leg.

"God, sorry. Sorry, sorry," he exclaims, as shocked as I am, a phone glued to his ear. "Sorry, Danny, I'll have to call you back," he says into the receiver as he offers me a hand up and ends his call. But I do not take his hand, I just stare, because I've seen this man before. I've seen his photograph smiling back at me from the Moon Finch "About Us" page. But more important I've heard this man's voice before on a muffled audio recording that I would give anything to be able to forget.

I rise quickly, desperately trying to keep my expression neutral because this is the man who raped Emily Bryant and got away with it.

He looks at me concerned. "Are you okay?" he asks.

I struggle for words. He's being so normal, he's being so nice. "Am I okay?" I repeat. "Yes, I dropped my comb." I bizarrely hold it up as evidence.

He smiles. "And your comb's okay?" he jokes.

The joke catches me off guard; I remind myself that he doesn't know me and he doesn't know that I know what he did.

"Ha, yeah," I reply with a halfhearted chuckle. "It's good."

He nods, then his demeanor suddenly changes as something clicks into place in his mind. "It's Mia Eliot, isn't it?"

My heart skips a beat; he does know me. He knows exactly who I am. I feel Jane waking up inside me.

"Yeah," I answer with a strident confidence I do not feel. "It is. Have we met?"

He shifts his weight. Clearly, we haven't. "No, but I saw *Eyre*. I'm one of the producers over at Moon Finch, Ben Cohan. *Eyre* was fantastic by the way. You've got a . . . a real connection with the lens, it's great to watch." He studies my elaborate hair. "You're here for the *Galatea* screen test."

"Just on lunch break. But yeah."

He nods knowingly. "That's great. Great to hear. You're great for this," he says, gesturing to the comb in my hand.

If he says great one more time I'm going to scream.

"*Galatea* was on our slate," he continues, "before Kathryn. We did a lot of development on it before we handed it over. But Kathryn is the best, she's got a good eye. Hey, listen, we'd love to get you in for something at Moon Finch soon, too, you know."

I bet you would.

He grins. "I'll send some stuff over to your agent. You in LA for long?"

Actors and crew from other productions bustle by on their way to the canteen; we're not alone here, and I'm not in danger, but I feel it. My entire body is telling me to walk away from this man, but Jane holds fast. "I'm playing it by ear out here," I manage. "One day at a time."

He lets out a laugh, probably mistaking my rudeness for dry British humor. I can feel my anger building beneath the surface. Jane's anger, my anger. I need to get away or I'm going to do something stupid. I try to shake off the images in my mind associated with his voice.

"Well, maybe you can pop by my office sometime this week," he continues, oblivious. "We'll see what we can find for you." He gives me a grin and it's the final straw.

"I think you know a friend of mine," I say brightly. "Emily Bryant?"

I watch his face melt from polite interest into slow understanding. I catch the light behind his eyes flaring in horror before quickly covering itself.

"Emily Bryant?" he repeats politely as if he has no idea who I'm talking about. He's a good actor but I'm better.

"Yeah, Emily Bryant. She's a good friend of mine. I think you met her at New Year." I don't know why I'm doing this but I can't stop myself. I want to see him squirm. I want to see him pay even if it's not my debt that needs to be repaid.

I watch him try to normalize what is happening until he works out that acting normal is no longer an option. His expression suddenly darkens and he steps closer, threateningly, all sense of the polite man I met a moment ago gone. "I don't know what you think you're doing but you need to stop," he says, his tone low and aggressive. I've rattled him.

Instead of feeling triumphant, I suddenly feel the vulnerability of my position. Even in a crowded place this man, now unveiled, seems dangerous. I take a step back, opening up space between us. There are witnesses everywhere, there are security cameras all over this lot, I know I'll never be in a safer, more protected place with this man. So if I want to say something, now would be the perfect time.

"Why is she hiding? What did you say to her to make her disappear?"

Ben's eyebrows rise. "What? I don't know what you're talking about," he mutters, scanning the faces passing us by. "You need to drop this," he continues, his voice low, "you don't know what you're talking about." Then a thought seems to occur to him. "Wait. How long have you been in town? What, like a week? Two weeks?"

His eyes are serious, his expression insistent, and I find myself answering, "A week."

"And Emily is a new friend, I'm guessing?" he asks, his tone unremitting.

"Yeah," I admit.

"Yeah, well. In that case, you don't really know Emily at all, do you? If you only met her a week ago, you don't really *know* her." There's something about his tone that makes me pull up short.

He must pick up on my hesitation because he presses on. "Don't feel too sorry for her. She's not who you think she is: look her up. Watch some of her old stuff. You'll see. You have no idea what you're getting into here. You're not going to help her, or yourself." His tone is calm but threatening. "Let this go. You've got a good thing going here. Cut your losses. Or you make a move, because you'd better believe we're ready."

A studio buggy beeps as it whizzes toward us. Ben holds my gaze silently for a moment more before striding away. I stand shell-shocked as the studio buggy whips around me and rattles off.

Back in the dressing room I'm hooked and buttoned into my final costume, Eliza pre-makeover, poor, down-at-the-heel flower girl. I wish more than anything I had a moment to myself, because as much as I hate myself for falling for Ben Cohan's words, I now have an intense need to look Emily up. Could there be more to the story than I'm aware of? It seems ludicrous that I haven't looked her up already but what with one thing and another, it honestly hadn't crossed my mind until he suggested it. And now I can't think straight.

Hair and makeup dirty me up and then I'm led straight to set to shoot the final scene of the day. Standing in first positions waiting for action, I push away my desire to pull out my phone and google. I try to block out the sea of unfamiliar faces looming in the half-light beyond the camera and the studio lights; I try to block out my thoughts of Ben Cohan and Emily Bryant. I squeeze my eyes shut, clench the handles of my flower basket until my fingerless-gloved hands ache, and force myself back to Edwardian England, Covent Garden, pre-war, pre-iPhones, pre-all-of-this.

I hear *action* and just like that LA slips away, my own life slips away, and I am the person I am supposed to be.

ON WRAP THE STUDIO BELL gives a final peal and a smattering of applause comes from around the set. I momentarily bask in the afterglow of a job well done.

The director pulls me into a tight hug. She grins and whispers, "Out. Of. The. Park."

And in spite of everything, I smile.

Back in the dressing room, I de-rig from costume as quickly as I can and slip back into my normal clothes.

Kathryn pokes her head around the door. "Are you decent?"

"I am," I say with a chuckle, and Kathryn makes her way into the room as flustered wardrobe assistants slip out past her.

She plonks down on a chair with a satisfied sigh. "Well, young lady, that was fantastic. I don't know if you noticed but we had some set visitors in that last scene. I hope you don't mind but I invited a bunch of suits over to the lot to check you guys out. They loved you both together. Great chemistry."

I stop mid-face-wipe. "Yeah? You think?" I ask. I hear the hope in my own voice and flush slightly at the sound of it.

She holds my gaze and nods meaningfully. "Yeah, I do. Of course, we'll have to wait for the rushes and get a general consensus, but it's looking good. Unless something completely untoward happens on Wednesday then I think we might be in business, kid."

"Wednesday, is that when the screen-test viewing is scheduled?"

"It is, why? You're not planning on jetting off before then, are you?" she jokes.

I turn back to the mirror and continue to gently remove my makeup. "No, no way. If you need me, then I'm here," I say, and I realize the truth: if I want to stand a chance of landing this part then that's what I will have to do.

In the safety of my Uber home I pull out my phone. I let Cynthia know I can't leave until Wednesday now and then I finally pull up Google. I can't find a photo of Emily online but I unearth a link to a short film on Vimeo. I pull my headphones from my bag, slip them over my ears, and press play. The sleeping face of a woman, though it's not Emily. It's funny, I assumed Emily would be the main character in this, but I guess there's no reason she should be. The pillows and bedsheets around her are crumpled and the camera pans up to the apartment window. Outside, we see New York. The low rumble of a passing train and the girl's eyes open. The scene flits to the woman rushing quickly through a chilly fall Central Park on her way to work. I don't know the lead actress's name but there's something vaguely familiar about her. I watch on as her day unfolds, as she witnesses an incident in the park, and as it colors her day until, in the final scene, we realize the incident actually happened to her. It's a good short but Emily's not in it. I scroll back through the credits and there's her name. She must have had a tiny role; I must have missed her. But the credits don't mention any other names. Only Emily Bryant as Anna.

Who the hell was Anna? I don't even know what the lead character's name was supposed to be let alone the background actors.

Then slowly comprehension hits and the hairs on the back of my neck stand on end. I press replay on the film. The face of the beautiful woman sleeping fills the screen, brunette, late twenties, peaceful. The lead character is called Anna. Anna is played by an actress called Emily Bryant. The girl I am looking at on the screen is Emily Bryant. Oh my God.

I look away staring unseeingly at the highway blurring past the window. The realization burns bright and urgent and terrifying in my mind. I've never actually met Emily Bryant, have I?

I look back at her face on my phone. Then I open another tab and search for more photos, or videos, or anything. At first it's impossible to track down anything, and then I find a pasta commercial on YouTube. The description mentions her name, the date posted was May last year. It's more recent than the short film. I click the video and watch: a woman dances elegantly around her kitchen with a wooden spoon as she prepares dinner for her bemused family. It's the same girl, her hair longer, perhaps a shade darker. I pause the video, her face filling the screen as she sits at the table proudly smiling. And then it hits me.

Sweet Jesus. I know who she is. I know where I've seen this face before. I *have* seen Emily Bryant before. I've seen her in the photo I took from her apartment, the photo on her nightstand; the photo of the two women hiking high in the hills above Hollywood. I was right about one thing: Emily *was* in that photograph; she was just the one on the left instead of the one on the right.

Which means I never met Emily—it was Marla I met five days ago at that audition.

Ben's words come back to me: *Emily's not what you think she is. You have no idea what you're getting into here.*

I shudder at the thought of what that could imply, for Emily Bryant and for me.

30

Who Are You?

ALL I HAVE TO GO ON IS A FIRST NAME AND A FACE.

Back in the apartment, two hundred results come up for "Marla" when I search for her on IMDb. But I have time. I sift through the list, removing names that are variants on Marla. I ignore crew, non-actors, and those with credits pre-1990. There's a chance she could be older than me but she can't be more than thirty-five at the max.

I narrow down the list to twenty-one possibilities. I flick through their pages studying their photographs, but do not find her. Thirteen of the twenty-one do not have photographs on their pages. I'm sure she was careful to remove any photographic evidence, especially on such a mainstream public site as this.

One by one I search Google for each of the remaining names. Some names come up immediately, actresses who have worked enough to leave a trail of publicity or production stills in their wake. I study face after face. Some older, some younger, some blond, some of different ethnicities, some successful, some not. The volume of careers, or lack of them, when seen in quick succession takes its toll on my psyche. The flickering question of why I am here, so far from home, so far from the people who love me, quivers inside me but I push on.

After an hour I have three names left on my list. Marla Sinclair, Marla Kaplan, Marla Butler.

Sinclair only has two credits: Woman in Crowd, in a 2011 Christmas rom-com I've never heard of, and Communion Girl, in a 2001 slasher movie. Both parts are essentially extra roles so I'm guessing this isn't Marla.

Marla Kaplan's credits look more promising. Nine television credits in total, with depressingly two-dimensional character names like: Hot Friend, Vampire Girl, Mila's au pair, Nude woman, and Girl.

Marla Butler's credits look plausible too, though in a different way. Most of her credits come from the early 2000s and the character names, such as Young Iris, Young Cassandra, and Cute Girl, indicate she was a child actor then. She clocked up an impressive twenty-six credits before a hiatus in 2012. Then a fresh crop of short film and cameo roles since 2019 brings us up to date with a small role as a hotel receptionist in a recent Bond film. This Marla is slowly starting to get somewhere.

I scour the Internet for photographs of both Kaplan and Butler. I can find a few production stills from Butler's younger roles but she's a kid and it's impossible to tell if it's actually her. The little girl in these films runs from about five years old to ten.

I find a still of Kaplan from her Vampire movie, her hair highlighted, her features similar to those of other Marlas, but she's only crouched in profile on the edges of the frame, not the focus of the photograph. It could be my Marla, though.

Either of these women could be.

A thought occurs to me. It might be worth searching Vimeo again, this time for one of the Marlas instead of for Emily.

I tap in Marla Butler's most recent short film credit, but nothing comes up. I try another title. Again nothing.

Exasperated, I try simply typing in her name. A result appears. It's a scene from a 2011 teen movie called *She's Got Class.*

The names of two actresses in the scene are written in the video's description box. Amy Rogers plays the lead and Marla Butler is her co-star. This could be her.

I click play. Two sixteen-year-old girls huddled on school bleachers, they're cold, sleeves pulled down over their hands, cheeks rosy and noses sniffle-y. They discuss a group of characters we don't know. Marla is brunette, Amy redhead. It's hard to tell yet. The characters seem close but something has come between them. From their conversation I gather their issue is a boy. Amy is a straight-A student while Marla's character looks cooler, more complicated. Something Amy says causes Marla to sigh and look off into the distance. I watch as she shuffles out a soft pack of cigarettes from her hoodie and reaches for her lighter. And then she does something that takes my breath away.

Cigarette held loosely between two plump lips, she cups the end from the wind, then flicks her lighter open and on in one smooth roll of the wrist. I sit bolt upright as she flicks it closed. She did the exact same thing on that bench in the sunlight, five days ago, the same reflexive, fluid motion. A movement she must have made a million times throughout her life. It's her. The teenage girl I'm watching, Marla Butler, is the woman I met at that audition.

I'm up and pacing the apartment living room. What am I supposed to do with this information? I know what I'd like to do, I'd like to fly home and never see any of these people ever again, but I can't leave LA until after Wednesday. And would I ever forget the ghost of Emily's voice in that audio recording, asking her attacker to stop? Fighting for her life? Can I forget that? Because try as I might to imagine Emily is still alive, I can't.

But I also can't imagine the girl I met a few days ago could be a killer. Even in the footage Lucy showed me, she never looked threatening. But then as Lucy said, she's clearly very convincing when she needs to be.

Perhaps whatever happened when Emily and Marla last met

ended in an accident and Marla didn't know what else to do but fill the gap Emily left behind?

But then where does that leave me, if that's true? How far could Marla go to protect her secret? She's already broken into my apartment, tampered with my car.

My phone rings—it's Cynthia telling me she's found me new accommodations starting tomorrow morning until Wednesday. Which means only one more night in this building. One more night in an apartment that Marla has repeatedly broken into. I shudder at the thought, but I know she's not stupid enough to come back to the building now that I'm onto her.

Of course, I don't have to stay here tonight. Nick texted me earlier to invite me over for dinner. I didn't think I'd be hanging around long enough to do that, but it looks like I'm stuck here for a bit longer. I text him back accepting the invite. I could always ask him if I could stay over later if I felt unsafe. I'm sure he has spare rooms or a couch, it's not like I have to sleep in bed with him in order to stay over. Of course, I realize at some point I am going to have to let him know I'm returning home.

I stare out at LA from my gigantic apartment windows, my eyes finding the tall tombstone letters emblazoned across the Hollywood Hills in the distance. Almost a century ago an actress who missed out on the role of a lifetime went to meet her friends and was found three days later dead, bloated, and unrecognizable in a ravine. Emily Bryant's face flashes through my mind. Nobody reported the actress who jumped missing either. An unknown female hiker found her. No one had even raised an alarm until then.

Before I can chicken out, I type a text and press send.

Today, 4:03pm

Marla, I spoke to Ben Cohan. I need you to tell me what happened to Emily. I know she disappeared in Jan & I know who you are. You need to tell me what's going on or I will report this.

I stare at my words for a second, and remind myself that I am safe here. She cannot get me, building security knows not to let anyone up, especially her, and now that my security monitor is repaired and my door code has been reprogrammed, I am safer here than ever before. And it's only one more night.

My phone pings in the silence, sending a chill straight up my spine.

Today, 4:04pm

Okay.

Whatever Ben told you he told you to protect himself. You're not safe now he knows, trust me. I can explain everything. It's not what you think, I promise you Mia. Will you meet me?

I stare at her words, and the pulsing gray dots beneath that tell me she is waiting for my response. My thumb hesitates over the keyboard. And then I type.

Today, 4:36pm

Yes. I will but only in a public place.

Her reply is almost instantaneous.

Today, 4:37pm

Okay. And then, if you want, I can take you to Emily.

31

Preparations

MONDAY, FEBRUARY 15

MARLA WANTS TO MEET ME AT ELEVEN-THIRTY TONIGHT AT THE 101 Coffee Shop by Emily's apartment. I'm reticent until she tells me it's the best she can do, she can't meet me in the daytime but she won't tell me why—which only heightens my suspicions. But what can I do? If I want to meet her, if I want my questions answered, I have to go. I comfort myself with the thought that at least I've been to the place we're meeting and I know that it'll be safe and not too quiet even at that hour.

I think about canceling my new dinner plans with Nick, but then I still need to eat tonight and a bit of company can only be good. I'll just stew in my own juices here otherwise.

It should only take me half an hour to get to Marla in Hollywood if I leave Nick's by eleven P.M. I'll have to make sure I restrict myself to one drink at Nick's house, so I can drive. Enough to calm my nerves but not enough to dull the senses, which given how well our first date went might not be such a bad idea anyway. The last thing I need to add to the equation tonight is the chance of getting laid.

Miguel calls up to the apartment to let me know that a mechanic from Audi has arrived. I head down to the car park where I find Miguel reading a copy of *Movie Maker* under the valet counter. He slides it surreptitiously out of sight as I approach and tells me the mechanic is already working on the car, and assures me he's got it under control. He suggests I go grab a coffee in the café opposite the building and pop back in ten or fifteen. Knowing nothing about cars and thankful for the free pass, I head over the road.

In the café two uniformed police officers catch my eye as they wait for coffee at the counter. I feel myself tensing even though I've done nothing wrong. Although, I suppose, I am now involved in a serious crime. I have listened to an audio recording of a rape; I have heard evidence and I know the victim disappeared shortly after the assault and her only friend in California took her place. Is not coming forward if you have knowledge of a crime a crime in itself or is it just morally questionable?

I watch the officers talk as they wait for their orders, weapons on their hips. I don't think I'll ever get used to seeing guns strapped to people in such everyday settings as cafés and shops. I try to imagine a local policeman back home in England wandering down a high street with a semi-automatic weapon capable of instantly killing without trial or real repercussions. But all my mind can muster up is some kind of ineffectual Frank Spencer or Rowan Atkinson character, and the idea morphs from chilling to ridiculous.

It's funny to be scared of guns given my job. Given the number of times I've worked with firearms on TV shows. I know how to load one, aim it, dismantle it, and reassemble it. Most actors do. You learn on the job, hours of safety briefings with weapons specialists and armorers for a single scene with a gun. All so that you look like you know what you're doing. Even if you don't.

I find myself wishing I had one for this meeting with Marla. The hour, the circumstances, and my uncertainty about her involvement in Emily's disappearance are making for a perfect storm of fear. A gun, just as a prop, not to use, heavy in my pocket, lifeless and bullet-free. A last resort. I think of Marla's text and the implication that I'm not safe from Ben. It's impossible to know at this stage who I'm more at risk from. Could Ben have had my car tampered with? Or are the pair of them in on all of this together? Either way I'd like to know I have a way of protecting myself tonight even if I know it's all a bluff. I just need something to show that could buy me a second to run away.

Of course, there's no way a tourist like me would be able to get hold of even an imitation weapon in this country. So hopefully I won't need one. I'm not going to need any protection in a public place. I'd only need it if I let Marla take me to Emily. But then the sensible thing to do is to just not go with Marla if I feel unsafe.

Back in the car park the Audi mechanic pulls the repaired car around and talks me through the issue. Tampering isn't mentioned, of course, though it turns out there was a loose ECU relay, the small pluglike electrical unit that controls the functions of the car. It was an easy fix once he worked it out, he tells me. He just had to reconnect the loose connection.

"It just happens sometimes." He shrugs. I wish I had his confidence.

Two hours later, dressed and carrying a nice bottle of wine from Guidi Marcello, I slip into the driver's seat and set off for Nick's house.

The journey up to Bel Air is an education, the location setting off alarm bells in my already frazzled mind. It's the same affluent area of North Hollywood that hosted the New Year's Eve party that changed Emily and Marla's lives. But I tell myself Nick is no Ben Cohan. Not everyone who lives in Bel Air is necessarily a monster. Regardless, Mulholland Drive mansions, under-lit and monstrous, peek out from behind lush jungled gardens, mock-medieval Gothic turrets spiraling up and out through tree lines with only their tips visible behind dense, shrouding vegetation. Fever-dream architectural structures made a reality with cold hard cash and pure bloody-mindedness. I try to picture the inhabitants of each house as I glide past their edifices. Some might say they have more money than sense, but winding through the night, these wild extravagancies go some way to giving Hollywood its dark magic, the blue velvet background on which to mount its iridescent stars.

I can't help wondering if Nick was aware of that party on New Year's Eve. Was it near his house? Could he hear the pounding of music from where he was? Could the low rumble of voices and shrieks of delight reach him?

I take the sharp corners and blind bends carefully, terrified of the barrier-less drop and jagged hillside flanking the unlit road ahead.

The satnav informs me the next turning is Nick's but as I approach and slow I see no turning for the house—only a thick cedar fence running flush to a whitewashed wall. I slow to a crawl. It's only as I pull up to it that I see the fence is actually a gate with a tiny gray call button mounted at car window height. Above it blinks the tiny black iris of a security camera. I lower my window and pop my head out, trying to catch a glimpse over the wall, but it runs straight up fifteen feet high, obscuring everything beyond.

I assumed Nick was rich, producers tend to be, but I had no idea he was this rich.

I take a fortifying breath, check myself in the wing mirror, and push the gate call button. A buzz then silence, save for little bursts of birdsong from the surrounding canyons. The button's edges glow green and the cedar gate glides back, sliding into the whitewashed wall. I close my window, slip into gear, and crawl into Nick's immaculate herringbone-bricked driveway; beyond it his concrete-and-glass house glows, welcoming, into the night. I can see straight through its glass walls to the rugged canyon beyond the living room where an open log burner hangs suspended from the ceiling. The building itself seems to float, suspended in the air, on the rock of the hillside.

I park, grab my wine, and head for the already open front door. I think fleetingly of my one-bedroom Victorian flat back in Clapton and wonder why, unlike Nick, I have so little to show after almost three decades on this planet.

Nick greets me with an effusive warmth that instantly settles me, and after a whirlwind tour of the house, we crack open the wine and he pours us both a glass. He looks good, laid-back casual in a soft cashmere sweater and trousers, no suit in sight, his tousled hair just the right side of messy. For the first time since we've met, I'm not wearing shoes with a heel and I notice how much taller he is than me, his chest broad and strong. There's an unspoken frisson between us tonight, we're both unsure if we should be picking up from where our date left off the previous night or if we should be starting from the beginning again. I sip my wine and compliment the house.

"Yeah, I got it about two years ago. Can't take any credit for the design. The previous owner had it built but never moved in. Sold it brand-new. I got a steal, if I'm honest."

I grin, taking it all in. "I won't ask what constitutes a steal in this case!"

He chuckles and seems to relax slightly. "How was today?" he asks.

He means the screen test but unsurprisingly that's not the first place my thoughts go. I consider telling him everything that happened today: about Emily, about Marla, about meeting Ben Cohan earlier, about the break-ins and threats and car tampering.

But then he'd either tell me to stay out of it like Ben did or, worse, ask me why on earth I hadn't gone to the police sooner. I would have to explain my plan, which I know is dangerous and pig-headed, but I can't leave LA until Wednesday and I want, no, I need to know what happened to Emily. I need to know how I'm involved in all this, and then once I know I'm going to wait until the last possible moment and report everything just before I leave.

I take another sip of wine and answer his question. "I don't want to jinx it but I think the screen test went really well!" I beam.

He gives a cheer of triumph and high-fives me with gusto.

"Yeah," I continue. "And I took your advice. I went to Guidi Marcello; thanks for the tip-off. He was great, my co-star. He just made the scenes so easy. I've got to stick around here until the test screening on Wednesday for an answer but hopefully they'll offer a contract then."

He nods, something on his mind. "And after that?"

The question throws me slightly. "After that . . . ?"

"Are you staying in town?"

"Oh." Oh shit. I realize what I just said and how it must sound to him. "No," I admit. "I'm going to head back home if I get it . . . or if I don't actually." I give a sad smile.

He thinks for a second then smiles. "Okay then. I guess this might be all the time we have, so we'd better make the most of it," he says, rallying. "In which case, I want to show you something. Come with me."

He takes me by the hand and leads me through the living room, down a spiral staircase, and out onto a large terrace that hangs over the sheer drop of the canyon. It's a clear night and stars are visible as I follow him over to a crackling firepit.

Nestled in the low bank seating, we cradle our wine and talk, the conversation fluid and easy. After a while Nick disappears back into the house and returns with a platter of cheese and various other delicious-looking finger foods. We dig in and the conversation turns once more to me leaving LA.

I'm going to miss this. Our growing ease, this need to talk and be heard by each other. I am achingly aware of his warm protective arm over my shoulder, the scent of him, the skin of his neck enticingly close. If only I could take him back to London with me. I know we barely know each other but I've never felt this close to someone this quickly. Even George.

"It's not all bad out here, you know," he jokes.

"What? The weather again," I say.

He laughs, nearly losing his mouthful of wine.

"Wow. Now, that is damning." He chuckles. "Okay, and what? The industry's so different in London?"

I study his face—he genuinely wants to know.

"I'm going to be honest," I say, before hesitating. "But first, let me just say, you are excluded from this. It's just weird out here. It's too nice on top and too mean underneath." I sigh, exasperated. I know I can't tell him what's going on right now but other words come that in a strange way seem to mean the same thing.

"Everyone here is obsessed. And not with the work. With the win. You know. Whatever it may be. I haven't had a single conversation about an actual movie anyone's seen or a play they've enjoyed, it's just all about acquisition, like a land grab. For intellectual property, for narrative control, for any control, to get to play a role just in order to be eligible for other roles, in order to get nominated, in order to get bigger roles, in order to start executive producing, in order to . . . ad infinitum. It's a mad scramble. It's a Black Friday sale. Just more, more, more."

He's grinning at me. "And you don't like that?"

I can't suppress a smile. "Correct, I don't like that."

He pops an olive in his mouth gamely. "'Cause a lot of people do like that." He crunches.

I giggle. "Yes, I know. I know they do. And I've met those people, I know them."

"But you think they're wrong?" He's prodding me on.

"No. Not wrong. I don't know what's going on in their lives. But I don't want to be one of them. I guess I'm only just starting to wonder what exactly we're all hoping to find at the top of the ladder when we finally get there, you know?" It's strange, it's the first time I've articulated that thought in my life, but hearing myself say it I understand it's been creeping up on me since George left.

Nick watches me scramble for words to explain why I can't wait to leave this godforsaken place. And again, I think about telling him the whole truth. But then that would change everything between us.

He senses my flip in mood. "What is it? Just say it," he encourages.

I watch as soft flames lick the edges of the logs in the firepit, their heat on my bare ankles.

"Do you know someone called Ben Cohan, Nick?" I ask, avoiding his gaze.

I feel him tense next to me. There's only the pop and crackle from the firepit and then he speaks. "I've met him a couple of times, yeah," he says, his tone tight. "Why?"

"I met him today," I say, turning to look at Nick. His features, usually so quick to shift to a smile, are fixed in a frown.

"Okay . . ." he prompts.

I don't know how far I'm going with this but I let the words come. "I've heard some things, about him." In my tone there's a question.

"Yeah, I'd take those things at face value."

"They're true?"

He leans forward. "Did something happen?" he asks.

I shake my head. "Not to me."

"But to someone you know?" he asks, his concerned tone only slightly masking his anger.

"Sort of, it's hard to explain. But you think the rumors about him are true?"

Nick gives a definitive nod and drains his wine. "Yeah, he's fucking weird. That whole outfit. His business partner, Mike . . . It's best to just to steer clear of the pair of them unless you wanna get fucked one way or another." I cringe at his jibe and his expression changes instantly.

"Sorry, sorry. Jesus. I didn't mean . . . Completely inappropriate. Sorry."

I shake my head. "It's fine, I get what you meant," I reassure him. "Tell me about his business partner, Mike."

Nick pours himself another glass of wine and tops up mine. I don't have the heart to tell him I won't be staying long enough to drink it.

"Mike handles the money, the legal, Ben's the figurehead. They met at college, I think, kind of an odd partnering from the beginning, but it seems to work. They make a good team, I guess. Ben goes crazy, Mike tidies up." Nick clocks my raised eyebrows. "Yeah, there was a thing last year, a rights issue that got out of hand. The rumor was that Ben had some . . . connections. When a certain rights option ended, all the other competing bidders suddenly seemed to dry up. Moon Finch cleared the field. They all got scared off. His connections paid some visits, apparently, made some calls. That kind of thing."

I think of Emily, obliviously turning up to meet these two men with her little audio file and her demands. How scared she must have been as she tried to play a game she didn't know the rules of—one that, given their connections, she never stood a chance of winning. Nick alludes to witnesses, competitors, paid off or warned off, some more heavy-handedly than others.

"You believe that?" I ask. "That they'd do something like that?"

Nick shrugs. "God, after everything that's come out in Hollywood over the last few years, it wouldn't surprise me at all."

"Then why doesn't anyone do anything? Say something?" I know I'm hardly the one to be arguing this point but here I am arguing it.

"Payoffs. NDAs. Fear. Lack of evidence. It's a gamble, it could ruin you just as easily as it could ruin them."

"Oh," I concede.

I catch sight of the time on his watch. It's nearing eleven.

I head to the bathroom, and Nick offers to go upstairs to grab me a coffee. I'm going to need to leave in the next fifteen minutes, but the idea of meeting Marla at this point fills me with so much dread I consider dropping the whole thing. I could just stay here with Nick and forget all about Emily and Marla and everything that's happened over the last week. I could just curl up here safe with him. I could take Ben's advice and drop the whole thing.

But what about Emily? And now that I'm involved, will the whole thing drop me even if I drop it?

I take a look at myself in the low-lit bathroom mirror, in my lace camisole and jeans, bare skin cooling now that I'm away from the warmth of the fire. In the half-light I look like her, Emily. Just as much as Marla looked like her, or Joanne, or any slim, white, brunette actress I've seen in any audition waiting room anywhere in the world. We're all the same no matter how different we are; that's the point of casting brackets.

The truth is I'm scared but I think I have to go. Not because I'm a daredevil; I'm not. But because I'm already involved in this. I don't know how I fit in to Emily's story yet but I need to find out if I'm in real danger and from whom. Because someone has already tampered with my car. Of course I'm scared. I'm no hero, I'm just a nearly-thirty-year-old actress from Bedfordshire. All I'm actually good at is pretending I'm different people and remembering lines. I know the bad things that happen to "difficult women." And right now I wish more than anything I had some way of protecting myself.

I check my watch quickly and make a decision, slipping quietly out of the bathroom and back along the corridor I came down. I pause as I pass the master bedroom.

I don't know why I'm so certain I'll find it there. Perhaps because Nick lives alone, perhaps because the nearest help is a dark and winding drive away.

My gaze flicks back up the corridor into the house and I hear the tinkle of cups in the kitchen upstairs, coffee being prepared. Here's my chance.

I stride into the room, heading straight for his bedside cabinet. If there's one here I'll just borrow it. I won't even load it; it'll be a visual aid, nothing more. But one that might just get me out of a terrible situation if it unfolds.

I slide out the bedside drawer carefully. There's only a remote control. *Huh.* The sounds of the coffee machine being used drift down to me from upstairs. I think fast, dashing across to the other side of the bed and rolling its bedside drawer open. I stop abruptly as its contents rattle loudly. This could be it.

I inch the drawer out bit by bit, careful not to make too much noise, the drawer's contents slowly unveiling themselves. Condoms, mints, pocket tissues, batteries, painkillers, loose change, another remote. Then I spy the edge of a small cardboard box, the rattle of small metal bullets inside, and finally, I catch sight of what I'm looking for, the corner of a dark metal object. Nick has a gun. Throwing a quick glance back to the door I carefully take it from the drawer.

The handgrip reads SIG SAUER and the slide tells me it's a P938 9mm Para, which I know from countless armor talks means it takes Parabellum bullets. I check the gun's safety: it's on. I run a full safety check just like I've done a hundred times on set in front of grim-faced firearms captains. Safety on: check. Mag empty: check. I do not take bullets. Bullets will only open up a whole new set of problems.

I will bring it back. It's insurance more than anything else; something to show and run.

As I said before, I always thought the story of my life would be a coming-of-age story and I suppose, in a way, it is, even if I got the genre wrong. But the thing that never occurred to me, until now, is that I might not even be the main character.

I carefully store the Sig into the snug inside pocket of my bag, close Nick's drawer, straighten the sheets, and head back out to the terrace.

32

The Truth

TUESDAY, FEBRUARY 16

I ARRIVE AT THE 101 COFFEE SHOP PAST MIDNIGHT, HALF HOPING SHE'S already gone, and park in the darkest spot farthest from the warm glow of the entrance.

I shrug on a sweater then pluck the Sig from its pouch. I release the mag, checking once more that it is safe, and then reflexively check the chamber too. My breath catches; I forgot to check it at Nick's house. A single gleaming bullet stares back at me from the ejection port. Nick must have left one in the chamber. I pop it out. I don't know how I missed this, nerves maybe, but it changes everything.

I pause for a second staring down at the shiny bullet in my lap. I could load it. But if it's purely a deterrent, then why do that? I'd just be asking for something to go wrong. But then what if the deterrent doesn't deter? If push comes to shove, couldn't a warning shot be more useful?

I think of Chekhov's gun. The theatrical trope that tells actors and playwrights: Never place a loaded gun on the stage if it isn't going to go off. Don't make promises you don't intend to keep.

I peer down at my now loaded gun. Apparently, Hemingway hated Chekhov's "loaded gun" advice. If every loaded gun in every story ever written had to go off then there would be no new stories.

A bell tinkles as I enter the 101 but nobody looks up, the diner music muffling my entrance. I scan the customers. Mainly men, various shapes and sizes, sit up at the counter.

The whites of a chef in the back, only his chest visible through the kitchen serving hatch. Two waitresses, one wiping the countertops, another refilling coffee. A middle-aged woman at a window booth tucking into a basket of sweet potato fries while quietly working on a crossword, reading glasses low.

Farther into the restaurant, I see the back of her head. Her long glossy chestnut hair twisted up into a bun, the back of her ivory neck visible through fallen strands. Marla. My stomach flips. The woman I've been looking for since she disappeared six days ago. The woman I thought was Emily Bryant. Emily's best friend.

I make my way over and slide wordlessly into the booth opposite her. Then I catch sight of her face and recoil before I can stop myself. She's definitely the girl I met at the audition six days ago, but the right side of her face from eyebrow to cheekbone is a smudge of deep-purple bruising. The delicate skin around her eye socket is swollen and puffy. She's tried to cover the worst of it with concealer but the livid colors beneath are impossible to hide. A deep cut punctuates her right eyebrow, the wound beginning to scab over.

She darts a reassuring hand across the table as I pull back, her cold fingers circling my wrist gently but firmly. "Relax," she coos. "It's fine. It looks worse than it feels." She smiles but the motion makes her wince.

I let my shoulders relax and place my bag down carefully beside me as I take in the damage to her face. She studies me with interest now too, the woman who has been doggedly tracking her for almost a week.

"Who did it?" I ask.

She knows I mean her face. "Who do you think?"

I think Ben Cohan. Probably not Ben himself, someone Ben knows.

"He sent someone, didn't he?" I ask, and she nods almost imperceptibly. "Was it Ben or Mike who arranged for that to happen to you?"

"Same thing," she answers. "You heard the recording?"

"I did."

"So you know what happened that night."

"Yes. And then Emily tried to blackmail them?" I clarify.

She nods again and it occurs to me that talking must be painful, damaged muscles aching under bruised skin.

"She played them the tape," she says, her voice low. "She contacted a few other girls at the party. She had an actual witness, someone saw Ben's assistant spike a drink. If she needed it Emily had a witness. But she said she'd drop the whole thing if they made it right."

"And what would make it right?" I ask.

"A job. She didn't want a trial. And she didn't want the payoff she knew they'd offer her. And by God did they offer her a payoff. She wanted what she came to LA for in the first place. The price was too high but she figured she'd already paid it so she should get something in return. And they'd done it for other actresses."

"What? Given them jobs after they'd . . . ?" I blurt before I can temper my question. Marla nods. "Then what went wrong this time?"

She falls silent as menus arrive; she doesn't speak again until the waitress is safely back behind the counter.

"The recording. The fact she had one. They wanted it. She wouldn't give it to them until she was actually on set, in costume, deal done. She didn't trust them. So she wanted to keep the evidence until they delivered."

"But she could have kept copies. Not told them," I argue.

Marla chuckles then winces. "They would have known. They wanted to send someone over, they wanted to wipe her hard drives, look through emails. That was part of the deal. They'd already taken so much from her, she wasn't going to let them into her home, into her life as well."

"So she said no?"

"Yeah." Marla rips open a bright-pink Sweet'N Low, tipping it into her black coffee. "She told them she'd hand everything over once filming was complete. That way they'd have to reshoot the entire movie if they wanted to pull out of the deal, and there was no way they'd do that." She pauses, her mug halfway to her mouth. "She was a good enough actress, by the way, good enough to handle a role like that. Genuinely good. They wouldn't have had to reshoot for that reason."

Was. Was good enough. The words hang in the air between us.

I don't suppose she'll have much of a career to come back to if she ever comes back. I'm sure they'll make sure of that. I take a moment to steel myself before I ask, "What did they do when she refused to give them the recording?"

She looks out of the diner windows to the LA streets beyond our reflections. "They acted like that was fine," she says simply. "They said she could keep it until she was sure." Marla's eyes glisten in the warm diner light. "And they offered her three possible roles. Great roles, lead roles. They got her hopes up, you know. But she was careful. She recorded that meeting too, their deal, everything they said. And when they told her they'd changed their minds, she told them exactly what she'd do with her two recordings." Marla pauses, savoring the memory of Emily outsmarting the two men who thought they controlled everything.

"She had them by the balls," I say, pushing her.

Marla frowns. "Who knows," she answers. "It certainly focused them. They said the deal was back on, and they told her the role they'd give her. All she had to do was go in and sign her contract . . . and then she was gone."

"She disappeared after signing?"

"She wasn't replying to texts, calls, anything. At first I assumed the meeting had just gone badly, that they'd pulled out again and she was distraught, but it wasn't that." She breaks off. "I should have gone straight over to her apartment but I didn't. I waited until the next morning. The cleaner let me in but Emily wasn't there. I couldn't get through to her so I logged into her laptop. I found her using her phone tracking app and I texted her to stay put, that I was coming."

"Where was she?"

"She had to disappear. She's still there. If you want I can take you to her."

Marla's words send a shiver down my spine; it's impossible to tell if she's offering to take me to meet a living person or to visit a grave. I think of the gun in the bag beside me and the safety it could afford me.

"Where is she?" I ask carefully.

"Not far. A fifteen-minute drive." I try to gauge her intentions but she seems to have no vested interest in me coming one way or another. "I told Emily about you. About how you got involved. How you've tried to help. She knows you've been looking for her. I'm sorry you're involved in all this, we both are. But she just can't risk coming back yet, talking to the police yet. We both can't risk it. It's not safe. I'm sorry I can't be clearer about everything but it's her plan. It's hers to explain. I can take you if you want me to? But it's up to you."

I study Marla's face, tired, battered, and bruised. What she's done for Emily is extreme. She's been hiding her and I assume muddying the trail she's left behind, risking her own safety and almost certainly her own career. I wonder if I would do half as much for a friend in need. Or perhaps I'm misreading the situation; I'm painfully aware Marla can be very convincing when she needs to be. What if she's the one responsible for Emily's disappearance in the first place, what if all of this is a lie? But I've met Ben Cohan, and I've seen what's lurking under his professional veneer. And I can see Marla's face right in front of me, bright with bruises, full of barely concealed fear for her friend. Perhaps I'll live to regret it but something tells me I need to trust her. We can all talk about the sisterhood until we're blue in the face but here's my moment to actually do something. If Marla can take me to Emily—if I can see her with my own eyes—then I'll be certain. I'll know I've done my bit. And if I need to, as soon as I'm ready to leave LA I'll bring the whole house of cards tumbling down around me.

"I'll come," I tell Marla, my tone firm, "but I'm going to follow you in my own car."

She takes a second to mull over the idea.

"Of course, if you'd feel safer. I totally understand." She reaches into her purse, pulls out a $20 bill, and wedges it under her coffee mug to pay. "Shall we?" she asks, moving to rise.

"Whoa, whoa, whoa. Wait," I say, placing my hands on the table between us. "I just need to get some things straight first. Why did you drag me into this? Last week you pulled me into this whole situation, didn't you—?"

Marla places a hand on top of mine, and I stop abruptly.

"I didn't drag you into this at all. You were already part of it. You just didn't know you were." She shakes her head, bemused by my lack of insight into everything she's been explaining.

She pats my arm. "The emails, the apartment, us meeting that day. You really haven't worked any of it out yet, have you? What you are to Emily, what you are to me?"

I stare at her dumbfounded as the meaning of her words sinks in.

I am part of a plan I do not understand. And I have been since the day we met.

I open my mouth to speak but she cuts me off.

"But it's *her* plan, I'll let her explain—"

"No," I interrupt, "you explain it to me. Now. Or I'm not going anywhere."

Marla nods. "Fine. Then I guess we're done here," she says simply. And with that she rises and turns to leave.

33

Up into the Darkness

TUESDAY, FEBRUARY 16

I FOLLOW HER TAILLIGHTS NORTH, AWAY FROM THE BUSY BOULEVARDS OF Hollywood, to where the roads thin out, becoming bumpier and darker, as we ascend into the hills. I have no idea where we're heading. However reckless agreeing to follow her may sound, I need to know how I am involved in this. And what exactly this is.

Marla's car begins to slow ahead of me. She pulls in at the side of the road behind a string of darkened cars, and I pull up behind her as she kills her engine.

Outside in darkness the few far-flung streetlights offer only pools of half-light and shadows. In the distance behind us I see the twinkle of the city's lights over the treetops.

I turn off my engine and slip Nick's gun from my bag, checking the safety before plunging it into the pocket of a jacket from the backseat. I root out my phone and pop it into my other pocket then stop myself. I don't know why I haven't thought of it earlier but I slip it out again and open the Voice Memos app, press record, and drop it back into my pocket. It can't hurt to follow Emily's own example. Just in case.

I watch Marla exit her vehicle in front of me and wonder what on earth could connect her and me, what could connect all of us? I guess I'll find out.

I pop my door and take in the street around me for the first time. Emily could be in any one of the darkened houses lining this rough track road. It's after one A.M. on a Tuesday; the inhabitants of all of them are most likely fast asleep in their beds. I get a sudden pang for home: for my pokey Clapton flat and my saggy bed with its soft brushed-cotton bedsheets.

Marla gestures, motioning up the road. We need to keep going on foot from here.

She wouldn't tell me where she's leading me but from the satnav it looked like we were heading up toward the distant edges of Griffith Park. As we make our way farther up the road, though, I see we've come to a dead end; we must be going into one of the houses.

Marla crosses the road and waits for me, leaning on a locked jade-hued oxidized gate. I cannot see the house beyond her but this must be it. I jog to catch up but as I reach her she turns from the gate and continues along the blank white wall toward the dead end. I turn back to the green gate, confused, and when I look back to Marla she is gone. Only the whitewashed wall stares back at me. I pause for a moment unsure what to do when suddenly her head pokes out, seemingly through the white wall itself. Taken aback, I approach slowly to discover that there is a narrow, staggered opening in the wall, with a rough-trodden path leading up into Griffith Park.

A hidden entrance. No guard, no gate, just an opening in a wall.

"Keep up," Marla says, her voice brusque, as she strides away up the sharply inclining path. We head into the darkness, branches scratching at our legs and hands. After we spend an indiscernible amount of time climbing the path, it seems to open up ahead, a single streetlight visible. As we rejoin a tarmacked path, I look up and see it for the first time, looming on the hillside directly above us, massive and inescapable, bone white in the light of the moon. Its letters forty-five feet high spelling out: HOLLYWOOD.

I stop in my tracks and stare, hairs on end. It gives me the creeps. The world's biggest tombstones jutting up into the night sky. I have never seen it this close up before. I've never even seen a photograph of it this close up. Our tour certainly didn't come this close. I remember the guide telling us about the string of protests at the sign over the last few weeks. The broken fences, the vandalized cameras. Perhaps that's why we're meeting Emily here: no cameras.

A hushed call from Marla snaps me out of my reverie. She gestures emphatically ahead along the road—we need to keep moving, keep going up a tarmac road leading away from the sign. It's with some relief I realize that it is not our final destination.

I catch up with Marla, allowing myself some space to hang back just in case. The streetlight behind us melts away and darkness swallows us again. My senses heighten as we ascend; every sound around us is amplified. I finger the cool metal of the Sig Sauer in my pocket and remind myself that if something happens, I'll need to act fast. I try to settle my breath to counteract the fizz of adrenaline coursing through my body as we pound on up.

Then in the distance, I see lights. High up, a bright-red beacon pulsing, the kind you'd find on a signal tower. What looks like a relay tower or some kind of electrical station hoves into view at the end of the road. Fences circle it high with barbed wire, official signs, and security lights. Is this where Emily is?

There are no cars on the road, no signs of life.

Perhaps we will be meeting her here. I let my mind run with the idea. There's a chance she's fine, just in hiding, and this is the only way she agreed to meet. Perhaps she has been working with the police all along to bring down a whole ring of Ben Cohans. I let my mind color in the picture with bright and hopeful colors. Perhaps Emily decided to expose everything. But there my mind and I splutter to a halt.

"I'm not going any farther until you tell me what the hell we're doing here, Marla."

She turns quickly. "Shush, Jesus Christ. You need to keep it down." She marches back to me and grabs my wrist. "This way," she insists, gently tugging me off the road and down another steep bank toward one of the fences. Then I see it. The whole of LA spread out before us, glittering like an earthbound constellation, the sight of it taking my breath away. I realize we've come full circle and now we stand directly behind the giant letters of the sign, their towering metalwork climbing straight up into the clear night sky. I feel dizzy as I look up, my warm breath clouding in the night air.

Marla has continued along the metal fence to a jagged opening, the wire caging curling back on itself, the ground around it and beyond littered with empty cans and bottles—the detritus left from the recent influx of protestors. There's no one here now, though, just us and the metallic jangle of the fence as Marla steadies herself against it. She throws me a look before stooping down and edging through onto the hillside of the sign.

I zip up my jacket pockets containing the phone and Nick's gun then warily duck through the wire and out onto the steep dusty slope beyond.

Marla has descended the slope as far as the base of the letters and is making her way briskly along to the end of the sign. I carefully scramble down, struggling to keep up as I watch her disappear out of sight behind the final letter. It's funny how the mind adjusts in order to normalize situations: back in the 101 Coffee Shop I hadn't thought for a second I would be doing this now. But I am and my mind is slowly and inexorably coming around to the idea that at the end of our hike I might see Emily, but Emily won't see me.

I stumble on the loose dirt, snatch in a breath, and catch myself on an outcrop of grass, a tumble of loose earth scattering off down the dark slope beneath me. I look up to see Marla's head reappear around the final letter. She's waiting. I get my bearings, recheck my pockets, and get moving.

I come to a halt beside her at the giant D at the end of HOLLY-WOOD.

"How are you with heights?" she asks, looking up at the letter.

She can't be serious. I follow her gaze up and about a yard above our heads a ladder begins. I see now as I look along the staggered line: each letter has its own white ladder beginning about ten feet from the ground and leading all the way up.

"You're joking," I erupt.

She looks at me calmly. "It's fine, kids go up it all the time, it's just a service ladder. It's perfectly safe." She cranes her neck up into the night again. "We need to get up there. You see the platform at the top. I'll go first if you like?"

She goes to move farther up the slope but I stop her. "You told me we were meeting Emily. Emily's not here, is she?" I demand, urgency clear in my tone.

She looks down at my hand on her arm, and when she looks up her eyes sparkle with tears in the moonlight. "No. No, she's not here," she says, a deep weariness seeming to crack open inside her as she stares out at the twinkle of LA beyond the sign. "I needed to get you to come here with me. I needed to tell you what happened, Mia. I need to tell someone what they did. What they did to her. I'm sorry I dragged you into this, but I promise you, you were already involved. I knew you'd never come if I told you." I feel my stomach lurch. Emily is dead. They killed her. Marla tricked me into coming here and Emily is dead. Her heartbroken eyes find mine. "I miss her so much, she was my friend, Mia. A real friend, we went through a lot. And she never let anything get her down. I've never known any-one like that before." She swipes at her wet cheeks with the sleeve of her sweater and looks up at me. "Will you come up with me? I need to show someone, someone else needs to know what happened, you can see her from up there."

Oh God. I shudder at her words. An image of the broken body of the actress who jumped from the sign flashes through my mind. I'm not really sure I want to see Emily anymore.

"How am I involved, Marla? You need to tell me."

"You know who killed her. Emily," she says, simply. "It's some-one you've met, someone you know."

The hairs along the back of my neck rise. Does she mean herself; did she kill her only friend? She can't mean that, she means someone else. My thoughts race through the new faces I've met this past week. Ben Cohan leaps instantly to mind. Ben Cohan and Mike. But I haven't even met Mike. I scramble for other options, and then my blood runs cold. Does she mean Nick? Is Nick connected to all of this?

Nick who I met years ago and forgot. Nick the producer. Nick who was so pleased to see me that first day when I thought I'd lost Emily. Nick who knows everyone in this town and has worked with everyone. Nick who lives in Bel Air. Nick whose house I just came from and whose gun lies snug in my pocket.

Oh shit.

Now that I think about it, he's been there from day one. When Marla disappeared at the audition he was lurking outside. No wonder she ran. I remember how interested he was in the missing girl; how eager he was to hear any news on the subject. His late-night emergency visits to the studio to deal with troublesome actors. I realize I have no idea what he's been up to since the beginning. I think of the way his arm pulled me close on the terrace and I cringe deep inside at the thought. How could I have read him so wrong? I so wanted Nick to be the man I saw that I must have ignored anything that conflicted. Why didn't I just ask him tonight if he'd ever worked with Ben Cohan? But perhaps I'm lucky I didn't.

"Nick Eldridge and Ben Cohan?"

Marla holds my gaze unflinching, and I feel my heart sink. "Yes," she confirms. "Will you come up and see?"

I gaze up at the platform nearly fifty feet in the air. God knows what I'll see up there. If there's a body up there or in the ravine, surely someone must have found it by now.

"Tell me what Nick had to do with this, Marla. I need to know."

"I want to show you first."

She scrambles past me, climbing slightly higher up the rocky slope, then positions herself carefully on a knotty outcrop of vegetation and teeters there for a moment before reaching across to brush the lowest rung of the letter's ladder. The fingertips of one hand just able to touch. She leans back away from the ledge, takes a breath, and then throws herself forward, off the outcrop. My heart skips a beat as she flies forward, in momentary free fall, before a palm slams down on the ladder's rung. For a second she hangs precariously by just one hand before the other finds the metal and she heaves herself up fully onto the ladder.

I've never been scared of heights but now, here, in the darkness, I am. Scared of the darkness beneath us, scared of Marla, but most of all scared of what she has to show me. But I need to know what Nick did, how bad it is, and how the hell I'm involved in all of this.

I slowly clamber up the slope to her starting ledge and shift into the same position. I try not to think of the six-foot drop if I can't reach the rung and the immeasurable darkness of the canyon beyond that. I take a breath and plow forward, stretching out for the chipped white paintwork of the ladder. I feel the contents of my zipped pockets shift with the movement. For a moment I am untethered, the night air all around me, my empty hands grasping at nothing before a palm thwacks onto the rung, its cool metal hitting hard. I immediately twist my body and claw my other hand up to safety too, breathless.

Then with tight aching arms, I engage my core to heave up, desperate to get my feet onto something in order to distribute the weight.

Once my feet make contact I rest my hot hands, looking up to watch Marla carefully ascending. She turns back, sensing I've paused.

"You okay?" she calls back.

"Yeah." I catch my breath and continue.

The wind grows in strength as we rise. I watch carefully as Marla sidesteps from the top of the ladder onto the strut-platform surrounding it.

Beneath me the ground is no longer visible in the darkness. Instead I focus only on the rungs in front of me, but as I reach the final rung my head crests the top of the letter and the glittering blanket of light that makes up Los Angeles comes into view. I catch my breath at the twinkling beauty of it laid out beneath the clear night sky. Beside me Marla shifts to make room on the thin platform, wedging her body between the waist-high metal of the sign and the support strut behind her. Once she's comfortable she reaches into her pocket and pulls out a packet of cigarettes.

With incredible focus, my limbs completely reluctant, I shift my weight around the ladder, lodging myself between the strut and the corrugated metal of the letter to join her on the thin platform.

I rub my aching knuckles, clawed from clenching the rungs too tightly, and watch as Marla lights a cigarette, ridiculously at ease forty-five feet above the dark hillside. I pat my zipped pocket instinctively for reassurance as she slips her lighter back into her jeans and takes a deep drag, casting her eyes out across the Los Angeles skyline.

I take it in too, the brilliant fluorescence of civilization against an otherwise black landscape, the American street grid system glowing as far as the eye can see out across the horizon. I search for the distant glinting of the Downtown high-rise buildings, hoping to locate my own building among them. But a tendril of smoke floats past and I turn my attention back to Marla, who is watching me.

"Thank you by the way," she says. "You kept looking for me, didn't you? You didn't know me but you kept looking for me. I appreciate it; that you were worried. It means a lot. You're a nice person." She offers me a cigarette from her packet; I shake my head. "Didn't think so." She smiles and slips the pack away.

"Where is Emily, Marla?" I ask.

She raises her arm, index finger pointing out across the darkness, like the ghost of Christmas future, off into the distance. I follow its trajectory. She's pointing southwest from where we are to a patch of darkness on the otherwise twinkling horizon. I squint, slowly making out a glint of moonlight in the black. My brain struggles to make sense of it; it's a body of water. A lake perhaps. "Is that Silver Lake?" I ask.

"Lake Hollywood," she answers inscrutably in a puff of cigarette smoke. There's an air of Lewis Carroll's Caterpillar about her. I study her angular features, catching a flash of her bone-white teeth as she lifts her cigarette to her full lips once more.

On second thought, she's more Cheshire cat.

"Lake Hollywood used to be a reservoir. Drinking water," she continues, a world-weary tour guide. "Now it's just a backup reservoir for forest fires. But it's deep. A hundred and eighty-three feet. I looked it up once. Nearly the height of the Leaning Tower of Pisa. She's somewhere under there." Marla stops talking, her glassy eyes trained on the distance as she takes a final drag on her cigarette and tosses it into the darkness in front of us. I watch its burning tip sail through the air and bounce away into the unknown.

Silence hangs between us until she speaks again. "I followed the tracker signal there. The last place her signal registered was from the dam road." She turns to me now. "I looked until it got dark. Found the phone in a bush near the banks. Dirty, out of battery, but fine. Whatever they did, they did in a hurry."

Her eyes are glistening again. Before I can open my mouth she speaks.

"They killed her and dumped her in the lake, I know they did. Like trash. I went back to her place to charge the phone. To follow the trail, the tracker's trail, to work out her last journey . . . to end up there. Under all that water." She pauses to pull out her pack of cigarettes again. She lights one in that same fluid way I've come to recognize. "Emily went to meet Moon Finch, God knows what they told her, but when she left everything must have seemed fine. She stopped for lunch at a roadside diner near the studio. That's where they took her. That's where I found her abandoned car, days later, in the diner parking lot. I don't know if there was a struggle or if she went with them willingly. I searched that diner, the parking lot, everything, for some clue to what happened, believe me. I looked for any trace of her, her hair, blood, anything. But I'll never know.

"The tracking app shows that after she left the diner without her car someone drove her all around LA. If she was dead already, or alive, I don't know. She still had her phone on her, registering a signal, but she didn't try to call for help, she didn't dial anyone. Then around four A.M., they took her to the reservoir, and that's where the signal stopped."

I try to keep my tone neutral as I speak though every fiber in my body is screaming to know. "And Nick was involved? Nick helped Moon Finch? He was the one looking for you the day we met. He thought you were Emily and you were still alive?"

She turns to me sadly then looks away. Eyes cast out to the lake, she nods.

A wave of dizziness hits me. Nick isn't the man I thought he was. All this time he's been watching me, waiting to see what exactly I knew about Emily's disappearance. I think of our conversation about Ben Cohan earlier this evening, Nick's arm wrapped firmly about my shoulders, and I shudder. "Why didn't you go to the police, Marla? Why didn't you tell them all of this?"

To my surprise Marla lets out a laugh. "Because things are a little different in this country than they are in yours, I think." She turns to me now. "I'm not like you. I might look like you, I might be able to fit in around people like you, but we may as well be a different species. We aren't the same. Everything I have in my life I fought for, tooth and nail, do you understand? Being in care, foster homes, juvenile. I was in and out of one thing or another until I was seventeen. My last foster mom. She'd been an actress, a failed one, but she pushed me. And it started to work. I suppose looking like this helped." She swirls a finger in the air around her bruised but beautiful face. "But the police don't tend to listen to people with my kind of record. At least not in this country. I didn't fancy my chances as a reliable witness in a court case against one of the richest production companies in America. Trust me, they would've destroyed me on the stand. They would have gotten away with it and I didn't want to trash a career in the only good thing in my life. That's why I didn't call the police. The police aren't for people like me. They're for people like you. But don't think for a second—" She breaks off emphatically. "—that I let them get away with what they did to Emily. I picked up her car, I moved into her apartment, I changed agents using her name, and I started to go to auditions as her. I changed all her head-shots to mine and then I waited. When they thought they were safe I emailed Moon Finch. As Emily." She lets out a giggle of pure joy. "I hope it scared the absolute shit out of them. God, to have been a fly on the wall when Ben and Mike read that email. As Emily I told them I'd been away but now I was back and looking forward to working together just like they'd promised. I don't know if at first they thought maybe Emily *had* survived somehow or if they knew who I was from the start, but boy did they invite me into their office fast. And I went in, with a copy of her tape recording from New Year's, and a copy of her tape recording from their meeting. And on top of that I knew what they'd done to her. Where they'd put her. I had all the cards. They were so fucked. Because as far as the rest of the world was concerned, I was Emily Bryant. And if they said I wasn't Emily, if they said I couldn't possibly be Emily, then they would damn well need to explain why I wasn't and how they knew it. I had them over a barrel."

Marla fingers the bruise beneath her eye delicately before taking another deep drag of her cigarette.

"And that's where you come in." She tips her hand in my direction. "No, actually, that's where Kathryn Mayer comes in."

The mention of Kathryn Mayer's name throws me for a second. What could Kathryn have to do with Ben Cohan and Moon Finch?

And then a cascade of thoughts fall into place. How could I have been so stupid?

Galatea.

Ben Cohan told me himself, *Galatea* was originally a Moon Finch production, they developed it, they did the pre-production on it, and then Kathryn Mayer joined the studio, swept in and laid claim. Moon Finch had *Galatea.*

I speak as the thoughts form. "They promised Emily *Galatea*?"

Marla smiles at my leap of logic. "They promised Emily *Galatea*. And then they promised it to me," she says, wry disappointment in her voice. "I could not believe my fucking luck when they gave me that script." She beams, basking in the memory. "No feeling like it. Nothing. I can't imagine how Emily must have felt when they first offered it to her."

We're all connected by one part. The role of a lifetime. A role worth dying for.

Maybe even a role worth killing for?

The reality of my situation finally dawns on me. Marla might not be responsible for Emily's death, but that doesn't mean she won't be for mine.

I force my right hand into my pocket and let it find a position on the gun's grip, my thumb finding the safety and testing its give. I remind myself there is a bullet in it and inch my thumb away again. It's odd how calm I suddenly feel, forty-five feet up in the air with a woman who wants what's mine and clearly has a very different moral landscape from me.

I watch her stub her cigarette out against the corrugated sign, my mind finally piecing it all together.

It's as simple as this: Marla found out Kathryn was eyeing me for the lead in *Galatea,* she looked me up, she knew what I looked like, and when she saw me at an audition she made friends. She read me like a fucking book, tried to get me to go ahead of her so she could steal my apartment key, read my emails, break into my apartment, but I wouldn't go first. I went out to the meter. Since we met she'd tried everything she could short of incapacitating me to stop me from testing for her role. She deleted my emails, distracted, scared, threatened, and impeded me, anything to keep me from that part. So in a way, I suppose it had to come to this. I can't say she didn't try to warn me.

"You tried to stop me from testing."

She gives me an apologetic look, her tone eerily lighthearted as she jokes, "Yeah. But it didn't work, did it?"

"No, it didn't."

"And here we are."

My mind races to catch up. "And Nick? He helped you?" I feel my head lightening, vertigo swimming around me.

Marla shrugs. "You keep bringing him up but I have no idea who he is. You seemed into the idea, though."

Oh God. She lied. She dragged me up here with garden-variety lies. I feel my anger flare. I think of how quick I was to assume that all this was somehow to do with Nick, and then I feel a tight clench of guilt too. Why would Nick be involved with a man he clearly told me he found repugnant? My grip tightens around the gun. His gun. The only thing I have up here to protect myself. And now that I think about it, Marla told me Ben was responsible for her bruised face.

"And your face? They didn't really do that either, did they?" I ask, trying to sift truth from lies.

"The video call from Moon Finch came after I'd returned your phone to your bag in the waiting room. I was about to head to your apartment. I knew they were still pitching me to Kathryn, and I knew it was between you and me. They told me they were going to back down. Kathryn wasn't taking recommendations. They told me they'd get me something else. I told Ben that was unacceptable. I told him to try harder. I did this to my face and sent him a picture." She clocks my expression and smiles. "It's not as bad as it looks. I took Advil."

"Why would you do that to yourself?"

"Leverage. Proof of what he did to me." She shrugs. "He just needed another nudge in the right direction. And photos of me beaten up along with everything else I have on them paint a pretty damning picture, don't you think?"

Marla's reason for hiring Joanne shifts into focus. "You couldn't collect Emily's things from me looking like that," I suggest.

"Not exactly. I had already been Michelle at your apartment. I would have been recognized. But you're right, I did need Joanne to take Emily's place for a few days. In case questions were raised too soon. I didn't want the deal to screw up. And I needed her to keep you busy and to return the car on CCTV."

"Why did you bring me up here, Marla?"

"Good question. When you went to feed the meter I took your phone—you really need to be careful who's watching you type in your code, you know. Everything's on phones these days. I took it to the bathroom, I found your address, I took your key, I emailed your building, I read your recent searches. Where you were going, what you were planning. Search histories tend to give you a good feel for where someone's head is. Recent breakup, running away, trying to escape what happened but they're always there at the touch of a button, right? The happy couple. I've seen her, I know how you must feel. Losing a job, losing a boyfriend."

"I haven't lost a job," I counter, my words drifting away on the breeze.

"And you've got a bit of an obsession with that story about the actress who jumped off the sign, haven't you?" she continues regardless.

Instinctively my hands grip tighter onto the steel of the sign as a massive surge of adrenaline sweeps through me. The girl who fell from the sign. The realization hits me physically, momentarily knocking my balance and sending a fresh wave of vertigo through me. That's why she's brought me here, to the sign, because of the girl who jumped.

"You're scared now, aren't you? I'd never heard of her, her story. But I looked her up. It's a good plot. Lots of pathos and bathos. That telegram offering her the new part the next day. Sad." She gives a mock grimace. "So here we are." She gestures out into the darkness. "I tried to ward you off. I gave fair warning. But you wouldn't stop. Which means I can't. Too many people have given too much for this part and I'm not going to let you sweep in at the last minute and steal it from under us. You don't deserve this like she deserved it. Like we both deserve it. I get the chance she missed. I am getting out of this hole. *I* am getting this part, not you with your nice life and your nice family and your other options. Emily and I were out here too long, we worked too hard to walk away when we're this close, when we've sacrificed so much. I never wanted it to come to this but you haven't left me any choice."

I feel the blow contact my face sharply before I see it, the pain intense and shocking. My balance fails me but thankfully, wedged between the struts and sign, it's impossible for me to fall. Instead my body slumps into the strut as I try to catch my breath and make sense of the situation. My vision fuzzy, I shake open my eyes just in time to see her elbow come down on me again. I dodge instinctively, her arm only grazing my shoulder this time, but I can now feel the hot trickle of blood from my nose and the bright taste of blood in my mouth from that first connecting blow. I can't feel the side of my face at all. My breath comes in ragged desperate gasps as I watch her raise a boot to kick.

Frantically I fumble for my pocket and tug out the gun wildly, catching it on the fabric and jolting the seam hard, tearing it in order to release it. I swing the barrel out into the air between us unthinkingly. She freezes, her face a mask of surprise.

Thinking only of my life I flick off the safety as calmly as my shaking hand will allow me to, my face a tingling, bleeding mess. With a quick swipe against my shoulder I remove the blood from my mouth before speaking.

"Here's what we're going to do, okay," I say as clearly as I can, my smashed and swelling face already making talking hard. My voice sounds weird. "I am not going to shoot you for a part. No one is dying for a part. Do you understand me? You have to stop. You have to leave me alone. There are other parts, other people. Even if I walked away from this role today you wouldn't get it, Marla. That ship has sailed. Kathryn has the film, not Moon Finch. You're playing with fire but if you really need this then go back to them and take whatever lead they offer. It doesn't have to be this one. Either way, this stops. I want you to go." I twitch the barrel of the gun toward the ladder. "Go now. I'm leaving tomorrow. You won't see me again. But if I see you, if you follow me, I will protect myself, do you understand?" My hand has stopped shaking but the quake is now inside me, deep in my core muscles, like shivering in the cold. Marla studies me, unsure of her next move. "If you go now, I won't report this," I push on. "Any of it. I don't want to be involved. But if I see you again, I swear to God, I will make sure they put you somewhere that you can't ever get to me. Do you understand?"

Marla looks at me quizzically. I wonder if she believes me. If I'd believe her were the tables turned. I don't even know if I believe myself. Because right now all I want to do is call the cops as soon as she's gone.

She looks at me silently until I pull back the hammer on the Sig and finally she speaks. "I'll go," she blurts. "But I'm going to need your word. Your *word*, Mia," she repeats with unassailable firmness. "If you go to the cops, if you get in my way, I will find you, do *you* understand? And next time you won't have a gun."

I feel my breath tighten in my chest. I believe her. She will kill me. Like Ben Cohan killed Emily. I will disappear. Of course, I can't be sure she won't try to do that either way; she could come for me again, anytime, any day, this woman who can pass for other people. Even if I reported this the police aren't going to be able to immediately protect me from her. The legal system doesn't work like that. People aren't locked up without evidence.

I think of the iPhone buried in my pocket recording all of this, seconds ticking over seconds. This is my only evidence. Everything that's happened out here. And that evidence will show I brought a stolen weapon to meet a stranger in the middle of the night. The best protection from Marla I could hope for pre-trial would be a restraining order, and something tells me Marla might not take that entirely seriously. I taste the blood in my mouth as the dark drop all around hazes in and out of focus. My thoughts come hard and fast, terrifyingly clear in their logic: the only way to be truly safe, to know for certain that this woman could no longer be a danger to me, would be to pull the trigger. Here, now. I could claim self-defense.

Fear fizzes through me at the mere idea of it, and I squeeze the gun's grip tighter as if I suddenly might do something crazy. But I'm not like her; I'm not willing to kill for this. I'm not that kind of person. Am I?

"You have my word," I tell her. "What you do is up to you. But you need to leave me out of it."

"Agreed," she replies.

And with her words I realize what I've just said, my statement making the recording in my pocket purely a form of evidence against me. I have verbally acknowledged that I will not report her crimes if she promises to leave me out of them. It's a promise I make her take at gunpoint.

She begins to shuffle out of her wedged-in position between the two struts and sidestep carefully along the metal beam beneath us, taking as wide a berth past me and my weapon as possible, one foot painstakingly placed next to the other until she is almost close enough to reach out and touch. My eyes follow her every move, aware that at any moment she might lunge and grab the gun or knock it from my hands as she passes. My stinging face is a clear reminder of how dangerous this woman is and the precariousness of our current location. Once past me she pauses momentarily, steadying herself before moving on. She takes a deep breath and steels herself before swinging around onto the ladder. And that's when it happens. Half on, half off the rungs, eyes still locked with mine, she loses her footing. I see the horror flash in her eyes as first one foot then the other slips from the rung. She drops, catching her own weight hard in her arms as she hangs two-handed from the top rung. And without thinking I am pitching forward, gun in one hand, as I grab for her flailing form. I reach her struggling body, her eyes desperate as she tries to find her lost footing.

But as my hands fly to help her I catch the look in her eyes, too late.

The air is knocked clean out of me. Her feet having easily found purchase on the ladder—she was never really in any danger—has freed up her right hand, which is now gripped viselike around my throat. The impact of her hand leaves me spluttering for breath as my windpipe burns under her tight hold. Without an option, I release the gun, my hands flying up to the choke hold on my neck. My weapon, my only lifeline, skitters onto the grating of the platform.

I stumble back as she pushes me hard against the metal of the platform away from the ladder, my breath knocked from me again. She slams me again, violently, onto a strut. The raw corrugated steel of the letter's lip digs painfully into my mid-back as she tilts me backward over the front of the sign. She's going to push me over. My eyes dip down into the darkness nearly fifty feet below; the sheer drop from this height at this angle will almost certainly kill me. I feel a sharp whip of panic as I struggle against her, trying to prize her fingers from my throat as her nails begin to break the skin. Unable to free myself from her grip I hook a foot under one of the metal struts to stop her pushing me any further as I gasp for breaths that just won't come. Then from the deep recesses of my memory I recall something I learned in an after-school self-defense class years ago. Instantly I stop struggling, I stop pulling away from my attacker and burst toward her instead.

Caught off guard Marla loses her balance, her hands flying out to brace herself, releasing my throat as she staggers back.

I gasp in a desperate lungful of air, pain ripping through my throat. But I know I only have a second before she is back on me. Without hesitation I act, moving to her and whipping *my* elbow hard into *her* face this time, the full force of my weight behind it.

She reels, her hands blindly grabbing for the strut and clinging for life as her left foot misses the platform edge. She stumbles forward to catch herself as her other foot follows suit. It's her turn to panic now, still disoriented from the blow, blood pouring from her nose. She catches herself half on half off the platform. She hangs, fingers clawed, white-knuckled, into the grating of the platform floor in front of me. She writhes desperately trying to heave her weight back up to safety but the angle is wrong, her shoulders not strong enough. Her eyes blaze up at me in disbelief. This isn't how she thought it would go. She tries again to kick her legs back up onto the platform, but each swing loosens her grip. Then a realization passes like a shadow over her face. She knows she can't get back up without my help.

I grab for her arm with both hands. The impulse comes from somewhere animalistic deep inside me rather from any rational part of my brain. The part that saves. The part that tries.

"I've got you," I rasp at her, my throat raw, my face swollen. A wave of relief floods her face and she kicks out once more for the platform to save herself.

Then, as if in slow motion, her leg finds the platform and she grins, grabbing my jacket and lurching me out over the drop. Without thinking I release her arms, bring my hands down hard on her grip on my jacket, and close my eyes as her fingers release and she topples backward out of sight.

Silence, and then the sound of an impact on the slope below. It doesn't end there. I hear as she tumbles on down into the ravine beneath the sign. I fly over to the front of the sign to look but I only catch the movement of branches and vegetation far below in the darkness. I stare after her, my labored breath catching and hanging in warm fog around me.

Finally the ravine below falls silent but for my rasps and the sound of blood pounding in my ears. Marla's gone. Disappeared again. My gaze is pulled up by the silent light of Hollywood glittering just out of reach beyond the hills and past the sheen of Lake Hollywood. I let the silence fill me. No screams, no rustles, no motion from the darkness beneath. There's a chance she could have survived. I should call an ambulance.

Hands trembling, I try to loosen my phone from my zipped jacket pocket but, in shock, no matter how hard I try, my fingers won't work properly, the joints too stiff and jittering.

I look down at them, shaking and bloodstained, and I realize how incredibly lucky I am to still be alive. And just like that the tears come.

34

Clearing Up the Mess

TUESDAY, FEBRUARY 16

IT'S ONLY WHEN I GET BACK TO THE CAR AND SEE MY FACE REFLECTED from the driver's-side window that I realize I can't possibly go back to the apartment like this. I look like the only survivor at the end of a horror movie: a wild thousand-yard stare, the front of my marl sweater stained, smeared with blood and hillside dust, my swollen bloodied face and tangled hair caked and crusted brown and red. I can't go anywhere looking like this. I can't speak to the police like this. I don't look like someone who watched a girl fall from a sign. I look like someone who pushed a girl from a sign.

I turn from the car to survey the houses and driveways near where we parked. I try to ignore Marla's car parked just ahead of mine. I try to block it from my mind.

I see what I'm looking for two houses down. The driveway is overgrown, there's no car parked there, and I see the green snake of a hose lying tangled near an untended hedge. Perfect. The house looks vacant, the blinds are open, and no nightlight comes from within. Its disheveled garden hints that it might not have been occupied for some time. I approach with caution but, noting the lack of furniture through the front window, I figure it might be safe to gently turn on the wall-mounted hose tap. The reassuring sound of water greets me.

I slip off my jacket and sweater and lay them on the overgrown grass. I locate the cracked flowing end of the garden hose and brace myself for its icy blast as I bend forward to wash the blood and dirt from my hair. The water hits me viscerally, a punch of cold, prickling my scalp and burning white-hot through me. I shake the water through quickly, hurrying the process, and then delicately turn the flow onto my numbed face, my croaked breath catching at the hit of cold. My bruised and bloodied eyes, nose, and mouth are grateful, after the initial shock, for the cooling stream. Likewise the throbbing skin around my neck calms under the icy splash. As soon as I'm satisfied that I've removed the worst of the mess, I shut off the tap and quickly return the hose to its pile. I don't want anyone wandering outside to find me, a soaking-wet actress with a swollen and bruised face wearing nothing but jeans and a silk camisole. I grab my soiled sweater, turn it inside out, and gently dry my tender face, and my hair, as best I can. Then slipping my unscathed jacket back on, and balling up the offended sweater, I head back to the car.

Inside I crank up the heat to full blast to settle my damp shivering body and get some life back into my limbs. I'm in shock, I know that much. I've researched the physical effects of it for various roles so I recognize it when I feel it. The short high breath, the sense of unreality, the inability to concentrate, trembling, cold, and a thirst. I grab my water bottle from my bag under the passenger seat and glug greedily until the plastic bottle crackles empty under my grip. I dig out a plastic bag from a side pocket and stick my balled-up sweater inside it, stowing it safely in the footwell.

I check myself in the rearview mirror, my skin gray-white in the dim street lighting, my wet hair hanging in thick damp coils. A drowned actress. My thoughts flash to Emily deep beneath the surface of the lake. I shake off the thought.

My lips are tinged blue and swollen from Marla's blow, and the bridge of my nose is wider than usual. I touch it gingerly and wince.

I feel the hot blast of the car heater beginning to loosen the joints in my hands and feet, my trembling slowly starting to subside. This will have to do for now, I can't stay here any longer and run the risk of attracting attention. I can only pray that I haven't done so already.

I fish the car keys from the tight confines of my jean pocket and start the engine.

EVERYTHING FEELS LIKE A DREAM as I drive. The car slips anonymously onto the 101 south, joining all the other nighttime traffic flowing toward Downtown LA. The strange lights and billboards of Hollywood add to the surreal nature of this odd journey. I try not to think about what just happened, but imagined images of Marla's broken pale body flash through my mind as I drive.

I left her.

I may not have meant to but I did.

Somehow, I don't know how, I made it to the bottom of that ladder. I jumped the final six-foot drop onto the hard dust of the hillside. Ankle twisted, wrists jarred, and body shaking like a leaf, I sat in the dirt and stared unseeingly into the darkness, shock sweeping through me. After a while I stood up and started to the car, the walk longer and darker on the way back.

In my lap, as I drive, my phone nestles unused. Somewhere back in the darkness Marla remains.

I come off the 101 and tap a waypoint destination into the car's GPS. I need to do one more thing.

After five minutes of sailing through nighttime streets the warm lights of my destination loom ahead, glowing out into the night, as I carefully turn off the main road and follow the little lane that loops around the building to a small hatch. I lower my window and order some food.

Parked in the car park, I perfunctorily eat until the food is gone then carefully place my bloodstained sweater inside the brown McDonald's bag, covering it with my used wrappers and rolling down the brown bag's top. I grab my baseball cap from the glove box, put it on, and hop from the car, just a girl grabbing a late-night snack and disposing of her litter.

BACK ON THE ROAD, FIVE minutes from the apartment building, I pull off my hat and look up at my reflection in the mirror once more, the streetlights here stronger. My face is a mess. There's no hiding it: something clearly happened to me tonight. Something very bad. There won't be any other way to explain it. Unless there *is* another way to explain it.

I know I'm not thinking straight because when the idea comes, I know it's crazy but I also know I'm going to do it anyway. There's only a tinge of fear at the thought of executing this brand-new plan where I'm pretty sure there should be a tsunami.

Regardless, I decide it's happening. I scan the two lanes ahead for a suitable vehicle and catch sight of a garbage truck. I make sure my seatbelt is fastened, switch lanes, and let my foot floor the accelerator.

The impact into the back of the garbage truck fires me forward sharply, my already tender face buffeting into the instantly deployed front and side airbags. Then, rebounding, my skull whiplashes back into the headrest behind me, knocking the air from my lungs, my horn blaring the whole time. Winded, I sit in the ringing muffle of the car and wait for someone to come and check on me.

The garbagemen are beyond kind. They move my car to the curbside and sit me down, checking I'm okay. An ambulance is called. I explain the car had problems with its relay yesterday, I don't know how it happened, I tell them, the brakes just didn't seem to work.

Aside from me, no one is hurt—I couldn't have hit the stationary truck at more than twenty miles an hour, but that was enough. My whole body aches. I pop my jacket collar up, hiding the bruises already blossoming around my neck from Marla's hands, and when the paramedics arrive I'm careful to only let them touch my face, explaining away my wet hair as a late-night swim. Of course, I am Breathalyzed—I don't blame them, the shuddering state I'm in I'd expect no less—but the alcohol reading is negative. My glass of wine at Nick's house was over five hours ago now. I exchange insurance details with the city sanitation workers and once everyone is convinced that I'm safe to drive, I slowly crawl the car back the final two streets to the Ellis Building.

An overwrought Miguel sits me down and fetches me a sweet tea as I tell him all about the accident. When my story is clear and settled and the state of my face explained away, I finally take my leave.

Upstairs in the apartment, I fish out my phone, which is still recording. I stare at the numbers still flying forward. I recorded everything. Everything she said, everything that happened tonight, all time- and location-stamped. I press stop on the recording. I press delete. I empty the trash. And it is gone. I hastily barricade the front door in case, somehow, that broken body rises in North Hollywood and comes to find me. I strip off my clothes, shower, and collapse into bed.

I'M WOKEN BY MY MOBILE phone ringing from the pile of discarded clothes in the bathroom. I haven't moved an inch in my sleep and it seems like only a moment has passed since I let my eyes droop shut.

I shift in the bedsheets, my whole body aching as if I've been in a car crash, which makes sense because I have. I bat my eyes open. Sunlight streams in through the edges of the bedroom blind, and everything that happened last night floods back into my mind.

I lurch up into the empty room, nausea crashing through me. She tried to kill me. Marla tried to kill me like the girl who leapt from the sign. She tried to get rid of me using my own Google history, and fevered imagination, as a weapon. My hand flies to my burnt-out throat as I launch into a cataclysm of excruciating coughs.

Images of Marla's white-knuckled hands and her face as she fell back disappearing from sight. I repress the urge to retch—the pain too intense for my battered throat. I stumble out of bed, lumbering my way out to the pile of clothes and the ringing phone.

Leandra at Audi. *Oh, fuck, the car.*

I decline the call.

They already know I destroyed their beautiful car. I wonder, vaguely, how they found out so quickly but then assume Miguel must have called them again after last night. He was pretty angry about the Audi mechanic giving me back a "faulty" vehicle. But then it's just as likely that the garbagemen have informed their insurance company of the accident.

I notice the time and bolt upright. It's four-fifteen in the afternoon on Tuesday. I've been unconscious for twelve hours. I only meant to rest my eyes.

Marla's body has been up on that hillside for over twelve hours. Another wave of nausea overtakes me and my head swims as I let it pass.

My thirst, already extreme last night, is now uncontrollable and I scramble to my feet heading to the kitchen and gulping greedily from the tap. Next I open the fridge and sit cross-legged on the cool kitchen tiles as I gorge myself on cheese, cold cuts, and whatever else I can reach. I haven't eaten in over seventeen hours and those seventeen hours have been the most traumatic of my life. I let snapshots from last night flash through my mind as I stuff cold olives and leftover salad into my mouth.

The cold breeze at the top of the sign, the smell of Marla's cigarettes, the shimmering surface of Lake Hollywood in the darkness. And then the blood, my blood, dripping down onto the gray marl of my sweater, the uncontrollable shuddering inside me. Marla's face inches from mine, her eyes, the warmth of her breath on my cheek before she disappeared into the void. The sound of her soft body hitting the earth forty-five feet below and tumbling, twisting down, down, down into the dusty valley, unable to stop, unable to save herself. I pause, a chunk of Brie halfway to my mouth. *Could she have survived it? Should I have gone back? Should I go now?*

I try to think rationally, morally, legally. *Was it my responsibility to save her if the impact didn't kill her?*

She tried to kill me but I certainly didn't intend to do the same. I only pushed her because she was trying to drag me down with her. I could feel my own feet slipping and I knew she'd never stop. Even if it killed us both. I let her fall to save myself. *Is that okay?*

Lost in thought, I finally pop the waiting chunk of cheese into my mouth. It will have to be okay, I decide, because that is what I did.

But I didn't call the police, did I? I didn't call an ambulance. If I was so sure I did the right thing . . . wouldn't I have called someone to help us afterward? I could have even called anonymously but the thought never crossed my mind at the time.

I don't think calling an ambulance would have helped her, a quiet voice inside me answers.

No, but that's the way things are done, isn't it? If someone has an accident you call an ambulance.

You did what you thought was right at the time. You did the best you could, the quiet voice answers. That's all you can ever do.

AFTER SHOWERING I EXAMINE MY damaged body in the mirror. The swelling around my nose has gone down; in its place a sickly green-yellow bruise now runs horizontally from under one eye straight across the bridge of my nose to under the other eye. An eye mask of bruising. Another livid purple-and-red contusion under my right eye, a small cut in the middle of my lower lip. I don't remember when, but I must have bitten down hard on it at some point. My unremoved makeup is now clogged under my eyes, my skin sallow, and my freshly rewashed wet hair adds to the horror show. I push my hair to one side and look at my aching neck, the skin blood-blistered and bruised, scabs already forming where Marla's thumbnails broke the flesh. I rifle through my washbag and pull out a tube of antiseptic cream, too late by far but the act of gently applying the cool cream gives me the illusion of clawing back my own body. Across my left shoulder and running diagonally over my chest is the blood-blistering and bruising caused by the seatbelt last night.

I cover my neck with my hand. Without the neck injury everything can be explained by my car accident last night, if it comes to that.

I dry my hair and put on a high-necked sleeveless top and jeans in silence as I work through a plan in my head.

Basically, I have three options now.

One: I go down to the station and I tell them everything that happened, beginning to end, and face the possible consequences of what happened to Marla.

Second: I call the police anonymously and say I saw something in the ravine under the sign. Just like the hiker who found the actress that jumped did in 1932. Then I would leave them to find Marla's body and construct a narrative themselves.

Or third: I pack, make my excuses, and go home. After all, I've been involved in a car accident; no one would begrudge me leaving LA on the basis of that. I'm sure even Kathryn Mayer and the studio will understand.

I know which option I'd prefer. Every instinct in my body is telling me to go home, right now. There is no way I can meet Kathryn Mayer or the producers looking like this. And I have no intention of handing myself in at a police station. I have the perfect excuse to leave LA today. A bruised face and body. A damaged voice. A trauma.

I fire up my laptop and wander into the living room with it. Outside the sun hangs low and sickly over the smog of the city and yet somehow, it's still beautiful.

My phone pings. A message from Nick, oblivious to all that has passed, thanking me for a wonderful night last night and asking if I want to grab a coffee later.

I feel a deep twist of shame. I was so quick to assume the absolute worst of Nick on that dusty hillside last night—that he could have done such terrible things—when the truth is he might be the kindest man I've ever met. I have no idea what to say to him right now, though, so I leave the message unanswered. I remind myself that I still have something of his—but I'll have to cross that bridge when I come to it.

I set about searching for a flight back to London. I'm leaving, there's no two ways about it and I'm not waiting for permission. I find a possible red-eye and call the airline and book a ticket for 9:05 tonight.

I check the oven clock in the kitchen. I need to be at the airport by 7:05 to check in.

That doesn't give me much time to do what I need to do.

I dash back into the bedroom, haul my suitcase onto the bed, and stuff everything I own into it. I tip everything from the bathroom unceremoniously into the mess of the suitcase and close it up. I shove my laptop, passport, headphones, and book into my handbag and drag everything out into the hall.

I sweep the rest of the apartment for left items, scoop the remaining contents of the fridge into the bin, and place the Audi keys and welcome pack into a cloth bag to leave at reception. Ready to go, I pull out my phone and dial.

Cynthia picks up after two rings. It's the middle of the night back in London. Her voice is thick with sleep but her tone is suddenly alert. Calls in the dead of night are rarely a good thing.

"Cynthia, hi. It's Mia," I croak. It's the first time I've heard my voice out loud since last night and it almost sounds like a joke, a crank call. I try to gently clear my throat before continuing but it makes no difference to my voice. "Listen, don't worry, I'm fine but I had a car accident last night." I hear her shift up in bed on the other end of the line.

"Are you okay? What happened?"

"I'm fine," I answer but the sound of my own voice loosens

something inside me and the intensity of everything that's happened over the last few days hits me. I try to stop it but my voice is emotional as I speak. "I'm fine. I'm just a bit banged up and not exactly audition-ready but . . . I'm alive," I answer, relief heavy in my voice.

"And the other guy?" she asks. I know she means the other car in the crash but I think of Marla nonetheless. I force myself back to my story. "I rear-ended a garbage truck," I say. I'm not sure if it's my own flat delivery, my relief at speaking to a friendly voice, or the bizarre facts of the situation but I let out a laugh and Cynthia does too. I welcome the second of levity it affords me.

"My face is a mess and as you can hear, I won't be bagging any musicals in the next couple of months but otherwise I think I'll be okay."

"Thank God!" She sighs heavily.

"Listen, I changed my flight, I'm flying back tonight." I pause, considering how best to phrase this. "I need to go home, Cynth."

"Of course," she coos. "I totally understand. I'll sort everything out with everyone over there. Just leave the apartment keys there. I'll deal with it all."

"The car's—" I begin.

She cuts me off. "Don't worry about the car, what matters is you're safe, besides that's what insurance is for. I'll deal with it. We'll sort it all out once you're back in London. It's nothing to worry about."

"Okay. And Kathryn, the screening, will that be okay?"

Cynthia pauses down the line; I hear her duvet shift. "Listen . . . you've been involved in a car crash. I mean, come on. It's perfectly understandable that you'd want to fly home, see your own doctor, be around your family. I can't imagine it being a problem for the studio but to be honest, if it is then . . . well . . . fuck 'em, frankly."

I feel my eyes prickle warm and sharp. I can't express the affection I have for Cynthia right now. A smile breaks across my face in spite of everything that's happened in the last few days. "Thanks, Cynth."

I'm going home.

. . .

My bags lie waiting by the door as I fish the unused Sig from last night's jacket. I wipe it down carefully, removing the hillside dust as well as my fingerprints. I remove the bullet, wipe it clean, and carefully reinsert it, wrapping the whole gun tightly in a clean dishcloth before slipping the snug package back into my handbag. I ball up the jacket, double-bag it, and deposit it in the trash. From what I can see, it doesn't have any blood on it, but it's sweaty and dusty and frankly I'd rather never see it again.

I scan the empty apartment. I'm ready. I tap out a message to Nick.

Today, 5:02pm

Are you at home? Something happened last night. Was involved in a car accident. I'm fine just bruised. I'm flying home on the red-eye tonight. It'd be great to come say goodbye before I go x

The message registers as read, gray dots pulse as he types. I imagine his concerned face, his concentrated expression. I'm really going to miss him.

OMG. What happened? You should have called me! Where are you? Hospital? Home? I'll come over now. I had a sense something was off.

I smile stupidly at the screen; he cares about me. He has no idea how much he's helped me already—but he can't come here, I need to get to his house. I need to get his gun back to his house, back in its drawer, and the sooner the better.

I'm okay. Can I drop by your house on the way to the airport? Just leaving my place now.

Then I add—

We need to talk.

His gray dots pulse . . .

Of course, I'll head back there now. Is everything all right? Are you sure you're okay?

Yeah, just shaken up. I'm getting an Uber over now.

Great. See you there.

I order my Uber, jot a phone number from the LAPD website down onto a scrap of paper, then lock up the apartment and haul my bags down to the lobby. A different receptionist is working today, someone I haven't met before. I hand over the apartment key to her and explain that I'm traveling back to London and someone will be in touch soon to sort everything out. Then I duck my head into the valet station and give Miguel the biggest hug, explaining away my departure and saying a proper goodbye.

Outside the sun begins to set as I hop in my Uber, an unexpected dread brewing inside me as I head to Nick's to play out the last step of my plan.

Around West Hollywood I catch sight of what I've been looking for through the car window and ask the driver to pull over. I trot back along the sidewalk to an old public phone booth and pull out the crinkled scrap of paper with the phone number. It's the LAPD twenty-four-hour anonymous hotline, anyone can call in and report a crime anonymously.

I'm calling Marla in then running. I curse myself for not having done so from day one instead of getting back in contact with Officer Cortez. But what's done is done and I don't have time to berate myself now. I'll have an eleven-hour flight to do that. I take a breath and key in the tip-off number.

An automated system tells me to disclose the state, city, or area I am calling in relation to then asks me to hold for an operator.

A fizz of fear flutters through my veins when suddenly I'm connected to a human voice.

"Crime Stoppers USA, how can I help you?" a female voice intones. The immediate reality of a person on the end of the line, and the question, throws me for a second. I have to actively reassure myself that there is no possible way she could know who, or where, I am. Or what I've done.

"I'd like to report a crime," I stutter.

"Okay, ma'am, and what's the location you're calling for?"

I tell her and she redirects my call. Another woman answers, her voice bright.

"Los Angeles Regional, how can I assist you?"

"I'd like to report—something."

"Okay . . ." she prompts.

"There's a body." The words sound awkward and harsh. "It's in the ravine in Griffith Park. Beneath the sign."

"I see," she says, her tone sober, careful. "And are you there at the scene?"

"No. I was hiking earlier. I saw her in the ravine."

"It was a woman you saw? Can I ask when this was?"

"This morning."

"And the body is female?"

"Yes."

"Did you call an ambulance at the scene?"

"She must be dead," I hear myself say, the facts bald and heartless. "I think she'd fallen. A long way. She must be dead. Somebody needs to go and get her." I recoil at my own choice of words but it will not serve the situation to be emotional.

"I understand, I'm sorry you had to witness that, that must have been traumatic." I'm sure her consoling words must follow a call-center script but I still find them a comfort. "If you can give me as exact a location as you can, then we can get someone down there as soon as possible. I can give you details of a counselor if you feel you need to talk to somebody about what you witnessed today?"

I decline but tell her as accurately as I can where to find Marla. I can only pray that given the relatively short time she has been outside in the elements someone, somewhere, will be able to identify her. I give the operator as much information as I can before hanging up and heading back to my waiting Uber with a fresh crime report number scrawled carefully onto the back of my scrap of paper.

NICK IS WAITING FOR ME in his driveway. He clocks my bruised face as I get out and looks at me horrified.

"This happened just after you left my house?" he asks, clearly filled with guilt.

"Well, it happened Downtown actually. I rear-ended a garbage truck at a traffic light." I shake my head. "I don't know how it happened, something wrong with the car's relay again I guess, or something. Someone explained it to me but I was out of it," I tell him.

He pulls me into a gentle bear hug, careful not to squeeze or crush my battered body. I let myself sink into him, though, and listen to the sound of his calm heart beating through his chest for a moment. God, he feels good. Like being at home already.

Nick whisks me and my luggage inside insisting he'll drive me to LAX himself. He offers to make me a tea and—seeing it as an opportunity to nip downstairs—I accept, letting him head off to the kitchen while I head to the bathroom.

Downstairs, I head straight for Nick's bedroom, listening for breaks in his activity upstairs. I carefully unwrap the Sig, wipe it down once more, and place it gently back into its drawer.

I hear him heading toward the staircase, his pace slow, teas in hand, and I dash as quietly as I can to the bathroom to make a show of finishing up. I pull the door open and he's leaning against the wall by the doorframe, two mugs in hand. He holds my gaze as I stand in front of the blocked doorway.

"What did you want to tell me?" he asks, finally, sipping his tea.

I frown, unsure what he means.

He gives me a soft smile. "In your text you said you wanted to talk to me about something."

I had wanted to tell him how sorry I was for leaving so suddenly after we'd been getting on so well, but now, standing in front of him, even the idea of doing that ignites a hot flush that moves with lightning speed up my neck to my pummeled face.

His eyes are on me, watching carefully, patient and quietly amused. "Were you planning on telling me you took my handgun yesterday by any chance?" he asks gently. "Because I'm guessing it's back in the drawer now, right?"

I straighten at his words but can only respond with dumb silence, caught red-handed and lost for words. He looks at me expectantly though not angrily.

"Yeah, it's back in the drawer," I answer, wincing at the sheer awkwardness of the exchange, my eyes searching him for a reaction. ". . . Sorry?" I add. It's a question.

He holds my gaze. "Okay," he says after a pause. "Is that it?"

"I'm sorry, Nick," I repeat.

He nods. "Right, I mean, I wish you'd just asked." He sips his tea, conscious of the oddness of the conversation but clearly keen to keep things on an even keel. "I'm dying to know why you needed it."

I remain silent, bathed in a weird kind of shame I haven't felt since childhood. He's not reacting like I thought he would. He's acting like I borrowed his toothbrush.

"You didn't use it, I'm guessing?"

"No," I confirm with a firm shake of the head. "Definitely not."

"You know there was a bullet in the chamber, right?" There's the lightest shade of worry in his tone.

"Yes, well actually, no I didn't. Not at first, but then yes."

He's quiet for a second, seeming to put the pieces together. "Is this something to do with Emily?" he asks.

"It is."

He waits for more but I can't give it to him, not unless I tell him everything. He lets a fresh silence stretch out before speaking again. And for the first time in the conversation he sounds genuinely concerned.

"Did you make up the whole Emily story, Mia? Is there something else going on with you? Something I should know about?" He looks worried, hurt even, and I find my resolve wobbling.

"No, I didn't. She was real. I went to meet a friend of hers last night. I was worried the friend might have been responsible for Emily's disappearance in some way." I cobble truth muddied with half-truth. It's all I can give him. "Turns out she wasn't responsible for Emily, not really. But I didn't know beforehand and I was scared. I know it was incredibly reckless going, taking your gun. Dangerous and illegal and I lied to you and stole from you but I just wanted some sense of security, I suppose."

He studies my face, his expression unreadable. "And can I ask if everything is all right now? Are you all right? Should I be worried?" He indicates my face.

I had almost forgotten how I must look to him. A pale English-woman covered in bruises and cuts telling him everything is just peachy.

"I wasn't fine. But I am now, it's all . . . resolved. None of it should be a problem anymore," I reassure him gently. Because Marla and Emily are gone and in a few hours I will be too. I choose my next words carefully. "I've told the police about it. It's all in their hands now. Nothing more for me to do." Nick's concern returns at the mention of police, so I reach for the first almost-truth I can find to reassure him. "It was just an overzealous stalker, you know, so. But nothing happened to me. I'm fine. No one got shot." I offer a muted smile. "I'm sorry, Nick," I repeat sincerely.

"Ah," he says, that narrative seeming to make sense to him given the little he knows. "No. I'm sorry you thought you had to go through this whole thing alone. You're all right now?" Another wave of guilt washes through me as I continue to tell lies by omission.

"Yes, I'm fine," I say, waving away the evidence clearly visible on my bruised face. "The car crash was me. I mean . . . it was entirely my fault. I just wasn't concentrating. And I knew there had been a problem with the car earlier but there's just been too much going on out here. I wasn't focusing. I'd just been to see her. I'd left her and I—" I break off as the image of her falling from me flashes through my mind. In a way I'm telling him the truth although hopefully my confession sounds more like a tired driver blaming herself for a car accident than anything else. I change tack, moving from facts to feelings because at least I don't have to lie about those. "I need to go home. It's been too much, out here. After *Eyre* everything's just been crazy. And then George. And here I am—" I catch Nick's subtle flinch at the mention of George's name. It's the first time I've mentioned the breakup though I'm absolutely certain he's seen the photos of George with Naomi in the tabloids by now. I bluster on. "I was trying to run away from things, not just George but all of it, being alone, that life I was left with, like if I could just keep busy enough everything would be okay. I think I kept myself a little too busy. And now I just need to go home, you know. To cry, to settle, to get over him and heal properly—I *really* like you, Nick. I'm sorry it happened this way. I'm sorry this situation got so fucked up. I'm sorry I'm so fucked up."

"Hey. Listen. This is Hollywood," he counters, a slow smile building, "you're going to have to trust me when I say you're not the craziest person I've ever met, Mia. Hell, you're not even the craziest person I've kissed."

I laugh in spite of myself, my face pinching tight.

Emboldened he continues, "When you're ready. When you're back home and you're thriving and happy and healed. When *you* want. Can I see you again? Back in London?"

My already haywire emotions reel off in every direction. It takes all of my willpower to hold it together. To hide my surprise, my happiness, my relief that I haven't ruined whatever this is. *He still likes me. Trusts me. Wants to see me.* Even though he knows something very strange has happened, and he knows I'm weird and a bit broken, and that there are certain things about me that I can't tell him just yet—somehow, somehow, he still likes me.

He mistakes my silence for something else and keeps talking.

"However stupid it sounds, I've genuinely never met anyone like you, Mia. You've got this rock-solid core, this strength inside you. People can see it. You know yourself. Do you know how rare that is? It's something special." He shakes his head, trying to find the words. "And whatever's been going on. I know you'd tell me if telling me was important. Maybe I'm naive, or delusional, maybe, but I trust you that you know what you're doing. You've got a good head on your shoulders. It's funny, with you I always feel like we're working toward something together, does that make sense? Like we're always just picking up the same long conversation we've been having since we met—" He breaks off, suddenly self-conscious.

I take a slow, calm breath before speaking—a movement in the mirror beside me catches my eye and my attention flicks to the figure reflected in the glass beside me, her bruised face, my bruised face, Jane Eyre's bruised face, our eyes wild and lost but still just about holding it together—and then, reader, I answered him.

35

Everyone's a Winner

SUNDAY, MAY 16 (THREE MONTHS LATER)

THE HOTEL SUITE IS EMPTY NOW AND THE COMFORTING RUMBLE OF metropolitan London seeps in through the hotel windows. Faint horns honk in the distance, and building work burrs on with the roll and shudder of traffic in the city streets below.

I stand and assess the woman before me. In the hotel's floor-length mirror, finally alone, I take in what hours of preparation and hard work have created.

I turn, the sparkles of my Tom Ford gown catching and refracting the light up into twinkling shimmers on the hotel's high ceiling. The delicate fabric clinging tight and then falling loose over the contours of my frame made six inches higher with towering Aquazzura heels. I wobble slightly as the sharp stilettos sink too deep into the thick pile of the suite's carpet.

It's almost exactly three months since I left LA, three months since I watched Marla tip back into the darkness and disappear.

I inspect my face for evidence of that night but my bruises are long gone. No traces of the trauma inflicted that night remain—except maybe the look behind my eyes, but then no one would know to look for that except me.

About my healed neck are £1.8 million worth of diamonds on loan from Boodles. The burly security guy assigned to guard it—and, I suppose, as a consequence, me—is stationed just beyond the suite door in stoic silence. He'll follow the small army of stylists, hair and makeup artists, and assistants down the hall, waiting for me to emerge, and escort me, from a distance, down to the red carpet just across the road from this hotel.

I think of the crowds gathering right now outside the Royal Albert Hall, the BAFTA television crews, the journalists, presenters, and public. The long gauntlet of the red carpet, the massive banks of photographers with walls of flashes. Tonight's show will be televised live, with only a three-minute delay. The idea of it both thrilling and nauseating.

I look down at my index cards again, my acceptance speech. Should I need one. My scrawled-out handwriting will be my only protection against the vast waves of nerves that I know will crash through my body if my name is called from the podium. That long walk to the stage—past the smiling faces of make-believe superheroes, historical figures, faux-gangsters, and rom-com best friends—to the moment I've worked my whole life for. Maybe.

I run through the speech cards again one last time, my hands shaking. Let's call it excitement.

The speech is short but packed with thanks.

I know how lucky I am. Now more than ever, to even be alive. Luckier than ever after everything that happened, after almost losing myself, after looking into the darkness and seeing so many near-identical faces staring straight back at me.

I am so, so incredibly grateful, but—and there is a *but*—I know none of this is real. This industry is not fair, the price is so often higher than the reward. I've won some things but more often than not, I've lost. We all have. And there should be a limit to what we are willing to lose along the way . . . after all, we'll need something left once we get there.

Marla lost everything. Emily too. I wish—award gown on, and on my way to the ball—I could have told them that it feels good but it's not worth losing everything for. This. Standing here, covered in reflected and refracted light. I can tell you firsthand this feeling is only the same one you felt when you won a gold star in school, or when your mum said she was proud, or when you won a sports match. Don't get me wrong, success is a great privilege, but standing here I can tell you it's not what I thought it was before I had it.

They never found Marla's body. They found something else instead.

Once I got back to London, I checked my report number every day until it was removed from the system. Case closed. No body was found in the ravine beneath the sign on that day. No body, no crime.

Marla disappeared one last time.

But Emily Bryant's body *was* found. In Lake Hollywood. Apparently, another anonymous tip-off. Nothing to do with me. God knows who called it in, but the LAPD dredged the lake. I remember wondering if Ben himself might have done it to finally close the circle. How he could be sure of maintaining his innocence I do not know. Though without Emily, her recordings, or her best friend I'm not sure how much ties him to her.

They found Emily's body in a weighted suitcase 180 feet beneath the surface of the reservoir. A homicide investigation was opened.

The story was on the news for a few days. Her postmortem showed the cause of death to be an overdose of heroin; she was dead long before she entered the water. Some speculated that she had been an addict, that she could well have overdosed accidentally or deliberately with someone who then tried to dispose of her body. But Emily was no drug addict. Looking at her glowing headshot on the news, that much must have been clear to everyone.

I waited on tenterhooks for an international call, every day expecting to hear Officer Cortez's voice, but the call took another month to come through.

I had begun to relax, to think that somehow I was irrelevant to Emily's story. After all, she was long dead before I even arrived in LA.

It was hard for the coroners to pin down exactly how long Emily Bryant had been dead, though, having only the rate of her decomposition to go by, the lower temperatures this year apparently slowing down decomposition while the high level of bacterial life present in the lake water may have potentially sped it up.

I read everything that surfaced online, becoming once again an expert on Emily. I worked out the time line, her disappearance, my arrival, my departure. My first phone call with Cortez about Emily would have come five weeks after her actual death, making me an unlikely suspect or witness. Though my story of a look-alike might be far more concerning.

When Cortez finally called me she walked me back through what I had told her in February. I reminded her of the part of the story where she herself assured me on the phone that the police had ID'd Emily in her apartment and told me she was fine. Placing the blame right back on the LAPD's doorstep.

Cortez asked me who the friend of Emily's was that I had spoken to about her disappearance. I told her I could not remember her name. I kept my answers vague, the time and the distance from those seemingly unimportant events doing most of my work for me. I do not know if Cortez managed to get footage from the Ellis Building of Joanne pretending to be Emily, but it seems unlikely. Lucy told me they wiped the tapes after a month. I'm pretty sure the footage of Joanne would only be another dead end for the LAPD. Joanne didn't know who hired her. Even if Cortez traced the bank account that paid Joanne, I'm sure it would only lead back to Emily's bank account anyway. Marla had access to everything through Emily's computer and phone.

Who knows where that laptop and phone are now. It's unlikely Cortez found them back in Emily's apartment, and who knows where Marla was staying. I try not to think of Emily's empty rooms, those wilted plants, the bowl full of moldy fruit. My emails and texts to Emily are all lost along with those audio files.

I gave my statement to Cortez again: twice. Leaving out anything to do with Marla and anything that might incriminate me.

That call was a month ago and I haven't heard a thing more. I check the news less these days. I try to forget. But every now and then I get scared. I expect another call, from Cortez, the call that unravels everything I've said and lands me in something I can't ever get out of.

And there's another thought that haunts me, the fact that Marla's body was never found. I think of the nighttime animal noises up in Griffith Park and perhaps that's my answer, but there's a tiny part of me that wonders if, somehow, Marla got away. If somehow her fall was broken on the way down and somehow, she tumbled to safety and then woke the next day, severely injured but alive. I know it's not possible but there's a magic and a terror to thinking she might still be out there, a ghost in a city of visitors.

It must have been true, what Marla told me about her childhood, because no one has missed her. There were no reports on Marla. Emily's family was plastered across the papers after her body was discovered, photos of her grieving father. He had filed his own missing persons report on Emily a week after Marla fell. That whole time he'd thought she was fine because Marla was texting him back as Emily. And when she stopped Emily's dad noticed. Cortez must know someone was impersonating Emily but without real evidence, or even a name, Marla's trail must have gone cold.

But Marla didn't kill Emily. Moon Finch killed Emily. It's odd being able to see things from the other side. I watched with interest as a few weeks after Cortez's phone call Moon Finch was quietly bought out by another company. Ben Cohan and his business partner, Mike, moved on who knows where. Did they cut their losses or were they pushed? I don't know if without that recording, or a witness, any of it could even be traced back to them. The most I can hope for is that what happened with Emily and then Marla scared them enough that they'd think twice before doing anything again.

I start on *Galatea* in two weeks. I got it. After everything. I'm excited to do it, of course, but I'd be lying if I said the sheen hadn't rubbed off the role to an extent. It caused too many people too much heartbreak to still feel like an entirely good thing. I'm not so sure about the actor's life anymore either. But things have a habit of changing quickly, don't they? For now, I'm happy pootling along. Happier than I've ever been.

Nick moved over to London a couple of weeks ago. We did long distance for a couple of months but we hated it. Now he's renting a warehouse flat in Dalston, just down the road from me, and I'm basically living there with him. He's got plenty of productions to keep him busy over here and though he moans about the weather, I can tell he loves it.

There's a knock at the hotel suite door, the bleep of a keycard, and Nick's head appears around the door.

"Mia?" he asks, coming in tentatively. He hoicks the sleeve of his immaculate evening suit and checks his watch. "It's time. You ready to go?" He looks perfectly handsome in every way, my American man, my plus-one.

"Yeah," I whisper and clear my throat, tucking my cue cards carefully into my clutch.

I told him everything that happened after I saw Emily on the news. I told him about Emily, Marla, the sign, my stupidity, and the craziness. The aftermath and the crash. The only part of the tale I skipped was the part where I brought my fists down hard on hers and watched her grip loosen.

In Nick's story she slips. In Nick's story I am innocent. I prefer Nick's version. He only told me things I already knew. Not to get involved unless I'm asked to, not to offer anything that might incriminate me. To protect myself. To protect us.

Nick holds the door wide and I gather my things. If I don't win tonight that's okay. If I don't ever act again then that's okay, because I'm alive and free and no longer alone. I count myself lucky, even with all my flaws, with all my failings and sorrows and hopes and dreams. Whatever happens tonight, it's going to be okay.

• • •

SNAPSHOTS OF MEMORIES. NICK'S WARM hand in mine leading me down the red carpet then setting me free. Microphones, questions, camera flashes, and umbrellas. Crowds of faces. The fizz of champagne and the pinch of sequins on skin. An auditorium of people I recognize but do not actually know, jokes and the sound of a thousand people's laugher, the swell of music and then some words I can't quite make out. Nick looks to me, his eyes alive with meaning, he stands and I find myself standing too.

A camera races up the aisle toward us and I lean into him, terrified, to whisper, "Did they say me, Nick?"

He laughs, his eyes full of love. "Yeah, yeah, they did, Mi." He kisses my cheek. "Now get up there."

The walk is long, a blinding tunnel of nerves and unbridled happiness. The warm imprint of Nick's kiss still on my cheek.

And finally, I am standing before them all, and I am speaking and they are laughing and I know I will never forget this moment and yet I realize I am forgetting it even as it happens. I lift the heavy statue and it feels so real, just like I knew it would.

A photo shoot backstage. I pose with my prize, eyes aflame, then retrieve my phone from an assistant to get my own shot. There's a message on screen. The code Californian. My blood freezes in my veins but I do not let my smile crack. I'm a good actor; I have a statue to prove it.

But as I'm led into the press interview room, I carefully read the message once more.

36

Coming Soon

FRIDAY, NOVEMBER 11 (18 MONTHS LATER)

WE'RE SITTING IN THE DARKNESS OF THE CINEMA; THE LIGHTS HAVE dipped and Nick is squeezing my hand. The diamond ring he gave me on bended knee in the middle of a blustery Millennium Bridge gleams in the half-light. Life is good.

I got no more messages after that night. The number was disconnected. I've since tried to push its words from my mind.

The cinema screen curtains widen for the theatrical trailers to begin. *Galatea* premiered in London and New York last week to fantastic reviews, but I wanted to sneak into a real cinema tonight, to see it in an everyday setting, surrounded by the public, and see if it can pass their test. If real audiences actually like it.

The chatter thins around us as the trailers before the main feature start to play.

I give Nick's hand a squeeze and take in his handsome face in the flickering screen light, and then a voice I recognize fills the cinema. The hairs on the back of my neck rise. Instinctively I turn to the screen and it's there that I see her face.

Marla Butler.

She stares back at me in celluloid. Alive. Not just alive but re-splendent. Her smile beaming across the forty-eight-foot-wide screen as one of the pre-film trailers plays. She's in a period costume drama, a drawing room comedy of matters, her ringleted hair bouncing above her extravagant Edwardian costume, as she dances. An American heiress, a literary adaptation. My breath is caught in my throat. She looks beautiful, every inch a movie star. My mind races to the text message I received that night months ago.

Sun May 16, 9:48pm

Congratulations. And thank you for keeping your promise.

At the time I'd racked my brain for other explanations, of who it could be, what it could mean but of course my mind had always snagged on Marla. Because I made her a promise at the top of that ladder. I had half-forgotten. In the heat of the moment I had promised her that if she went away, I wouldn't ever go to the police. If she left me alone then I wouldn't ruin things for her.

I watch the cinema screen mute. Spellbound as she laughs, dancing and scheming her way frenetically through the trailer, electro-punk Vivaldi pulsating over it all. Oh my God. She did it, I realize with a shiver fluttering up my spine. She made it. She got what she wanted. She got her deal. And I kept my promise, whether I meant to keep it or not. I didn't ruin things for her. My story has always ended without her name being mentioned.

The music crescendos as Marla grins straight down the barrel of the lens at me, at the audience, and winks. Then the screen flashes to black. I clock the old Moon Finch logo. One of their last productions before they folded.

I pushed her that night but she survived. She must have watched me win that award on another screen somewhere. And she sent her message. As a warning, I suppose, or as a thank-you. Either way a reminder to keep my promise. A reminder of how much skin I have in the game. How much skin we both have in the game.

The trailer's credits burst up with the promise that the film will be COMING SOON.

God help us all.

And then I spot it, in black and white—above-the-title billing— INTRODUCING ANNA SANDERSON.

She changed her name.

My eyes travel to Nick in the darkness. He is watching the screen oblivious, and I realize he never actually met Marla. He has no idea.

I take in the rest of the mesmerized faces around us and realize I am the only person here who recognizes this woman. Who knows what she's done.

And I have promised to spare her if she spares me.

Acknowledgments

It seems inevitable now that as an actor/author I'd eventually get around to writing a story based in the acting world. And here it is . . . it is both the most researched and least researched book I've ever written. While I wasn't fact-checking with a neuroscientist as I did with *Mr. Nobody,* or watching hours of scuba diving videos, researching flight paths, and gorging on South Pacific documentaries as I did with *Something in the Water,* it could be argued that I've been undercover for the past sixteen years! Hopefully I've managed to convey a little of the raw excitement and bald terror of a first-ever pilot season for readers, bound up here in a what-would-you-do psychological thriller.

Acting is a strange job and LA is an even stranger place but then . . . wouldn't the world be a little less sparkly, a little less interesting, without it?

There are a lot of people to thank for bringing about this book.

Firstly, a very special mention goes to my daughter. I finished the first draft of this story in the British Library at eight months pregnant so we very much wrote it together. Thank you, cookie, for not kicking me too much and, later, for allowing me to work on edits during your nap times.

Huge thanks to my wonderful husband for the lockdown shift work, cheerleading, and for being an all-round dreamboat. There's no one on earth I'd rather self-isolate with/share deadlines with than you!

Thank you to everyone at PRH for their fantastic work on bringing this book to fruition during a global pandemic and all the logistical trickiness that that entails! I'd especially like to thank my fabulous editor Kara Cesare, whose wonderful notes and clear eye kept me going in the right direction.

Special thanks, too, go to my brilliant agent Camilla Bolton at Darley Anderson. I still can't thank you enough for responding to that first email I sent back in 2016 and for everything that has happened since.

About the Author

CATHERINE STEADMAN is an actress and writer based in London. She has appeared in leading roles on British and American television as well as on stage in the West End, where she has been nominated for a Laurence Olivier Award. She grew up in the New Forest, Hampshire, and now lives in North London with her husband and daughter. Steadman's first novel, *Something in the Water*, was a *New York Times* bestseller with rights sold in over thirty territories. Film rights have also been sold to Reese Witherspoon's production company, Hello Sunshine. Steadman's second novel, *Mr. Nobody*, was published in 2020. *The Disappearing Act* is her third novel.

Twitter: @CatSteadman
Instagram: @catsteadman

About the Type

This book was set in Bembo, a typeface based on an old-style Roman face that was used for Cardinal Pietro Bembo's tract *De Aetna* in 1495. Bembo was cut by Francesco Griffo (1450–1518) in the early sixteenth century for Italian Renaissance printer and publisher Aldus Manutius (1449–1515). The Lanston Monotype Company of Philadelphia brought the well-proportioned letterforms of Bembo to the United States in the 1930s.